T0157864

Is It Too Late?

Lyla Clarke

Order this book online at www.trafford.com
or email orders@trafford.com

Most Trafford titles are also available at major online book retailers.

Printed in the United States of America.

ISBN: 978-1-4669-3578-5 (sc)
ISBN: 978-1-4669-3579-2 (hc)
ISBN: 978-1-4669-3580-8 (e)

Library of Congress Control Number: 2012908089

Trafford rev. 05/21/2012

 www.trafford.com

North America & international
toll-free: 1 888 232 4444 (USA & Canada)
phone: 250 383 6864 ♦ fax: 812 355 4082

Dedication

This book is dedicated to three people that I have tagged with the description *Lovers of Life*. First would be my son Graeme. From the day he could speak everything in Graeme's world was a "wow" the first time he saw it, touched it, or experienced it. He is now at the end of his teens and beginning the life of an adult and I'm happy to report the "wows" still happen. Turbo sleds and Suzuki 4x4s are his latest "wows."

My beloved "Uncle Ole" Pedersen was the first person I can remember thinking, "here's a man who finds something to be thankful for every day of his life." He was a part of my life from birth and continues to be a positive influence despite his passing from cancer several years ago. Fond memories of sharing the joys of nature, discussions of ecological issues, religion, politics and life in general are his legacy to me. Despite his illness he was still thankful for all of life's goodness.

Daniel Carter was a young man that entered my life as a co-worker several years ago. His enthusiasm for life was contagious and seemed uncontainable. Daniel was killed by a hit and run driver while crossing a street one night in September 2010. He was an intelligent young man full of potential and dreams whose death is genuinely mourned. I have borrowed Daniel's name for the character of Dabria's father, whom I've created to be a man of intelligence and integrity with the added bonus of a great sense of humor. Daniel Carter, you and your laughter will not be forgotten.

Acknowledgments

I would like to thank several contributors of this book. First and foremost would be my good friend Krista, who coincidentally (or not) just happens to be a private practice lawyer and one of my staunchest supporters. Frozen cocktails on the patio at the lake helped us through a few hours of necessary edits. Thank you, Jacqueline (a Legal Aid lawyer) for providing me with fodder for the "special scenes" and for pointing out my obvious legal mistakes. Thank you, Helen, from Victim's Services for your input. Thank you, Constable Ducette for allowing me to "borrow" you name. Thanks, Shelley, for allowing me to create a character that holds your real life position as Deputy Director in the Correctional System. Thank you Nicole for several years of beautiful Gel nails. Thanks to my readers: Jennifer, Maryjane, Jacqueline, and Cathy (who suggested I add an epilogue).

Thank you, Auntie Doreen for days and days of editing and Uncle Ken for keeping us fed and watered while we worked. And last but not least special thanks to Brandi Sidoryk of the band *Sydney York* for allowing me to name this book after a song she wrote titled "Too Late." *Sydney York* is a talented group of three young women who create and perform avant-pop music. Check out their website and their music. You won't regret it.

Prologue

Hmm . . . . music. Hmm . . . . hmm . . . . hmmmmmm. Elevator music? Hey, I know. It's that Bach stuff. That's weird. I never listen to this shit. Wow, bright lights! I can't see a thing. Hey, where am I and why am I so cold? Yah, ... *why* am I so cold? Shit! I can't feel my hands . . . . or my feet. I can't move! I can't even turn my head!! Holy shit, am I dead? No. No! My heart is pounding. I can feel it. I can hear panting. I can *feel* myself panting. I must be alive. What's wrong with me? Wait. What's that . . . . a scraping sound? A door opening? Footsteps . . . . coming closer. I feel a draft. I *can* feel! I'm scared! This is NOT good!

God, my tailbone hurts! I must'a been laying here forever. And this ain't no feather bed. Something cold . . . . something hard. Oh my God, ... I'm naked!!! No wonder I'm so cold. *What* is that gross smell? Toilet cleaner! Why can't I move? Where the hell am I and how did I get here? Hey, a face. A FACE!!! I know you! Remember me? Help me! Help me!! I'll be good from now on. I promise! No more tricks. I swear! I'll do anything you want. Please. . . . You can't hear me, can you? I can't hear me!!!! Why can't I speak?

"Hey, beautiful, are you comfortable? Warm enough?"

No! I'm cold. Very cold! I can feel sweat running down my forehead into my hair. I'm sweating, but I'm freezing. Why are you strokin' my cheek? I can feel that, too. Stop. Please stop! Hey, stop!! You're creepin' me out. Why can't I move? I'm gonna die . . . . aren't I? I'm gonna die!! Shit, I think I just peed myself.

"Just relax. Don't cry," the voice gently coaxed as the hand brushes my tears away. "You're even prettier than I remembered. I'm so sorry. I know you trusted me." The hand moves from my cheek down my throat and across my breast. "I haven't taken very good care of you. Have I? I'm going to wash you and make you smell nice again. I remembered the lavender. Do you like lavender? I used to. My . . . . you *are* dirty! It's okay. You'll smell like your old self in no time. I'm being very gentle. Please stop crying. It won't help. I can't let you go but I promise I *will* set you free. I'm sorry. I won't ever hurt you . . . . I promise. I'm very good at some things. Very gentle. Don't be afraid. It will all be over soon."

Stop touching me! Stop touching me!! STOP . . . . TOUCHING . . . . ME!!!!! HELP ME! HELP ME!! HELP!!!

Chapter 1

"Damn it," Dabria cursed under her breath as she registered the flashing red and blue lights of the "ghost car" in her rear view mirror. She was already late and being pulled over wasn't going to help matters. She coasted over to the shoulder of the road and parked. A headache had started to throb behind her left eye about half an hour ago and not wanting to waste any time by stopping, she had tried to ignore it. Eventually, as the throbbing had increased she had given in to the inevitable. She was going to have to pop a pill to make the pain go away. Apparently digging through your purse and trying to drive at the same time as you blaze past an unmarked police car *forces* that cop to pull you over. Years ago her best friend had coached her on how to avoid encounters of the unfriendly cop kind. The wise advisor solemnly stated, "Never break more than one law at a time or you're just asking for trouble." That advice had been handed out after he had received hefty fines for speeding and having open liquor in his car. Today's two broken laws would be speeding and erratic driving. One, if not both, were bound to get her a ticket.

Temporarily forgetting why she was stopped on the side of the road, because she was so engrossed in her search for an Advil, she jerked when she heard knuckles rapping on her side window. As she looked up with a frown she recognized an R.C.M.P. badge held in front of the window. Depressing the button to roll it down, she dug through her purse for the information she knew the officer would request. Before the officer could speak Dabria thrust her documents at him with one hand while she continued to search for the Advil with the other.

"I assume you know why I'm pulling you over?" a gravelly voice questioned her sternly. An unfamiliar jolt of awareness arrowed straight to her gut! No, ... not exactly her gut, and not exactly unfamiliar. It was more like her core and it was more like . . . . rusty. It was a sensation that hadn't been felt in a very, verrrry long time. Wow . . . . it must have been a twinge of sexual attraction!

As she slowly swiveled her head to focus on the officer, rather than her purse, she was startled by the vision before her. The officer had returned his badge to his pocket and she now had an unobstructed view of the "man behind the badge." Staring back at her were cold cobalt blue eyes in a rugged, beard stubbled face framed by a sun-bleached blond mop. A giant Viking dressed in the modern day clothes of jeans and a well worn coffee-colored leather jacket towered outside her window. His unconventional appearance drove the frown right off her face and an unguarded expression of female appreciation replaced it. A grin instantly spread across his face and promptly brought Dabria's focus back to the situation at hand. Her features immediately smoothed into her usual expressionless mask. Annoyed that he had observed her involuntary appreciation of his attributes, she again thrust her license and insurance at him. He accepted the documents and clearing his throat, wiped the smile from his face.

"Yes," Dabria didn't pretend innocence. "I was speeding."

"Do you know what the speed limit is on this highway, and do you know how fast you were going?"

"No, ... and not exactly. But, I'm sure you do," Dabria responded dryly.

"The speed limit is 100 km/hr and I clocked you at 150 km/hr. That'll get you a speeding ticket, and the erratic driving as you sailed past me, will get you a court summons for Dangerous Driving. Can you explain why you were weaving back and forth across the yellow line?"

"I have a headache and I was searching for some Advil. Please give me the ticket and the summons and I assure you I *will* attend. As you may have noticed I'm in a bit of a hurry and see no further need to continue to create a hazard on the side of the road. Thank you, Officer," Dabria abruptly dismissed him. She reached to take the ticket and looked up at him impatiently.

"I'm sorry, but I need to go back to my car to run your plate and print your copies up. I'll try to be as quick as possible, Ma'am." He flashed another of those cheeky heart-stopping smiles. As he turned she noticed a single dimple adorning his left cheek.

The pint-sized sprite he had left fuming in the car behind him was why the term *exotic* had been coined. Her skin was a flawless canvas of warm liquid honey. Her flashing toffee colored eyes and satiny dark chocolate locks made her a morsel Morgan would love to gobble up. Dabria might have an angel's name, but she certainly did not have the anticipated disposition of one. This was one individual definitely worth investigating further. He glanced back and caught her checking out his rear-end from her driver's side mirror. He chuckled out loud as he slid into his seat.

Ma'am!!! Silently fuming she knew she shouldn't have taunted him, or used her courtroom voice on him, or reminded him of why she was speeding in the first place. It was up to the discretion of an officer to issue a warning, an actual ticket, or write up a court summons when pulling someone over for driving violations. She knew better than to let her emotions dictate her behavior. Her haughty attitude could only serve to force him into prolonging her wait, making her ticket fine as large as possible, *and* practically guaranteed the issuing of a summons. From previous experience she knew that police usually ran licence plates before they approached the vehicle since part of their safety relied on knowing vehicle ownership, if there were any outstanding warrants or tickets for that owner, and if the vehicle was stolen. He was deliberately stalling, which was justified, given her arrogance. Great! Now he had just caught her checking him out and was laughing at her. She resumed her search for the damn bottle of pain medication and after taking a couple of pills she rested her head against the back of her seat and began to massage her temples to try to relieve some of the tension.

Two of Dabria's many talents were her skills of observation and her ability to hear the nuances in a person's speech. Her instincts told her that the officer often received a similar reaction to his appearance, and that he was amused by not only that reaction, but also her attempt to dismiss him. With a huff of disgust she continued to massage her temples. My gawd, those eyes were something else though. Popping her head up off the seat she suddenly realized that this might actually be the first time ever that a man's voice had forced her to acknowledge that she was a sexual being. Another knock on the window abruptly brought her back to reality. This time, carefully schooling her features, she opened the window and waited with a feigned appearance of relaxed patience for him to finish their encounter.

"Since you obviously have pressing business in our fine city and I don't want my tardiness to color your impressions of us, I tried to be as swift as possible, Ma'am." Again that mocking smile graced his countenance. "You will be required to appear two weeks from today at the Provincial Court House to plead your case or acknowledge your guilt for sentencing. I hope that won't be an inconvenience for you, since I see you're visiting from out of province."

Dabria neglected to correct this misinformation, since she was concentrating on trying to distinguish the unique scent of cologne that had just wafted past her.

"I'm sure you're aware that I will also be attending. Please pull over next time you need something out of your purse and slow down. Until we meet again, have a nice day . . . . *Ms.* Abdulla-Smythe." With a slight bow he handed her the summons and ticket and swaggered away. Wow! The arrogance practically rolled off of him. Cocky bastard!

Dabria glanced down at the ticket to check the amount of the fine and to look for the officer's signature. The ticket ended up being a warning only, with no fine, which was a surprise, and the signature, of course, was illegible. She wasn't worried though because she knew once she described him to her new coworkers someone would be able to identify him: blond curls, blue-black eyes, a dimple, a tight rear end that begged to be squeezed, impressive stature, and no apparent rings. Fleetingly, Dabria wondered what he looked like under all those clothes. A fling with him might just be the way to kick-start her new life! After being engaged for years the freedom to pursue a "no strings" affair was definitely a tantalizing temptation.

Round one went to the Viking. Round two would be Dabria's victory. The courtroom was her domain and he was about to find out she would not be bested there. Restoring her purse to order, she glanced behind and waited for his car to pull out. With a wave of his hand he indicated that he was waiting for her to pull out onto the highway so that he could follow her into town. Silently applauding his strategy, she executed a thorough and prolonged shoulder-check and then pulled onto the highway to resume her journey. Ten minutes later, with him still following her, Dabria approached the city limits. Before they reached the first set of traffic lights he pulled up into the lane beside her, and as she glanced to the right he gave her a salute and then turned off to circle back onto the highway. Dabria continued on to the Legal Aid Office to explore her new digs and meet her new coworkers. There would be time enough to plot her next move after she was settled.

~ ~ ~

Dabria spent the next week familiarizing herself with her new surroundings both at work and in her new city. The apartment she had rented was small but served the purpose for now. She had contacted a real estate agent and was looking for property at one of the local lakes. Prince Albert was in a boreal forest called Nesbitt Forest and the surrounding area was called Lakeland. There were several lakes within a 100 km radius of P.A. and when she had interviewed for the job after taking a tour of them, she had settled on Emma Lake. Its proximity to the city would ensure a short commute each day and grant her access to breathtaking scenery to use as the inspiration for one of her hobbies. Although the main purpose for this move was to strike out on her own and prove to herself and her family that she could survive and provide financially for herself, she was not above using the inheritance she had received upon David's death to purchase a property. Her house would not simply be a residence, but could become a healing place. What better way to put that money to use.

Since no one out here knew who her family was, she was free to cultivate friendships based on her own preferences. The last six months of infamous publicity had taken their toll on Dabria and she just wanted to hide away and lick her wounds - while allowing herself just to be. The stifling image she had been forced to portray all of her life had overshadowed her true self. Those restrictions no longer applied. Dabria embraced her new found freedom and relished the anonymity she would be able to experience here.

Once she had unpacked the necessities and gotten a feel for the city, using her female coworker's recommendations, she made appointments for a complete make-over. She had her mane of luxurious locks lopped off and donated to a real hair wig manufacturer for cancer survivors.

She had streaks added to the trendy pixie cut, taking her appearance from classically beautiful to chic. The look was stunning. She had a manicure, a pedicure, and a massage. She purchased new glasses which she believed added the elements of intelligence and controlled confidence to her new look. With a business suit on and four inch heels Dabria's new court image said, "Don't mess with me!"

~ ~ ~

Dabria's first morning of work dawned sunny and warm. It was the first of March and although not officially spring yet, the weather mirrored Dabria's mood of expectant optimism. The Legal Aid Offices were situated in a three-story, turn of the century boardinghouse made of red brick with painted white masonry accents. It was built into the side of a hill. The main entrance, at ground level, featured a round reception desk with an ample supply of mismatched chairs that served as seating for the offices' varied clientele. A supply room containing a copier and posting machines, client interview rooms, a washroom, and a couple of offices could also be found on this level.

The second floor contained several more offices and a washroom. The third floor held three offices for the senior lawyers. There were two boardrooms in the middle that the lawyers used for staff meetings and conferences. Both of these rooms opened onto a white alabaster balcony that served as the roof for the second floor back offices. The balcony and the second floor offices that it sat on overlooked the park-like atmosphere of the backyard. The basement, which contained files and records, opened onto a cement patio. The front yard had been paved to make client parking spaces. The acre backyard was enclosed by a six foot high brick and wrought iron fence. The fence was bordered on the inside by huge old maple and oak trees. Younger birch and willows dotted the property and offered shade for benches strategically placed under them. The house next door had been purchased several years ago and bulldozed down to make a staff parking lot. It was unusual in Prince Albert for an historical building such as this one to be renovated and used as a business. More often than not, in the past, old buildings were torn down rather than renovated. Dabria learned that a judge's family had privately owned the property and upon his death it had been willed to Legal Aid. A trust fund was in place to cover the costs of building renovations and yard maintenance.

Dabria's office was on the second floor and was one of several converted bedrooms. She was lucky to have a corner office that had opening windows facing the backyard. The floors, doors, and door and window casings were original refinished hardwood. The windows and furnishings, however, were new. The room was small, but roomy enough to contain a large honey oak veneer U shaped desk with a credenza, a file cabinet, a coat rack, and two beige cloth client chairs. Dabria had remembered that the windowsills were wide enough to support plants and so she had bought two plants the night before to bring with her. Today she wore lower heels and slacks rather than her usual attire of skirts. She brought her framed degrees and diplomas in the box with the plants. She also hauled in some framed black and white prints and a couple of her paintings for the walls.

After making a few trips back and forth to the car, she set her items on a chair and surveyed the room. Sitting on her desk was a box containing a new laptop, some cables, and a mouse. Beside the box sat a printer, printer paper, cartridges, and a phone. The windows housed functional cream colored venetian blinds. Walking behind the desk she discovered a plastic chair pad on the floor which would make the rolling movement of her chair easier. The only thing missing *was* a chair for her. She hung the pictures and frames with the nifty picture hangers she had brought and set the plants on the sill. She then unpacked the computer and connected it to the cables hanging out of the wall. As she crawled on her hands and knees under her desk to thread the cables she heard footsteps and looking towards the door she saw a pair of shiny black wingtips peeking at her. Scooting backwards out from under the desk, she popped up and was greeted by the Legal Aid Area Director, who was also the staff's Senior Counsel.

"Good morning, Dabria. Welcome aboard," he extended his hand. "Are you finding everything all right? I had hoped to have your computer hooked up before you got here but I just haven't had time. Do you need some help?"

Dabria dusted herself off and shook his outstretched hand.

"No, thank you, I'm finding everything just fine. The only thing I seem to be missing is a chair," she responded with a smile.

"This office used to be a storage room and as you're the first person to use it since it's been renovated we haven't purchased a chair yet. Go buy yourself one and we'll reimburse you up to a hundred dollars. If you pick it out, then it'll fit you properly. Once you've had a chance to get settled I want you to come to my office so that we can talk about the cases I'll be handing over to you."

Brad reached into his pocket. "Here are your keys for the front door and this is the security code. You have access to our offices twenty-four hours a day, seven days a week. I know that coming from a private practice you're accustomed to putting in hours that far exceed a normal forty hour work week. Our lawyers are no exception. However, we're very flexible here to accommodate for family obligations, personal appointments, etc. All you need to do is make sure our reception desk knows when you're out of the office and when you expect to return, whether for personal reasons or for court. Each lawyer has a mail box behind the reception desk for client messages, memos, and notices. Please check it at the beginning of your day and every time you return to the office. I know texting is the more popular mode of communication these days but it is often easier for me to simply dictate a memo and have my assistant distribute it. Do you smoke?"

"No."

"The facility is non-smoking. So, if you have a client who needs to smoke, take them outside into the backyard. There are tables and ashtrays out there. There's a side door on the main floor leading to stairs that descend onto the patio and a water cooler and coffee counter on each floor. The coffee pots indicate the time they were made so check that before grabbing a cup. Everyone and no-one is responsible for the pots, so if the coffee is out or old, please make a fresh pot. That's all I can think of for now. I'll see you in a bit."

Chapter 2

Before Dabria had a chance to head upstairs knuckles rapped on her door and what could have passed as a polished lawyer from the TV show *LA Law* strolled into her office.

"Hi, my name is Craig Marten. You're obviously our new lawyer."

Dabria accepted his hand and smiled.

"You guessed right—Dabria Abdulla-Smythe. You can call me Bree, if you like." Dabria had decided the less prim and proper name might help to make her new coworkers more comfortable with her. Her full name was useful in the courtroom but she felt people would think she was being pretentious in this relaxed, more informal environment. Bree was the pet name her childhood companions, Matthew and David, had for her when they were alone. It was a name her mother had forbidden, saying it sounded common. Since it brought back fond memories for Dabria and she wanted her new life here to be happy, she figured Bree was a good place to start.

Craig couldn't believe his luck. What a nice piece of eye candy this addition to the staff was. There were no rings . . . . that was a good sign. Hopefully, there were no boyfriends waiting in the wings either. Craig believed that the first man in always had an advantage. Never let it be said that he wasn't a pro at taking advantage of every opportunity that presented itself.

"Bree, it is," he readily agreed. "Have you met any of the other staff yet and did anyone give you a tour?"

"I stopped in last week and I met Jaimie, the receptionist. She did the honors. So besides Brad, you're the first lawyer I've met. Thanks, for asking."

"How do you know I'm a lawyer?" he questioned with mock innocence. "I could be a paralegal, a court runner, or even one of the secretaries, or rather, I mean *Executive Administrative Assistants.*"

"I've been a lawyer several years now. I can spot 'em ten miles away. But good try," she chuckled.

"Can I get you a coffee while you're setting up?"

Since she hadn't had a coffee yet today, she nodded in agreement. "Black, please."

His attempt at flirting was amusing but it wasn't going to get him anywhere. Dabria had never dated lawyers and wasn't about to start now. She had always believed that one of the reasons her parent's marriage worked so well was because they had different careers. Her mother's career had begun as a psychiatrist and had turned into a homemaker and a socialite. Caroline and Daniel, Dabria's father, each brought something new to the relationship every day. When Daniel came home and Caroline asked about his day he took the time to add to the previous day's drama at the lab just as Caroline then recited the events of her day. The different environments each worked in kept the interest level up for both of them when they were together in the evenings. Dabria knew she would settle for nothing less than the relationship her parents shared. Communication, respect, and pride in the other's accomplishments contributed to the obvious love they still had for each other. Similar backgrounds and the shared belief in the importance of her father's research also strengthened their commitment.

Dabria and Caroline had a tenuous relationship. To be fair to her mother, Dabria had to acknowledge that the reason Caroline had become a homemaker was out of love for her family. Caroline truly believed she would be more of an asset to her family and society in general, if she focused her attentions on fulfilling the physical and emotional needs of her husband and daughter rather than working out of the home. Basically, she had laid aside her dreams of saving the world and concentrated on the needs of her family instead. Although Dabria was unsure if that was a path she would ever follow, she did respect her mother for the choice she had made. There had been times though that she wished her mother had patients to worry about rather than concentrating so much on her daughter's life. Now was one of those times. Although Dabria appreciated the support from her family, especially during the time immediately after David and Matthew's deaths, she now felt suffocated by it.

Dabria was brought back to the present as Craig returned to her office with a full coffee cup in hand. While Craig continued to chat her up one of the female lawyers knocked and with Dabria's nod, walked in. There were ten lawyers currently working for Legal Aid. Besides Dabria there were only two other women. Brad had given her a brief run-down of staff before she had signed on. Dabria checked her mental notes and assumed that this was Sarah. Sarah was the unmitigated opposite of Dabria. She was exceptionally tall, thin almost to the point of emancipation, and blue eyed with long straight blond hair. Sarah looked like a stereotypical Scandinavian skier while Dabria was a petite, curvy, exotic looking mulatto. Sarah's specialty was family law. Since that was also Dabria's she knew that the two of them would often be working together or, at the very least, be collaborating. Dabria extended her hand as Sarah drew near. With a grin a mile wide Sarah grabbed Dabria's hand and pumped it enthusiastically.

"Morning, Craig," she acknowledged Mr.GQ. "I'm Sarah and I'm into family law. I heard you are, too. Brad's been promising us another family law lawyer for a while now. I'm so glad he found you. Has anyone shown you around yet? I'm expecting a client call PDQ but then I don't have any clients scheduled until after lunch so I'd be more than happy to help you get set up." As she stopped to take a breath Dabria cut in.

"Thanks, Sarah, that would be great but I have a meeting with Brad first. I'm pretty much set up already but we could go out for lunch? Oh, and please call me Bree."

"For sure, I'd love to. My office is #203. Just pop in when you're ready to leave." With a wave for Craig she swiftly swept out of the room.

"Sarah is nothing if not enthusiastic," commented Craig dryly. "Did you get all that before she *leapt* away?"

"Of course. How long has she practiced family law? She's definitely eager."

"Only a year, so the harsh reality of it hasn't settled in yet. I started off in family and soon discovered I just didn't have the stomach for it. Criminal law is much less emotionally draining."

"You sound jaded."

"Not jaded necessarily just realistic about my own limitations. I can sleep at night without worrying that my client's safety is in jeopardy because a judge won't put a restraining order on her abusive husband. How about you? How long have you practiced?"

"About seven years. You?"

"Ten all told." Craig stood up. "I hate to cut this short but I have to head out myself. I'm in the middle of a trial so I can't offer up any support or socializing this week. How about you meet me for a drink Friday after work?"

"Not to assume anything, but I just want you to know I don't date lawyers."

"Now there's a challenge if I ever heard one. Let's just call this: two coworkers getting to know one another. I'll call you Friday afternoon. Have a great week, Bree."

"Thanks. You, too."

Dabria finished setting up her computer and then headed to Brad's office. The third floor offices were twice the size of the second floor ones. The room's focal point was one wall of floor to ceiling bookshelves that were full to overflowing. His desk was also twice as big and the client chairs were larger and more comfortable than the ones in Dabria's office. That didn't mean to say the office was in any way extravagant looking, unlike the partner offices from her last firm. This one did, however, exude a feeling of integrity and instilled a sense of confidence in the person looking in upon it.

"Grab a seat, Dabria, or would you prefer Bree? I heard you talking to Sarah when I passed your office."

"Either one is fine."

"Alright then, I prefer Dabria. All of the cases you'll be working on for the next little while will be ones that were already assigned to other lawyers. Because of the overwhelming caseload we've had them adjourned. Not all of them are family law. If you have any questions the name of the original lawyer is at the top of each file. Some of them unfortunately have rescheduled court dates in the very near future. One, in fact, is this afternoon. The lawyer that interviewed the accused is no longer with us and his notes regarding that interview are sadly lacking in content. If after reviewing the notes you need another adjournment, I'm sure the judge will be willing to accommodate us since it is no fault of the client that his lawyer has abandoned him. The next most pressing case is scheduled for Friday. It's going to be overwhelming for awhile since Legal Aid isn't like a private office. We rarely have the option of declining a client's representation even if we're swamped." Brad pointed at a pile of files perched precariously on top of the two drawer filing cabinet by the door.

"Do you have the copy of the revised court dates?"

"Yes, I grabbed what was in my mailbox and breezed through the contents before coming to your office."

"Great. The location of each session is listed under the cases. Your first appearance is at the courthouse in town. Do you know where that is?"

"Yes, it's in the middle of the traffic circle at the top of the hill on Central Avenue. Actually, when I was in private practice in Alberta I represented a client that needed to appear here. That original trip to PA was what sparked my interest in applying for this position," she volunteered.

"Interesting," Brad commented without asking for details. "Get a parking pass from reception before you leave and they'll explain where you park. Apparently, your client is next to impossible to contact so let's hope he shows up at the courthouse in time for you to find him and at least introduce yourself. I'm sorry to dump this on you but there's no one else that can go. I'm off to court myself this afternoon. If you have any questions relating to things other than your cases ask the receptionists. They're both from PA so they should be fountains of information." Brad rose from his desk and motioned towards the pile. "Take the top file and I'll have someone bring the rest down to you shortly. There's nothing quite like jumping right in to force the first day jitters away, is there?"

"Thanks for the opportunity to prove that I'm the right person for the job," Dabria responded.

"I have every confidence that you'll serve this office well," Brad smiled and settled himself back into his oxblood, leather, wing-back chair. Lawyers may have desks and file cabinets that looked like they were dragged out of some bargain basement but they generally had expensive, extremely comfortable chairs for themselves. Brad was no exception. Although Dabria had been advised that she could buy herself a chair and be reimbursed she had every intention of spending a lot more than the office's budget and planned to make up the difference herself. But, she made a mental note to herself, it couldn't look better than Brad's. Dabria understood office politics very well. She would find a smaller black one with less buttons. She grabbed the flimsy file on her way out of the door and proceeded to the stairs.

Once back in her office, she grabbed a client chair and pulled it behind her desk. When she flipped the file open she was dismayed to discover there was less in the file than even she had anticipated. The client's name, address, and phone number were typed onto the first page. The previous lawyer had made a notation underneath which simply read, "Client pleads not guilty to all charges, claiming he was not driving stated vehicle." The next page was a copy of the list of charges: exceeding the posted speed limit, driving with a suspended license, driving under the influence, and undue care and attention causing dangerous driving. If the police officer could positively identify the suspect then her client was obviously guilty. She hoped that he showed up at court early enough for her to explain that to him. Strangely, his charges were similar to hers. She checked the officer's signature and *not* surprisingly it was a carbon copy of the signature on her summons. How ironic that her first court appearance in town would be representing a suspect charged with offences by *the Viking*.

Dabria dialed the number listed in the file and counted ring number seven as a knock at her door brought her back to earth and she looked up in time to see a stack of files with legs attached entering her office.

"So, where do ya want 'em," the muffled, unidentifiable voice requested?

"On the chair will be fine. Just give me a sec," Dabria directed as she hung up the phone and jumped up to skirt the desk and clear the other chair off.

Once the pile was plopped onto the chair Dabria discovered a rotund, red faced, balding, and bespectacled gnome of a man. He yanked a handkerchief from his pocket, wiped his brow, and then cleaned his glasses while he squinted at her. After returning his glasses to their perch he thrust his hand at her.

"Howdy. My name's Barry . . . . Barry Bainbridge. I heard through the grapevine that we had an addition and I decided to check out the little girl with the big name."

"Hello, Barry. Just call me Bree."

"That fits you much better. My office is next door to yours. If you need anything just holler. I'm preparing for a particularly dry corporate trial and I'd welcome any interruptions. Got lunch plans yet?"

"Yes, thank you."

"Next time, then. My wife, Melinda, meets me most days but occasionally I'm at loose ends. Back to the grind." With that he toddled out the door and was gone.

What an interesting creature. Not only was he almost cartoonish looking but his drawl was contrary to the image, making him even more of a character. Dabria could picture him wearing a red gnome's hat, riding a hobby horse, waving and hollering, "Y'all come back now, ya' hear!" The fantastical image made her laugh out loud. She wondered what his wife looked like and if they had children. Gazing over at the pile on her chair she instantly sobered. She was afraid there was enough work in those files to keep her occupied for a very long time to come. Although she loved her career she wanted to cultivate some kind of a social life here as well.

Seizing the top ten files, the list of court dates, and a calendar, Dabria started to wade through the mess. Before she knew it, lunch was upon her. Grabbing the file she needed for court that afternoon, her coat, and her purse, she headed to Sarah's office. They parked on the street behind the courthouse outside a building with a very appealing architectural design. Sarah was happy to enlighten Dabria that this was PA's best kept secret when it came to home cooked food. It was a quaint three story, turn of the century row-house that had a colorful history. The old timers knew it as the long time neighborhood whore house and tended to steer clear. The nouveau YUPPIES or BOBOS, Bourgeois Bohemians—so coined by author David Brooks—frequented the renovated structure and didn't attempt to sway the locals to their way of thinking.

Each floor was a different color. The walls of floor one were painted butter yellow, floor two - key lime, and floor three - sky blue. All had wide base-boards, doors, window casings, and stair rails painted stark white. A dumb-waiter had been installed allowing for easy transport of both full and empty plates from the main floor to the third floor and back. The dining rooms were populated with well used, intimate tables for four and mismatched chairs. And they were all full. Sarah and Dabria finally found an open table on the third floor. There were specific menus for each day of the week with only three options per meal. There were two different fresh desserts each day. All five items were posted on the board as you entered. The prices were no higher than your typical fast food meal. But, there was a huge difference in presentation and quality. The taste more than made up for the speed of a drive thru. Sarah's claim had just been substantiated.

Along with the divine cuisine came Sarah's commentary on the office staff. Both were equally tasty. Dabria was enchanted by the straightforwardness and lack of pretense of her lunch companion. It was a nice change from the double speak she was used to navigating both at her mother's social soirees and at her previous work place. Dabria wasn't required to talk. A simple nod or smile was encouragement enough for Sarah to continue her narration. There were ten lawyers, two administrative assistants, five legal secretaries, and four paralegals. The court runner duties were shared by the legal secretaries and the paralegals. Once Sarah had run through the staff she stopped and took a long drink of water, no doubt to fortify herself for the next phase of her oration. It was then that Dabria dove in.

"I met an R.C.M.P. the day that I arrived in town. Well, actually, he pulled me over. Anyway, as it happens, he's the arresting officer of the client I'm representing this afternoon in court. I can't read his signature but if I describe him to you do you think you might be able to identify him? I'd like some insight into how to cross examine him."

"Sure, I know several of the R.C.M.P. In fact, I'm dating one. Fire away."

"O.K. He's thirty-something, well over six feet with curly blond hair, and blue eyes. The day I met him he was in street clothes and unshaven so I'm guessing possibly a plainclothes detective. What I'm trying to figure out is why he would be issuing traffic tickets to not only me but also our client."

"I've never even heard of him let alone seen him. I know there have been some new transfers in within the last couple of weeks. Kent, that's my boyfriend, has been on holidays. Do you want me to ask about him and see what I can find out?"

"Yes, please, but do it discretely. I don't want him to know." Dabria glanced down at her watch. "I'd better get moving. I have to try and find my client before court starts and according to Brad that could be a bit of a challenge."

"You go ahead. Lunch is on me today. I'll meet you back at the office later. Good luck!"

"Thanks. I don't think luck is going to help this client at all. Thanks for lunch. I'll catch you later." With a goodbye wave Dabria skipped down the stairs and made her way out into the sunshine and across the street to the rear of the courthouse.

Chapter 3

Dabria walked around to the front and ascended the wide granite stairs of the intimidating sand-stone brick courthouse, adorned only by thin wrought iron accents and granite window casings. It looked like the perfect backdrop for an 18th century "horrid" novella. As she walked through the oversized, weathered brass and glass double doors she was greeted with a foyer containing three-story high cathedral ceilings, classic grey and white marble floors, and a fan shaped marble staircase with an age darkened oak banister leading to the second floor. Thousands of hands would have smoothed their way down it or pulled their masters up it over the course of the last hundred years, inadvertently polishing the surface to a glowing sheen. As she surveyed the ground level, worn oak benches placed strategically outside of several sets of smaller double doors came into view. A similar set up appeared on the second level. Smaller staircases flanked the outer walls of the second floor leading to the third floor. Modern antique replica lighting was suspended by cables from the cathedral ceiling. Similar styled light sconces were attached to the walls on each level. Sunlight streamed in through the second and third storey windows. The initial impression of gravity and solemnity had continued inside the walls of the imposing structure.

Although the casual observer would possibly classify the setting as bleak and uninviting, Dabria found it inspiring and comforting. She knew these hallowed halls would have seen many dramas unfold over the course of their existence. Some would be tragedies and some bittersweet victories. Dabria was proud to call herself a lawyer and humbled by the knowledge that her passion and devotion to her calling could have a positive impact on those she represented. She had a responsibility to her clients that she did *not* take lightly. In some instances a client's very life could be transformed by her dedication to their case or lack of it. This felt like home - like she belonged here. It was the same feeling that had washed over her the first time she had entered the foyer a year and a half ago. With a deep breath Dabria pushed aside her musings and concentrated on looking for her client. Although the halls and entrance had been occupied by several people previous to her arrival, their presence and the noise they made just now registered into her consciousness.

As Dabria's gaze swept the lobby she noticed two young men of the approximate age she was looking for, chatting and leaning against an outer wall. As she approached them, the one with his back to her turned around and Dabria realized that the two were identical twins. Suddenly the plea of "not guilty" made sense. It was either a case of actual mistaken identity or at the very least they planned on using that as their defense. As she continued to advance the one closest to her straightened up and extended his hand.

"Hi. My name is Mark. Are you my new lawyer?"

The file name had been Mark, but her gut instinct was telling her this was *not* Mark. She had learned to always listen to her instincts.

"I'm sure I'm not *your* lawyer," she slowly enunciated with a glare, daring him to contradict her. "I am looking for *Mark* Simmonds," she emphasized as her scrutiny swiveled to his brother.

"Of course. How clever of you to determine that I'm not Mark without ever having met us before," the young man admiringly commented. "This one's a lot smarter than the last one, Mark. She'll definitely be able to convince the judge that that silly cop has no idea who he arrested. I told you everything would work out fine."

"And you are?" she questioned with disdain.

"Matt."

"Okay, boys, let's find a room with some privacy so you can tell me all about it before we get into court." There were several single open doors straight ahead and turning on her heels Dabria made her way towards them, knowing full well that the boys would follow. Once inside she closed the door firmly, sat down, opened the file, and placed it on the desk in front of her. She glanced at her watch and determined she needed to get to the truth in the next fifteen minutes. Gesturing for the boys to sit down, she began her interview.

"Let me just clarify that I won't represent you if you lie to me, again. So, Mark, let's start at the beginning and tell me the truth. Oh, and by the way, I *will* know if you're lying. You aren't my first client and I didn't just pass the Bar yesterday. Let's begin with you stating your name, just like you'll have to do when we get into court." Dabria directed her instructions to the brother who, up to this point, hadn't spoken.

"Mmmmmmy . . . . mmmy . . . . my nnnname . . . . name is Mmmmmmark." Mark's stuttering was pronounced enough that there was no way the boys could get away with mistaken identity if he spoke in court. This was, of course, their plan.

"Okay, let's cut to the chase here, shall we? Who was actually driving the car?"

"Iiiiiit . . . . it was me," Mark responded emphatically but without conviction.

"Did you speak to the R.C.M.P. at all during your encounter with him?"

"Yes."

"So he knows that you stutter?" she bluntly inquired.

"Ooooof . . . . ooof . . . . of course," he declared.

"Do you stutter when you're drunk?"

"Huh?"

"I said, do you stutter when you've been drinking?"

"Uhhhhhhh," Mark stalled and his eyes darted towards his brother. In that instant Dabria knew that just as she had suspected, it was actually Matt who had been driving. When he was pulled over instead of taking his punishment he had pretended to be Mark just so that his identity would come into question.

"Okay, do you remember me saying don't lie to me again? Well, you just did. So I guess you better find yourself *another* new lawyer." With that, Dabria closed the file and stood up.

"Noooo . . . noo . . . no wait," Mark stood up and reached out a hand to stop her from leaving.

"Mark, shut up," Matt advised threateningly.

"You . . . . you . . . . you shut up," he pointed his finger at his brother. "The reason I have a suspended license is be . . . be . . . because of you. I'm tired of covering your ass. You get caught doing st . . . st . . .

stupid things and then use me to get out of your messes. I can't afford to get caught lying to a judge. I want to make something of myself and it's hard to get a job when you have a criminal record. Lying is hardly the way to accomplish that goal. I plan on telling the truth today. No more "mistaken identity" or twin switch . . . switch . . . switching."

"Funny how you were happy to do it as long as I was gettin' you laid. I don't remember you complainin' then," Matt countered.

"All right, boys, that's enough. Matt, were you driving the night the R.C.M.P. pulled the Mustang over?"

"Yes," Matt mumbled.

"Were you drunk?"

"I had been drinking," he hedged.

"Did they do a breathalyzer test?"

"Yes."

"Did you blow over the limit?"

"Yes."

"Have either of you ever had any other drunk driving charges laid against you before?"

"No," Matt responded while Mark shook his head.

"All right, this is what is going to happen. Mark and I are going into the courtroom to face the judge. Matt, you will sit at the back of the courtroom. The charges against Mark will be read. They will ask for a plea. We will plead "not guilty." The prosecution will call their witnesses and they will relate the events of the evening including the arrest. They will be asked to identify the accused. After I have cross-examined them the prosecution will rest and it will be our turn. Mark will be called to the stand. After reciting your name I will ask you to describe your activities on the night in question. You *will* tell the truth. Once the prosecution is finished their cross examination I will request that you be fingerprinted again to compare to the prints that were taken the night of the arrest. That will prove that Mark wasn't driving since the prints won't match."

"Ahh, actually that could be a problem," Matt said.

"Why is that?"

"Well, then they're gonna know it was me!"

"*That* is not my problem nor is it Mark's. Mark is the one being charged with things he didn't do. It *is* my job to make sure he isn't convicted of those charges."

"Wh . . . what will h . . . h . . . happen to us?" asked Mark.

"Well, Mark, you may be looking at Obstruction of Justice since you knew that Matt was driving your car and didn't report it. The R.C.M.P. has the option to press for jail time. However, if you fully cooperate from now on you could end up with public service. If the R.C.M.P. decided to pursue Matt he may face charges related to the events of the night of his arrest. Those would obviously be Driving Under the Influence, Obstruction of Justice, and impersonating you. So, gentlemen are we ready?" she inquired seriously.

"Yes, Ma'am," Mark declared decisively, without stuttering.

Again with the Ma'am! Good gawd! Maybe it was time to check into the cost of a couple of Botox injections, Dabria thought with a grimace.

"Whatever! I'm not stickin' around to make it easier for some pig to take me in. I'm outta here," Matt defiantly declared.

Matt bolted from the room in front of Dabria and Mark. He pushed past an officer that looked alarmingly familiar to him as he hustled out the front door of the courthouse. With Mark trailing behind her, as she made her way up the staircase, a distinctively familiar scent assailed her nostrils and Dabria knew who followed her before she heard the rumble of his voice from behind. Butterflies instantly fluttered as awareness prickled up her spine and a trail of goose bumps rose on her forearms. Thankfully, she was wearing long sleeves. Twisting her head she confirmed that *the Viking*, not Matt, was on the stair directly behind her.

"I see you're early for our date," he murmured softly as he moved up to walk beside her.

"Our date?" she questioned with a raised eyebrow.

"Our court date, of course," he added with that smug smile. "I didn't expect to see you for another couple of weeks. And, look at you! You got a make-over and everything. You shouldn't have gone to the trouble. I liked you well enough the way you were. I'm sure you think the new hairdo and the glasses will make people take you more seriously and that you'll appear less approachable . . . . more intimidating. I, however, think they just make you look like more of a challenge." Again with the killer smile! "I never could resist a good challenge."

Today he was clean shaven and in uniform. Unfortunately, he was even more attractive. There really was "just something about a man in a uniform." The quote popped into her head as she tried to focus on walking up the stairs without tripping.

"I guess it's your lucky day then, isn't it. We'll see how you fair across the floor from me, this afternoon."

"One of your twins bumped into me as he beat it out of the courthouse. His very existence may lend support to your "not guilty" plea. However, I too, may have a surprise up my sleeve."

"I never doubted that for a second. I have every confidence in your ability to get the right man."

Morgan's instincts were sending off warning signals not to casually dismiss her remarks. She was obviously trying to tell him she knew the truth behind the twins' story and she would not be caught unaware in the courtroom. He was going to have to stay on his toes to keep ahead of this one.

"Thank you, for the support," Morgan acknowledged. "Occasionally both sides can win *and* achieve a common goal at the same time. Let's see if, in fact, we do have a common goal."

"I'm pretty sure you and I do not have a common goal. My goal is simply to *promote access to justice through the process of quality legal assistance.* What's your goal?" she flashed him her first real smile as she stopped, turned, and stood one step above him defiantly looking him directly in the eye. It was saucy and sexy and immediately changed her from cute to ravishing. The stab of lust he instantly felt focused directly on his crotch and he felt his penis twitch. Since Mark had caught up to them she turned away from Morgan and directed Mark to follow her down the hall.

"We're in Courtroom Two." She pointed towards a door to the right of the stairs. As she walked away from her still nameless *Viking,* she flung over her shoulder, "See you inside," very effectively ending their conversation. He let her consult with her client and after making no attempt to hide his thorough inspection of them, he walked in the other direction.

Morgan had done a lot of research since their initial meeting and had discovered that there was much more to Ms. Abdulla-Smythe than the very pleasing package that he watched from across the hallway. Dabria had recently taken a position at the Legal Aid Office in town as one of their Family Law Lawyers. He knew she had moved from a small community in Alberta. After checking with the detachment there, he was taken aback to discover that she had been investigated in the harassment and attempted murder of a female Conservation Officer. Although no charges were laid, apparently there was still some question as to whether or not she had actually been involved. The accidental death of her fiancé precipitated the harassment and murder attempts. The conclusion to the whole sordid affair was the murder of one of her fiancé's lovers and the fatal shooting, by the R.C.M.P., of one of their childhood friends.

In the last six months drastic changes to her life had obviously occurred. The fact that she had removed herself to another province, far away from the nightmare, was hardly surprising. Since he had done his research alone and the results obviously had no bearing on her traffic violations, he decided to keep the findings to himself and would continue to keep her secrets unless circumstances dictated that he reveal them.

For now he would keep a very close eye on Ms. Smythe. Since he had made no secret of his attraction to her he planned on watching her for both personal as well as professional reasons. It would be interesting to see how today's proceedings unfolded. Morgan was an excellent judge of character and his intuition was telling him that she was trustworthy and honest. He hoped her behavior in the courtroom substantiated his instincts.

Moments later the doors to Courtroom Two were unlocked and opened. The bailiff entered the hall and requested that lawyers and clients for the upcoming case numbers proceed into the courtroom. Their case was the first on the docket. Dabria and Mark walked to the front of the courtroom and sat at the table provided for the defense. The prosecution lawyer settled himself at the desk opposite. The judge entered the courtroom and the gallery, lawyers, and their clients rose collectively upon the bailiff's instruction. The proceedings were called to order. Dabria was whispering to Mark to stop fidgeting and missed the arrested reaction of the judge as his eyes initially skimmed over her and the courtroom. Stillness surrounded him as he continued to stealthily sneak glimpses of her while he settled himself on his perch above the assembly before him. The charges against Mark were read and the judge asked for his plea.

"Not guilty," Dabria said with absolute certainty as she stood beside her client.

"And who might you be?" Judge Richard Reynolds inquired of Dabria.

"My name is Dabria Abdulla-Smythe and I am Legal Aid Counsel representing the defendant."

"What office do you work out of? You have never appeared before me, have you?"

"No, Your Honor, I have not. Today is my first day at the Prince Albert Legal Aid Office."

"Where did you come from?"

"I came from a private practice in Alberta, Your Honor."

"I see. Have you had adequate time to review this file? I understand this case has already been postponed once."

"Yes, Your Honor, I am confident that I can effectively represent this client."

"Fine, let's proceed then. Shall we? Mr. Avery please present the Crown's case."

The prosecutor called Morgan to the stand. After Morgan was sworn in the prosecutor then began to question him as to the events that transpired on the night in question.

"For the record, Officer, please state your full name, title, position, and place of employment."

"My name is Detective Morgan Vaughn. I am a Detective for the Royal Canadian Mounted Police, Prince Albert Detachment."

"Detective Vaughn, please relate to us the events that occurred on the evening of November 23, 2011."

"I was returning from surveillance duty and was waiting on Buckland Road to turn onto Highway 222 on my way back to the detachment. A 2010 yellow Ford Mustang with license number "H-O-T T-O-O" raced past me, obviously exceeding the speed limit. I immediately pulled out in pursuit and as I switched on my flashers the Mustang increased its speed and passed a slower moving vehicle ahead of it. I continued my pursuit and requested back-up at that time. The Mustang passed several vehicles and maintained its excessive speed. After traveling approximately five miles the driver seemed to realize that I was following him and finally pulled over. I approached the car after running the plates and determined that it was registered to a "Mark Simmonds." My search informed me that Mr. Simmonds' licence was suspended. His driver's licence picture was displayed for my information. When I arrived at the window of the car the driver opened his door and all but fell out. I helped him stand up, and since there was a great deal of traffic, I asked him if he would consent to a blood alcohol test in the back of the cruiser that had just pulled up, instead of trying to do a sobriety test on the side of the road. He mumbled and finally stuttered out an answer that I took to indicate his agreement."

"Do you mean he was so inebriated that he was stuttering and couldn't speak, Detective?"

"I thought that might be the case at the time but once he sobered up he continued to stutter."

"His speech obviously had nothing to do with allegedly being under the influence then. Did it?"

"No, it did not."

"What happened next?"

"I helped Mr. Simmonds into the back of the cruiser and asked him for his licence and registration. He indicated they were in the console of the car and I could go retrieve them. Officer Bailey accompanied me to the Mustang while Officer Mackenzie supervised a breathalyzer test on Mr. Simmonds. It was determined that his blood alcohol level was .14 and exceeded the legal limit. The licence and registration were for Mark Simmonds. I asked him if he was Mark Simmonds and he replied that he was. At this point we read Mr. Simmonds his rights and arrested him for Driving Under the Influence, Driving While Suspended, Exceeding the Posted Speed Limit, and Undue Care and Attention Causing Dangerous Driving. He was handcuffed and then transported to the holding cells. After being processed at the station he passed out before exercising the right of one call and was left in the cells overnight to sleep it off."

"What did you do with his car?"

"His car was towed to the R.C.M.P. holding compound and locked inside."

"Is there anything else you would like to add, Detective?"

"I found it odd that his stuttering seemed to be extremely pronounced at the time of arrest and seemed to almost disappear the next morning."

"How did you manage to hear him speak the next morning, Detective?"

"Since I was on a night shift I made a point of waking him up and releasing him before my shift ended at 8:00 a.m. It was almost like he forgot to stutter when he first woke up. Then suddenly he seemed to recall the situation he was in and the stuttering became extreme again."

"Are you saying you think he was acting?"

"It did seem that way."

"Objection Your Honor," Dabria exclaimed as she rose from her seat.

"Ms.? . . . . what do you want me to call you?" Judge Reynolds inquired gently of Dabria.

"Ms. Abdulla-Smythe, Your Honor."

"Ms. Abdulla-Smythe?" the judge questioned with a raised eyebrow. "Fine. What is your objection?"

"Detective Vaughn can't make an assumption like that based on his two interactions with my client. My client would have been under extreme stress because of the events of the previous evening once he realized where he was. Stuttering is often accentuated by stressful situations."

"Sustained. Councilor, do you have any further questions?"

"No, Your Honor. Thank you, Detective Vaughn." The prosecutor sat down.

"Do you wish to cross-examine, Ms. Abdulla-Smythe?"

"Yes, Your Honor, I do."

"Please proceed then."

"Detective Vaughn, you said that you questioned the sincerity of Mr. Simmonds' stuttering. Why would you do that?"

"As a detective I am trained to look beyond the obvious, to follow my instincts, and to investigate further if the facts don't seem to add up. I had a roommate in college who stuttered. When he drank alcohol his stuttering became less pronounced because the alcohol made him less self-conscious. In the case of Mr. Simmonds, although his blood alcohol level was well above the legal limit, his stuttering was extreme. That was inconsistent with my previous personal experiences. Since the licence plate of Mr. Simmonds was "Hot Too" it naturally occurred to me that there probably was a licence registered as "Hot One." Upon doing a search I determined that there was indeed a "Hot One" licence plate and it was registered to a Matthew Simmonds. Further investigation revealed that Matthew and Mark were related. In fact, they are identical twin brothers."

"What did you think was the purpose of the *insincere* stuttering, Detective?"

"Obviously, the one I had arrested was trying to be the twin that stuttered."

"How do you know that both twins don't stutter?"

"My investigation revealed that the boys had no family but I was able to confirm where the boys graduated from high school. I went and spoke to one of their teachers. Mrs. Francis verified that only one twin stutters and that it was Mark."

"So if Mark was the one that stuttered and the young man that you arrested not only stuttered but also claimed he was Mark, then why would you question his identity?"

"Mrs. Francis also told me that while in her class the boys often tried to switch identities. Since she has a set of twins of her own, she knows that even identical twins have characteristics that distinguish one from the other. Their handwriting was telling as well as the content of their "in class" spontaneous prose assignments."

"Did you bring some writing examples from Mrs. Francis' class for the court to examine as evidence?" The gallery chuckled, as did Dabria.

"Of course not. But, she did let me read copies she had kept. The difference in the boys was extremely apparent. Mark's short stories had a common thread of integrity and morality. Matthew's stories were about deception and the joy derived from that trickery."

"What are you trying to tell us, Detective Vaughn?"

"I believe that Matthew was driving Mark's car and pretending to be him so that Mark would take the fall for the drunk driving?"

"Detective, can you identify the person you arrested on the evening of November 23?" Dabria asked.

"No, he's not in this room." A collective gasp rose from the gallery. The shuffling and muttered comments created a din in the courtroom.

"If the gallery cannot contain itself I will clear the floor," Judge Reynolds threatened. "Excuse me for interrupting, Councilor," the Judge leveled a penitent smile upon Dabria, "but are you saying the gentleman sitting before the court is not Mark Simmonds, Detective Vaughn?"

"No, I'm sure he is. I'm saying the gentleman I arrested that night *claiming* to be Mark Simmonds is not in this courtroom."

"So who did you arrest and where is he, Detective Vaughn?"

"It would be Mark Simmonds' identical twin brother Matthew Simmonds."

"And what, pray tell, would lead you to that conclusion?" the judge demanded.

Dabria had been standing directly in front of Morgan while she questioned him. She now turned and sauntered back to her table. Once there she resumed her stance in front of her chair.

"Mrs. Francis also told me that Matthew suffered an injury as a toddler and he developed Horner's Syndrome which has caused him to become a heterochromiac," Morgan answered the judge's question but his focus never wavered from Dabria.

"What the heck does that mean?" the judge inquired, obviously losing patience with Morgan's courtroom antics.

"It means that Matthew has one blue eye and one brown eye while Mark's eyes are both brown."

"I still don't understand, Detective Vaughn. Isn't there such a thing as colored lenses these days?"

"Yes, Your Honor, there is. The young man that I released from the R.C.M.P. cells on the morning of November 24th woke up with only one bloodshot eye. I, myself, wear contacts and I know that if I sleep with them in, then in the morning my eyes are dry and often bloodshot. I watched Matthew that morning before his release. Initially he carefully rubbed his right eye but apparently that didn't relieve the dryness so he then popped the contact out, spit on it, and then replaced it. In the time it took him to do that I observed that his bloodshot eye was blue. The twin of the man sitting in front of me bumped into me as he hurried out of the courthouse just before the proceedings started today. He had different colored eyes. The gentleman sitting before us does not."

"Detective, are you claiming that you believe the man sitting before us with charges against him is not in fact the perpetrator of the crimes?"

"That is correct, Your Honor."

"So why the heck didn't you say something earlier instead of wasting all our time with your recitation of what you consider to be your amazing detecting abilities?"

"Because, Your Honor, until I actually sat up here and looked closely at Mark I wasn't positive that I was right."

"But now you are?"

"Yes, Your Honor, I am."

"Therefore, if you are correct, Detective, then fingerprinting my client and comparing them to the prints of the gentleman you arrested should clear up any question as to my client's innocence. Would that not be a logical conclusion?" Dabria swiftly questioned Morgan.

"That is correct," he agreed.

"Is your client agreeable to being fingerprinted, Ms. Abdulla-Smythe?" Judge Reynolds asked.

After consulting with Mark, Dabria stood.

"My client would be more than happy to provide the court with a set of his fingerprints, Your Honor."

"Fine. I adjourn this case until the prints of the gentleman sitting in front of me have been collected and compared to the prints that were taken the night of the arrest. When the results return from the I-Dent lab we will reconvene. If, at that time, the defense can prove the prints don't match, all of the aforementioned charges against Mr. Mark Simmonds will be dropped. I don't doubt, however, that new ones might be laid against both of the gentlemen involved."

Chapter 4

After dismissing her client with new instructions, she gave herself a mental pat on the back. Her first representation as a legal aid lawyer had gone well. As she walked down the courthouse staircase her cell phone vibrated. She continued out of the doors, stopped on the outside steps, and answered it.

"Hello."

"Ms. Abdulla-Smythe? This is Colin from REMAX. I've lined up some listings for you out at Emma. Can you do viewings this evening?"

"Colin, please call me Bree. I'd love to do viewings this evening. What time and where do we meet?"

"I can pick you up at your place around 5:30 p.m. How does that sound?"

"Can I just meet you out there? I'd really like to drive around a little and familiarize myself with the lake. The best way to do that is to drive yourself, ya know?"

"Sure. How about meeting at the Old Trading Post at 6:00 p.m.? Do you know where that is?"

"Yes, I'll see you then," Dabria turned to skip down the stairs. At the base of the town's war memorial slouched Detective Vaughn. He appeared nonchalant, but in reality was scrutinizing Dabria's every movement. She was definitely a mouth watering little package. Acknowledging that she had finished her call and was therefore available to him, Morgan straightened and ambled over to her. Sunglasses obscured Dabria's view of Morgan's eyes, but that telltale dimple indicated that he was trying to suppress a grin.

"So, Ms. Defense Attorney, I don't see a little black Tiburon in the parking lot. Was that also sacrificed as part of your *Total Make-Over?*"

"The Tiburon was the first part of the *Total Make-Over*, Detective. I've always wanted an inexpensive but sexy little sports car. So, I traded in my *very* expensive, *fairly* conservative Palladium silver colored Mercedes Coupe Roadster."

"Are you kidding me?" he exclaimed with disgust as he shook his head. "You do realize that the Roadster was ten times the car your Tiburon is?"

"Maybe. In fact probably, but I don't need to drive a high performance, snob mobile here. Beauty is in the eye of the beholder and anyway, I love the look of my new wheels *and* I blend in better."

"Blend in?"

"This isn't Calgary, Detective. I'm trying to fit into my new community."

"Point taken. So where is the little devil? Parked at the office?"

"Yes."

"Do you need a lift?"

"Thank you, no. It's a beautiful day and I prefer to walk back. It's only a couple of blocks. I believe my Professor in Law 101 told us the very first day of class that it's not a good idea to fraternize with the enemy."

"The enemy? Ms Abdulla-Smythe, I take offence to that. I would not consider myself your enemy. Do you feel threatened by me?"

"No," Dabria scoffed. "Hardly. Let's just agree that our next encounter will see us on opposing sides of the courtroom with opposing views on what we want the outcome to be."

"You may be wrong regarding what my hoped for conclusion is," he taunted her with a smirk. "I guess you'll just have to wait and see."

"Detective Vaughn, although you've also recently moved here maybe you can answer a few questions for me." Ignoring Morgan's apparent sexual innuendo she changed the direction of the conversation back to business. Damn it. She realized she'd just revealed that she must have asked about him and at the very least, knew he was also a new-comer to the community.

"Shoot," he encouraged with a twitch of his lips. He obviously had caught her slip.

"In all my years of practicing I've never come across a judge that allowed a witness to postulate the way you did today."

"Me either," he agreed.

"Is that a common practice here? Or is it peculiar to this judge? And how did you know he was going to allow you to do it?"

"I don't believe it is common practice. I can't tell you if it's peculiar to him since this is the first time I've appeared before him," he answered each question in order. "And I had no idea he was going to allow me to do it."

"Then, why did you investigate the boys that thoroughly?"

"It's what I do, Ms. Abdulla Smythe."

"On every case?" she questioned with bewilderment.

"I certainly try to. You'd be amazed by the things I've dug up over the years."

"I'm sure I would. How do you find the time? Researching is very time consuming."

"Well, up to this point my entire existence was focused on the job. It was how I've managed to stay alive for the past two years."

"I don't understand," she asked quizzically.

"That's another story for another day," he effectively put her off as he backed towards his cruiser.

"Have a lovely afternoon, Detective." Dabria took her cue to leave and with that she turned away from him and headed back up the hill. She could feel his eyes on her as she walked out of sight. A shiver of dread raced up her spine. How deeply had he dug into *her* past? And what did he know?

Once back in her office, Dabria dismissed any thoughts of Detective Vaughn, read through several of the case files she needed to prepare for, made notes, and confirmed trial dates. The rest of the afternoon flew by and when Sarah poked her head in to say goodbye Dabria was startled to discover it was after 5:00 p.m. Before she could sprint away, Dabria reached out her hand and motioned for her to sit down.

"Sarah, have you ever appeared before Judge Reynolds?"

"Have I! Was he your introduction to P.A.'s courthouse?"

"Yes," she didn't bother to correct Sarah's assumption that this was her first visit since it wasn't really relevant at this point.

"How was that?"

"Unusual would be the word that comes to mind."

"Yup, that would be one word. He's very eccentric and we all dread coming up before him."

"Why?"

"You go into court thinking you're prepared and sometimes everything goes well. The next time your whole strategy will go to hell in a hand-basket. I've not only appeared before him but also sat in on some of his sessions. The man is brilliant and he scares the crap out of me. How did it go today?"

"I served the client's needs well and guaranteed that he won't pay for a crime he didn't commit."

"So, despite Judge Reynolds, you're happy with the outcome?" Sarah questioned with a raised eyebrow.

"Yah, I am," Dabria confirmed with a nod of her head.

"He's not typical of the judges in town. So don't worry. Sorry, but I gotta run. Kent is waiting for me."

"Thanks for making me feel so welcome today," Dabria commented.

A huge grin split Sarah's face. "Any time," she promised as she disappeared into the hall.

Dabria gathered the files she would be working on overnight and stuffed them into her well worn, chocolate brown, soft as butter, leather briefcase. As she entered the foyer she noticed Jaimie the receptionist was leaving and held the door open for her.

"So, how was the first day?"

"It was better than anticipated. Thanks for asking."

"I see you found a hairdresser. I hardly recognized you this morning without all your long hair."

"Thanks for the name. I think Brandy did a great job. Don't you? What do you think of the nails? I talked her into taking me on as a nail client as well."

"Ya, it's okay. I just can't believe she allowed you to cut it all off, though. I think it was better before. And the nails aren't really my thing."

"She didn't have much choice since I told her that's what I wanted. And as far as the nails, they *are* my thing and she does an excellent gel. Anyhow, as I'm sure you've heard before "the customer is always right." Well, I have another appointment so I'd better run. See you tomorrow,"

Dabria waved her freshly decaled and buffed nails as she hustled out to her little black devil car and headed for the lake. Jaimie was certainly comfortable in expressing her opinions. At least Dabria would always know where she stood with her. Her honesty might come in handy. It was certainly a switch from the predictable platitudes Dabria was used to, she thought with a chuckle.

It was a beautiful winter day. A lot of the snow had already melted and it looked promising for an early spring. The roads were dry and traffic was light as she sped out of town. The only way Dabria could guarantee she wouldn't go over the speed limit was to set the cruise and then sit back and enjoy the journey. She was bubbling with anticipation as she cruised on down the road.

Emma Lake was actually made up of three lakes attached by channels. The first lake was the largest with a channel wide enough to allow the passage of several boats at one time between it and the second lake. The channel between the second and third lake, which was the shallowest, however, was very narrow and only two boats could meet while slowly navigating through it. On a low water year the best way to travel between the two lakes was single file at a fairly fast clip since the boats then planed out and skimmed over the top of the water. Each lake had its own advantages and disadvantages. The third lake's big plus was that only the south side of it was developed or ever would be. This made it very private, but much of it was reedy with a soft bottom. It was great for fishing for northern pike since they liked the reeds and it was perfect for water skiing since it was almost always calmer than the other two lakes. Cottage owners were no longer allowed to change the natural state of the shoreline, due to new conservation laws. If you had rocks and reeds in front of your cabin you were stuck with rocks and reeds in front of your cabin. Adding sand and removing the rocks and reeds destroyed fish breeding grounds as well as nesting sites for the many waterfowl that populated the area, including the Common Loon. Kenderdine Camp, owned and operated by the University of Saskatchewan, was located at the end of the row of private cabins. It was an art camp that invited accomplished artists from all over the world to teach aspiring artists their trade. In the middle of the lake sat Fairy Island that was also owned by the U. of S. It was used by both the artists and biologists. The biologists studied marine life, plant life, bird life, etc. of the northern lakes.

The second lake's claim to fame was the Provincial Campground. There were more cabins on this lake than the third, since both sides of the lake were conducive to swimming, and sand beaches had been created along the lakeshore many decades ago.

The first lake contained the three largest public sand beaches and the surrounding area enjoyed the majority of the lake's various amenities. However, it was also the most populated and therefore, the busiest, particularly on the weekends during the summer. Since it was larger and therefore, less sheltered, as well as heavily used by boat traffic the lake was rarely calm.

As she pulled into the parking lot of the Old Trading Post she noticed a big sign displayed over the boarded-up building explaining that they were closed for the season. A smaller sign, extremely weathered, stated that they would be re-opening May 1. The Old Trading Post was one of several local businesses at the lake that catered to the summer traffic. It was like the stereotypical general store that sold everything from fishing licences and tackle, to fresh baked goods, to beautiful tie-dyed beach dresses. They also had DVD and Play Station Rentals for those rainy days at the lake. Dabria knew this because the locals in the Village of Christopher Lake, the lake closest to Emma, had filled her in when she had been doing her scouting trip before she took the job. According to the village entrepreneurs and some very friendly locals, there was only one store at Emma and one at Christopher that actually stayed open over the winter. Most of Dabria's shopping would have to be done in Prince Albert before she left town after work, since even those stores closed by 6:00 p.m.

Directly across from the Old Trading Post was the Emma Lake Golf Course. It was an eighteen hole golf course that apparently was booked up at least two days in advance. Dabria wasn't a golfer but her mother was and she knew that once she got set up out here, her parents were going to want to come out for a visit. She needed to find things for her mother to do so that time wouldn't drag. Dabria's interests lay more in the direction of water activities. She loved to swim, kayak, and snorkel. Her hobbies also included amateur photography and watercolor painting. Therefore, living at the lake surrounded by water and forest was an obvious choice for Dabria.

Colin pulled in behind her right on time. He jumped out of his car and climbed into hers. He showed her the listing sheets of the properties they would be viewing. When he suggested she follow him she told him to lock up his car and that if he directed her she would drive the two of them from site to site. Grinning broadly, Colin readily agreed. Colin was a thirty something, ring-less, "ginger" with chocolate brown eyes, and a dusting of freckles. His boyish good looks made him appear much younger than Dabria knew he was. The real estate's web page stated that he had been an agent for fifteen years. Colin was charming and funny and Dabria totally enjoyed the mild flirtation he attempted as they looked at each property. Starting off with the least expensive and the least appealing they moved their way up to the most expensive and the supposedly most appealing. She knew this was all part of the game. Since she had no other plans for the evening, viewing these different properties at the various beaches allowed her to get a better understanding of the layout of the area. She knew as soon as they drove up to the second last listing that this was the one.

Detective Morgan spoke of trusting his instincts. Dabria's instincts were screaming at her to sign on the dotted line. Unbeknownst to Colin, Dabria considered the place hers the second she rounded the front of the cabin and visualized herself sitting on the deck with her morning coffee, gazing out upon the crystal clear water of the first lake, surrounded by spruce, aspen, and birch trees. The property was a double lot on Guise Beach, with trees lining three borders and the lakeshore forming the fourth. A break in the trees in two spots on the back side of the lot allowed for the semicircle drive-through driveway into the property. The owner had built a double wide log garage with a garage door on each end of it so that you could drive right through it. On top of the garage was a guest suite. Dabria asked to see the suite first. The logs were unfinished and weathering and almost matched the color of the obviously older cabin. Stairs on the side of the garage facing the lake led up to a deck that rose above the roof of the actual cabin, giving one an unobstructed view of the lake. It was the ideal place for a painting studio. The suite had two bedrooms, a bathroom, and a multipurpose room with space for sofas, etc.

The cabin was also built of logs, but Colin claimed, a hundred years before the garage. The front deck was supported by pilings made of water worn rocks which matched the fireplace that graced one of the side walls. The deck itself was made of weathered, pressure treated wood which enhanced the look of the tiny tired cabin. The cabin itself had been built and used by trappers at the turn of the previous century. There were four other similar cabins around the lake, Colin informed her. Two had been maintained in their original natural state while three had been stained various colors to give them a more updated look. Dabria preferred the mottled grey color as it seemed to belong amongst the aspen and birch. Colin told her that when the previous owners had lifted the cabin to put it onto a cement foundation some of the original mortar had dislodged and they discovered that newspapers from 1907 had been stuffed in between the larger gaps in the logs to keep the mortar in place. The appearance of the rustic exterior was deceptive. The entire cabin had been re-mortared, rewired, and re-roofed. Hot and cold water had been plumbed in and an in-floor heating system installed about ten years ago. The cabin itself was only about seven hundred square feet, but it was large enough to accommodate a bedroom, a three piece bathroom - with a very modern jet tub - and an L shaped cooking and eating area with a living room. It was the perfect place for a single person or even a couple. With the suite above the garage there was even a place to escape to if you got cabin fever.

The cabin had its own well with drinkable water and a holding tank for both black and grey water that had to be pumped out by one of the local septic pumping companies. A small shed off to the side of the lot, in between the cabin and the garage, contained the external natural gas-fired boiler that heated the glycol for the in-floor heating as well as the radiant heat for the suite. It also heated the water in the hot water heater. Sections of dock were piled up along the shore waiting to be put back into the lake as soon as it thawed. Colin assured her she would be able to hire help to set the dock up and take it back down again in the fall. She could also hire plumbers from the area to maintain the boiler and well. Although she couldn't confirm his claim that the property had a beautiful sandy beach and pebbly walk since it was presently snow-covered, she took his word for it since the remainder of the property was exactly what she was looking for. Apparently, there was next to no lawn as the owners had tried to keep the property as natural as possible. The ground was supposedly covered by pine needles, leaves, moss, and rock. That suited Dabria just fine since gardening wasn't one of her fortes.

Dabria allowed Colin to show her the final property. It was a two year old, twenty-five hundred square foot, three-story Cape Cod built into the hillside on one of the high lots. It had every modern convenience and more. You walked into the second floor of the house at the back of the lot and walked out the doors of the first floor on the lakefront. It was shiny and clean and truly beautiful, with floor to ceiling windows, and a wrap around deck encircling the second floor that provided an amazing view of the first lake. Dabria hated it. It reminded her of her old life. It was too perfect, too clean, and too new. Convinced that this was the property Dabria would be purchasing, Colin continued his sales pitch by adding details about the area's amenities that were within walking distance.

The year round Emma Lake Resort was a really only a hop, skip, and a jump from the Cape Cod, Colin claimed, if Dabria ever got lonely and needed a friendly face. It housed a small convenience store, a bar, a restaurant with take-out, and a round dance hall built out of logs. Their *Available Services Board* posted in the parking lot also boasted first class boat, party barge, canoe, and kayak rentals as well as rentals of tubes and water chairs. The establishment sat perched on the hill above a beautiful public beach where volleyball nets were set up directly below the expansive balcony of the bar. In the winter they hosted snowmobile poker rallies and company Christmas parties. In the summer there were fish derbies, volleyball tournaments, live bands on the weekends, the occasional comedian and hypnotist, and the annual July 1st fireworks display from the beach. Cabin owners from around the lake would navigate their boats over after dark and anchor out in the middle of the first lake to watch the enchanting, a-h-h-h-h-h evoking display from on the water.

Colin raved that they served the best chicken wings in all the land and if you were looking for a spiked hot chocolate after a chilly cross-country ski or snowshoe you couldn't find a better place to sip it than curled up in their loveseats in front of the roaring stone fireplace in the bar. Since the resort was situated even closer to the tiny log cabin, Dabria had listened intently to Colin's testimonial.

She suggested they make their way over to the resort to try out those famous chicken wings and see if they knew how to brew a pot of tea. Once their orders had been placed, Dabria shocked Colin by asking him to draw up an offer to purchase the little old log cabin. Despite his surprise he readily agreed. Possession date was listed as negotiable. Waiting for financing wasn't an issue since Dabria would be paying cash for the property and she was pretty sure she could find a good lawyer to finalize the sale. She planned on moving in two weeks. That should give the present owners enough time to move out. Dabria would start looking for furniture on-line once she got back to the apartment tonight.

Colin was right. The wings were excellent and although the tea left something to be desired the bartender explained that he didn't get much call for tea in this establishment and assured Dabria he would get it right the next time she came in. By 10:00 p.m. the deal was done and Dabria was the proud new owner of the antique cabin. Life was going better than Dabria could have ever hoped. Things were falling into place as if they were meant to be. Dabria dropped Colin off at his car and with a wave, headed back to town. As Colin watched her drive away he shook his head and marveled at how wrong he had been regarding Bree and what she would purchase. The only reason he had shown her the property she ultimately bought was because the lots were prime and he thought she might be interested in bulldozing the cabin and building her own. He learned today that even after years of observing his customers and their buying habits, occasionally one of them could still surprise him.

Bree was an intriguing collection of contradictions. During the entire viewing process she had maintained a reserved, almost impassive demeanor. She asked pertinent questions and gave yes and no answers but volunteered very little. Although he was attracted to her physically his subtle attempts at flirtation went unreciprocated and he had initially concluded that she had the personality of a rock. Her responses were distracted and definitely uninspiring. Colin had anticipated having to continue to lead and support any dinner conversation that occurred. That impression swiftly changed once he began the process of filling in the blanks of the offer to purchase. When he was forced to ask questions in order to fill out the appropriate paper work Dabria suddenly became extremely accommodating with both information and conversation to the point that she could have actually been called animated and extroverted. By the time both buyer and seller had reached an agreement Dabria was downright exuberant. Not only was she gorgeous and smart, but she could also be funny and personable when she felt like it and that made her sexy as hell. Once the purchase of her cabin was concluded and she was moved in Colin planned on initiating a more intimate relationship. The challenge of bedding Bree was too hard to resist.

Chapter 5

The remainder of the week Dabria spent poring over files, interviewing clients, and generally familiarizing herself with the rhythm of her new office. Her next court date wasn't actually until the following Tuesday. Jamie continued to amuse Dabria with her unflattering comments regarding Dabria's choice of apparel and her general appearance. Then, Friday afternoon, shortly after lunch, Craig called.

"Hey, Bree, how's it going?" he inquired. "Are we still on for dinner tonight?"

"Sure," she responded. "What time and where?"

"How does Shay's sound? It's a tiny little restaurant with a fantastic menu and a quiet, subdued atmosphere." Shay's was the perfect place to have an intimate conversation with someone while you attempted to seduce them.

"What's the dress code and what time do you want to meet?"

"Dress is semi-formal and I'll pick you up at 7:00 p.m."

"I'll meet you there, Craig. I'm an independent gal and I like to have my own wheels. Thanks for the offer of a lift, though." Dabria's response swiftly reaffirmed her initial declaration to him that she did *not* date lawyers and that this was in no way to be misconstrued as a date. Although, she had only been seriously involved with one man, namely her fiancé, Dabria was not naïve when it came to men. She would be seduced only if she chose to be seduced, not because she was too inexperienced to realize what was going on. No man would play her for a fool a second time. Dabria wondered if she shouldn't simply decline the invitation and any future invitations from Craig. Some guys had a hard time taking no for an answer. Experience from representing women who were divorcing controlling men led her to be more cautious than most. She made the snap decision of sticking with the original appointment and determined she would have a fun evening out regardless of Craig's agenda. He graciously accepted her choice of meeting rather than picking her up and silently vowed to entice her into wanting to pursue him rather than appearing to pursue her.

When quitting time rolled around Dabria packed up her stuff and leisurely returned to her apartment to scan her wardrobe for something appropriate to wear that was classy but not provocative. Most of her dress clothes fell into that classification since Dabria had been raised to dress conservatively, not flamboyantly. She chose a light caramel colored ultra-suede long sleeved pant suit. The tailored jacket accented her curves and with four and a half inch matching suede pumps Dabria unwittingly presented a picture that was not only extremely feminine but also very sexy. With her glasses off, her eyes, framed by her luxurious dark brown lashes, were truly remarkable especially since they were the exact color of the suit. She finished the ensemble off with coffee colored wood earrings and a necklace made out of a coconut shell. By the time she freshened herself up and dressed it was time to leave for the restaurant. She looked up the address and drove to the first social event of her new life.

When Dabria pulled up outside the restaurant and parked she recognized Craig stepping out of a silver Mercedes. She smiled as she recognized the car as being the same model she had just sold. It was a CL600 Coupe and retailed for around a hundred and fifty grand. David had talked her into purchasing it just before he died. Unlike Craig, for David it wasn't so much a status symbol as it was a high performance vehicle that combined Dabria's need for speed with comfort and safety. Knowing what Legal Aid lawyers salaries were, Dabria assumed that Craig either had another source of income or his need to impress others surpassed his need to eat. Dabria unconsciously noted that Craig and Morgan were almost polar opposites despite both being exceptionally tall and good looking. The simplest way to describe Morgan was to say *Viking*. The best one word description for Craig was *metro-sexual*. He slid out of his car sporting obviously styled dark hair, what appeared to be a fresh manicure, and wearing a chic tailored avocado colored silk shirt with a casual black blazer and black slacks. Black wingtips finished the polished look. Maybe too polished?

The exterior of the eatery was extremely unremarkable. Floor to ceiling privacy glass windows prevented any insight into the interior of the establishment and a modest *Shay's* was poised above the single solid wood entrance door. Dabria had been to restaurants similar to this before in many Canadian cities. It reeked of understated class. Again Dabria questioned Craig's agenda. Unless you were very comfortable financially this was not a place you picked for a casual dinner with a friend. As they walked inside Dabria wondered if Craig had made a reservation since the ad in the phone book said reservations were recommended.

"Martin Reservation for two at 7:00 p.m.," Craig announced as the hostess approached them.

"This way, please," she directed with a smile. She led them to an intimate table in the back corner of the restaurant. The lighting was muted and conversation from other tables drifted over in a low murmur. A harpist was melodiously playing a classical piece on a raised dais in the opposite corner of the room. Various mediums of art were strategically displayed around the room and upon closer inspection Dabria realized they were all for sale. This may be just the venue she was looking for to display her own "works of genius." Candles glowed on each occupied table and not surprisingly each table was occupied. The establishment only had sixteen tables and each waiter was responsible for four. Their waiter approached, introduced himself as Niall, recited the evening's specials and then requested their drink preferences.

"What are your house reds?" Dabria inquired.

"We have a lovely Australian Shiraz and a Canadian Merlot."

"I'll have a glass of the Merlot please. Which winery, by the way?"

"I believe it is Mission Hill, Ma'am," Niall responded.

"That sounds great, and by the way how old are you, Niall?" Dabria's question totally threw off not only the waiter but also caused Craig to swiftly raise his head from the liquor menu.

"I'm thirty-four."

"Hmmm, ... I'm thirty-two," she informed him "which means I'm younger than you." The waiter politely waited for her to elaborate while he regarded her quizzically. "I know that "Ma'am" is a term of respect. I, personally, have always considered it appropriate for mature women, but since I've been called "Ma'am" twice in less than a week and I know I'm not in any way a matron I'm starting to question the meaning of the word. Either I look much older than I actually am or once you hit thirty you're automatically classified as "a woman of a certain age." I had hoped to not be a "Ma'am" for at least another twenty years. So, which is it?"

Craig visibly relaxed. She giggled when she realized he must have thought she was hitting on their waiter.

"Which is what, Ma . . . . I mean Miss?" the waiter squirmed.

"Am I old or do I just look old?"

"Ah lassie, ya won't be trapping *me* now," Niall lay on a Scottish brogue. "What would ya like me to be calling you then, m' lady?" he inquired with a wink.

"I honestly don't know but there has to be something better than "Ma'am". M'lady is certainly safer, Niall, isn't it? How about you just call me Bree for now and I'll think on it."

"Aye, m' lady, Bree it is," he agreed with a flourish and a bow. "And for you, m' lord?"

"Please bring a carafe of the Merlot and you can call me Craig."

"Vera weal," the waiter backed away and headed to the bar.

"Feeling old, are you?" Craig questioned with a grin.

"No. Actually, I feel like life is just beginning: new town, new job, new home, and the opportunity to make new friends. It's actually very exciting," she stated. "So tell me all about yourself." Dabria was a master of drawing people out while she revealed very little of herself. She listened intently to Craig and continued to ask him questions at opportune times thereby encouraging him to monopolize the conversation without making it obvious. As the evening wound up she had learned not only the things he told her but also she determined his façade of bored, jaded, public defender was just that, a façade. Despite Dabria's initial reservations Craig had turned out to be an excellent dinner partner. She discovered she actually liked him and could envision them being friends. This dating thing even if it was supposed to be a casual supper out with a co-worker was fun. Maybe she could play the field a little and actually see what was out there in the world of potential boy toys.

Although Craig claimed that being hauled to the theater and to art exhibits left him cold he became quite animated when she volunteered that she had recently seen the musical JERSEY BOYS and had loved it. When he admitted that he had also seen it she asked his opinion on several of the scenes. Despite his attempt to downplay his enjoyment of it the enthusiasm with which he spoke disproved his attempt at ennui. Dabria thoroughly enjoyed the evening and even though she was looking for new adventures it was a comfort to know that she needn't leave the parts of her old life that she enjoyed behind and that when she wanted to see a play or view an exhibit she could ask him to go with her. You might be able to take the girl out of the city but you can't totally take the city out of the girl.

As they prepared to leave Dabria insisted on paying for her meal and since Craig's new plan was to use reverse psychology to seduce her, he put up no resistance. Niall, who had continued his brogue for the remainder of the evening, questioned whether Bree had come up with a better way of addressing women "of an indeterminate age" and since she had been totally focused on Craig she confessed she hadn't. She promised him she would pop in one day and let him know if she found a better moniker.

As Dabria drove away Craig reflected that he couldn't remember an evening ever passing so swiftly in the company of a gorgeous female without any physical interaction. They had talked, or rather he acknowledged, he had talked while she listened for almost five hours. The only things he could definitively say about her were that she was an excellent listener and interrogator, that she loved the fine arts, and that she was a big tipper. Oh, and he mustn't forget that she had the most wonderfully unexpected bubbly laugh and twisted sense of humor. When he asked if they could do this again she surprised him by immediately agreeing. They hadn't set a firm date but when he suggested the following weekend she said, "Call me." It was going to take a bit of persuasion to get her to open up but Craig relished the challenge.

By Saturday night she had everything organized for the next week, so Dabria decided to take Sunday off and go do some shopping in Saskatoon. She visited the Mendel Art Gallery and bought some new paint supplies. She walked Broadway and bought a funky new pair of shoes and some great costume jewelry made out of leather, wood beads, and pounded metal. She wandered down Spadina Crescent along the river to the bandstand and spied an organic restaurant advertising a walnut pesto vegetarian pizza and chai tea lattes. That sounded too good to pass up. The scent of cardamom wafted up and teased her senses as she "people watched" from her window seat. She closed her eyes, inhaled deeply, and mentally hugged herself. If she could just commit to appreciating simple pleasures more often maybe she could find joy again.

Wanting to hit some of the smaller furniture stores on the way out of town Dabria finished her lunch and headed out. After surveying the merchandise displayed by a family owned furniture crafter she determined that getting custom-made pieces was a more attractive avenue for her tiny cabin than trying to find ready-made that would fit. The furniture designer of the family asked that Dabria take pictures of the inside of the cabin and email them as well as the dimensions of each room. That way she could design furniture that would complement the cabin rather than overpower it. Dabria could still support the P.A. merchants by buying furniture for the loft from them. Dabria decided on the drive home that she would buy furnishings for the loft right away but use them in the cabin until the handcrafted pieces were finished. As she journeyed back to Prince Albert her head was full of decorating ideas and she couldn't wait to get started on the list of things she was going to need. Setting up her first home on her own was so exciting she could hardly contain herself.

Chapter 6

Dabria spent Monday morning preparing for Tuesday's court date which involved the custody arrangements for a baby boy whose parents were both still teenagers. This one was very different from the last male client she had represented in a custody case. It was that client that had originally led her to Prince Albert. Today's client was a young father who himself had been raised by a single parent, was struggling with school, and was working part time. The baby's mother had left school and was the primary caregiver at this point. She was hoping to get some evenings free so that she could continue her studies. The pressure on Dabria's client was extreme. He was working every day after school and every weekend to provide the *baby momma* with some child support. Between that and school there was simply no time to spend with his son. A compromise needed to be reached, so that he could work less, spend time with his son, and allow the mother evenings for some night classes. Dabria was confident that they could reach an agreement.

Dabria's last custody case had also been one handed over to her. The original lawyer in that one had retired and the client agreed to hire Dabria as the replacement. That case involved a father who was working a province away to try to support his family, since the company he had worked for here had shut down. His working schedule was eleven days away and three days at home. With traveling time this actually only allowed him two days off. So, although the wages he sent home permitted his family to live in the lifestyle to which they had become accustomed, he wasn't there to share it with them.

In his case there were four children all of whom were involved in various extra-curricular activities. The mother had basically been operating as a single parent for the past two years. With two hormonal teenage girls in the family and two younger boys in hockey she was overwhelmed with discipline issues as well as stretched to the limit time-wise to fulfill her family's physical and emotional needs. This had led to loneliness, frustration, and bitterness on her part. When a widowed father from one of the boy's hockey teams had offered her companionship and support it had unfortunately turned into an affair for her. Dabria had planned to simply finalize the divorce arrangements and clarify the custody schedule. It just should have been a formality since the father was only home for two days every second weekend anyway and the mother was more than willing to allow the kids total access to their father at that time. Since the kids had gotten used to not seeing their father on a daily basis nothing had changed for them other than they now had a new man around the house every day and a new little brother. However, it wasn't that simple.

Once Dabria had met with the father she recognized that he was clearly heartsick since he had only been trying to be a good father and husband. As Dabria saw it, a much better solution to the whole problem would have been for the father to take a lower paying job closer to home. Although the family would have had to make some lifestyle adjustments, the marriage and the family might have still been intact and the kids would have learned the valuable lesson that money is *never* more important than family.

When the alarm on her phone sounded she knew that she only had a half hour until court time. She set her reflections aside and realized she didn't have time for lunch but she could fit in a call to the real estate agent. She asked Colin if he could get her back into the cabin to take pictures so that her furniture could be started. He jumped at the opportunity to spend another few hours with her and assured her the owners wouldn't mind. They arranged to meet after work.

Dabria met the young father at the courthouse and proceedings moved swiftly to a mutually beneficial conclusion. Ironically, as Dabria stopped to grab a "salad to go" from the grocery store she ran into the very client she had been thinking about that morning.

"Ms. Abdulla-Smythe," he greeted her with a stunned exclamation. "I never expected to see you here again."

"Hello, Mr. Thomas, this is a surprise," she offered him a genuine smile and a sincere handshake. "I live here now. I liked the area so much when I was here last time I decided to relocate."

"Are you practicing here?"

"Yes, but I'm no longer in private practice. Now I'm with Legal Aid."

"Oh, for a moment there I was hoping I would be able to rehire you."

"Sorry, but unfortunately I don't think you would qualify."

"Probably not," he acknowledged with a sigh. "Since you're no longer my lawyer maybe we could grab a coffee some time?" he asked hopefully.

"Maybe," she hedged.

"A lot of things have changed in the last year and a half and since you helped with the custody I'd love to let you know how things are going now."

"You know what, that doesn't sound like a bad idea, Mr. Thomas. Give me your number and I'll give you a call once I'm a little more settled," Dabria promised. Although Marshall Thomas was a former client he was ultimately a man that Dabria respected and actually liked. He also wasn't hard on the eyes with sun weathered skin, brown hair, hazel eyes and a tall rangy build like the ranchers whom she had often come into contact with in Alberta.

"Please call me Marshall," he invited.

"Then you must call me Bree," she encouraged. "I don't know anyone here and a familiar friendly face is not something that I should let slip by." They exchanged numbers and Dabria returned to the office.

As Dabria munched on her salad she recalled her first meeting with Marshall, two years ago, in her office in Rocky Mountain House. At that initial meeting Marshall had walked into the room and given Dabria a firm handshake. In that moment based on instincts only, she had made a swift, but accurate character judgment. This was not the typical broken, defiant, or angry man like she had represented in other divorce proceedings. He was a proud, hard working, honest man with a purpose. Marshall Thomas was well over six feet and radiated strength. Although he towered over her, Dabria had felt no threat. The man's aura was one of *gentle* strength.

Dabria flashed back to that initial meeting.

"Please have a seat, Mr. Thomas. Can I get you something to drink before we begin?"

"No, thank you. I'm fine."

"What can I do for you today?"

"As I am sure you have already determined the lawyer that was representing me from your office has retired and he recommended you. My wife and I are separated and in the process of finalizing our divorce. Basically the only details left to attend to are final custody arrangements for our four children."

"Mr. Marty did indicate that you may be retaining me and so I took a quick glance through your file. According to the notes in there you're set for court next Tuesday morning at 9:00 a.m. in Prince Albert. Is there any problem with you attending?"

"No, however, I've had a change in circumstances and therefore I would like to modify the proposal."

"No problem. That's what I'm here for. Why don't you explain your new situation?"

"My brother passed away recently and I've inherited the family farm as well as a substantial amount of cash and assets. Since we had originally farmed the land together, after our parents died, it seemed only natural to me that I quit my out-of-province job and return to farming. I now have a residence that is close enough to my children that they can stay overnight and for extended periods of time without interfering with their schooling or their activities. Since we have already established joint custody I simply want to arrange to have the kids every second week. The farmhouse is old but was well maintained and is large enough for them to each have their own bedrooms. Since their welfare has always been my primary concern and I believe the court is aware of that, I was hoping that changing the arrangements might be a possibility. I would, however, request that my child support payments be reduced since they would be living with me half of the time."

"I think that's a reasonable request and I have no problem presenting it to the court. Is your ex-wife or the children aware of the proposed changes?"

"No. I didn't want to say anything to the kids until the actual arrangements were finalized. Jeanine may be aware of my brother's death but I'm not sure of that either, since the two of them didn't get along. He was a bachelor and a very private man. There was no funeral because he had requested not to have one. To my knowledge the kids are unaware that I will be moving back and taking up farming again. I know it's not going to be easy for them to adapt since they've created a life without me over the past two years, but I do believe that it's important for not only me but also for them that we develop a stronger relationship."

"I agree with you. Children need both of their parents whether they're divorced or not. You do realize that because both the girls are over the age of twelve they can request to stay solely with either your ex-wife or you?"

"Yes, I'm aware of that but I'm hopeful that they will choose to spend time with both of us."

"Right. Let's get down to the business then of setting out specific custody guidelines for the future, such as school holidays, vacation times, etc. How do you feel about that?"

"Works for me."

Dabria and Mr. Thomas had spent the next hour fine tuning the proposal.

"Thank you, so much for your help, Ms. Abdulla-Smythe. I'll see you next Tuesday." With another firm handshake Mr. Marshall Thomas rose and stepped out of Dabria's office.

One week later Dabria had entered the Prince Albert Courthouse for the very first time. She swiftly scrambled up the stairs as the day was cold and overcast with a howling gale force wind that whipped biting little shards of sleet into her face. The foyer was virtually empty and those people that she did see were scurrying off to where they needed to be rather than casually conversing with clients and colleagues. Although there was a definite chill in the air the interior of the courthouse had been both awe inspiring and strangely comforting to Dabria. As she hurried up to the second floor she had noticed Mr. Thomas waiting calmly for her outside the courtroom. His quiet self-contained air bolstered Dabria's confidence in her ability to help him achieve his goal. With an optimistic, encouraging smile she had greeted him and they entered the courtroom together. His ex-wife and her lawyer were already present. Dabria got herself and her client settled and waited for the judge to appear.

After the preliminaries were attended to Dabria had presented Mr. Thomas' new circumstances to the court and put forward his request.

She was pleased to learn that this was the judge that had presided over the divorce. Providing that Mr. Thomas' demeanor during the divorce proceedings had been similar to what it was today the judge should look favorably upon his request. He sat at their table attentively and respectfully listening to the hearing. The ex-wife was quite obviously not pleased and had begun to furiously whisper to her lawyer. When the judge asked the opposing counsel if his client had an issue with the father's proposal, her lawyer stood up and asked for a court appointed social worker to do a "home study" and implement "Voices of the Children." Dabria had forewarned her client that these proposals would probably be put forward. In layman's terms it meant the social worker would inspect Marshall's home and interview the children regarding their thoughts and feelings to the requested arrangement. Marshall readily agreed to the terms. However, he had requested a reduction in support if the custody arrangements were approved since he would now have the children half the time.

His ex vehemently rejected the idea of reducing the child support. Dabria had quickly pointed out that since the father's income was unpredictable at this time the new amount offered was in fact very generous. The likelihood of her client continuing to make the income he had previously was questionable. He was now a farmer as opposed to his past career as an oil field consultant.

The judge issued the order for the recommendations and strongly urged the ex-wife's lawyer to counsel his client to accept the reduced child support. He apprised her of the fact that if she forced the issue she exposed herself to the risk of having to actually *pay* child support since she had a job with confirmed income and her ex-husband no longer did. The judge indicated this case be adjourned until the new information was obtained, at which time he would then deliver his verdict. Dabria had secretly breathed a sigh of relief. Regardless of how prepared she might be there was often the possibility that ex-wives or ex-husbands could throw a monkey wrench into custody proceedings.

As they had left the courtroom Mr. Thomas' ex-wife began to rail at him in the hallway. Her lawyer tired to steer her away from the open door of the courtroom that was within the judge's hearing. Rather than argue with her in public, Mr. Thomas indicated that they could possibly be shown to a more private place for them to discuss the situation. Dabria and the other lawyer readily agreed and a private room was quickly obtained. Mr. Thomas continued to maintain his composure during her rant. Since he was not fighting back she had eventually calmed down and while both lawyers looked on, he very coolly responded.

"Despite the fact that you were the one that broke our vows and sought comfort outside of our marriage without trying to come to some kind of compromise with me, I agreed to the divorce, the child support, and the joint custody without a fight. I did that for three reasons: I knew I was partly to blame for not recognizing how unhappy you were, you obviously were in love with someone else, and it was in the best interest of our children to not drag things out. I have *never* stopped loving our children nor have I ever put my own needs and desires ahead of theirs. That is why when I had the opportunity to move back to be closer to them I took it. If our children didn't mean everything to me I would have sold the farm and continued working away with the previous agreement. I didn't propose this new arrangement to get back at you. I suggested it so that I could strengthen the relationship I already have with our children and to participate in their daily lives. I may have been an absent father but I don't believe anyone could accuse me of not being a loving father that tried to stay involved despite the physical distance that separated us." With that he rose and walked towards the door. He had stopped and turned back towards his ex-wife.

"Jeanine, do what you know is right for them," he quietly but determinedly implored. Then he left the room. Jeanine softly began to weep as Dabria bustled out of the room to follow her client. She caught up to him just inside the entrance as he bundled his coat up to face the elements.

"I'll contact you as soon as arrangements have been made. Might I suggest that you give your kids a call and explain to them what is going on and that you are available for them if they need you."

"Now that I know there might be a chance of my proposal being accepted I have every intention of contacting them immediately. Thank you, for everything you've done. I don't mean to bolt out of here but I've said everything I need to and I'd rather not give Jeanine another opportunity to bitch me out, today." He then briskly shook her hand and headed out the door. As Dabria turned to fasten up her own apparel she realized that Jeanine and her lawyer had been making their way down the stairs behind her as she and Marshall spoke. No wonder he wanted to "get the hell out of Dodge." Jeanine's lawyer approached Dabria alone. He formally introduced himself and then assured her that the proposed reduced child support was agreeable to his client. Dabria thanked him and then braced herself for the onslaught of the storm as she pushed through the entrance doors.

Marshall's proposed arrangements had been approved and that had basically been the end of her involvement with this client. When she had resigned from private practice and relocated she had sent out a blanket letter to all past clients informing them that she was no longer with the firm but that the remaining lawyers would be happy to help them with any future requests. She did not divulge where she was moving to or what she would be doing. She obviously had not totally forgotten about Marshall since it was his court case that had brought her to the city in the first place. But Prince Albert *was* a city and she hadn't considered that she and Marshall would bump into each other. It was not an unpleasant encounter. The coffee date should clarify if the *happy ever after* for his ex-wife was fantasy or fact and who knew what may result from a little cup of coffee and conversation.

~ ~ ~

Dabria spent the remainder of the afternoon working on other client files. At 5:00 p.m. she packed her stuff up and headed for the lake with her digital camera. Colin had arrived before her and the cabin and loft were ablaze with lights. The owners had already moved out and the cabin was empty. With Colin helping her measure and no furniture to impede their progress, she was finished in less than half an hour. She also took pictures and measurements inside the loft to help her with the furnishings and window coverings she needed to get in P.A. Although Colin suggested stopping for a bite at the resort—hoping to further their involvement—Dabria declined explaining she had briefs to attend to at home and planned on having a working supper. Colin was disappointed but graciously acquiesced.

Once back in town she downloaded her pictures and sent the necessary ones with the measurements to the furniture guru in Saskatoon. She worked until 10:00 p.m. and then fired up her laptop to do some web searching for interior design ideas. By midnight she had compiled a list of things she needed that were sorted into three columns; things she already had, things she could buy in town, and things she needed to look for elsewhere. She also made herself a list of the different tradesman she needed to get in touch with regarding her water and heating needs, her internet hook-up, phone and utilities transfer, etc. Between work and the impending move she was going to be a very busy little girl for the next several weeks.

The next morning when she was back at the office she went in search of Sarah to see if she was interested in ordering in a nice hot, loaded pizza for lunch so that she wouldn't have to brave the cold again until she left for the day. Sarah was all for it and asked if her boyfriend could join them. Since Dabria was interested in meeting him she readily agreed. Perhaps she might also gather more information on the *Viking*. Sarah said she'd order and have Kent pick it up on his way over.

At noon a grinning Kent showed up with two loaded pizzas in tow. They set up lunch in one of the conference rooms on the third floor while Dabria grabbed cans of pop from the vending machine.

"Kent, I'd like you to meet our newest lawyer, Dabria Abdulla-Smythe. Bree this is my boyfriend, Detective Kent Ducette."

Kent was a little under six feet and while Sarah was almost as tall, she was pale, blond, and willowy while he was dark haired, dark skinned, husky, and of aboriginal descent. They made a striking pair.

"It's a pleasure to meet you Ms. Dabria Abdulla-Smythe," Kent pronounced with an exaggerated bow.

"Please call me Bree," Dabria chuckled, amused by his antics.

"Thanks, I think I will," he assured her as he reached out and shook her hand.

They all sat down to indulge in the serious business of pizza eating. The girls chatted and chomped while Kent wordlessly wolfed down several pieces. Once his hunger had been appeased he sat back and drained his coke in one swallow. Although Dabria had been an only child, she had grown up with David and Matthew and was therefore used to witnessing the awesome ability of men to single-mindedly polish off any food in sight. Despite her tiny build, she could pack away the groceries almost as well. Her metabolism was such that she hadn't wavered from her present weight for the past ten years. She was convinced that this was so, in part, because she speed walked a minimum of two miles every morning, come rain or shine, and she did free weights every second night at home. Apparently Sarah's appetite was just as healthy since between the three of them they managed to polish off both pizzas.

With a satisfied belch, Kent excused himself, wiped his non-existent moustache and leaned forward to rest his arms on the table.

"So, tell me all about yourself, Bree. Where are ya' from, who're your people, and what're you doing here?"

"Oh, for heaven's sake, Kent, stop interrogating her," Sarah admonished.

"I don't mind," Dabria responded. "But I do expect the same courtesy back."

"For sure," Kent agreed.

Dabria filled him in on the basics, including the fact that her fiancé had died. She left it up to him to uncover the details if he was so inclined. She knew that although he may not care, Sarah would definitely be curious. It would be interesting to see how much of her past followed her.

Kent very courteously informed her of his background. Despite the questions the lunch was basically relaxed and Dabria left feeling comfortable and welcome. After bidding her boyfriend farewell, Sarah popped into Dabria's office to apologize for the grilling. Dabria brushed it off assuring Sarah she had not been offended in any way.

"Sarah, it's his job to know what riff raff is moving into his territory," she teased.

"Riff raff!" Sarah exclaimed outraged, as she scrutinized Dabria's grinning expression. "Oh, you're kidding," she realized as she sank into one of Dabria's chairs.

"Sarah, I know you want to believe the best in everyone, but everyone has secrets and not all of those secrets are pretty."

"So, there's more to the story than you told us?"

"Of course," she confirmed with a nod as she opened a file. "Isn't there usually? I hate to end our little visit but I really need to prepare for court tomorrow. I'm facing Detective Vaughn on my Dangerous Driving charge and I need to be at the top of my game in order to get the charges dropped."

"Oh, my goodness! I forgot to get some info out of Kent about "your cop." Did you want me to find out before tomorrow?"

"Sarah, don't worry about it. It was simply curiosity."

"No way. I'm going to see what we can find out. I'm sure he's done his homework on you."

"I doubt it. It was a speeding ticket. I didn't kill anyone. He would have no reason to investigate."

"Unless his interest in you wasn't only professional? Besides, he's a detective and that's their job to investigate. You told me he went way beyond what was necessary regarding the twins. It's not that hard to get info on a person if you know where to get it from."

"I know. I just can't imagine he would go to the trouble," she shrugged. "Sarah, don't bother asking Kent about Detective Vaughn. I don't want to make this simple matter into something it's not. I'd rather base my opinion of him on my own observations."

"You're probably right. I better let you get to work. Thanks for the lunch date." Sarah shot out of her chair and out of the office.

Since Dabria wanted the new people in her life to form their opinions of her based on their observations rather than on her past, she acknowledged that she owed those same people that same privilege. Although she knew that a person's past affected their future she also knew that the assumptions people made knowing only some of the facts weren't always correct. Dabria had every right to question the integrity of those people she chose to allow to get close to her. But, despite the betrayals and the broken heart salvaged from her last intimate relationship, she refused to allow the pessimistic attitude that everyone lied and led double lives. Dabria's instincts told her that Detective Vaughn was someone she could trust. Her greatest regret was that she hadn't followed her instincts years before and that she hadn't asked David questions that should have been asked. She would give Detective Vaughn the benefit of the doubt. But, she *never* made the same mistakes twice.

Chapter 7

Dabria was scheduled to appear during the morning session of court. She dressed in full battle gear wearing a fitted, black with white pinstripe, two-button tab jacket with a classic, double vent, ultra-fitted, knee length matching skirt and a stark white, collared, long sleeved, button down dress shirt with black pearl buttons. She wore black hose and five inch black pumps and her jaunty new glasses. She might be going down today but not without making an impression. When she surveyed her appearance in the mirror she saw a determined, confidant professional. That, of course, was not Jaimie's impression.

"You aren't wearing that to court are you?" she questioned with a raised eyebrow.

"Better this than go naked, don't you think?" Dabria teased.

"You look like a high priced hooker," Jaimie spat out as she turned away.

"Well, it's too late to change now," Dabria commented before she slipped out the door. Wow, Dabria had no idea that her attire would trigger that kind of emotional reaction. Jaimie herself wore very conservative, unflattering garments and Dabria wondered if she hadn't been sexually abused. It was like she tried to make herself as unattractive as possible but still maintain a professional appearance. She obviously tried to downplay the fact that she was female and it was hard to determine her age. Dabria remembered Sarah's comments regarding Jaimie. She had said that she was shy and seemed unresponsive to any of Sarah's friendly overtures. Dabria wouldn't classify Jaimie as shy or unresponsive. She certainly didn't hold back when it came to Dabria's appearance. Oh well, she'd have to analyze Jaimie another day. Today her every thought needed to be focused on a certain detective.

Like Jaimie, Morgan's impression was different than the one Dabria sought when she had dressed that morning. However, unlike Jaimie, his was far more flattering. He watched her enter the building and take off her overcoat and then with a predatory gleam in his eyes he followed her ascent. She was the sexiest thing he had ever had the good fortune to be able to chase down. He knew she was dressed for battle. And he smiled inwardly as he tried to gauge her reaction once she realized his intentions.

The maximum fine if convicted for Dangerous Driving was $2000 and up to five years in jail. Since he had made his point by charging her and forcing her to prepare a defense for herself the obvious solution to this situation now was for him to *drop* the charges against her. Forcing the suit by making her defend herself would serve no purpose other than to find out what her defense might be, which was unquestionably self-serving. He didn't want her to be convicted and if she hadn't provoked him the day he pulled her over, he would never have charged her in the first place. He would have simply issued her a warning and given her the speeding ticket instead.

With a tilt of her head she acknowledged his presence as he entered the courtroom and sat beside her. She was in the back row and sat ramrod stiff waiting for their case to be called. Her briefcase rested on the seat between them. She refocused her eyes straight ahead and appeared immersed in the proceedings. He inhaled deeply and savored her unique scent. It was a combination of spice and citrus and her natural musk. There went that twitch in his pants again. Now he was going to have to concentrate on something other than her or embarrass himself when he stood up. He cleared his throat and focused his attention on the disheveled elderly gentleman two rows ahead of them that was industriously picking his nose. That image immediately cooled his heating ardor.

Dabria couldn't believe his nerve. First he plopped himself down beside her and then he all but sniffed her. If he was trying to disconcert her it wasn't working. She should probably just sniff him right back and see what kind of reaction that elicited from him. And so before she lost her nerve, she did. With no attempt at subtlety she turned towards him, leaned in, and inhaled. That was a mistake. She hadn't consciously acknowledged it until just that moment that his scent had already imprinted itself into her memory. It was a combination of sandalwood, nutmeg, and strangely enough, tobacco. She had never seen him smoke but that didn't mean he didn't. It sent her libido into overdrive and she unconsciously crossed her legs and squeezed her thighs together.

What the hell was Ms. Dabria Abdulla-Smythe trying to do to him? Not only had she just leaned into him and all but inhaled him, but then, she had provocatively crossed her legs which automatically drew his attention directly to her crotch. With clenched hands he forced his eyes to refocus on the old gold-digger in front of them. Was she actually hoping to distract him enough that he wouldn't be able to testify? If that was her intention she was going to be hopping mad once the judge read his statement.

Thankfully, the next case up was theirs. As Dabria rose to make her way to the front Morgan continued to sit and prevented her from moving past him.

"In the case of The State versus Ms. Dabria Abdulla-Smythe all charges have been dropped. Case dismissed."

Dabria had been subtly, but ultimately unsuccessfully, trying to motivate him to either stand up or move so that she could get past him. Morgan had deliberately ignored her. Once the bailiff's words sunk in, she stilled and with eyes flashing murder, she stared directly into his twinkling ones. Morgan calmly stood and once he reached the aisle he stepped back so that she could precede him from the courtroom. She was seething. Once the doors to the courtroom had closed she crooked a finger at him indicating that he follow and she led him to one of the interview rooms. After he had entered the room behind her she very quietly closed the door and with her back pressed against it let him have it.

"Why in God's name if you planned to drop the charges did you not inform me so that we could both have avoided this total waste of time? I would hope that you have better things to do than to spend taxpayers' money trying to teach me a lesson. That was what this whole drama was about, wasn't it?"

"Actually, I'm on my own time now. I'm on night shift so the only thing our meeting was interrupting was some sleep time."

"How nice for you," she stated sarcastically. "I'm not going to give you another second of smug satisfaction. I do have work to do and clients that actually need my help, so if you'll excuse me I think I'll put an end to your little party."

"Have dinner with me," he declared as she turned around and grabbed to open the door.

"What?" She gritted out as she stopped. She whipped back around and glared at him. "What did you say?"

"You heard me and you're simply stalling to come up with an excuse even though we both know you want to. Come on. It's one dinner which will allow me to apologize properly." Morgan left the other side of the room where he had casually propped himself up on the windowsill and was moving towards her. She had the uneasy feeling that he was stalking her.

"Apologize for what. You aren't sorry for forcing me to appear this morning." She moved away from the doorway and back into the room trying to anticipate his next move without revealing that his approach was unnerving her.

"No, I'm not. It's for this." He stopped right in front of her and taking the knuckle of his forefinger he raised her chin so that she was forced to look up at him. She instantly stilled and the look in his eyes froze her to the spot. She waited breathlessly for him to tilt his head and kiss her. She knew from the first moment she saw him that if he ever attempted to kiss her she wouldn't stop him. She licked her lips and of their own accord they parted . . . . anticipating. He did lower his head and as her eyelids drifted downwards he gently, leisurely slid his tongue along the fullness of her lower lip. As she unconsciously leaned towards him, he released her chin and stepped back. He reached out and steadied her as she jolted back to reality and opened her eyes. With a clenched hand she immediately tried pushing away from him, resisting the temptation to run her fingers over her licked lip. Morgan was easily within striking distance and as she raised that same hand to smack him he grabbed her wrist.

"I'll apologize for not finishing what I just started. But this is neither the time nor the place to get into this. Fortunately, for both of us, I couldn't go another day without a taste of you. I promise you retribution if you are up to the challenge of a night out with me." He released her, crossed his arms, and sat down on the table in front of her. "Ladies choice as to where we go and what we do."

Dabria took a deep breath and stepped away from the wall. She thought for a moment and then a gleam entered her eyes.

"Fine. Paint-balling. Saturday afternoon. Are you man enough to play war games with a little girl, Detective Vaughn?"

"I was raised with two sisters. I know how bloodthirsty women can be. Let the games begin, Ms. Abdulla-Smythe, or should I say continue." He stood up, opened the door, and held it for her.

"I'll book a time and leave a message at the station."

"This is my cell number. Call it instead." He handed her a business card that he whipped out of his breast pocket, with a hand written number on the back.

"Do you give that number out to just anyone or were you planning on giving it to me all along?"

"I'll let you figure it out. See you Saturday." With that he waltzed through the door, skipped down the steps, and out of the court house. As he swaggered past the Cenotaph, Dabria was reminded of the tale she had read regarding the placement of the monument and the courthouse itself. Apparently if you were convicted of your crime and sentenced to death you were hung on the exact spot that the memorial now resided. Since the courthouse was at the top of the hill, all of the townspeople could stand at the base of the hill and witness the hanging. Dabria wondered if she was about to inadvertently witness her own metaphorical hanging.

~ ~ ~

As soon as Dabria got back to the office she left a message for Sarah to call her when she was free and she returned to the duty of serving her clients. Less than an hour later, Sarah appeared in the doorway. Dabria had removed her blazer and unbuttoned the cuffs of her blouse and rolled them up. She was much more relaxed than she had been an hour ago.

"Hey, what's up?" Sarah asked as she sank into a chair.

"Have you ever paint-balled before?" Dabria asked.

"You mean played war games out in a field somewhere?"

"Yes."

"Actually, I have. We played when I was in university."

"Would you be interested in playing again this weekend?"

"Sure. Where and when?"

"I have to find a field and book it for sometime Saturday afternoon and with your help, I'm going to try to get a team together."

"So, what's the occasion?" she inquired. "Hey, you had court this morning with "your cop", didn't you? That wouldn't have anything to do with this, would it?"

"Firstly, he's not "my cop" and secondly, it definitely does have something to do with this morning."

"What happened? Did you amaze them with your brilliant arguments?"

"There was no opportunity for brilliant arguments. The charges were dropped and the case dismissed."

"So, why didn't someone call and tell you that?"

"That was my very first question once we left the courtroom."

"He also appeared?"

"Yes. I think the whole point of the thing was to teach me a lesson."

"That's a little extreme, don't you think? I think there was more to his agenda than that."

"Reallllly?" Dabria asked sarcastically with a raised eyebrow.

"Okay, smarty pants. What's the deal with the paintball?"

"He challenged me to a date and gave me the freedom to pick the time and place. I chose to pick an event rather than the usual supper and a movie."

"Bree, I have the feeling that you picked this particular event for a very specific reason. Am I right?" she questioned as she cocked her head to one side. "Let me guess. Number one, you're the Paint-ball Champion of Western Canada. Number two, not only do you plan on kicking his ass but you plan on doing this publicly since paint-ball is usually a group activity. Number three, this *is* a group activity so you aren't forced to deal with him one on one. How am I doin' so far?"

"Well, I don't think there even is such a thing as a Canadian Paint-ball Championship but I do know my way around the game. Bringing him down a peg or two in front of his peers wouldn't be a bad thing, and you're right about me wanting to keep this as a casual gathering rather than an actual date."

"You're falling fast, aren't you?"

"Let's just say I need to maintain some distance and hold Detective Vaughn off. I'm not really sure that I want a relationship with him and I definitely haven't figured out what kind of relationship it should be if I did."

"Right. So let's pretend I believe you and we'll concentrate on the paint balls. Let me do some asking around about not only the available facilities but also who's interested in playing with us. I'll get back to you before the end of the day. Does he know you're finding a team?"

"Not yet. That's why I called you right away. If we can find players he also needs time to get a team together."

"Kent is off Saturday but if he finds out that cops are playing on the other team we'll probably lose him to them. Wish me luck." Sarah scooted out the door.

Dabria returned to her files and when lunch rolled around Sarah called and invited her to join her and some of the other woman from the office. They met at Boston Pizza and once orders were taken Sarah settled down to the very serious business of recruitment. By the time lunch was done Dabria had a team of six, and coincidentally the paint-ball place was owned by one of Jaimie's friends. Only three of them had played before and so they decided to get together an hour before the actual game began to play a mini game of their own. They discussed gear and equipment and they were all surprised to discover that Dabria had not only the required safety equipment but also several guns and a custom-made suit. She promised to help them collect what they needed and assured them they would be able to rent rather than buy the safety equipment. As they headed back to work there was a buzz of excitement in the air.

Jaimie booked the place for two hours and had a list of rental equipment faxed over. She buzzed Dabria with the go ahead to inform Detective Vaughn of the arrangements. All six players were woman and all were single. Two of them had boyfriends that they assured Dabria would play for the other team. So Morgan really only had to find three other players. She called and left a message on his cell phone before she went home for the day. After returning to the apartment and changing into sweats and a T-shirt she went into the storage room in search of her gear. All of the equipment was stored in a huge Rubbermaid plastic tub. She hauled it into the living room and began digging through it.

The facility allowed you to bring all of your own gear with the exception of the paint balls, which had to be purchased there. Dabria's suit needed to be washed and she needed to refill her CO2 tanks. She removed the two-way radio headset from her helmet and made a mental note to ask the girls in the morning if they wanted to use radios or not. The memories evoked by the unpacking were bittersweet. David, Matthew, and Dabria had played war games of one sort or another for over twenty years. She loved being outdoors and the adrenaline rush of stalking and shooting for fun surpassed even her "need for speed" in her car. She hugged her suit to her chest and closing her eyes relived the last time she had used it. It had only been six months ago and it was at a facility near Rocky Mountain House. When the three of them played with others they always played together as a team. Not surprisingly they were unbeatable.

It had been fall and the weather was cool. Snow had come early but the ground wasn't frozen yet. The debris underfoot was soggy and limp and cushioned one's footfalls. Although the deciduous trees were leafless and camouflage tricky at least crackling leaves didn't reveal locations as both teams stalked the other. It was a perfect day with the sunlight streaming through the trees and the crisp air filling her lungs as she played. It was later that night that Dabria had met the station's new conservation officer, Annah. She was David's new partner and ultimately the catalyst for the destruction of Dabria's two best friends. As emotions began to overshadow Dabria's memory of the perfect last game she chased the sadness away. Dabria would not allow Annah to destroy those memories. She continued her perusal of the tub and set aside the things that needed attention. Just then the phone rang.

"Hey, so I got your message. We meet at 5:00 p.m. and we play until 6:00 p.m. What's this about a team?" Morgan asked.

"I thought it would be fun if we got together a couple of groups and played against each other. I've found five others to play with me and two of them have boyfriends that can play on your side. You just need to find three other players. I assume you've played before?"

"Yes, and I'm guessing you have, too."

"A couple of times. If you give me a fax number I'll have Jaimie send you over a copy of their rates and rentals."

"Sounds great. Don't think that being sore will be an excuse for avoiding dinner afterwards."

"I wouldn't dream of it, Detective Vaughn. See you Saturday." Dabria clicked off and after shoving her suit in the washing machine decided to make herself some supper and settle in for a night of more homework.

Chapter 8

The rest of the week flew by with court appearances, client interviews, and hours spent researching. Dabria was glad when Friday finally rolled around. Sarah popped in and invited her to a join some friends for a girl's night out. They were planning dinner and a chick flick. Dabria readily agreed since the thought of spending one more night at home working on the piles of files left her cold. She had made a respectable dent in about half of the piles and was hoping to continue at her current pace until the initial backlog was cleared up.

She hurried home and changed into jeans, roper boots, and a forest green chenille sweater. They met for a leisurely supper and then watched a sappy movie before heading out to the bars for an evening of dancing and people watching. Sarah was DD or designated driver for the night so Dabria was free to have a couple of drinks. Between the dancing and the tequila shots the evening came to an end all too soon. Dabria actually had a great time. She danced almost every dance, which did not go unnoticed by more than a few people in the crowd. Niall, her little Scottish waiter from Shay's, was one of the first to snag her. Colin, the real estate agent, and Craig, from work also had a turn on the floor with her. Although Colin sent her over a drink with a request to join him, Dabria respectfully responded that it was girl's night out, so maybe another time. Craig was more in tune with women than that and didn't attempt to interfere with the girls and their fun. Last but not least, a very sexy looking bookish type drew her onto the floor for a waltz. The second he coaxed her into his arms a shiver of alarm raced up her spine. This guy was sexy but a sense of foreboding descended on

Dabria. Her instincts were on full alert by the time the dance was done. Before she could decide whether he was a real or imagined threat, Sarah, who had been dancing beside them, announced that she was tired and asked if they could call it a night. Dabria agreed and politely, but with a distinct feeling of relief, declined his offer of another dance. The girls decided to hit the washroom before leaving. As Dabria walked out of the bathroom she was alarmed to discover that a brawl had broken out. She watched the melee from the hallway and tried to call 911, when she observed a young man pull a knife out of his hoodie. One of the bouncers ran right into her in his hurry to attend to the commotion. Being half the size of him she was violently flung against a wall. Banging her head, she crumpled to the ground as her cell phone skittered across the floor.

~ ~ ~

Kent and Morgan both happened to be coming off shift when they heard there was a disturbance at one of the bars in town. Kent had sought out Morgan and introduced himself just a couple of days before after being recruited by Sarah for the paint ball challenge. Morgan now volunteered to accompany Kent when they learned that ambulances had been called and Kent indicated that this was a bar Sarah and he frequented. After trying unsuccessfully to reach Sarah, Kent bolted from the car as soon as they stopped in the parking lot, yelling over his shoulder that Sarah's car was there. Morgan quickly followed him as two city police cruisers and the ambulances came screaming in behind.

The scene that greeted the men was one of frenzied brawling. Chairs and tables had been pitched aside while two bouncers tried to hold their own against several drunken, aggravated patrons. While some of the bar's clients left, most of them were still inside cheering for one side or the other. As they entered Kent went directly to the bar and demanded that all the lights be turned on and the music turned off. Sarah saw him stride past her as she sat on the floor holding Dabria's unconscious, bleeding body in her arms. She called out to him but the noise level was so great he was unable to hear her plea. Immediately after exiting the bathroom and seeing Dabria slumped on the floor next to the entrance she had placed a 911 call. Dabria's back was against a wall and someone was kneeling over her. By the time Sarah had pushed her way past several fleeing people and reached Dabria, the person had disappeared. Several more police officers entered the bar and as they contained the situation, Sarah was able to flag down one of the paramedics to assist her. Kent finally spotted Sarah when she stood up beside the paramedics as they lifted a body onto a stretcher. She walked out with the EMTs holding the hand of the patient. Kent shouted to Morgan then headed for the ambulance. By the time both men made it outside Dabria had already been loaded into it. Sarah was about to jump in beside her when Kent yelled her name. She turned around and Kent was startled by the blood smeared all over her shirt.

"My Gawd, are you hurt?" he barked as he grabbed her and feverously began to check her out.

"I'm fine. This is Bree's blood," she assured him.

He pulled her into his arms and as she hugged him she realized that another plain clothes cop was standing behind Kent.

"Dabria's hurt and they're taking her to the Vic. I'm going to ride in the ambulance. Can you follow in my car?" she asked Kent.

Morgan pushed forward.

"Dabria?"

"Yah, Dabria!" Sarah confirmed as she pulled herself up into the ambulance. "Are you Morgan?"

"What? Yes," Kent's companion replied. "That's Dabria in there? What the hell happened? How serious is it?"

"All I know is that when I found her she was unconscious and bleeding, but now she's awake. I'll explain at the hospital. I have to go." Sarah moved farther into the ambulance so that the EMT could close the door. She sat down beside Dabria and the ambulance took off.

Morgan made a dash for his car with Kent fast on his heels. The men made it to the hospital seconds after the ambulance pulled up. Once parked, they rushed into emergency and after showing their badges were ushered into the waiting area outside Dabria's examination room. Sarah was there pacing and wringing her hands.

"Tell me what happened," Morgan demanded without waiting for an introduction.

"Bree and I had a *girls' night out*. We went for supper, to a show, and then decided to go dancing. It was just after last call and we were getting ready to leave. We went to the washroom. She left before I did. When I walked out I saw someone sitting on the floor, with their back against the wall and someone crouched over them. It wasn't until I got closer that I realized it was Bree. People had started rushing out of the bar and by the time I reached her whoever had been there was gone. She was unconscious and bleeding."

"Bleeding from where?"

"Her head . . . . her face. There was so much blood," Sarah shuddered and Kent reached for her hand. "I saw a gash on her forehead, but I don't know if that's all or not. She came to as the EMTs were loading her onto the stretcher."

"Did she say anything?" Morgan prompted.

"She said she had a headache and the EMTs asked that she just lay still and not talk."

"Is there a doctor in with her now?"

"Yes. They asked me to leave while they examined her."

Suddenly the curtain to Dabria's cubicle opened and a nurse stepped out. As she attempted to pass them Morgan stopped her.

"Excuse me. Can you tell me how Dabria's doing and can I see her?"

"Are you family?"

"I'm an R.C.M.P. and her boyfriend. She has no immediate family in P.A."

"I see. I'll check with the doctor then and let you know." With that she continued to a supply room, returned with the needed equipment, and disappeared again behind the curtain. Morgan strained to understand the murmur of voices he could hear. Within moments the curtain reopened and the nurse gestured for him to come inside.

Dabria lay on a hospital bed with her head elevated and her eyes closed as a doctor sutured together the gash on her forehead. An attempt had been made to clean off the majority of the blood on her face but the front of her sweater was soaked with it. Although Morgan had been exposed to many accident victims before and knew that forehead cuts bleed profusely, the scene in front of him was still unsettling. Dabria's normally vibrant fawn colored face was pale and combined with the dark red blood and forest green sweater she appeared as a garish caricature of her usual self. Quietly the doctor spoke to her as he stitched.

"You shouldn't be concerned that you can't remember the events directly before the accident. That's normal. Now, once I'm finished with this I'm going to cut off your sweater and we're going to send you for a CAT scan just to confirm that you haven't received a more serious concussion than I suspect you of having."

Dabria opened her eyes and discovered Morgan standing behind the nurse. She smiled weakly and the doctor swiveled to see why she was smiling.

"You can come and hold her hand, if you like," he said to Morgan. "She's being very brave though without you. I can't give her any freezing, except numbing spray, since she's been drinking and yet she hasn't uttered so much as a whimper."

Morgan moved to the other side of the bed, picked up Dabria's hand, turned it over, and kissed it. He pulled up a stool and sat beside the bed holding her hand in both of his. Dabria closed her eyes again and squeezed his hand occasionally as the stitching continued. A single tear escaped as the doctor tied off the last suture. Gently using the pad of his thumb, Morgan brushed it aside. The doctor grabbed a pair of cutting shears and swiftly sliced Dabria's sweater from bottom to top. She re-opened her eyes, and the doctor and Morgan helped her sit up so that they could pull it off her and discard it. Dabria's bra was also saturated so the doctor snipped it off, too. Under normal circumstances being bare-breasted in front of an audience would have made Dabria extremely self conscious. At this point, however, her head was pounding so intensely that she really didn't care. The nurse stepped forward and she and Morgan helped Dabria into a hospital gown and then a wheelchair. Morgan picked up her hand again and held fast to it as they maneuvered her down the hall to the scan room. Not a word had passed between them this entire time. Dabria had discovered that talking only made her head hurt more. Since she was in obvious discomfort Morgan knew from dealing with other head trauma victims not to speak unless she initiated it.

The nurse requested that Morgan remain outside the room while the scan was being taken. Not long after the doctor came out and spoke quietly to Morgan.

"My nurse tells me you're an R.C.M.P. Is that correct?"

"Yes," Morgan replied. "I'm off duty right now, though. Why do you ask?"

"The gash on your girlfriend's forehead is not really a gash. It's actually a slash. She was cut with something very sharp. The wound is even, clean, and deep. It's not consistent with someone running into her with say a sharp ring or something like that. It's more like she had already been knocked out and then someone took a scalpel or a box cutter to her. I don't believe the cut was an accident and I've seen cuts similar to it before."

"What are you saying? Who had similar cuts?"

"The *scalper victims*. Those three young women all had a similar hairline cut."

"I'm not working that case and I've moved here recently so can you give me a rundown on the details."

"Sure. Most of this information is public knowledge anyway. Three young women have been found over the last two years raped and murdered. All of them have been scalped. Her forehead cut is similar to those. It is directly below her hairline, so on the upside, her scar will be easily hidden."

"Are you telling me that someone actually thought they could scalp a person in a crowd of people?"

"No, but it's still the same kind of cut. I just thought you might want that information."

"Thank you. I do. I may be back with more questions if we can find a witness."

"Absolutely. I'm here to help."

"Doctor, does she know the particulars of the cut?"

"No. I saw no purpose in disclosing that information to her at this time."

"I appreciate that. Thanks."

After reading her scan the doctor returned to the room with Morgan and explained to Dabria that she did indeed have a concussion but it wasn't life-threatening. However, he did suggest that she spend the remainder of the night in the hospital. When she protested that she would prefer to go home he responded by stating that unless she had someone there to wake her up regularly he wouldn't release her.

"I'll stay with her and promise to wake her up when necessary," Morgan vowed. When Dabria offered up no resistance to the idea the doctor agreed to sign the release. He mentioned to Morgan that she had already vomited, and if she did so again, he needed to contact the doctor. He also told Morgan that by Saturday evening her headache should have subsided substantially. Morgan gently settled Dabria into a wheelchair and then pushed her back to the emergency entrance. Sarah immediately rushed up to the wheelchair. With a motion of his head Morgan indicated that she tone down her inquiry.

"Hey. How's the head, Bree?" Sarah asked quietly as she squatted by the side of the wheelchair.

"It's the worst migraine I've ever had," Dabria whispered with a grim smile. "Do you have my purse?"

"Yes. Are they releasing you?"

Morgan took over the conversation at this point to spare Dabria from having to speak.

"She's being released on the condition that I stay with her the remainder of the night and I wake her up every couple of hours." He shrugged out of his coat and wrapped her in it. Kent ran to pull Morgan's car around and they buckled her into the front seat. Morgan dropped them off to pick up Sarah's car and he assured them that he could handle Dabria from there on. When they arrived at her apartment Dabria walked out of the car and up the stairs on her own steam. Once inside her unit she eased off his jacket and told him she was taking a shower before lying down. He made her keep the door of the bathroom open just in case she passed out again and then went to dig through her cupboards to find some tea.

Taking advantage of the fact that she couldn't hear him while she was in the shower he called the detachment and requested the name of the detective in charge of the murdered girls' investigations. The dispatcher told him it was Detective French and that his next shift started at 8:00 a.m. Morgan informed the dispatcher that he may have some relevant information and to have the detective call him. In record time Dabria rinsed herself off and carefully washed her hair. Morgan signed off as he heard the shower stop. She wandered into the kitchen wearing what looked like an oversized night-shirt and was wrapping up in a brilliant embroidered green blanket. By now the tea was ready. Morgan guided her over to the sofa, grabbed a fleece blanket to drape over her, and handed her a cup. The tea had cooled enough to drink and as Dabria took a sip she discovered he had laced it with honey and vanilla.

"My mom used to make it for us like that when we were feeling off. It always made me feel better."

"Thank you, for volunteering to stay. Being home and being clean, even without the tea, is heaven compared to staying at the hospital," she softly whispered her gratitude.

"I can tell you're beat, so drink up and then off to bed."

"If it's okay with you I'd rather sleep out here because that way I can keep my head elevated on the arm of the sofa."

"Dabria, it's wherever *you*'re most comfortable that matters. I'll be fine. Go to sleep."

"If you're hungry," she said, "fix yourself something to eat. If you can't find anything exciting in the fridge there are meals in the freezer."

"Thanks, I don't mind if I do." Morgan moved back into the kitchen and by the time he had rustled up something to eat Dabria was fast asleep.

She looked almost back to normal despite the stitches. Curled up into a ball at the end of the sofa her color was better and the wrinkles of pain that had lined her face were smoothed out in sleep. After refueling himself, Morgan set the alarm on his watch and went in search of a blanket he could use. He glanced fleetingly into the spare room as he walked past, but stopped abruptly and returned to it when he realized there were several guns laid out on the floor. Crouching down to inspect them closer he realized they were paint-ball guns. Also laid out were CO_2 tanks, a helmet, a face and neck shield, battle boots, and a camouflaged padded suit. Beside the helmet were a two-way radio headset and a couple of paint-ball hoppers. All of the equipment with the exception of one gun, had battle scars. Morgan knew when she suggested this as a date that she had obviously participated in the sport before but he hadn't realized that this girl was one serious paint-ball enthusiast. There wasn't going to be any paint-balling in Dabria's immediate future, but he silently promised himself that they would be facing off against each other in the not too distant future.

With a chuckle he continued his search for a blanket. Although Dabria had only been here a couple of weeks he assumed she would have more unpacking done. The spare room was stacked high with unopened boxes and so was her bedroom. The only covering on her bed was a bottom sheet and a duvet. There were no personal items out except toiletries in both the bathroom and bedroom. No knick-knacks graced the living room coffee table or pictures were hung. It was all very sterile and impersonal. Morgan wondered if this was a temporary accommodation while she waited for a more permanent residence. Giving up on the blanket, he returned to the living room and settled himself at the opposite end of the sofa. His only other options were to sleep in her bed in a different room, or to stretch out on the floor beside the sofa. He rechecked his alarm, laid his head back, and stretched his legs out to rest on top of the coffee table, which was actually an antique steamer trunk. As he drifted off to sleep he wondered if over the years that trunk had contained as many secrets as he knew that Dabria kept.

~ ~ ~

Dabria was awakened by an unfamiliar sound. As she blinked the cobwebs away she realized it was the sound of gentle snoring, and it wasn't coming from her. Sprawled at the other end of the sofa was a big, gorgeous, hunk of a man that was obviously exhausted. Dabria leisurely scrutinized her sleeping partner. It was nice to be able to devour his features uninterrupted and unobserved. He was dressed in a well worn, button down, blue striped dress shirt that had the top two buttons undone and had been pulled out of the waist of his jeans. His dirty blond curls were even more tousled than usual. Beard stubble enhanced the ruggedness of his chin and jaw line. The crinkles that she often witnessed at the corners of his eyes, as he openly mocked her, were smoothed out in sleep and he looked totally at ease. She fantasized crawling over, straddling his prone figure, and slowly undoing the remaining buttons to explore the muscles of his chest and arms while she nipped at his neck and ear lobes. The urge to wriggle over and discover if his chest was furred or hairless was almost more than she could control. As she unconsciously licked her lips and her fingers twitched her mind raced. Morgan's watch alarm went off and Dabria almost jumped out of her skin. Guiltily, she quickly closed her eyes and pretended to sleep.

Morgan sat up and stretched, unaware that Dabria was awake. As he reached over to wake her he noticed she was flushed. Thinking she may have a fever he carefully placed his hand on her forehead. Not expecting him to touch her Dabria jolted which caused his hand to brush over her stitches. He instantly drew back and cursed under his breath. She opened her eyes.

"I'm okay. You didn't hurt me."

"You were flushed. I was checking to see if you had a fever," he explained. Suddenly understanding dawned. "You were watching me sleep, weren't you? And you're blushing because you almost got caught. Am I right?"

"Don't be ridiculous. I was sleeping until you touched me," Dabria protested.

"Yah, ... whatever," the crinkles at his eyes predictably reappeared. "At least you're awake now. Can I get you anything?"

"What time is it?"

"It's 5:00 a.m."

"Since I'm not about to send you out in the cold at this time of the morning and I seem to have woken up easily why don't you go sleep in my bed. I'll be fine out here."

"Only if you join me," he taunted.

"I think that's a little premature, isn't it? We've never even been on a date. See, if you knew me better you'd realize that I don't fall into bed at the drop of a hat."

"Well, let's rectify that problem then. You can ask me anything you want and I get to return the favor. That way, before this day is over, we should know each other well enough that we can begin the physical part of our relationship."

"We don't have a relationship."

"Of course we do. I told the nurse that I was your boyfriend and that's why they released you into my care. I never stretch the truth, unless of course it's absolutely necessary," he assured her. "Where do you want to begin or do you want me to start?"

"Can I make myself another cup of tea and go to the washroom before we get into whatever it is you feel the need to tell me?"

"Of course. I'll start the kettle. By the way, have any memories of what happened last night surfaced yet?"

"No," she responded glumly.

"Don't sweat it. It'll happen." Morgan turned back to the stove.

Dabria had been trying to remember what had happened at the bar since she came to on the stretcher. So far, leaving the bathroom was her last conscious thought until she heard Sarah talking to the EMTs.

The doctor had warned her that it might take time for the memory to return. He told her not to stress over it and that it would eventually come back. Being a cop, Dabria knew that Morgan wouldn't let it go until she was able to relate every detail. Hmm . . . . Morgan. Now what was she going to do about Morgan?

Dabria knew that they were eventually going to be lovers. It was simply a matter of timing and strategy. The question was should she simply not overanalyze the situation but instead go with her instincts? David had been the only other man she had ever been with and although that had started off wonderfully, and she had no regrets that he had been her first, it certainly hadn't ended up the way she'd expected. Maybe it would be better to enter into this with no expectations and just take things as they happened. The problem was that her lack of experience would be apparent to Morgan and he would question it since it was possible he knew of her terminated engagement. Was she willing to open herself up to those questions and how should she respond, or should she declare her inexperience before anything happened? Chastising herself, she acknowledged that she had never been known to be faint-hearted. She was thirty-two years old, she wanted him, and he obviously was attracted to her, so why not take the plunge.

Since she was in the bathroom anyways she decided to brush her teeth and swipe on some deodorant. Her hair was sticking up all over but it was close to her normal styled appearance without any product and it was clean and soft. "So now," she pondered, "how does one go about seducing someone that you told two minutes ago you weren't easy?" With a sigh she decided not to force the issue and to let things progress naturally. Although she'd rather jump him than talk to him maybe that wasn't the most prudent approach.

She found him still in the kitchen when she returned and since she discovered she was suddenly starving she dug through the cupboards for something to munch on, letting him handle the task of the tea.

"Did you eat before?" she asked.

"Yes, but I could have a snack if you're looking for something for yourself."

"I guess my invalid status has just been dropped since I have now fallen into the role of woman making man food."

"I'll do it if you tell me what you want," Morgan looked at her with exasperation.

"I was kidding. I don't know what I want yet but I certainly have no argument with making you something."

"How about I get out of your way since this kitchen is hardly big enough for one, let alone the both of us?"

"Sounds good. You can start telling me your life history any time."

"In a hurry to get the formalities out of the way so that we can get down to the good part, are we?"

"You know it," she brazenly agreed.

Spurred on by her obvious good mood and playful flirtation Morgan proceeded to give her the Reader's Digest version of his life.

"I was born on Salt Spring Island in British Columbia thirty years ago to loving parents named Natalie and Michael. My father was a fisherman and my mother is an artist. I have two sisters named Shona and Amy. Shona is married to a banker and lives in Vancouver with her twin baby boys. Amy is a potter and lives on the island with my mother who has MS. My father was killed in a fishing accident when I was sixteen and instead of carrying on the family tradition I decided to try my hand at earning a living doing something that was less work, less dangerous, and more financially rewarding than my father's career."

"And being a cop was it?"

"No," Morgan chuckled. "That wasn't the career I initially chose. My friend and I started a lovely little Cannabis grow operation hidden on the island. It required little work and produced more than adequate funds. That is, until we got caught. The R.C.M.P. that busted us gave us the option of cleaning up our acts or charging us with Production of a Controlled Substance. If convicted there was a maximum penalty of seven years in jail."

"You were growing pot in the bush?" Dabria questioned with amazement.

"Well, yah! Anyhow, since I didn't want my mother finding out I agreed to clean up my act. After destroying all of our plants and turning over our scavenged equipment we were not so gently persuaded to replant our plots with native vegetation to discourage other entrepreneurs from following in the footsteps of our ill-fated venture. Since this was the winter of grade twelve the cop helped me fill out scholarship applications, university application forms, and student loan forms.

Although neither Drew nor I were dummies we definitely hadn't been excelling up to this point, so the chances of getting a scholarship were slim to none. However, our marks were good enough to get us accepted into the Faculty of Arts and Social Science at Simon Fraser. Since mom was now a single parent I qualified for loans. Drew's parents were island hippies so he qualified as well. In conclusion, Drew is now a successful architect living in Toronto and I am following in the footsteps of the man who turned me from a felon into a fine, upstanding, productive member of our society."

"After your first year what did you take at University?"

"Commerce. And then Law."

"You're a lawyer!" Dabria exclaimed.

"Yah, but I don't like to be inside so after passing the Bar and practicing for a year I joined the R.C.M.P. and decided to put my knowledge to a different use."

"So, you've only been a cop for a couple of years then," Dabria calculated.

"Actually, I graduated when I was seventeen, so after getting my degrees and articling for a year I was only twenty-five. After I finished training in Regina my first posting was just outside of Toronto. I was there for four years before transferring here."

"So, if you've only been with the force for four years, how did you make detective so fast?"

"It was a combination of things, my background in law, plus the fact that I became an undercover cop after two years. The undercover part occurred because I apparently make a good criminal. Who knew!" he exclaimed sardonically. "When I transferred here I was promoted to detective because of my undercover work."

Dabria had quit foraging in the kitchen and sat down with a tray containing cut up fruits and veggies, cheese, crackers, and pickles. She pushed his feet off the trunk and laid the tray on it. Oblivious to the fact that Morgan was enjoying the view of her plump unfettered bouncing bosom beneath her green blankie, she slipped onto the sofa and then reached for some apples and cheese. As she sat back and munched she gazed at him expectantly and waited for him to continue.

He grabbed some carrots and waving one at her declared, "You're up."

"That's it?" she questioned.

"For now," he confirmed. "Your turn."

Chapter 9

Dabria was surprised he had revealed so much of himself to her. It was flattering that he felt comfortable enough to do so. However, she didn't feel obligated to offer details about her own past. She continued to nibble on the crudities she had set out while she glossed over the basics. She explained her own family situation and then told him that she had grown up with David and Matthew. She told Morgan that she had been engaged and that David, a conservation officer, had died during a mountain rescue gone bad. She also disclosed that Matthew, a friend of both theirs, and also a conservation officer, had died after being shot by the R.C.M.P. Knowing how much he seemed to love to investigate, she naturally assumed he had done a background check of her as well. Since Morgan was a member of the same police force and his access to information would be almost limitless, there was no point in keeping the basic details from him. The question was how much more had the Rocky Police Force volunteered regarding their theories surrounding last year's debacle.

"I see. Do you want to talk about what happened?" Concealing any previous knowledge he had of her, he prompted her to share more.

"Not really. Let's just say it's a lengthy, convoluted story. I wouldn't wish the last six months of my life on my worst enemy." Morgan was relieved she had told him that much of the truth. She hadn't elaborated beyond the bare facts, but he hadn't expected that she would actually tell him as much as she had.

"That would, of course, bring us to the reason why I moved here. After losing my two best friends amid scandalous rumors, innuendos, and furtive, suspicious glances the only choice I had was to leave Rocky. Although my parents thought the obvious choice should have been to move back to Calgary, the thought of being surrounded by family and well meaning friends was smothering. I needed to get out and make a new life for myself."

"So, why here? The world was your oyster, and you could have chosen anywhere."

"Actually, I represented a client who had a court appearance here a couple of years ago. When I went on the internet and looked for job postings I discovered they were looking for a family law lawyer for Legal Aid. The job was close to scenic lakes, the city was small, and the cost of living was acceptable for the wages that were offered. Plus, the big bonus was that absolutely no one knew me, my family, or the boys." Reaching for a handful of carrots she inclined her head and inquired, "And you? Why did you come here?" She crunched as she waited for his answer.

"Well, after living the hectic life of the big city I was looking for something a little more pastoral and like you I was attracted by the lakes. I missed the water and being undercover I hadn't had any personal time to take advantage of the lakes around Toronto. Although, there's no deep sea fishing here I can still kayak, snorkel, and indulge in lake fishing."

"I've never kayaked on the ocean but I have on lakes and in rivers and I love it. My kayak is in the storage room."

"Can I see it?"

"Sure," Dabria slid off the couch and padded over to the closed door off the kitchen. Inside was a bright orange and yellow ultra-light kayak, with a padded seat and water proof GPS attached to the front of it.

"It's smaller and shorter than the ones I'm familiar with," Morgan said.

"Chances are," Dabria stated cheekily "so am I."

"Chances are," he chuckled.

"I needed something light that I can carry myself. This is the lightest I could find, plus it's virtually unsinkable. It's served me well. We'll see how it performs on Emma." Dabria backed out of the room and closed the door.

"So, you can tell me it's none of my business if you like, but I wondered why you haven't unpacked yet. I noticed packed boxes in every room."

"Every room, huh?" she flung over her shoulder as she headed back to the living room. "I bought a place out at Emma Lake and since I move in soon it didn't make sense to unpack anything."

"I was looking for a blanket," he claimed in his defense with his arms thrust out, palms up.

"Didn't find one, did ya?"

"No, but I did find your not-so-hidden arsenal."

"Do you like my guns?" she asked beaming as she rubbed her hands together.

"They're impressive. Do you get out much?"

"It's been about six months since I've had a chance to play. Telling you that it's a favorite pastime of mine probably isn't a surprise since I'm sure you checked out *all* of my equipment."

"Have I!" he affirmed. Dabria doubted he was referring to only her paint-ball gear. "But, unfortunately you won't be using any of it later today. Mind if I borrow a couple of the guns to try out?"

"No, help yourself. Did you find three others for your team?"

"No, I could only get two guys, so I planned on playing one short. I guess we're even now."

"Since I can't go, will you wear my helmet camera and film for me so that I can watch it tonight? I'll make supper for us while you're gone," she bribed.

"I didn't see a camera with the rest of your stuff."

"I got it as a gift and haven't actually used it yet, but I know where it's packed," Dabria yawned.

"Sure. Now, I think that's enough talk for a while. How about you crawl over here and sleep on top of me and that way I can keep your head elevated with my chest and stretch out on the sofa at the same time."

"That is the lamest come-on line I have ever heard," Dabria chastised as she looked at him dubiously with one eyebrow cocked.

"It's no line. Come on, I won't bite, and believe it or not, it's against my moral code to seduce defenseless lawyers. I promise," he vowed with one hand over his heart and the other raised like he was being sworn in. "Come to think of it that's an oxymoron isn't it—a defenseless lawyer."

"Ha! Ha!! You know what? I'm too tired and sore to argue. Make yourself comfortable and then I'll lie down," she chuckled.

Morgan didn't have to be told twice. He reset his alarm and then swiftly swung his legs over and scrunched himself down so that he was lounging back on the sofa. He undid his belt, pulled it off, and dropped it on the floor beside him. Dabria flung the blanket over top of him and as she approached he opened up the blanket to let her slide in under it. She was still encased in her green wrap and although she should have felt awkward she was surprised to discover that it seemed natural and that they fit together quite nicely. Laying her head on his chest she snuggled in and promptly fell asleep. Morgan wasn't so lucky. With a jolt he was reminded of a conversation he had overheard between his sister and his mother not so many years ago.

"Mom, how did you know that Dad was the one?" Shona had asked.

"It was very simple, Shona. We just fit," his mother had replied.

He hadn't thought much about it then, but suddenly it seemed to make sense. There was so much they didn't know about each other and they had only met a few weeks ago and yet somehow he knew Dabria "just fit." He had to believe she was innocent of the suspicions the Rocky Mountain House Police Force still had about her. Although she was holding back the details of her past, he couldn't envision her actually carrying out the scheme they suspected her of being involved in. Wrapping his arms loosely around her, he relaxed. Rome wasn't won in a day and neither would Dabria be. His father had always told him everything worthwhile involved patience, hard work, and faith. He wished his father could see what he had grown up to be. Morgan drifted off with a smile on his face and a new challenge to conquer: Dabria Abdulla-Smythe.

~ ~ ~

The vibrating of Morgan's cell phone woke him up a little after 8:00 a.m. Not wanting to wake Dabria, he simply reached into his pocket and turned it off. She sighed, wriggled, and then settled down again. Since her sleep didn't appear coma-like he decided to let them both sleep for another hour. At 9:00 a.m. when the alarm sounded it immediately woke both of them up. She shifted and stretched like a satisfied kitten. His body had decided there were things it would rather be doing than just sleeping and as Dabria became aware that some parts of Morgan's anatomy were harder than others she took the initiative and began to unbutton his shirt.

"Are you sure you know what you're doing?"

"Yep," she confirmed. "Any arguments?"

"Absolutely none. Carry on."

Dabria repositioned herself so that she was in fact straddling Morgan and sat up. He laced his fingers behind his head and let her explore. She opened one button at a time and once she was finished she peeled the shirt back and smoothed her hands up his chest and across his pecs. He was mostly hairless with a treasure trail shooting from his belly button down to, as of yet, unchartered territory. His chest and stomach were sculpted and firm without being muscle-bound. She leaned in and began to kiss and lick up his neck, along his jaw line, and over to his ear lobe. Without touching his lips she made her way back down to his chest and focused her attentions on his nipples. She could tell he was rock hard and probably uncomfortable. So, as she laved his right nipple she scooted her butt down past his crotch and moved her hands to unzip his jeans and pull apart the folds to give him some breathing room. Then she scooted back up so that she was actually sitting just below his balls.

At this point Morgan hunched his shoulders and grabbing his shirt from behind his neck he pulled it off and flung it onto the floor. He then placed his hands on Dabria's hips. Dabria sat up and undid the twist of her wrapper, letting it fall off. Morgan slid his hands slowly up her sides under her night-shirt pulling it up as he explored. Once he had gently cleared the top of her head he dropped the night-shirt onto the floor. Suddenly, Dabria placed a hand on Morgan's chest signaling they stop.

"Too fast?" he questioned with resigned regret as his eyes devoured the tantalizing sight before him.

"No, I just realized something I haven't thought about in a long time. I'm not on any birth control and I don't have any condoms. Do you?"

"Sorry. I've got to say, the thought of being prepared for this didn't occur to me. I guess we're done, huh?" he stoically accepted with a sigh.

Dabria collapsed on his chest in a fit of giggles.

"Oh, I really don't think it's that funny," Morgan stated with a grimace. "Where is your shirt and stop rubbing up against me or you're going to get more than you're prepared for."

"I'm sorry. It's just that I was so worried about my performance that I actually forgot I shouldn't be performing in the first place. Honestly, Morgan I'm not normally a cock tease." Dabria climbed off and grabbed her shirt. "You know we haven't actually even kissed and yet I was preparing to do *the nasty*."

After tucking himself back in and zipping up, he strode over to her and gently pulled her into his arms. Dabria let out a squeak as he bent his head and began to very thoroughly kiss her. He started out teasing her as he had at the courthouse by simply rimming her lips with his tongue. Her lips parted with little encouragement and he nibbled first at her bottom lip and then peppered her neck with little pecks and licks. A moan slipped past her reserves and pushed him over the edge. He grabbed the globes of her perfect ass and ground her into him as he slanted his head and literally kissed her breathless. His kisses were now urgent and demanding—challenging her to give "as good as she got" and to match his passion. Just as suddenly as he began, he abruptly stopped, and set her away from him. Panting lightly she swayed. He reached out to steady her, but she pulled herself together by stiffening her shoulders and stepping back before he could touch her. With a satisfied smirk and his blue eyes gleaming, he chucked her under the chin with his knuckle.

"I think you'll be just fine for the day if I head home now. Just don't overdo it while I'm gone. I should be back by around 7:00 p.m. By the way, I *will* be prepared tonight just in case you decide to continue where we left off."

Morgan grabbed his shirt and belt on his way to the spare room. After redressing and picking out two guns, CO_2 tanks, and hoppers he returned to reclaim his coat. Dabria was standing in the living room holding a small box out to him. It contained the helmet camera.

"Be good," he demanded as he took the box from her and let himself out. She blew him a sassy kiss as he closed the door.

After Dabria had checked out her grocery supplies and decided what to make for supper she tidied up her appearance. The cut was so close to her hairline that she was able to do her hair in such a way that you couldn't see the stitches at all. After shopping at the grocers, the liquor store, and the pharmacy she was back at the apartment by noon. She had decided to get her own protection so that she was prepared if any opportunity presented itself again. She had mixed emotions about the aborted attempt she had made this morning. She didn't doubt that it would have been great but she wondered if it was premature. She decided not to reinitiate anything this evening. She'd leave the ball in Morgan's court for now. Snatching up a blanket and her shuka, she curled up on the couch again and grabbed another nap.

~ ~ ~

As soon as Morgan left the apartment he checked his cell phone. The 8:00 a.m. call had come from the detachment. He swiftly called back.

"This is Detective Morgan Vaughn. Are there any messages for me?" He listened as she ran down the list. "Please save them for me and could I speak with Detective French?"

"One moment," stated the dispatcher. The "on-hold" melody started while Morgan stowed Dabria's gear into the trunk.

"Detective French speaking."

"This is Detective Morgan Vaughn. I know you returned my call this morning but I couldn't talk then. If you've got a minute I'd like to stop at the station and pass on some information regarding an incident that occurred last night. It might be related to a case you're working on."

"Sure, come on in. Which case?"

"The three murdered women that were scalped."

"I'll have a coffee waiting for ya."

Morgan signed off and pulled out of Dabria's parking lot. Within minutes he was at the detachment. Raking his hands through his hair he determined he couldn't look any worse than when he was on a stake-out and continued inside. The receptionist recognized Morgan and at his request directed him to French's desk. After the introductions were done they got down to business.

"So, what've ya got?"

Morgan relayed to him Sarah's version of the events and then added what the doctor had told him. He explained that at this point Dabria had no memory of what happened and so unless they could scare up any more witnesses they were left with only Sarah's statements. He asked French if he could take a look at the file that had already been compiled regarding the three unsolved murders.

"A set of fresh eyes would be welcome. You may pick up on something that has eluded us. Sean Layden is the other detective assigned to this case. We're trying to get a task force assigned but with budget restrictions our request keeps getting denied. I expect things will change as soon as the mayor calls for an election this spring. Since we're working with the city police force on this if they suddenly get their budget upped the R.C.M.P. won't want to look bad and so I'm sure we'll get more man hours as well. Of the three women that have been found two were prostitutes and the third is a Jane Doe. At this point there hasn't been a big panic by the general public. Does Ms. Smythe know about the murders?"

"No. The doctor suggested letting her memory come back before we filled her in."

"I'll hold off until after the weekend. But, come Monday morning I'm going to be calling her in for questioning and I'll want to snap some shots of her forehead. What was the name of the doctor who worked on her last night? I'm going to give him a call and get him to give me a statement regarding his suspicions. Do you know who was in charge from the city force last night so that I can give him a heads up?"

Morgan gave him Dabria's number and the name of the doctor. He told him that the witness was in fact Detective Ducette's girlfriend and that he didn't know the cops that had arrived at the scene. French passed him the file to copy as they exchanged cell numbers. By the time Morgan was finished photocopying French had reached both the doctor and Sarah and set up interviews with them. He was presently on the phone with one of the officers that had responded last night. Morgan sank back into a chair opposite French's desk and waited for him to finish.

"Well, that was interesting. According to Officer Brown, Sarah wasn't the only witness. One of the waitresses saw Ms. Smythe leave the washroom. A fight had broken out in the hallway between the washrooms and the entrance to the bar. This waitress was standing on the platform reserved for the waitresses, in front of the bartenders. She heard the disturbance and turned around. From her vantage point she could see exactly what was going on in the hall because the lights are always kept on there. Apparently, it was a bouncer that ran into Ms. Smythe on his way to break things up. He's twice as big as her and since she didn't see him coming he basically bowled her right over. He knocked her into the wall and without sparing her a glance continued on to the fight. The waitress said she saw her slide down the wall and slump against it."

Detective French took a sip of coffee and then continued.

"She immediately had the bartender push the silent alarm for the cop shop and asked him to call 911 for an ambulance. Since the fight was raging on in between the waitress and the bathrooms, there was no way for her to get to Ms. Smythe. As she stood there helplessly watching she saw a man approach Ms. Smythe and then bend down in front of her. Assuming that he was helping the injured woman her attention wandered elsewhere and that was all she had to report regarding Ms. Smythe. As the brawl escalated she went behind the bar and remained there until after the EMTs left. Officer Brown said he would re-interview her, determine if she could describe the man, as well as, find out if she noticed if Ms. Smythe was bleeding before the man approached her."

"Great. Sarah wasn't even sure it was a man. If we're lucky, between the waitress and Sarah we may at least get a basic description of this guy."

"Officer Brown said he hasn't read all of the statements yet and that if he finds any other witnesses he'll let me know. I had him transfer me back to reception and left a message for Detective Hughes to call me Monday. He's one of the city cops working on the *Scalper Case*."

"Are there notes in here as to what information has been released and what hasn't regarding these cases?"

"No. Everything in that file has been released. When you're done with that, come back and talk to me and I'll fill you in on the rest. The "reserved info" file doesn't leave this office."

"Fair enough. Thanks for this. I'll see you Monday." Morgan scooped up his file and headed for home, a shower, and a nap before the big paint-ball challenge: Legal Aid versus the Cop Shop.

~ ~ ~

Dabria woke up again around 3:00 p.m. and called Sarah. She explained that although she felt better she wouldn't be competing with her team today. She did assure Sarah though that she would be attending the practice session at 4:00 p.m. She re-packed the remainder of her equipment and maps of the course layout, had some lunch, marinated some chicken breasts, and headed out.

As she pulled up into the parking lot she discovered that her team was already assembled and waiting for her. She grabbed her maps and headed into the paint-ball headquarters. Dabria was pleased to see that the office had a good selection of rental equipment as well as equipment for sale. She wouldn't need to lend any of her equipment out. Once the team was outfitted in their gear and had their weapons loaded and ready to go, Dabria took them to the shooting range. They only spent ten minutes there before moving out into the field. Dabria and each team member were outfitted with voice activated radios. They had divided into two teams; one of three and one of two. Each team had their own radio frequency. Dabria stood in a tower above the field and was able to see the location of each member of both teams.

As she watched them play a devious plot evolved and she descended the tower and called both teams together to put her plan to a vote. It was unanimous. Dabria would hide her car and keep a radio tuned to the same frequency as her team. Then she would return to the tower to tell them where the other team was hiding. They were so *totally* cheating but since it was only a game the thrill of them beating the all male team of experienced cops any way possible was too big an enticement to pass up. In order to pull it off Dabria would have to leave the tower, return her radio, and drive away from the facility before her team finished the game. The staff agreed to help her and actually went so far as to provide her with a second radio that allowed her to listen in on the other teams conversations without their knowledge.

Dabria was giddy with the thrill of beating the other team. She just managed to hide her car and make her way back into the tower as the first member of team "Cop" pulled into the parking lot. Her team had reassembled in the office and was nonchalantly trying on equipment as if they too had just arrived. The windows of the tower were luckily one way glass. The only way the boys would ever discover that they had been duped was if the girls' consciences got the best of them and they spilled the beans.

The game started promptly at 5:00 p.m. By 5:15 p.m. not a single hit had been scored by the "Cops" and yet they had each been shot at least once. Things really began to heat up. Dabria was literally laughing out loud as the "Cops" frustration became increasingly evident with their escalation of swearing. Men by nature were competitive. They had entered into this little game as a way to impress the female team with their prowess. By 5:30 p.m. it had become more than a game to them since it was obvious that the team of girls was not only holding their own but actually beating them. As they tried strategy after strategy the girls continued to elude their stalking and yet managed to sneak in hit after hit. By 5:55 p.m. Dabria knew she had to leave. So giving her team final instructions as to the other team's location she slid off her headset and ran from the tower out to her car. Sarah called her from the bathroom at the paint-ball complex not ten minutes later, just as Dabria was pulling into her parking spot at home.

"I have to talk fast because Kent is waiting for me. I don't think the girls and I have ever had so much fun. We surrounded them and walked right out into the open with guns blazing and annihilated them. It was the best feeling ever to see the shock on their faces. We're all heading over to BP's for supper and drinks to celebrate our victory. The guys have to join us or they come off looking like poor sports. I can't guarantee they won't get the truth out of us before the evening is over but even if this win is only temporary it was *so* worth the cheating. Thanks for a great afternoon. Have fun with Morgan. I'll call you tomorrow." Dabria could hear the other girls in the background laughing and congratulating each other. It sounded like even Jaimie had fun.

Dabria grabbed her equipment out of her truck and let herself into her apartment. She carefully placed the equipment where it had been on the floor of the spare room and then started supper. While the wine breathed, the chicken baked, and the rice steamed she listened to The Dixie Chicks and prepared a salad. At 7:05 p.m. Dabria saw Morgan drive up. Dancing over to the intercom with a grin she couldn't seem to wipe off she buzzed him up. She couldn't wait to hear his version of the afternoon's events.

Chapter 10

Am I dead yet? No!!!! Please, come back!!!! I know I'm going crazy. I can't stand his touch. I don't want you to come back because when you do I know he's not far behind, but I'm terrified that you won't come back and I'll die here alone. No one knows where I am. Is anyone even looking for me? Please God, if you help someone find me I'll change my life. Is it too late? I'll do anything. How long can someone live like this? I don't want to die. I hear the door. You're back!!! Oh thank God, it's just you. I hope this means he's not coming tonight. Why did you do this to me? I never did nothin' to you. You were always so kind to me. I thought you liked me. What does he have on you? Why don't you let me go? You never take any for yourself. You just watch. I don't get it.

"Did you miss me? I couldn't come last night. You're happy to see me. That's too bad because you're not the right one. I finally found her. I marked her for later."

Please say you'll let me go. I won't tell. I'll move away. What are you doing? What is in your hand? Not more drugs. Noooooo!!!

"I'm sorry. I'm so sorry. I hope I didn't hurt you. You can sleep soon. It won't be long. You've never looked so beautiful. Are you sleepy yet? He won't hurt you anymore, I promise. Are you cold?"

Huh, ... I'm not cold anymore. I'm floating. I'm dying. Why? Why? I'm not so scared anymore . . . . not so scared. I don't want to die but I'm so tired. So tired . . . . Don't go . . . . Don't go . . . . Stay with me. Stay with me. I'm floating . . . . Too late . . . .

"Don't cry. It's better this way. He can't hurt you anymore. Please, don't cry. I won't leave you. I'll stay with you till the end. No one should have to die alone."

Chapter 11

Morgan walked into the apartment carrying Dabria's equipment in one hand and a bottle of wine in the other.

"So, how's the head?" he inquired sympathetically as he sidled up beside her, set the wine on the counter, and gently coaxed her face up to his with his forefinger under her chin.

"It's not bad. The headache has settled down to a dull roar and the stitches pull a little but basically I'm fine," she responded with a smile.

"What did you do all day?" He let go of her chin, turned, grabbed the equipment he had left at the door, and took it to the spare room.

"Well, I slept for part of it and then I went out and got some stuff for supper."

"That's it?" he inquired from the other room.

"I didn't overdo it if that's what you're asking." When he didn't respond Dabria looked up from the salad and wondered if she had placed some of her equipment in a different place than it had been before. It was almost as if he knew she was lying. She shook her head. She was just being paranoid. There was no way he could know that she had been out at the paint-ball complex. "Is there anything you don't like in a salad?" she asked, to get him to respond to her.

"If it's not moving, I'll eat it. We weren't allowed to be picky eaters in my Momma's house. Having you cook is a definite plus," he informed her as he returned to the kitchen. "Can I set the table for you?"

"Sure. Are you going to tell me what happened this afternoon? Did my team make me proud? Plates and glasses are here and cutlery is in that drawer," she directed. "I opened a bottle of red wine to let it breath and there's a bottle of white in the fridge. Can you pour me half a glass of red?"

"Did you take any of that pain medication today?"

"Are you afraid I'm going to pass out in my salad?" she teased. "No, I didn't take any and I have no intention of taking any. It's really not that bad." She motioned him towards the table. "Grab a chair. We'll eat our salad first. The rest should be ready in about five. So, you didn't answer me?"

"Your team did exceptionally well. In fact, Dabria, if I didn't know any better I'd almost think there had been some kind of divine intervention."

"What do you mean? You're not actually trying to tell me that my team gave you a run for your money?" Dabria asked with affected disbelief. "By the way, did you tape the competition?"

"Ah ya, I did. What time did you say you ran downtown to pick up those few things?"

"I don't believe I did say. How's the salad? Can we watch the tape while we eat?"

"It's delicious. Pine nuts, right?"

"How clever of you. You're obviously a cook."

"I dabble in the kitchen. My mother could turn a potato, a hand full of herbs, and a fish into a different gourmet meal every night of the week. I learned from the best."

"So, like me, tonight's entrée is going to be graded?"

"I love food. And by the smell of things, you've passed the cooking test with flying colors."

"And the other?"

"Time will tell. Relax Dabria, this evening is supposed to be a stress-free affair. Nothing you say or do will be held against you since you can claim a head injury as your defense."

"Who said I wasn't relaxed?" Dabria questioned as she rose gracefully to serve the remainder of the meal. "So, were we gonna watch that tape?"

Morgan lay off the grilling and settled back to enjoy the sumptuous feast Dabria had prepared. He was a master at the art of interrogation and knew that lulling his prey into a false sense of security always worked in his favor. He topped off her wine, and then popped the tape into her machine. He primed himself for the gloating that he knew was about to begin. It was a simple deduction to assume that Sarah had already called Dabria to regale her with the highlights of the afternoon. However, Morgan knew that there was more to the win than simple good luck. Somehow Dabria had been involved and eventually he would get it out of her. She was laughing so uproariously at one point that Morgan was concerned she would actually make her headache worse, thereby putting an end to his plans for the remainder of the evening. Although he was sure she figured it was due to his bruised ego, he turned the tape off, and instead diverted her with his memories of growing up on Salt Spring Island.

It was like a mini world on the island, he explained. Ancestry of the islanders was diverse but the philosophy of the majority was similar. They all sought the uncomplicated, quiet life of living on an island surrounded by the splendor of the Pacific Ocean, with the added bonus of warm winters. There were roughly nine thousand people that ranged from First Nations, descendants of the original Hudson Bay recruits, hippies, and draft dodgers from the 60's and 70's. In more recent years the island had become a haven for retirees and artisans. Morgan was a direct descendant of a draft dodger and a hippie. Between his fathers' seasonal fishing and his mother's gallery his parents had provided him with everything a boy could want, living in paradise. That is until his father was killed and his mother was diagnosed with MS. That was the year paradise changed and the boy grew up, with some help from the local law.

The stories continued as Dabria and Morgan cleaned the kitchen and settled at opposite ends of the sofa. Dabria did share a couple of the escapades of the three musketeers but then a flashback of David laying cold and still in his coffin destroyed her reflection. Morgan had watched the play of emotions march, unguarded, across her face as the remembered happy times changed to pain and regret. Suddenly, as if a shutter had come down her features evened out and her expressionless lawyer mask was firmly put back in place. He immediately steered the conversation into a different direction.

"So, tell me about this new abode you purchased?" he urged.

Dabria was relieved and appreciative that he was sensitive enough to know she needed a change of topic. As the evening wore on he realized he had learned two very important things: one was that she was still grieving and the other was that the more tightly she was backed against a wall the less likely she was to reveal her secrets. Pushing her was not the way to discover her mysteries. Earning her trust would be more productive.

The two questions he needed answered were: was she still in love with her dead fiancé and was she capable of, and had she been involved in the stalking and attempted murder of another human being? He decided to let the little matter of the paint-ball game drop for the time being and set out to seduce her instead. As she described her new home he picked up one of her feet and began to massage it. She had changed into jeans, a sweater, and a bra, so getting her heated up might be a little more difficult than this morning. But, he was determined to give it the *Good Old College Try*. Morgan finished with one foot and moved onto the next while Dabria relaxed further into the sofa. The topic moved from the cabin to their hobbies, to movies, and on to music.

Morgan slid out from underneath her legs and brought the bottle of wine over to refill their glasses.

"If you're trying to reduce my inhibitions with the wine," she murmured, "don't bother. You're simply wasting good wine."

"I was hoping to loosen you up so that you weren't worried about your performance. I recall you making a comment this morning something along those lines. But, I can't image that being an issue." Morgan sat down and pulled her feet back up into his lap.

"Can't you now? Well, what if I told you I have only been with one man and that we hadn't been together for a while." A while! Huh! That was certainly stretching the truth. Try more like over a year.

"A while before he passed away, or just since then."

"A while before," she confirmed. "We were having some problems and let's just say things really "went south" when I discovered he was having an affair." That was the truth in more ways than one. When Dabria had discovered David's sexual involvement with Mathew she had been devastated. She had always loved David and the knowledge that he was gay was a hard blow for her to recover from. She promised to keep the boys' secret and naively became a participant in their charade. Since they were already engaged she continued the pretense to not only protect her friends but also to keep any would-be suitors at bay. The last straw had been when she discovered he had taken a female lover. That was when she ended their engagement. Unfortunately, that confrontation occurred only two days before David's death. It was the last time she had spoken to him. But for now, she would keep all of that information to herself.

"And you feel guilty because?"

"How do you know I feel guilty?"

"A wild guess."

"Well, you're right I do. The final words I spoke to him were ugly and hurtful. I honestly can't remember a time when I didn't love him and our lifetime relationship ended the worst possible way."

"Dabria, if he loved you as you deserve to be loved he never would have put you in that position. I think your years of loving him and your loyalty to him far outshine one moment of harsh words." Morgan stopped massaging her feet and looked directly into her eyes. "Why did you tell me?"

"I debated not saying anything but figured you'd wonder what was wrong with me since I was in my thirties, had been engaged, and yet was obviously unsure of myself. Explaining only made sense."

"So you've accepted that we will be lovers?"

"I knew that the day you pulled me over. There are only two things that would prevent it from happening. One is if you are married, and the other is if you have any unfulfilled homosexual tendencies that you'd like to reveal."

"No. I swear councilor, that I am a single, fully functioning heterosexual male that can't wait to show you how incredibly sexy you are." Interesting that her second deal breaker involved homosexuality he thought. Morgan's sources indicated there were rumors that David and Matthew were gay. "And, I have the protection, so there should be no need to abort the mission tonight."

"I've got back up if you run out," she volunteered.

"Do you want to switch roles or would you prefer to be the one in control?"

"I'd actually really like to have someone who knows what they're doing teach me."

"I'm hardly a player, Dabria. For the past two years I've been under cover—neither time nor opportunity for any kind of relationship. But since someone needs to start tonight I would be more than happy to make the sacrifice."

Morgan slid out from under her feet, stood up, reached down and took Dabria's hand. He pulled her to her feet and then swung her up into his arms. He switched off all of the lights on the way to Dabria's bedroom and then had her turn on the light on her nightstand. He eased her onto her bed and then stood in front of her. With no fanfare and without delay he started to disrobe. He removed his shirt first and then his belt. He pulled off his socks and unzipped his jeans. He removed a sleeve of condoms from his pocket, placed them on the nightstand, and then yanked his jeans off and kicked them away. It was all very methodical and relaxed. This was not how she had envisioned it. She would have predicted ripping off each other's clothes and hungrily feasting off of each other for their first time—a dueling for superior position. Maybe that was yet to come and he was simply trying to lull her into a false sense of security.

"Your turn," he prompted as he sat on the bed beside her, clad only in his boxers. Then he lay down with his hands clasped behind his head.

"I take it the foreplay was the foot massage!" Dabria inquired sarcastically.

"Hardly. I haven't even started yet. I just wanted to start with no clothes on the first time so that I can see every inch of you and you can see every inch of me."

"Oh," Dabria muttered perplexed. So that was his strategy. Make her crazy in lust for him so that she lost control first. She would fool him. She was so self conscious she was pretty sure that she wasn't gonna get a lot of enjoyment out of the nights' festivities. She decided to take the "road less traveled" and do her striptease backwards, not out of any attempt to be coy but because she had suddenly gone shy and it was easier to undress when she couldn't see him watching her. She was far from being any kind of a seductress. She stood up and walked over to her bureau at the end of her bed. With her back to Morgan she tried to pretend he was not there as she removed her jewelry first and then her clothing. Sadly, as each article was dispensed with, her level of anxiety increased. She removed the condoms from *her* pocket and placed them on the dresser. She then unzipped her jeans and shimmied them down her legs. She readjusted her black lace thong and then bent over standing on first one foot and then the other to pull her jeans off, providing Morgan with an unobstructed view of the perfect café au lait colored globes he had been fantasizing about for days. She straightened and with her back still towards him she pulled off her sweater, undid her bra, and dropped it to the floor.

Unconsciously, she closed her eyes and ran her hands over and under her breasts removing the imprinted feeling left by the bra, just like she did every night. It was a habit that was unintentionally erotic. Morgan's indrawn breath alerted Dabria to the fact that he was intently watching her. When she opened her eyes she was startled to discover that she was standing in front of the mirror on her bureau and that he wasn't only watching the show from the back but that he could also see the front of her. His eyes were locked on her hands—the hands that were still cupping her own breasts. She could feel the heat wash up her neck and over her face and it seemed to make her skin glow even more. A wicked thought flashed across her consciousness and she tentatively, gently squeezed and then watched as his eyes turned obsidian, his penis jerked inside his boxers, and the muscles in his arms went taut. Her breasts were the same beautiful café au lait color as the globes of her tantalizing ass, with dark brown areola and erect nipples that enticed him like decadent little chocolates just waiting to be devoured. An unfamiliar feeling of feline satisfaction enveloped Dabria. He was captivated by her! *Her actions* were increasing his level of arousal. That had never happened to her before. Deciding to test her ability to manipulate his reaction she removed her right hand from her breast and let it smooth down her flat belly to rest at the top of her next-to-nonexistent thong. Her eyes were glued to his face gauging the reaction she caused. His lips were pierced into a tight line that almost bordered on a grimace. She suddenly realized that his reaction was fueling her own increase in excitement. There was tightness in her core and she could feel dampness forming in her panties. This was enough passive torment for one evening. She needed to touch. Slowly she turned, crawled onto the foot of the bed, and knelt at his feet, like a supplicant awaiting instruction.

"Come to me and finish what you started this morning. Learn me. Get comfortable with me," Morgan persuaded huskily. "We have all night and all day tomorrow."

Dabria didn't need to be asked twice. With cautious eagerness she did as he suggested and crawled on top of him. Morgan was already obviously aroused but so far was able to hold onto his control. She started the same as this morning by smoothing her hands up his torso and across his chest, instantly turning his nipples into hardened nubbins.

"You're beautiful," she breathed.

"Thank you. So are you," he assured her.

She continued to touch him as she kissed him and licked him. The globes of her breasts brushed his chest and with each pass her nipples became more engorged. He realized that while she was pleasuring him she was unconsciously pleasuring herself as well. Dabria instinctively began to slide herself up and down his silk boxers and her breathing escaped in little gasps as she continued to kiss everywhere but his lips. Morgan moved his hands from behind his head onto her hips. He slowed her slide down and ground her into his crotch. With a shudder she opened her eyes and looked directly into his. Limpid melted toffee gazed into vibrant blue velvet. He raised his lips to hers and blew on them. The lure of his kiss drew her face instinctively down to his without him actually touching her lips. He rolled them both over so that she was on her back.

Morgan then treated Dabria to the same exploration and ministrations she had subjected him to. Her hands drifted over his shoulders and down his arms, continuing to learn him as he learned her. Morgan carried his exploration even further. He slipped her thong to the side and slid one clever finger into her moist folds. He stroked her and adding a second finger stretched her as he feasted on one nipple while gently kneading that breast. Involuntarily, her back arched and shockingly, without warning, her orgasm blossomed and starbursts flashed behind her closed eyelids. Dabria hands had curled around his biceps and her nails now dug in. It was so unexpected Dabria continued to cling to Morgan after the tremors had subsided.

"Oh, my God!" Dabria exclaimed.

"That was just the beginning," Morgan promised with a satisfied smile.

"That's never happened before," she gazed up at him as she relaxed her hands and reaching up cupped his face and smoothed her thumbs over his cheeks.

"You've never had an orgasm before?" Morgan blinked disbelievingly.

"No *man* has ever brought me to orgasm before," she clarified.

"A girl," Morgan leered with a glint in his eye and then almost instantly could have kicked himself.

"No person," she kindly let his faux pas slide. "Are all men turned on by the thought of two women?"

Ignoring her question he kissed her fiercely, almost like he was staking his claim. His lovemaking became more demanding and each caress, each suckle drew them both to the inevitable conclusion. He pulled off her thong and his boxers and feverishly she sheathed him in a condom while he continued to stroke her just before the point of orgasm. As he felt her tense he backed off and with one smooth thrust he impaled her onto him. My gawd she was tight! That was all it took to push her over the edge again. He stilled while she contracted and released in spasms. He held himself taut, focusing on not thrusting. Once her shudders subsided he allowed himself to move and swiftly he built her up again, one smooth stroke at a time, until he could no longer hold back. He pumped into her one final time, stiffened, and with a groan emptied himself into her. Still connected he rolled over so that she was on top of him. They both lay recovering from the maelstrom. Without moving from her position Dabria released a cleansing sigh.

"Are you okay?"

"I know this is going to sound corny, but I'm not kidding. I had no idea it could be like that."

"Despite what you may think the reality is it's often not like that."

"Point taken. Do you want me to move so you can go to sleep now?"

"Did you think we were finished?"

"Yes."

"Dabria, I'm not an old man yet. I can perform more than once a night."

"Oh," she cocked her head to the side and with a grin inquired, "can we do it again, like right now?"

"Yes," he chuckled. "But, let's try something a little different." Morgan slid out of her and made a quick trip to the bathroom. He returned all shiny and clean with a bottle of body lotion.

"Lay on your stomach," he instructed her. He straddled her and squirted a generous blob of lotion into the middle of her back. It was cooler than her skin and she squeaked in protest.

"Trust me, I'll have you and this lotion heated up in no time," he assured her. With firm even strokes he massaged her from rump to neck. When she was totally relaxed he raised himself off her, re-sheathed himself, spread her legs, and knelt behind her. With one hand resting on the middle of her back he used his other hand to coax her derriere up. In one smooth thrust he slid into her from behind. Being only semi-conscious the unexpected intrusion caused Dabria to arch up, drawing Morgan even deeper inside her.

"Oh!" she gasped.

"Am I hurting you?"

"No," she sighed.

"How does that feel?" Morgan questioned.

"Hmm . . . . different, but good."

"Lay your head down but keep you back bowed and let me teach you something new." Morgan stroked her and caressed her as he slowly penetrated and withdrew. As her breathing changed and her muscles tightened Morgan increased the speed of his thrusts. When her back arched Morgan thrust deep and held her tightly to him. She came with a gasp and then sagged. As her contractions continued to milk him he was pulled into his own release. With a growl he gritted his teeth and tried, unsuccessfully, not to bruise her hips with his clenched hands. This time he slid out and sagged beside her on the bed. Moving onto his side, he stripped off the condom, wiped himself with a facecloth he had brought from the bathroom, pulled her against him, and cuddled her spoon-like. With a shiver Dabria grabbed the duvet that had been pushed to the side and pulled it over them. Exhausted they fell asleep locked in each other's arms.

~ ~ ~

Dabria was awakened by the sensation of arousal. Her walls clenched as Morgan's hand caressed a trail across her breast, down her stomach, past her navel to the top of her pubis, and back. She squirmed and maneuvered herself so that she lay flat beside Morgan.

"Morning," he murmured as he moved in for a kiss.

"Hmm . . . ." She nuzzled his nose as he drew back. "What a lovely way to wake up."

"I can make it even better."

"Let me go to the washroom first."

"Okay."

Dabria slipped from Morgan's grasp and headed for the bathroom. After her potty break she quickly gave herself a sponge bath, rinsed her mouth with mouthwash, and fluffed her hair. As she opened the door to head back to bed she yelped as she walked headfirst into Morgan's arms.

"I figured I could also use a trip to the can."

Dabria scooted back to bed and waited for Morgan. She lay there wondering how she would go about asking Morgan what his feelings were regarding oral sex. Although she had performed that particular service hundreds of times the favor had never been returned.

"Are you ready for your education to continue, councilor?"

"Yes, ah . . . . I wondered if I'm allowed to make requests?"

"Your request is my command, m'lady."

"Cunnilingus."

"Is this a spelling game?"

"Funny," she retorted dryly.

"Actually, as luck would have it, that is one of my very favorite activities and that was exactly where I was headed. Lay back, close your eyes, and let me create new sensations." Morgan stripped the duvet from her gripped fingers, pushed her back against the pillows, and grabbed both her hands. He swung his leg over top of her and straddled her. He stretched her arms up over her head and wrapped the fingers of first her right hand and then her left hand around the headboard rails.

"Close your eyes and hold on," he whispered.

He started by kissing her eyelids and continued to move down her body kissing, licking, sucking, and blowing without ever touching her with his hands. Instinctively her body arched silently seeking his tantalizing ministrations. Her nipples pebbled and unconsciously she began to softly pant. As he continued his journey Dabria's legs intuitively relaxed and parted, coming into contact with his muscular thighs. He stopped his downward journey at her belly button and gently nudging her thighs wider repositioned himself so that his knees now resided between hers. He scooted backwards, farther down the bed, knelt at the end of it and continued his assault back *up* her body. He started with her toes, the arches of her feet, the insides of her calves, and on up the insides of her thighs. He draped her legs over his shoulders and positioned himself for maximum access to the part of her that although untouched at this point was eagerly awaiting him. She opened her eyes and the sight of him grinning up at her caused her to convulsively grip the rails even tighter and hold her breath. He leaned in and gave her one quick lick. Her back bowed and she gasped with pleasure. He grinned even more broadly and then determinedly got down to business as he continued to watch her reactions. When he saw one of Dabria's hands let go of the bedrail and move downwards toward him he stopped.

"Uh, uh," he chastised. With a nod back up he silently directed her to keep her hands away from him.

"Morgan, I need to touch you," she breathlessly complained.

"Close your eyes and focus on what I'm touching," he coaxed soothingly. She begrudgingly followed his directions. Each flick of his tongue and suction of his mouth brought her closer to the brink. She squirmed and thrashed her head from side to side as she softly moaned and panted raggedly. The onslaught continued mercilessly until Dabria was begging, arms taut, hands white knuckled from hanging on.

"Please," she didn't know if she was begging him to stop or to finish her off. She just knew that she couldn't continue on like this. Morgan continued to roll his tongue around the button of her clitoris. Around and around. Back and forth. Lapping and sucking—first smoothly and then with more enthusiasm. Her entire body was gently vibrating.

"Come for me," he entreated just before he placed his mouth on her one last time and sucked her over the edge into a shattering orgasm. Dabria actually cried out as it hit her. She was left lightly perspiring and spent in a boneless sprawl on her bed. Morgan licked his lips and crawled back up her. He took each arm, one at a time, massaging the stiffness out of them and kissing her palms as he drew them back down to her side. Her eyes were still closed and her breathing continued to saw in and out. He kissed her lightly on the forehead before rolling off the bed. Her eyes fluttered open and she reached out to him.

"Shhh, lay back," he tenderly whispered as he pulled the duvet back on top of her and let her doze off. He grabbed his jeans and with a contented grin headed for the kitchen to brew up a pot of coffee and read through the files he had copied the day before. What a lovely beginning to a Sunday morning.

Chapter 12

Two hours later Dabria woke up and realized she was alone. She grabbed her sea green shuka out of her closet, wrapped it around her nakedness, and followed the scent of coffee. She found Morgan lounging on the sofa intently reading what appeared to be a file.

"Homework?" she inquired as she poured herself the dredges from the coffeepot and made a new pot.

"Not exactly," he closed the file and set it down. "Have any memories resurfaced from the other night, yet?"

"Not even a "good morning" before the interrogation resumes," she gently chided him as she pretended to talk to herself. He rose from the sofa and wrapped himself around her like the shuka, as she poured water into the coffeemaker.

"And how are you feeling this morning, my eager little beaver?"

"Satiated. For the first time in my life I can actually use that word and mean it."

"Well, I guess I accomplished what I set out to do."

"I guess so. And you? Are you disappointed?"

"Are you kidding me?" Morgan exclaimed. "Friday, as I contemplated our impending Saturday conflict, I hoped to steal a kiss after impressing you with both my cunning on the battlefield and my skill in the kitchen. Not only did your team soundly thrash mine but I didn't get a chance to cook for you either, and yet you allowed me to seduce you and make love to you repeatedly. I don't think that constitutes grounds for disappointment. Do you?"

"Probably not," she giggled.

Morgan was charmed by the sound of her giggle. It was very girlish and contradictory to the image she tried to portray to the outside world. She tried to appear aloof and unemotional. He was flattered that she had chosen to show him her other self.

"Since you made supper will you allow me to impress you with breakfast?"

"Absolutely. And, by the way, I'm starved, so a bowl of cold cereal won't cut it. I feel like a shower. I'll be back in fifteen minutes." She took her cup of mud and sashayed down the hall with her shuka trailing behind her.

While she showered she thought about Morgan's question and realized she did have some memory. Quickly she finished, rewrapped herself, and returned to the kitchen.

"I *do* remember some things," she announced as she made her way over to the coffeepot. Wonderful smells wafted from the oven as she settled herself at the table. Morgan handed her a luscious looking fruit salad to start.

"Excellent."

"Wow, this looks delicious. Okay. As I was leaving the washroom I remember hearing a bunch of swearing and yelling. I peeked out the door and saw two guys wrestling in the hallway. They moved from the hallway back into the bar area. I continued out of the washroom and was cautiously watching them as I went towards the bar. Then I saw a guy on the dance floor pull a knife and so I started to dial 911. Suddenly someone hit me from the side. I remember dropping my phone—flying through the air—then nothing, until I heard Sarah talking to an EMT."

"Do you remember feeling any pain in your head or face?"

"No. I remember being hit and having the breath knocked out of me. Whoever ran me over didn't touch my head. I'm assuming my concussion is from hitting the back of my head against the wall." The understanding of what he was asking her suddenly emerged. "Then why is the front of my head cut?"

"Good question." Morgan settled in beside her with a fresh cup of coffee and a bowl of fruit. "Three women from the area have been murdered in the past year and a half and each one of them has been found scalped."

"What? Why haven't I heard anything about this before?"

"Probably because two of the women were prostitutes and one was a Jane Doe. The general public isn't too worried about their own safety when they believe that death is one of the hazards of the women's profession."

"And the Jane Doe?"

"It's probably assumed that she was also a prostitute."

"So, how does this relate to me?"

"The doctor that stitched you up told me that your cut was deliberate. It was accomplished with a very sharp instrument like a scalpel or a box cutter. The slash was very precise. Instead of it actually being a random slash it was more an incision. He was the one who told me about the *scalper murders* because your injury reminded him of them."

"Tell me exactly what he said," she harshly demanded as her stomach clenched and a shadow of dread settled over her. She clutched her coffee cup with suddenly bloodless fingers.

Morgan swiftly removed their fruit bowls to put them in the dishwasher and grabbed the file off the cupboard, but remained silent.

"Morgan?" she entreated.

He returned to the table with the coffee pot and the file.

"The doctor said that your incision was the same as the primary incision on the scalped women."

"What!"

He pried her fingers off of her cup and refilled it while she leaned ever closer to him.

"What's in the file?" she asked tightly as she perched on her seat and reached for the file.

"The file contains all the information the police have released on the unsolved murders. Detective French, from the R.C.M.P. allowed me to copy it so that I could read it and possibly come up with some insight."

"And have you? Can I read it?" she rushed on.

"Not yet. But I don't have all the information either. There is a second file that contains unreleased details that I can't remove from the station. And yes, you can read this one since the contents of it *have* been released to the public."

"So, after reading what you have, do you actually think there's a possibility that my injury is related?"

"Dabria, there's more to your story than what you've remembered."

"Let me guess, you found a witness?"

"A couple, so far. Sarah came out of the washroom after you and she saw someone standing over you. Before she could reach you there was a mass exodus of people from the bar. By the time she made contact with you the person was gone and you were slumped against the wall bleeding. Also, one of the waitresses confirmed what you just told me about being bowled over and knocked against the wall. It was actually one of the bar's bouncers that ran into you. She saw him hit you and watched you crash into the wall and then slide down. The bouncer didn't even acknowledge that he had hit you and kept on going to break up the fight. She couldn't reach you since the fight was between you and her so she had the bartender call 911 and request the cops and an ambulance. As she watched you from across the bar she saw a man approach you and then crouch down beside you. She assumed he was trying to help you and her attention wandered elsewhere. When she looked back over towards you the EMTs had arrived and were attending to you."

"So, let me get this straight. I get knocked out and the "scalper" just happens to be having a cocktail in the bar. He's close enough to see the incident and so he decides to take advantage of my state of unconsciousness and scalp me in a room full of people? Have I got that about right?"

"Yep."

"Are you kidding me?" she exclaimed. "What kind of a serial killer, who has successfully gotten away with three murders, would actually attempt something that risky?"

"The thing about serial killers is that they learn something from each murder. Most of the elements of the murders are repeated because the killer knows they work. Those similarities give each serial killer his signature. However, with each new victim the killer evolves and attempts riskier scenarios in the hopes of exceeding the last thrill. Although, at this point, I have no evidence to suggest this, my guess is that the killer has killed a lot more than three times."

"So, what you're saying is that I was a crime of opportunity, an experiment?"

"Precisely. I also know that the interval between murders lessens with each new murder. The first body turned up a year and a half ago, the second about ten months later, and the third about five months after the second."

"That means the last murder was about three months ago. Which would indicate he's gearing up for his next one?"

"Right."

"What did he learn from me?"

"That scalping live victims is a messy business."

"I think we need to get our hands on that other file before we make any more assumptions."

"I think you're right. The oven omelet should be ready by now. Let's finish eating and head to the station."

Dabria was impressed by Morgan's culinary expertise. The omelet was as delicious as the fruit salad. They cleaned up together and then both went back to the bedroom to finish dressing.

"What is this blanket thing you're wrapped in?" Morgan asked as he attempted to help her unwrap.

She slapped his hands away.

"If you actually want to make it to the station today you should probably keep your hands to yourself," she scolded. "The blanket is called a *shuka*. My father brought this one back for me from his last trip to Kenya. It's used by the Maasai as part of their traditional clothing. I've always had one and use it instead of a housecoat."

"It makes you look very exotic and kind of forbidden. Are you sure we don't have a half hour to spare? It's really turning me on."

"I promise I'll wear it for you again sometime. Right now I'd really like to learn more about those women."

"You're right. There's time enough for messing around later. I'll wait for you in the living room."

They stopped at Morgan's place so that he could shower and change on their way to the station. Morgan's condo was a surprise. It was a brand new pet free complex for childless singles or couples. Morgan was on the top floor of the four levels and had a corner unit with balconies on two sides. Floor to ceiling windows covered most of those two sides. Morgan had an excellent view of the river and the two bridges crossing it. The condo was ultra modern with curved walls, brushed nickel light fixtures, and whitewashed cabinetry. The fridge blended into the cabinets with its own whitewashed cabinet door. The stovetop with a Jenn-Air grille sat on the counter and the oven was wall mounted. The kitchen was spotless. Not even a cup in the sink.

Morgan's furnishings were sparse. He had a chocolate brown leather sofa and two Adirondack recliner chairs upholstered in a multicolored geometric design. A set of mismatched end tables and a coffee table were made of the same wood as the chairs. There was a huge pottery bowl on the coffee table and dried sea creatures on one of the end tables. Dabria loved the furniture and was intrigued by the pottery. It was a melding of greens and blues with an off centre splash of orange. The piece was exquisite. The creatures were actually a collection of cleverly crafted clay. At a glance they had appeared real. But upon examination it was obvious that they were man-made since each one had a cartoon face molded into it. Dabria noted that contrary to what you would think, Morgan's interests and personal space revealed an unexpected aspect of his personality.

Dabria moved back into the bare dining room. The only thing in the dining room was a stack of paintings resting against one wall. Since she dabbled in paint herself she was always drawn to others' works. The paintings were mostly oils, unlike the water colors she favored. The canvases almost exclusively depicted ocean scenes. Some were turbulent, some were calm, and all were abstract. There were three charcoal sketches as well—all portraits. Because there was an obvious resemblance to Morgan, Dabria assumed that the pictures were of his father and sisters. The work was good. Dabria felt Morgan's presence behind her.

"Your mother is gifted. I assume the pottery is Amy's. It's remarkable."

"I agree. They're both extremely talented."

"And you?"

"Oh, I think we both know where my talent lies. Don't we?"

Dabria blushed.

"Since I don't have several partners to compare you to, I guess I'll have to agree at this point."

"Trust me. You won't ever be *satiated* like that with anyone else."

"My, my, we are awfully full of ourselves today, aren't we? Right from our first encounter I knew you were a cocky bastard."

"I don't believe I harbor any false modesty. I know my attributes as well as my shortcomings."

"Do you actually have any of those?"

"Shortcomings? Of course. We all do. I'll let you discover them yourself. Are you ready to go?"

"Sure. The sketches are of your family?" she inquired as they exited the condo.

"Yah. They're several years old now as I'm sure you guessed. The girls were teenagers and she did the one of Dad right before he was killed. Shortly after they moved to the island she used to do charcoal portraits for the tourists to earn money. In the winter she painted for herself. A local saw some of her oils and persuaded her to let him show them to a friend of his. The friend owned a gallery in Vancouver. The paintings sold and requests for more prompted Mom to open her own small gallery and showcase only island talent. Then she started painting in earnest. Years later the girls had been over to a friend's house one day and saw one of her sketches. They came home and begged Mom for sketches of themselves. She put them off for days before their begging got the best of her and in a couple of hours she whipped off a couple of sketches of each of us. When I left home instead of taking photos I asked for those three."

"She didn't sketch herself though, did she?"

"No. She has no self portraits and I have no photographs of her either. Next time I'm home I've promised myself to get a whole roll of candid shots of her."

"You miss them and the island a lot, don't you?"

"You have no idea. If it were feasible for me to move back there tomorrow, I would. Unfortunately, there's no way for me to make a living there. For now I have to settle with a couple weeks of holidays a year."

They pulled up to the detachment and parked. Before Dabria could climb out of his Jeep Morgan lay a hand on her arm.

"Detective French is going to want to ask you some questions. While he takes your statement I'll see if he'll let me read over the other file. Even though I know you're going to want to, please don't bother asking questions about the other cases because I can guarantee he won't answer them. You're being a lawyer is definitely going to keep him from letting any restricted information slip. Let me find out what I can. Deal?"

"Can I reveal that you told me about the murders?"

"Sure. He's going to guess that anyway since I'm coming in with you. Just tell him what you told me." Morgan jumped out of the Jeep and joined her on the other side.

"Yes, sir," she saluted as she marched beside him.

"Funny, Dabria. Very funny." He grabbed her hand and they walked into the station hand in hand. He took her to French's desk. Detective French rose as he observed their approach.

"Detective French, I'd like you to meet Dabria Abdulla-Smythe. Dabria, Detective French." After the introductions were over, French motioned them into chairs.

"If it's okay with you I'd like to read that other file while you take Ms. Abdulla-Smythe's statement," Morgan stated.

"Sure." French unlocked a drawer in his desk and handed the file to Morgan. "Where's your desk?"

"Upstairs."

"I'd prefer to keep the file within my sight if it's okay with you. There's a vacant desk over there by the coffee machine. Feel free to use it."

"Thanks, I will." Morgan took the file and made his way over to the desk. Detective French turned his attention back to Dabria and got down to the business of taking her statement. Half an hour later they were finished and Dabria signed the statement he had printed off.

"Detective, if I can assist you in any way in the future don't hesitate to contact me," Dabria offered.

"Thanks," he smiled. "That's an offer I seldom hear. Since we know which bouncer plowed into you, did you want to press charges against him for assault?"

"No. I realize he was focused on breaking up the disturbance and there was no malicious intent on his part. However, I do have one request. Have you or will you be interviewing him?"

"Actually, I haven't yet. What would you like?"

"Can you just make him aware that bowling me over and then not checking on me could have had far worse consequences?" Dabria stood up.

"Trust me, I will." Detective French also stood up and extended his hand. "Thanks for coming in."

"My pleasure. Please tell Detective Vaughn thanks for the lift and that I'll walk home." Dabria shook his hand and left. Detective French made his way over to Morgan and sat down across from him.

"So? Questions?" he prompted.

"Many. I made notes."

"Great. Come back to my desk and let's get started. Ms. Smythe said to say thanks for the lift and that she'd walk home. How involved are the two of you, anyway? Is everything you read and every question I answer going to be passed on?"

"Involved," Morgan confirmed but did not elaborate. "And not everything," he assured him.

"At least you're honest. Do you trust her to keep this info between the two of you?"

"Yes. She understands the sensitivity of this information and it's not like she isn't used to dealing with discretion. If you're seriously concerned I'll give her a retainer making me a client of hers and then she'll be bound by her oath of confidentiality."

"Since this information is extremely sensitive I'd actually appreciate it if you would follow through with that. All right, I'll fill you in." French and Morgan spent the next hour hashing through the evidence. After talking to French, Morgan was even more convinced that Dabria had been attacked by *the scalper*. Her physical attributes mirrored those of his other victims. All the women were tiny in stature, all had short dark hair, all had voluptuous bodies for their height, all were non-Caucasian, and each woman had a cut originating in the same place on the forehead. There was more evidence supporting the theory that he was her attacker than not. The obvious deviations from past victims were her profession, her ethnicity, and the fact that she had been alive and in a crowd when he cut her.

Morgan discovered that the women had been scalped post mortem. They were all found with the femoral artery in their legs surgically severed. Other marks on them were bruises and puncture marks. It was determined at autopsy that all of the women had been drugged and that every drop of blood that could be drained out of them had been. The women had bled to death. They were stripped, scalped, meticulously washed, and then transported. Each woman was discovered naked, lying on their back on the banks of the river with their hands folded across their chest, smelling like lavender.

The investigators knew several things about this unidentified subject (unsub). First, he had either medical training or had carved up enough bodies to know exactly what artery and where to sever it in order to accomplish quick and maximum blood loss. Second, he had access to a building or a garage that was secluded enough that neighbors didn't question his habits. He had a four wheel drive truck to navigate the steep graveled slopes down to the riverbank. It had to be either a crew cab or have a cap over the box of it to transport the bodies. He had to have approached the local street walkers at least three times in order to have succeeded in enticing three of them into his vehicle. The attention to detail and the fact that he remained at large suggested that he had been at this a lot longer than eighteen months and that there were probably more victims than the three they were counting. A request for information pertaining to cases with similar idiosyncrasies had gone out to all other police departments in Western Canada. So far the Intel that had been received didn't appear to be related to these cases.

Morgan had gotten the directions to the locations where the three bodies had been found. All were in a secluded area close to the abandoned La Colle Falls project. Morgan decided he and Dabria needed to go on a fieldtrip. He thanked French for the privilege of being given access to the cases and headed out to pick up Dabria. He arrived at her doorstep just as she was walking up the sidewalk.

"Wow. I thought you were in better shape than that. It's like a ten minute stroll from the station. I must have really played you out last night."

"Hah . . . . again with the references to your amazing sexual prowess."

Morgan chuckled.

"I went for a *stroll* to the public library and I looked up the newspaper articles relating to these women. Not surprisingly, there was very little press for the first woman and unfortunately not much more for the second or third woman. Did you know that the first victim is the Jane Doe, not the third, as I had assumed? I have three burning questions after reading those articles. Are the police trying to minimize the panic of the public by downplaying the seriousness of this? Second, are they trying to reduce the infamy of this murderer so that, instead of increasing his victim count to show off his intelligence, they can flush him out before he succeeds in harming anyone else? And, third, am I totally overanalyzing this and is it simply that no one cares enough about these women to actually try to find their killer?"

"I can assure you that Detective French genuinely wants to find this guy and stop the killings. As for the rest of the police force and the politicians in this municipality I can't answer. Jump in. Let's grab some subs and head out on a fieldtrip. I'll fill you in on what I learned after you left the station." As Dabria hauled herself in Morgan remembered his promise to Detective French. "By the way I need to retain you as my lawyer before I can divulge any of the unreleased info."

Dabria immediately stiffened up. Slowly with eyes flashing she gritted out, "Are you indicating that you can't trust me with privileged information."

"No, Dabria. Detective French doesn't trust you," he informed her. "He just met you this morning so why should he jeopardize his investigation to satisfy your curiosity?"

"Because I have a vested interest in this case."

"So what? If I were in his shoes I wouldn't make you privy to the restricted details. Face it, if we weren't involved chances are, despite your attack, you wouldn't know anything about the serial murders. Who would have told you? Certainly not the Doctor? Definitely not French. The doctor would have notified the city police. They would have interviewed you regarding the attack but they most certainly would not have told you their suspicions."

"So, what are you saying, that I owe you so I better be good and keep my mouth shut?" she asked tightly with narrowed eyes and pursed lips.

"No, Dabria," he said with exasperation as he raked his hand through his hair. Boy, he had certainly ruffled her feathers but good. "I'm simply telling you where French is coming from. Come on. I'm not trying to pick a fight. I'm gonna tell you what wasn't in the original reports and I'm bringing you with me *because* you have a vested interest in this and I believe that a couple of fresh sets of eyes and ears may help this case and keep you safe."

She forced herself to relax as she allowed his words to sink in.

Watching her settle down he reached over and linked their hands.

"Dabria, will you be my lawyer?" he asked with a smirk. "A retainer doesn't have to be monetary, ya know. We could barter something. Special services for silence . . . . ?"

She squeezed his hand back.

"Agreed."

After picking up sandwiches and drinks they headed out into the wild blue yonder. Twenty minutes later they were gingerly traversing the slippery gravel and snow-covered trail. The trail wound its way down into the valley and a small clearing appeared close to the river. There were a couple of trails leading from the clearing to parts unknown. They decided to park and eat their lunch while they continued to discuss the case. Morgan grabbed his camera from his kit in the back and they headed down the path that appeared to lead to the "falls." La Colle Falls wasn't actually a falls at all. In the early 1900's a developer persuaded the city into building a dam that would harness the energy produced by the flowing river and create power for the new city. Unfortunately, the projected cost rose over three hundred percent above the original estimates and when government funding fell through the project ran out of money and the dam was never finished. What remained was a partially constructed cement barrier created to divert the flow of the river through turbines. It was sloped and rose about twenty feet in the air and jutted out about a quarter of the way across the river.

There were two rectangular cement pools on the other side of the wall that held partially frozen stagnant water. Graffiti covered most of the cement walls of the ponds right down to and below the existing waterline indicating that at some point the water level had been lower than what it was now. Half submerged dead logs, water weeds, and other bits of refuse were trapped in the murky rotten ice. The breeze whistled through the trees and swirled around the ponds. Despite the afternoon sunshine the pools lay in shadowed gloom. The place had an eerie, deserted atmosphere to it.

"This is not a happy place," Dabria shuddered as a shiver raced up her spine. She stuck close to Morgan and warily scanned her environment for unseen threats. "It's disconcerting."

"French claims teenagers have been coming down here for years and that they party and dare each other into swimming across those pools."

"You can't be serious!" she exclaimed. "I'm going to have nightmares just thinking about some kid in that water. Would you have been one of those testosterone overloaded teenagers that had to prove how tough he was?"

"Possibly," he chuckled. "Back then I would have done just about anything to impress the girls and beat out my rivals. If it's any comfort to you I wouldn't dream of sticking even my little toe in there now."

"Some comfort. If you actually considered going in there now, I'd suggest some kind of psych exam. I'm creeped out already and we haven't even gotten to one of the drop sites yet."

"We're close though. The first site is just a little farther down shore. French said there's a pulled up tree stump where the first one was found." Morgan reached out his hand and pulled her along behind him. "Come on. Where's your sense of adventure?"

"Back in the Jeep," she admitted.

They found the first site which was also shadowed and took pictures of the immediate area. As they continued their walk they came across an abandoned truck. Thankfully, it seemed to be parked in a clearing that was flooded with sunlight. Some of the chill had left Dabria but she was still uneasy.

"This is a strange place to leave a truck. I wonder how long it's been down here," she commented.

"I'd say not much longer than since last night."

"How do you know that?"

"There's only a skiff of snow on it. It snowed hard on Friday night and hardly at all last night. So, someone left it here sometime in between then. I'm going to call in the plate and find out if it's stolen. Don't go near it or touch anything close to it just in case," he instructed.

While he waited on the phone, Dabria cautiously continued on down the trail that wound back towards the river to prove to Morgan that she wasn't some sissy. Suddenly she felt the hair stand up at the back of her neck and a definite sense that all was not right overwhelmed her. She froze in her tracks and literally stopped breathing. Then she heard it. Her stomach clenched and she slowly silently sucked in a breath as the sound of gut wrenching sobs disturbed the tranquility of the pristine, sun-glistening, snow-dusted trail. She cautiously eased forward and peered around the bushes that concealed where the sound emanated. A man was kneeling on the ground, rocking back and forth as he held a body close to his chest. Dabria stood stock still while tears swiftly gathered as she tried to control the pounding of her heart and quiet her ragged breathing. The words of his anguished begging had registered and Dabria concluded that seeking Morgan's assistance was a safer plan of action than rushing in to assist the young man.

"Baby, please, ... please don't die. This is my fault, what have I done? What have I done?" the voice bawled.

Dabria silently backed away and hurried to catch Morgan before he called out to her as he followed her trail. She caught him just as he ended his call.

"Hey, find anything interesting?" he asked as he turned around to greet her. He quickly went over to her when he saw the look on her face and realized she was silencing him as she raised her finger to her lips. He stopped directly in front of her, grabbed her hand, and impatiently waited for her to get herself back under control.

"There's a young man holding a body down by the river and he's crying and begging it not to die. I think it's a woman because it has long blond hair," she shakily whispered while clenching her hands.

"I'm calling for back-up and an ambulance first," Morgan informed her. After notifying dispatch he pushed Dabria behind him and drawing his gun he followed her footsteps back to the tormented sounds. He indicated that she should stay hidden behind the bush as he approached the young man.

"Excuse me."

A wild eyed young man looking somewhat like a wounded, cornered animal swung his head around to Morgan. Tear tracks streamed down his face.

"I don't mean to startle you but you look like you could use some help. My name is Detective Vaughn. What can I do for you?"

With blood shot, glazed eyes the boy begged Morgan, "Help me, please help me. Megan's hurt. She's really hurt. Oh God . . . . please, Megan, please don't die!" the young man shook with agony as he sobbed and rocked.

Chapter 13

D abria heard every tortured word.

"Have you got any weapons on you, sir?" Morgan asked as he cautiously approached.

"What? Weapons? No, ... Um, just my hunting knife."

"Can you take it out for me and lay it on the ground."

"Didn't you fucking hear me? Megan's hurt. Help me!" the young man clutched her unresponsive body more closely to his chest as he shouted angrily at Morgan.

"I'm trying to help you," Morgan calmly assured him. "I've already called the ambulance. Now, just place your knife on the ground and I'll come over there and see what we can do for Megan. Okay? What's your name, son?" Morgan kept his gun trained as the boy pulled a lethal looking knife from his boot and flung it over towards the bushes by Dabria. After she heard the knife hit the ground she peeked around the bush and she saw the face of the young man. He was just a boy and obviously overcome with shock and grief.

"Cody," he blurted out. "Cody Saddleback. Please help me!" he keened as Morgan advanced towards him.

Morgan crouched down beside the girl and checked for a pulse. There was none and her body was not only cold but also stiff with the onset of rigor mortise.

"She's so cold," the boy said. "Do you have a blanket or something I can wrap her in? I put my coat around her but she won't warm up and I don't think she's breathing."

Swallowing convulsively Dabria swiped her tears away and forced herself to get it together. As she approached she removed her coat and silently offered it to the boy. He looked up.

"Thank you. Do you know CPR?" he implored as he clutched at Dabria's hand. "I tried but I don't really know what I'm doing and I don't think it helped much."

Morgan helped him wrap the obviously dead girl in Dabria's coat and then gave Dabria his own coat to put on.

"Can you tell me what happened, Cody?" he asked the boy gently as he crouched beside him.

Dabria surveyed the area while the boy talked. There was a snowmobile not ten feet away and tracks leading up to it from the river. The only tracks from the abandoned truck were Dabria's and Morgan's footprints. There was a set of footprints leading from the sled over to a disturbance near some bushes and then those same footprints leading back. It appeared to Dabria that the boy had driven up on his sled and discovered the girl lying near the bushes. He had run over to her, picked her up, and brought her back to the sled. There was disturbed snow around one side of the sled. She'd lay bets the truck belonged to the girl.

"Megan and I were supposed to meet here last night and I got delayed and couldn't come. I had warned her that I may not be able to get away but she was determined that last night be *the* night. I told her that if I wasn't here waiting for her to go back home and I'd meet her this afternoon instead. As I drove up off the river I found Megan laying here in the snow. She was unconscious. I don't know how long she's been here. I tried to get her onto the sled so that I could hold her and drive to get help but I can't hold her," the boy stopped talking and started rocking and sobbing again.

The clenching of Dabria's stomach had stopped, but the tightness had moved up into her chest and she was forced to turn away so the boy couldn't see the tears streaking down her cheeks again. The boy knew his girlfriend was dead but he just wasn't ready to let go of her yet. Dabria knew that feeling well. Despite her attempts to stem the flow, the tears continued to silently stream down her face as she listened to the agonized sobs of the heartbroken boy. Morgan spoke soothingly to the boy and then left him and approached Dabria.

"I need to take pictures before any more of the scene is disturbed. I don't believe the boy is a threat to you. Can you sit with him?" Morgan whispered knowing full well what he was asking of her.

"Of course," she responded hoarsely as she vigorously wiped her cheeks forcing herself to get a grip on her emotions. The wind had shifted while she stood waiting for Morgan and the distinctive scent of lavender wafted by. Dabria grabbed Morgan's arm as he turned away from her. He instantly stopped and looked back. "This is going to sound really strange but I can smell lavender. Can you?" she fearfully whispered.

Morgan inhaled deeply. It was there alright and a feeling of dread filled him. He nodded to Dabria and she moved back over to Cody. Morgan instantly began scanning the area around to find the location of the scent. He took pictures of everything Dabria had just observed. The boy had obviously found Megan and tried to put her on the sled. Because of the rigor he had been unable to hold on to her. Unwilling to admit to himself that she was dead he had stumbled with her over to his present resting spot and slumped into the snow while he mourned. Morgan called back to the detachment.

"Can you tell me what other licenced drivers may have access to the truck I had you run the plate on, besides the registered owner? I'm looking specifically for a teenage girl, first name, Megan."

"I have a Megan Thomas aged seventeen at the same address as the registered owner, a forty-one year old woman named Jeanine Thomas. Is that what you're looking for?"

"Unfortunately, yes," answered Morgan as he continued to visually sweep the area. Suddenly his eyes caught a flash of white that wasn't snow. Squinting, he discerned what looked suspiciously like the sole of a foot resting on the snow-covered ground not far from where the snowmobile was parked.

"We have a dead girl down here with her live boyfriend and I think I may have found something else, too," he reported. "I'll call you right back." Using his camera lens he zoomed in on the object and confirmed that it was indeed a foot. Following the foot backwards he established that there were two feet attached to a naked body that lay near a copse of bushes. The body was a female and she had been scalped. Dabria touched his arm and he jerked the camera away from the body and focused on her.

"What?" he roughly whispered as her touch had startled him.

"I simply wanted to ask if there was anything else I could do? Cody is wrapped up in his misery and my sitting with him at this point isn't accomplishing anything," she remarked. "But I can go back and sit with him if I'm disturbing you."

"I'm sorry," he raked his hand through his hair. It was obviously an unconscious habit of Morgan's when he was frustrated. "I didn't mean to bark at you. I found something else and it's going to change everything regarding this boy. I've got to call back to the station again. Can you just give me a minute?"

"Of course," she backed away and returned to the boy's side.

"This is Detective Vaughn again. I need to speak with Detective French," Morgan requested of the dispatcher.

"I'll just transfer you, one moment."

"French here," he answered almost immediately.

"Hey, this is Morgan. Get your team together. We have another body down at the falls. This situation is a little more complicated though since there is also a dead young girl and her grieving boyfriend sitting about twenty metres from the body. I've already called for an ambulance and backup but this has become more complicated than what I initially thought."

"Is the scene disturbed?"

"As I said, we're only a few metres away. Dabria is with me and neither she nor the boy is aware the body is even there. There are no footprints anywhere close to it nor is the snow around the body disturbed in any way. I'll take as many pictures as I can from the vantage point that I have and I'll wait for you to arrive."

"Since there will obviously be others there before I can get there, please keep them away from the body. I'm on my way."

French signed off and Morgan continued to take pictures of the body and everything around it. Once he was finished he gestured for Dabria to come over. Cautiously she advanced.

"I said I was sorry," he impatiently reiterated. "You don't have to approach me like a beaten puppy, for heaven's sake."

"Apparently, you're unaware of how truly formidable you look when you're upset. You have a scowl that would send lesser beings than I cowering into a corner."

"I didn't realize that. Please come here. I have something to tell you," he gentled his voice and held out his hand to pull her to him. He wrapped his arms around her and whispered into her ear.

"I don't want you to make any sudden movements or to cry out because I don't want to alarm the boy, but I found something else. Can you stay calm?"

"Of course," she responded, slightly miffed.

"I found another victim."

Dabria instantly and unconsciously stiffened up. Morgan stroked her back and held her close.

"I'm okay" she whispered as she clutched his shirt. "Go on."

"There's an ambulance and backup officers on their way as well as Detective French's team. We need to keep the initial officers and EMTs restricted to our path. Can you go back to the Jeep, wait for them, and then bring them here the same way we came?"

"Yes."

"Good. I'll stay with our boy. Have you got your cell with you?" he continued as she dug it out of her pocket. "I'll program my number in. Phone me as soon as you get back to the Jeep. Get in and lock the doors." He gave her a swift kiss and pushed her towards the path. The likelihood of *the scalper* remaining near the scene was remote but it was a possibility that Morgan needed to consider.

With Dabria gone Morgan concentrated on the situation at hand. If this kid hadn't already been in enough trouble the discovery of a scalped corpse, only metres away, wasn't going to help his case. Morgan stood slightly to one side of the boy and continued to survey his surroundings, mentally cataloguing everything he saw for future reference. Moments later his phone vibrated.

"I'm here and everything is quiet. How long before the back-up shows up," Dabria asked?

"I'm guessing any minute. Just keep the doors locked until they arrive."

"Morgan, if you're trying to freak me out it's working. You don't think the guy is still around here, do you?"

"You're making the assumption that Cody isn't our killer?"

"Don't be ridiculous! Of course, he's not *the scalper*."

"Could you swear to that in a court of law, counselor, or are you letting your emotions cloud your judgment?"

"Morgan!"

"It's not an unreasonable question, Dabria, and believe me it's going to be asked of you so you better prepare your answer," he advised.

"I will," she promised. Dabria signed off and after settling into her seat and locking the doors she dug through her purse looking for paper and a pen and made notes regarding what she had heard and seen over the past half hour. Absorbed in her recollections she was alarmed to discover vehicles suddenly appearing behind her. She hadn't heard their approach at all. As they came to a stop she jumped out of the Jeep, introduced herself, and led them to Morgan. The EMTs carried a stretcher to transport the girl's body. Dabria called Morgan to let him know they were on their way. Once they rounded the last corner Morgan coaxed Cody into letting the EMTs take Megan from him and lay her on the stretcher. They bundled her in. Cody was fine until they covered her face and made the move to return to the ambulance. He instantly went berserk.

"What are you doing?" he shrieked. "Save her. Help her!" He tried to pull out of Morgan's grasp slipping in the snow and pulling Morgan down with him. Morgan held on tight.

"She's gone, Cody," Morgan regretfully whispered. "She's gone. Let her go."

"I can't," he bellowed. "I can't let her go. She's my life!" He continued to struggle furiously with Morgan to escape his restrictive embrace. He wormed his way out of Morgan's arms enough to be able to give one good punch to the face. It was enough that Morgan momentarily lost his grip on Cody. Cody bounced up and started to charge after the retreating stretcher. Cody might have age on his side but Morgan was in top shape. He was known for his agility and speed and now he was pissed off. Morgan tackled him only inches from the last EMT. As Cody hit the ground all the fight seemed to drain out of him and he suddenly sagged against Morgan when he was yanked to his feet.

"She's my life," he raggedly declared with that dazed look back in his eyes. "I don't know how to live without her."

Dabria turned away with tears again coursing down her cheeks. That boy was no more a murderer than she was and she would bet her career on it. Morgan walked Cody back to the cruiser with one officer leading the way and Dabria trailing behind. Three of the other officers remained on site to continue the investigation. Within minutes of returning to the clearing French's car pulled in along with the coroner and the CSI Unit. What had started as a single case had turned into not only a potentially double murder scene but also the site of victim four and possibly five. Despite the fact that the coroner was there the EMTs continued to place Megan's body in the ambulance. She would be taken to the hospital morgue either way. With Cody obviously being distraught this was simply a kinder way of transporting her body back to town. After settling Cody into the backseat of one of the cruisers, Morgan requested that the officer also take Dabria back to town.

"I can wait for you," Dabria assured Morgan.

"Go back to town, Dabria. I may be here for hours yet and then we'll have to notify Megan's family. French will want to question you again, so try and get some rest. I'll come over when I'm done. I promise."

"Okay." She shrugged out of his coat and handed it back to him. "You're going to need this."

Morgan gave her a hard kiss and took the coat as she slid into the passenger seat of the squad car and closed the door. Not a word was spoken the entire trip back into town. Cody was locked inside his shock and grief and Dabria was reliving her own nightmares. The officer was observant enough to realize that Dabria was not interested in chatting. Half an hour later he pulled up in front of her apartment and dropped her off. She stepped out and let herself into the building. She turned around, waved at the officer from inside the locked glass doors, and watched him drive away with Cody slumped in the backseat.

She dragged herself up the stairs to her suite and drew a bath. She couldn't seem to stop shivering. She knew it was shock, so she made herself a cup of tea. She picked up the sugar bowl, paused, and then returned it to its shelf. Instead she opened the door to the pantry and pulled out honey and vanilla. If Morgan's mama thought it was good medicine then it was just the thing Dabria was seeking. She stripped and sank into a fragrant, steaming tub and sipped her tea as she soaked. Images swirled around in her head as she tried to relax. Resigned to the fact that she would not be resting until Morgan showed up she climbed out of the tub, dried off, and redressed. Knowing that she couldn't sleep she decided to make something for them to eat later. She cranked her stereo on and listened to a CD of Pavlo while she dug through the fridge. Next she grabbed her slow cooker out of the cupboard and aggressively started chopping vegetables to throw into a pot of soup.

~ ~ ~

The Crime Scene Investigators combed the scene for evidence around the site of Megan's body before moving on to *the scalper's* latest victim. Once they finished site one they moved on to site two and eventually allowed the coroner's office staff to remove that body. The positioning of that body, as well as the appearance of that body, was identical to the other three found along the shore. The scent of lavender clung to her. There was no doubt that she was another of *the scalper's* victims. However, the burning question was what had happened to Megan? Morgan hoped that the autopsy gave him the proof he would need to divert attention away from Cody. He knew in his gut, that Cody, a young Métis, was going to be implicated and probably charged with the murder of the beautiful blond teenager, if it was determined that she had in fact been murdered. He'd bet next month's pay cheque that *the scalper* was actually responsible. Since he was first on the scene and the incident had occurred outside the city limits Megan's case was officially his. The other victim was French's. Because of the bodies proximity to each other he and French were going to need to collaborate on both cases. Once he had finished up with his scene he wandered over to French.

"I'm done for now. Do you need me to stick around for anything or can I head back to town, inform the parents, get a positive ID, and then start interrogating the boyfriend?" asked Morgan.

"No. I'm good. I'll see you back at the station. I'll watch you interview your prime suspect before I decide to question him. Do you think he was even aware of the other body?"

"No."

"So, I'm guessing you don't think he's involved in the other killings."

"I don't think he's involved in any killing. But, I've been known to be wrong before. We'll see how this plays out. See you in a bit." Morgan left the riverbank with Detective Ducette and walked back to his jeep. He called Dabria as soon as he had maneuvered out of the valley and back up onto the highway.

"Hey. How're ya doing?"

"I'm fine. And you?"

"I've been better. We're on our way to inform the parents and to persuade them to come to the morgue to ID their dead child. Then we need to head over to the station and interrogate the obviously distraught boyfriend and determine if he killed the love of his life or simply arrived too late to save her. When we're finished all that, I'll give you a call," he promised.

"I'll be here. Who's going with you?"

"I'm taking Detective Ducette with me, and we're having someone from Victim Services meet us at the wife's house to stay with the family until extended family can arrive for support. Megan's parents are divorced so we'll have to make two calls. Apparently, her dad lives on a farm in between here and the city, so we'll stop there first."

An icy premonition skittered down Dabria's spine.

"Morgan, is Megan's last name Thomas?"

"Yes, why?"

"Is her dad's name Marshall Thomas?"

"Yes, ... Dabria what do you know?" His voice had taken on a sudden edge.

"I know Marshall. I'm sorry, Morgan, but I can't explain."

"Dabria, this not the time to be holding back on me. If you know something about this girl I need to know what it is," he encouraged urgently.

"I don't know anything about Megan," Dabria unequivocally stated.

"Let me guess client-lawyer confidentiality," Morgan commented with disdain. "Just be there when I call you later," he strongly directed.

Dabria immediately bristled.

"We both have jobs to do that aren't always popular, Morgan, and guess what, mine is just as important as yours. I would never deliberately impede an investigation so don't you dare insinuate that I would. Don't assume that for the sake of a client I would protect a killer of a teen-aged girl!"

"I never accused you of that," Morgan quietly stated.

Dabria silently kicked herself. She knew she was overreacting but for some ridiculous reason she had allowed herself to forget that cops weren't like other people. She had been under investigation by enough of them the past year that she should have remembered to be wary of them. Why, of all the professions in the world, had she chosen to end her years of celibacy with a man in law enforcement?

"Dabria," Morgan prompted her for an acknowledgement.

"I'll either be at the apartment or the police station. I'm sure you should be able to track me down," Dabria stated tightly and then disconnected.

Morgan sighed and continued down the road to complete an obligation he was sworn to fulfill. This was the worst part of his job and thankfully he had only had to do this once before. That time, however, it had involved the death of an elderly man who had been killed in a car accident. It wasn't as if this was only the second dead body he had seen or investigated but he had usually been the junior officer, so telling the family had been the responsibility of his supervisors. This was a very different matter. He had to tell a father, who probably didn't even realize that she was missing, that his seventeen year old daughter had been murdered. Then he would have to get back in his car and drive to town to tell the girl's mother the same thing. Would these parents ever recover from the death of their child? He knew that statistically speaking most didn't. Parents of dead children didn't care about statistics they just wished they weren't one of them.

Morgan pulled into the farmyard and was met by several barking, bounding dogs of obvious mixed breeds. As he pulled to a stop in front of the house a man exited the barn off to the left and called the dogs off. Morgan and Kent left the Jeep. Kent was in uniform and as they approached Mr. Thomas he called out to them.

"Afternoon, Officer, what can I do for you?" The dogs followed close behind.

"Afternoon, sir, my name is Detective Vaughn and this is Detective Ducette," Morgan introduced them as he flashed his badge. "We're looking for Marshall Thomas. Would that be you, sir?"

"Yes, it is." One of the dogs was standing beside Marshall and he stroked him while he quietly spoke.

"Do you have a daughter, sir, named Megan?"

"Yes," Marshall stated tensely as he stood stiffly by his dogs. "What's happened?"

"Is there someplace we can talk, sir?" Morgan inquired gently.

"We can talk right here just fine. What's going on and where is Megan?"

Expressionless, Morgan stood up straight and without pulling any punches or further beating around the bush he carried out his duty.

"I regret to inform you, sir, that this afternoon the body of a deceased young woman was found by the river near La Colle Falls. She has been identified as Megan Thomas."

Marshall's hand immediately stilled and he stopped petting the dog. With a strangled voice he inquired desperately, "Are you sure it's Megan? Who identified her?"

"She has been identified, sir, but we ask that you accompany us to the morgue to confirm it. Would you be willing to do that?"

"Yes, of course, but who identified her?" Marshall pressed.

"A young man claiming to be her fiancé," Morgan responded.

"What! I didn't even know she was engaged. What's his name? Is it that Cody kid? Did he do this?" Marshall's voice rose as he swiftly determined he may have someone concrete to direct his wrath against.

"The young man's name is Cody Saddleback," Morgan replied.

A strained moment passed while neither man spoke. Marshall's eyes drilled into Morgan's.

"I asked you another question, Detective," Marshall challenged. "Did he do this?"

"I cannot answer that, Mr. Thomas," Morgan replied.

"Can't or won't?" Marshall bit out.

"Can't," Morgan assured him, with a sigh.

"Let me lock up and get my truck," Marshall stated as he nodded his head in acceptance and turned away.

"Mr. Thomas, we would be more than happy to drive you into town and bring you back. I don't think that you should be driving. Do you?"

"You're probably right. I'll just be a minute." Marshall walked woodenly to the house, seized the door, grabbed his keys, locked up, and then returned to the Jeep.

"I'm ready. Please tell me what happened."

Morgan explained things as briefly as possible leaving out the details that Cody had repeatedly claimed he had been responsible for her death. He simply informed Mr. Thomas that he and Dabria had been out for a walk and had happened upon Cody sobbing and holding Megan's body. He also left out the part about the other body they found. Once they reached the hospital all three trouped in and made their way to the morgue.

The smell was always the first thing that hit Morgan when he entered a morgue. It was the distinct odor of embalming fluid—a combination of formaldehyde, methanol, and ethanol. The second thing was the lack of noise. The coroner was waiting for them in the outer office.

"Detectives, may I have a word?" he directed his question to Morgan and Ducette.

"Mr. Thomas, please have a seat. We'll be right back," Morgan promised him.

Wordlessly, the coroner led them to a private viewing room. He opened the door and gestured the detectives in. Out of respect for the family members this coroner often laid the deceased on a stretcher during the identification process rather than leaving them on the dissection table. Megan's body was draped with a pure white sheet. The first thing Morgan registered was the soft blonde tendrils of hair that fanned around her too still, too white face—a flawless face that was attached to perfect shoulders, arms, and hands that lay at her sides. As his gaze moved down the gurney it came to an abrupt halt.

A gasp from beside him confirmed that Kent had come to the same conclusion as Morgan. Megan Thomas had been pregnant. Quite pregnant! Morgan raked his fingers through his hair and cursed softly.

"I appreciate the heads up," he thanked the coroner. "Stalling isn't gonna make this easier. I'll tell Mr. Thomas before we come back," he informed Kent.

Marshall had not sat down but instead was pacing in the waiting area.

"Mr. Thomas, can we sit down for a minute?"

"I'd rather not. What's going on?" he asked obviously agitated.

"Sir, please have a seat," Morgan again requested as he indicated the bench behind them. Reluctantly Marshall sank onto the seat. Morgan took the chair beside the bench and Kent continued to stand, but off to the side.

"Mr. Thomas, I don't know if you were aware but it appears that Megan was pregnant."

Marshall blinked several times.

"What! That's not possible," he croaked. He closed his eyes briefly and his head dropped back against the wall. Suddenly, he straightened and surged to his feet. Morgan swiftly followed suit and Kent moved in.

"My Gawd, Detective, it obviously isn't Megan then." His hopeful gaze swung to encompass Kent.

"Mr. Thomas, if there has been a mistake we still need you to confirm that the girl is not Megan. Please, sir, can you follow Detective Ducette?"

With a detective flanking each side of him Marshall walked to the viewing room. Lying there on the bed, appearing to simply be asleep, was the body of his beautiful first born child. His child! Marshall's knees gave out at the same time as his hands tightened into fists and he flung his head back again. This time, a primordial cry of anguish burst from deep inside of him. It echoed off the walls of the sterile silent room as Morgan and Kent grabbed him before he hit the floor. They helped him stagger out of the room and over to a chair in the hall. He slumped into the chair, sat with his head in his hands, and bleakly wept. The detectives moved off to give him some privacy. Although Morgan was trained to be resistant to sliding into the slippery pit of a family's despair, Marshall's roar had hit Morgan hard. And now despite his fight for self control Morgan's throat automatically tightened with every rasping sob. After several minutes Marshall wiped his eyes, visibly attempted composure, and then stood up and cleared his throat.

"I need to see her again," his voice wobbled, but with conviction.

Not trusting his own voice Morgan silently led him back into the room with a nod. This time Marshall lovingly clasped Megan's hand is his and caressed her cheek as the tears silently streamed down his face. Again the detectives backed off and went to stand beside the door. Morgan watched Marshall continue to stroke his child's face as he quietly spoke to her. Feeling the tears gather in his eyes Morgan was forced to look away and blink them back. No father should ever have to do this. He was gonna catch the bastard that had killed this man's child and grandchild—the monster that had broken the hearts of Megan's father and Megan's young lover!

"We need to tell Jeanine," he informed Morgan without taking his eyes off of his child. "I'm coming with you."

"Absolutely, Mr. Thomas," Morgan had himself back under control.

Marshall placed Megan's hand on her swollen abdomen and covered it with his. He brushed the hair from her forehead, and gently kissed her as any father would kiss his cherished child. Then he straightened, and left the room with Megan's hand still resting on her unborn child. It was a memory Morgan would never forget. Silently they returned to the parking lot and headed off to the former Thomas residence.

When they arrived Megan's mother, Jeanine, was just pulling into the driveway. As she emerged from her car she immediately began to shriek at Marshall.

"I've been trying to reach you for hours. If you can't get yourself a damn cell phone could you at least invest in an answering machine so that I can reach you when it's necessary? Megan didn't come home last night and I'm *assuming* she spent the night at your place," she sarcastically spat. "Apparently, she's not at Candice's like she told me she would be. That girl seems to be lying more often since you moved back," she accused.

"Jeanine. Can we speak to you in the house, please?" Marshall gently asked.

Jeanine suddenly realized there were two other men with Marshall and one of them was obviously a police officer.

"Marshall, what's going on? I don't want to go in the house. Where's Megan?" Jeanine frantically began to look back and forth between the men as she backed away from them with her hands outstretched.

"Jeanine, let's go inside," Marshall coaxed. "Are the kids at home?"

"I'm not going inside. Where's Megan?" she screeched.

Another vehicle pulled in behind the Jeep. Marshall walked past Jeanine into the house forcing her to follow him. Morgan, Kent, and the Victim Services support worker, who had just arrived, filed in behind her. Once inside, Jeanine immediately turned to Detective Ducette and demanded, "Where is my daughter?"

Before Kent could answer Marshall positioned himself directly in front of her and answered.

"Megan was found down by the river this afternoon. She's not coming home."

"What do you mean she's not coming home?" her eyes again darted wildly between the people standing in her foyer, as she wrung her hands together. "Is she hurt? Is she at the hospital? I have to go to her." She attempted to pass Marshall. He firmly yet gently gripped her by the forearms and held her steady though she struggled for release.

"Jeanine, she's gone," he stated very softly.

"Gone?" she gulped. "She can't be gone."

A gasp from behind Morgan alerted him to the fact that someone else was in the room.

"Daddy," a small voice inquired. "Is Megan lost?"

Marshall cautiously released his ex-wife and crouched down to answer the question posed by the youngest of his sons.

"No, Nathan. Megan's not lost. She went to live with the angels up in heaven."

"No!" Jeanine wailed as she slumped forward in a faint. Again Morgan and Kent caught a member of the Thomas family before they hit the floor. Morgan picked her up and lay her down on the sofa. By this time the other children had arrived in the living room. Morgan and Kent left the support worker while she attempted to console the wailing mother. She had immediately taken over from the father as he was trying to explain to his other children that Megan had had an accident and wouldn't be coming home. The Victim's Services support worker would remain until the family reinforcements arrived. Morgan's last picture of the family was of the children clinging to their father while he watched their mother rock back and forth moaning, "No, no, no!!!!"

Kent savagely swore under his breath as they walked back to the Jeep.

"Ever had to do that before?" he asked.

"Once, ... you?"

"This was the first. Does it get easier?"

"No," Morgan informed him. "This was far worse than the last one. Maybe it's not supposed to get easier. Ya know?"

"Yah."

Chapter 14

Morgan and Kent drove back to the station in silence, each lost in their own thoughts. Once there they focused on the business at hand. Cody Saddleback. Cody was being held in an interrogation room, supposedly waiting to be questioned. In reality Cody was in a fog of grief and disbelief. If someone had asked him how long he'd been sitting there his answer would probably have been that he had no idea. He had actually been there for several hours. Morgan informed French that he was about to start with Cody. One of the junior officers on duty told him that Cody was in Interrogation Room One.

"Was he offered as much as a glass of water?" Morgan questioned.

"I don't believe so," the officer answered.

"Officer, are you aware that this boy just discovered his dead girlfriend in a snow bank and that he's probably in shock?"

"I thought he was a suspect?"

"Whether he's a suspect or a victim it's our job to treat him with some compassion and provide him with basic human needs such as a washroom, and a blanket, since he is probably both wet and cold, and either pop or coffee laced with sugar since he's probably in shock!" Morgan exasperatedly reprimanded the officer. "I don't believe any of those things could be called anything other than common courtesies. Do you?"

"No, Detective, probably not," the flustered young officer agreed.

Morgan and Kent walked into the room carrying a blanket, bottled water, and a sugar-laced coffee.

"Hey, Cody, how're ya doing?" Morgan asked.

Shaking himself from his stupor, Cody sat up and replied. "Fine."

"Do you need to go to the washroom before we get started?"

"No."

"Are your clothes wet?"

"I . . . . I don't know," Cody responded with a dazed look on his face. "I guess my shirt is." Cody was wearing waterproof snowmobile pants.

"I brought you a blanket if you want to take off your shirt and wrap yourself in it. I also brought you some coffee."

Cody removed his shirt and wrapped the blanket around his shoulders. Morgan had noticed cuts and scrapes on Cody's hands down by the river and wondered about them. With the removal of Cody's shirt several bruises were revealed and Morgan wondered about their origin, as well. Megan hadn't had a mark on her. Cody took the warm coffee and gulped it down. The door to the interrogation room opened and a second cup of coffee appeared. Morgan took it and passed it to Cody. This one was hotter than the first and he sipped at it cautiously.

"Okay Cody, let's start at the beginning. Why don't you tell me about Megan? How long have you known each other?"

"I've known Megan since Grade One. We've gone to school together off and on for all our lives."

"Why off and on?"

"Sometimes my mom would move back to the reserve and then I went to school there. Sometimes, before my mom remarried, I was in foster care and went to other schools."

"How long have you and Megan been seeing each other?"

"About a year and a half."

"What grade are you and Megan in?"

"Megan's in Grade 12 at the collegiate and I'm taking mine through correspondence. I got expelled two months ago for beating up a kid."

"What happened?"

"He was a football player that Megan used to date. He'd been trying to get her to go out with him again when he found out she was dating me. He called her a *Buck Fucker* as she was leaving school one day and started pushing her around. All of his friends were laughing at her and taunting her and egging him on. One of my friends ran and got me, told me what was going on, and then several of them followed me outside. Just as I was about to reach her, he pushed her hard enough to make her fall down. I made my way through the crowd and beat the crap out of him before a teacher stepped in. With my friends backing me, his friends wisely decided to simply observe the two of us rather than try to help him. Since I threw the first punch I was the one to get expelled."

"I see. So did Megan's parents know you two were dating?"

"At first her mom did and she was pretty cool but after the school thing Megan was forbidden to see me. Her mom said I was dragging Megan down and that she was just going to get hurt if she kept . . . . kept hanging out with me," Cody's voice stumbled. Gulping he looked up and stared Morgan right in the eye.

"She was right wasn't she?" he whispered. "I got her killed."

"Did you kill Megan Thomas, Cody?"

"No!!!! . . . . my God, no," he shuddered and returned to looking at the tabletop.

"Then you've got to stop saying that. So, what's been going on the last few months?"

"Megan and I decided that regardless of what everyone else wanted we knew we were meant to be together and we made plans to leave after graduation. I already had a scholarship to attend any university in Western Canada and Megan had applied and been accepted to both the U. of S. and the U. of A. We hadn't decided where we were going yet and then we found out Megan was pregnant."

"Then what?"

"We talked about it and Megan knew her mom would try to pressure her into getting an abortion. We love each other and the thought of destroying our child went against everything we believe in. We decided the only course of action was to move Megan onto the reserve with me until she graduated and then we could leave together and raise our child while one of us worked and one of us went to school. Since I'm treaty I qualify for funding for daycare and housing while I attend school. We had it all worked out?"

"Cody, Megan was only seventeen though. Her parents could have come and taken her back from you."

"Megan's eighteenth birthday is tomorrow. She figured if she hid the truck and told her mother she was staying with a girlfriend for the weekend she wouldn't be missed until Monday after school."

"So tell me exactly what was supposed to happen last night."

"I was supposed to meet Megan at midnight. She was going to drive the truck down to the river and leave it there and I was to pick her up with the snowmobile. Then we were going back to my house."

"You have a house?"

"Yah. When I turned eighteen I applied for a residence on the reserve and I got one. Megan and I have been fixing it up for the last six months. It was pretty bad when I first got it but it looks good now."

"Where did you get the money from to fix it?"

"Megan has an after school job and I work full time at the bottling depot. We worked on the house on the weekends."

"Okay. What happened that prevented you from meeting her last night?"

"My mom and her husband got into it. My mom called and asked me to come into town and take her back with me out to the reserve where she would be safe. Her husband is white and with the way he's treated her over the years he isn't welcome on the reserve anymore. By the time I got her out of the house and settled down at my place it was well after midnight and I couldn't leave her alone in case *he* showed up."

"Don't you have any other relatives on the reserve?"

"Yes, my mom's family."

"So, why didn't you take her to one of them?"

"Because she's my mom and I should be the one to protect her, not one of her sisters."

"Okay. What time did you leave to pick her up?"

"About 10:00 p.m."

"What time did you arrive back on the reserve?" Morgan asked.

"About 12:30 a.m."

"Did Megan have a cell phone?"

"Yes."

"Did you call her to tell her what was going on?"

"Yes. I called her right after I talked to my mom as I was heading into town. I told her I had no idea when I was going to be finished and that we needed to postpone things until noon today."

"What did she say?"

"She said she didn't want to wait that long and that unless I called her back before midnight saying that I couldn't meet her she was going to go down to wait for me anyway."

"Then what happened?" Morgan asked.

"I tried calling her at midnight and all I got was her voicemail. I left a message saying I couldn't be there and that she should call me the next day just before she left town to head for the river. Cell service down at the river isn't that great so I knew she would go someplace to check for messages if I didn't arrive shortly."

"If you were supposed to meet her at midnight and it takes half an hour to get from town to the river, why didn't you call her back earlier?" Ducette asked.

"I was a little tied up with trying to stop Mom's husband from trying to prevent her from leaving."

"Tell me what happened."

"There's nothing to tell," Cody stated defiantly as he unconsciously pulled the blanket closer around his body.

"Cody, what happened to your hands and why do you have bruises all over you?"

"I must'a tripped or somethin'."

"Look," Ducette interjected, "we're trying to help you here. Did you *get into it* with your mom's husband in the process of trying to help her leave?"

Up to this point, Cody had been looking everywhere *but* at Ducette or Morgan. He now raised his eyes and looked directly into Morgan's.

"My temper often gets me into trouble and so I don't think it's a good idea to talk about it. Do you?"

"I think if we can prove you received those cuts and bruises as a result of an altercation with your mom's husband that may actually help with your alibi?"

"Are you saying I need an alibi? Do I need to get a lawyer about now?"

"You can if you like but at this point we're simply talking. You aren't charged with anything?"

"No, but I'm pretty sure I'm your prime suspect?"

"I'm not going to lie to you, Cody. You are a suspect and until we can prove you have an alibi you'll remain so. Now, do you want to try answering that question? Where did you get the bruises and cuts from?"

"I got them from defending my mom. But, I'll tell you right now she's never going to stand up and say that. She's covered for him for years and even though he's beating her again, since I moved out, she won't ever stand up against him. So it'll be my word against his. I've already been charged with assault this year and there are a dozen people who could easily stand up and say they've witnessed my temper. *He* has never been charged with anything and with the exception of my mother and brothers and sisters there have been no witnesses to his abuse?"

"How old are your siblings?"

"I'm the oldest and actually the only one that isn't his child. The next is Kyle who is eight, Jessi is six, and Sam is four."

"Were the kids home when this was going on last night?"

"No, they were all at sleepovers with friends for the night."

"Have you ever been beaten badly enough to have to go to the doctor?"

"Sure, but mom would just take me out to the reserve and leave me with her sisters until I healed up. He does have rules. He doesn't break bones and he never hits you in the face."

"Have you ever told anyone what was going on?"

"Sure. My mom has only been with him for eight years. So I was ten when we moved in with him. The first time he "disciplined me" was with his belt. I knew that wasn't right and I told a teacher at school. Social services came over to the house and had a talk with both him and my mom. He apologized and claimed that since he had been disciplined like that as a child and had no children of his own he just figured that's what you're supposed to do. Because of who he is they told him and mom that if any other incidents occurred they would be forced to recommend parenting classes. That was it."

"Who *is* your stepdad, Cody?" Morgan asked, with a feeling of dread.

"He is not my stepdad!" Cody said emphatically. "He's my mom's husband. And his name is Richard Reynolds."

"*Judge* Richard Reynolds?" Ducette asked with a gasp.

"The one and only," Cody responded with a grimace.

"When was the second incident and what happened?" Morgan asked, disregarding Ducette's reaction.

"It was actually a few years later. Mom was the one that paid for it right after social services left and he told me in no uncertain terms that if I told again he'd beat her so bad the next time that she wouldn't be able to tell anyone anything again. My mom cried as she put me to bed that night and begged me to be good and not to say anything, because otherwise we'd have to move back to the reserve and she didn't want to have to do that. We had a real nice house then, she could buy me things she could never afford before, and people thought she was somebody."

"So you never said anything again. How often were you beaten?"

"Not so often when I was younger because he knew the school was watching and I tried really hard to be good so he wouldn't hurt her. Mostly if I was good he wouldn't hit her and I figured she was safe. But now that I'm older I know that I was wrong. When he wasn't hitting her in front of me he was raping her at night."

"How do you know that?"

"Because I would hear things at night and when I asked mom about it she said that's what men and women do in bed and that the crying out wasn't because she was being hurt. I know what kinds of sounds a woman makes when she's having sex and the sounds I heard coming from their bedroom were nothing like the sounds a woman makes when she is being pleasured."

"Then what happened?"

"I got older and he knew that smacking her bothered me more than getting smacked myself and I think he was afraid I might tell to protect her. So he returned to acting out his anger on me during the day and her at night behind closed doors. I could deal with that because I knew one day I'd be able to leave and hopefully take my mom with me."

"Have you ever seen him touch his own children?"

"No. It's just me and mom."

"Did your mom ever go back to the reserve before?"

"Sure."

"Could your aunts verify the appearance of your mother's bruises or of yours?"

"I don't know."

"So there's little way to prove that what you're saying actually happened?"

"That's right." Once Cody had found the courage to look directly into Morgan's eyes his gaze had never wavered.

"All right, let's leave that for now and get back to what happened after you left the message on Megan's phone. What time did you say that was?"

"It was about midnight. I had just left town and I knew there was no way I could make the meeting."

"So you went out to the reserve with your mom and went to your house."

"Yah, I sat with her until about 3:00 a.m. Then we went to bed."

"Did you try to call Megan again?"

"Yes, I went to call her again after I got home and realized then that my phone had been on vibrate. For whatever reason, I didn't feel it when she called me back. She left me a message saying she would return to town and that she would meet me at noon like I suggested. I tried to call back but her phone was out of range so I just left her a text instead."

"What did the text say?"

"Just, goodnight—I love you—see ya tomorrow."

"We found a cell phone at the site that we think may be Megan's. Can you describe it?"

"Yes, because I bought it for her. It's a pink chocolate phone with her initials on it."

"What's a chocolate phone?" Morgan asked.

"It's one of those phones that slide open rather than flip open," Cody replied.

"Okay, you sit up with your mom until 3:00 a.m. talking and then you both go to bed. Is that right?"

"Yes."

"What time did you wake up?"

"About 7:00 a.m. That's my normal time to get up so even on the weekend I tend to wake up then. I got up and made a pot of coffee while I showered. After I dressed I took a coffee and went outside to make a list of the things I'd need to get after Megan came. I had some food but we would need to buy healthier food for her. Mom got up about an hour later and I told her I was meeting a friend at noon. I told her she could either stay at my house or I would take her to one of her sisters."

"Why didn't you tell her what was really going on?"

"Because I was concerned that she, like Megan's mom, would try to interfere."

"What did she decide?"

"She asked me to drop her off at her sister's and promised me she wouldn't go back until the kids returned home. She believes she's in less danger if they are there."

"What do you think?"

"Up until now, I might have agreed with her, but after last night I'm not so sure anymore. He was really wound up last night."

"Do you know where she is now?"

"No. I haven't had access to a phone."

"Please give her a call before you leave. If your mom's already gone home we can drop over there and use you as the excuse for stopping in."

"What do you mean?"

"We have to check up on your alibi and the easiest way to do that is to interview your mom and see if she will verify that you were with her."

"And if she says she never left home?"

"Then we go to your Aunt's house and see what she has to say. Then we question your neighbors and her neighbors to see if any of them saw you and your mom either arrive or leave. What time did you drop your mom off at your aunt's?"

"At 11:30 a.m. in my truck and then went back to the house to jump on my snowmobile. I tried calling her again, and again her phone went straight to voice mail so I figured she must already be waiting for me. I arrived at our meeting place at almost exactly noon. She wasn't there, so I drove along the shoreline to see if her truck was parked where we had planned. I could see it from the river and all of sudden I had a really bad feeling that somethin' was wrong. I drove up off the lake onto the trail and I saw Megan . . . . ," Cody's voice broke.

"I know this isn't going to be easy, but it's very important to try to remember exactly what you saw before you reached Megan and picked her up," Morgan gently prodded.

Cody closed his eyes tight and Morgan watched as his hands convulsively gripped the blanket. He took a deep breath seemingly trying to steady himself. Then in a voice straining to remain even he recounted the scene that had met him.

"Megan was lying face up with her hands resting one on top of the other, on top of her chest. Her eyes were closed and except for the snow that had fallen on her she looked like she was sleeping."

"Did you notice anything else around her or hear anything unusual?"

Cody opened his eyes and again stared straight into Morgan's.

"The first sound I recall hearing was the sound of a madman screaming over and over again . . . . No!!!!!No!!!!!! Then I realized it was me," he explained in anguish. He closed his eyes again and hung his head. "I grabbed her up and tried to put her on my sled but she wouldn't bend. I staggered away from the sled, I guess, to try to take her to the truck. I dropped to the ground and that's where you and your girlfriend found me."

"Cody, we didn't come upon you until almost 2:00 p.m. Are you saying you held Megan in the snow for almost two hours?"

"I guess so," he responded forlornly. "It wasn't long enough. I want her back. I want to hold her and laugh with her and raise our baby together. Who could hurt her like that? She never did anything mean to anyone. She was kind and loving." Suddenly sitting up straight Cody vowed, "If it's the last thing I ever do I promise you I'm gonna make the freak that destroyed my family pay."

"Cody making comments like that isn't going to help your cause," Morgan warned. "Is there anything else you can think of that you should tell us?"

Cody shook his head as he removed the blanket from around his shoulders. "Wait," he grabbed Morgan's hand as he was about to leave the room. "There is something. Her ring! She wasn't wearing her ring. She always wore it when we were together. Please find it. Maybe it's in one of her pockets." He let his hand fall away and he continued to fold the blanket, lay it on the table, and then reach for his wet shirt.

"Don't put that on. I have a dry T-shirt you can wear. Just hang here for a minute while I go get it. I'll ask the coroner to look for the ring. If she doesn't have it on her we'll search her truck and then I'll go back and search for it on the riverbank. We'll do everything we can to find it, Cody," Morgan promised, trying in a small way, to comfort the young man.

Chapter 15

Dabria waited impatiently for the phone to ring. It was going on 7:00 p.m. and she hadn't heard anything. She had been sorting through boxes, mindless busy work really. Her only excitement had been making soup. At 7:05 p.m. the phone rang and although the display showed it was the R.C.M.P. detachment Morgan wasn't the one on the other end of the line.

"Ms. Abdulla-Smythe?"

"Speaking."

"This is Detective French. I understand you were with Detective Vaughn this afternoon when the bodies were discovered. Would you be willing to come in and give us a statement?"

"Of course."

"Do you need a lift?"

"No, I'll walk over. I'll be there in about fifteen minutes."

"I'd prefer that you not walk. I can send a car."

"No I can drive."

"Fine. Have me paged when you arrive."

Dabria turned her soup off, locked up the apartment, and briskly headed to the station. Detective French met her immediately upon her arrival and motioned her over to his desk.

"Thank you, for coming in, Ms. Abdulla-Smythe. It looks like I get to take your statement twice today. Can I get you anything before we start?"

"No, thanks, I'm fine."

"Okay. Let's begin basically from when you left here earlier today."

"Sure. Morgan, Detective Vaughn," she amended, "and I decided to go on a fieldtrip. We picked up sub sandwiches and drove out to the dump sites of the other victims. As we drove and then parked to eat, Morgan told me some of the information you had passed on to him."

"Such as?"

"Such as, where the women were dumped and how they were discovered. I know this information is privileged. He made me retain him just like you recommended. I have never broken a confidence before Detective and I'm not about to start now," she assured him. "We left the Jeep and followed a trail down to the La Colle Falls site. After surveying the vicinity directly around the dam we moved farther down the river to take pictures of where the first victim was discovered. As we made our way down the trail we came upon an abandoned truck. Detective Vaughn immediately called the plates in and since he was waiting for information I continued on down the trail. I realized suddenly that I could hear the sound of someone sobbing. I quietly continued forward to attempt to discover where the sound was coming from."

"At this point, why didn't you return to inform Detective Vaughn of what you heard?".

"Because I knew he was only a few hundred metres away and I didn't feel like I was in any danger. Since he was occupied I decided to investigate the crying on my own. As I peeked around a clump of willows I saw someone holding another person, rocking back and forth, and crying."

"Did this person say anything?"

"Sort of."

"What does that mean?"

"It means I heard him mumbling but I'm unsure of exactly what he was saying."

"Why don't you tell me what you think you heard?"

"I'd rather not."

"We'll come back to this in a moment. Then what happened." It was obvious to him that she was being evasive.

"I backed away from them and quickly returned to Detective Vaughn to tell him what I had seen and prevent him from making any noise that would alert them to our presence."

"And then?"

"Detective Vaughn moved in front of me and whispered to me to stay behind him and stay hidden. He approached the couple and offered his assistance. When the man turned around and I saw his face I realized that he was just a boy. I moved out from behind the bush and went to stand beside Detective Vaughn to help him."

"Did it not occur to you that this *boy* might be dangerous?"

"No."

"You can't possibly be that naïve given the profession you're in," Detective French asked her in disbelief.

"I felt no threat from the boy. His total focus was on his girlfriend and on his desperate, misguided hope that he could bring her back to life."

"You couldn't be sure that he wouldn't turn on you."

"I trust my instincts, Detective, just like I know you, as a police officer, must do."

"Let's move on," French suggested with a wry quirk of his eyebrows, clearly indicating that he thought she was crazy to have put herself in harm's way like that.

Dabria continued to relate the events as they occurred, focusing her narrative on the details of the scalped corpse and steering away from her interaction with Cody. Her only omission was Cody's remarks when she had initially stumbled upon him. She was *almost positive* she had heard Cody saying he was responsible for Megan's death. But, she *wasn't positive*, and she would swear in a court of law that she didn't believe the boy was guilty of actually killing his girlfriend, anyway. She truly believed that he was so overwrought by the discovery of his dead girlfriend that he blamed himself for her death and therefore, in his mind, he was just as responsible as the actual killer. She was determined to prevent Cody from being convicted of a crime that she intuitively knew he had not committed.

Down the hall Morgan was wrapping up his questioning. Cody had voluntarily allowed Morgan to fingerprint him and take a DNA sample. They had just passed hour two. The boy had acknowledged that Megan was dead despite the fact that he had yet to come to terms with that death, and the death of his unborn child. Morgan knew it would be years, if ever, before Cody forgave himself for missing their rendezvous. He advised Cody to steer clear of Megan's family and to return to the reservation so that Morgan would be able to contact him tomorrow. He strongly indicated that disappearing would not be in Cody's best interest, and then he released him.

"Where did you take Megan?" Cody asked as he paused in the doorway.

"She's in the morgue at the Vic," Morgan replied.

"I don't suppose I can see her?"

"I don't think that's a good idea, do you?"

"Probably not. Please, Detective, can you try to get me in to see her for just a minute?"

"I don't know, Cody. Her parents aren't going to want you anywhere near her, are they?"

"I love . . . . loved her," Cody asserted. "And she loved me."

"I believe you, Cody. But she was a minor and you have no rights regarding her."

"Please. I just wanna' say good bye," Cody pleaded. "She was gonna' have our baby."

"I'll see what I can do, but don't get your hopes up, Cody. Give me your cell number."

Cody fired off the number and then reached his hand out to shake Morgan's.

"Thank you, for trying to help Megan today." This young man was not the same distraught teenager that Dabria and Morgan had initially stumbled upon. Although he was still obviously reeling from the events of the day he had pulled himself together.

"Please call your aunt from the courtesy phone at the front desk before you leave the station. Do not speak to your mom or tell your aunt what's going on until I have a chance to talk to them. Okay? Do you need a ride home?"

"I can get one of my aunties to come get me," Cody assured Morgan.

"How about, if your mom is still on the reserve, I take you home and then I can interview her immediately?"

Cody nodded his head in acknowledgment, turned away, and continued out of the doorway and down the hallway.

"You know we should have detained him until we got word from upstairs?" Ducette declared as he laid a hand on Morgan's arm.

"He didn't kill that girl," Morgan stated with conviction as he shook his head.

"You don't know that for sure."

"I'd stake next month's paycheck on it"

"How do I know you're not independently wealthy and that this gig isn't simply a way to keep you occupied?"

"Have you seen what I drive?"

"Maybe the Jeep is simply one of your fleet."

"Yah, I have a fleet of ten year old vehicles."

"You just better hope that kid doesn't decide to go hide in the bush somewhere to mourn his girlfriend, or try to break into the hospital morgue, because if he does either of those things your ass is gonna be grass."

"Let's see where Cody's mom is hanging out and then get that interview out of the way. It would be great to be able to head home before midnight. Once the media gets wind of this, we won't have another day off until we solve it."

"I'm with you."

As Morgan made his way to reception he glanced over at French's desk and realized Dabria was sitting across from the Detective. He wandered over. French looked up and stopped writing as he became conscious of Morgan's approach.

"Can I help you, Detective Vaughn?" French inquired.

"No. Just stopped by to let Dabria know I'll be tied up for quite some time yet. I need to conduct some other interviews tonight. I'll call you later. Sorry to interrupt." With a nod from Dabria he turned around and headed back to reception.

"My mom is still at my aunt's and apparently is planning on staying the night. I didn't speak to her but I did talk to my aunt and she said she would keep mom there until I returned," Cody told Morgan.

"Sounds good. Let's go," Morgan led the way outside leaving Cody and Ducette to follow.

As they pulled into the aunt's yard several dogs came running.

"I can walk home from here," Cody offered.

"Are you sure?" Morgan asked. "I was going to let Detective Ducette drop me off to talk to your mom and he was going to drive you home."

"No. I'll walk. That way you can question both my aunt and my mom at the same time."

"Are you sure you're okay to be alone?"

"Yah, I'd rather be alone right now, anyway." Cody let himself out and headed for home with the dogs trailing behind. Morgan and Ducette walked to the Aunt's door and before they could ring the bell it opened.

"What do you want?" an elderly, stooped, aboriginal woman squinted at them from inside the house.

"Ma'am, I am Detective Vaughn and this is Detective Ducette and we wondered if we could ask Mrs. Reynolds a few questions. Is she in?"

"Leotie," a voice called from somewhere inside the house. "Let them in."

The woman shuffled aside and they entered. The house was warm and the fragrant smell of simmering stew assailed them. Morgan's stomach growled. The submarine sandwiches had worn off a long time ago.

"Would you like a bowl of stew, officers? Are you hungry?" that same voice offered. A woman was standing over the stove stirring a pot.

"Thank you, Ma'am, that would be great," Ducette answered for both of them.

"Please sit," she instructed, still with her back to them, as she filled two bowls with the steaming ambrosia. The elderly lady, presumably Cody's aunt, brought bannock to the table, and two fresh cups of coffee, and then sat down beside Ducette. As the woman at the stove turned and placed the bowls of stew in front of them, Morgan was stunned by her beauty.

"What questions do you have for me, officers?" she inquired as she gracefully settled into the chair beside him. Morgan understood why Judge Reynolds had been enthralled by Cody's mother. She was absolutely breathtaking. Her long straight glossy blue/black hair hung halfway down her back. Her statuesque physique was impressive in itself never mind the almost black almond shaped eyes and distinct cheekbones.

"You are Mrs. Reynolds?" Morgan asked just to confirm.

"Yes, but you may call me Nina, if you like. This is my sister, Leotie," she focused her attention on Ducette. Immediately picking up on this Ducette took over the questioning.

"Can you tell me where you were last night from about 11:30 p.m. on?"

"I was here and there."

"Here, as in, right here in this kitchen?"

"No. Here . . . . as in, on the reservation."

"And there?"

"There . . . . as in, at home."

"Were you here at 11:30 p.m. last night?"

"No. I arrived about 12:30 a.m."

"How did you arrive here?"

"My son picked me up in town and brought me out here."

"Your son?"

"Cody. The son who just stepped out of your police car," she stated quietly.

"Where did you stay last night?"

"At Cody's house."

"Was he with you all night?"

"Yes. Officer Ducette, why are you asking me these questions? Is there something you need to tell me about Cody? Why did you drive up with him and let him walk home? What's going on? Is it that girl again? Is her family making trouble?"

Ducette looked up from the bowl of stew he had just swiped clean with a piece of bannock. He popped the bread into his mouth and chewed slowly, never taking his eyes off of Mrs. Reynolds and obviously forcing her to wait on his reply.

"I need to know if you were with Cody the entire time between 11:30 p.m. last night and noon today."

Without a flicker or a twitch Nina stared Ducette in the eye and replied, "I was with him from 11:30 p.m. until noon today."

"Did you sleep last night?"

"Did I sleep? Well, actually, very little. I went to bed at around 3:00 a.m. and finally fell asleep around 5:00 a.m. I woke up at 7:00 a.m. when I heard Cody get up. I lay in bed until I smelled coffee and then joined Cody in the kitchen at about 7:30 a.m. We spent the morning together and then he dropped me off here around noon. Now," Nina sat up straighter, "tell me why you're here."

"Megan Thomas was found dead this morning down by the river and Cody was with her when she was found."

"No!" Nina swiftly jumped up knocking her chair over as she tried to back away from the news. "Why did you let him walk home by himself?" she asked frantically as she made for the door.

Ducette stood and blocked her way.

"Mrs. Reynolds, Cody asked to be given some privacy and I have a few more questions. Please sit down," he requested with his hand indicating she return to the fallen chair.

"But, I'm his mother. I should be with him." Nina made the last comment sound more like a question rather than a declaration.

Morgan righted the chair and he and Ducette stood until she returned and sat down again. She sat with her hands clenched around her coffee cup.

"Cody would never hurt that girl!" Nina vehemently asserted.

"We aren't saying that he did, Mrs. Reynolds. We just needed to confirm Cody's version of the events of last night."

"I was still awake when Cody's car drove by last night some time after midnight," Leotie volunteered. "He didn't leave the reserve again until around noon today on his snowmobile."

"How do you know that?"

"Cody has to drive past my house if he wants to leave the reserve by car or truck."

"As the crow flies, about how far is it to La Colle Falls from here?" Morgan asked the women.

"About ten miles," Nina guessed and looked to Leotie for affirmation. She nodded.

"Mrs. Reynolds, you asked me if there was some trouble with Megan. Why did you ask me that?" Ducette questioned.

"I know that Megan's mother wasn't happy about their relationship."

"How do you know that?"

"I saw her at a charity function just before Christmas and she asked me to keep him away from Megan."

"What was your response?"

"I told her that Cody was an adult now and what I had to say had very little effect on his actions. That was not what she wanted to hear. She grabbed her man and left the party."

"Do you know where Cody was heading when he left here at noon today?"

"No. Since he moved back to the reserve and got a place of his own he allows no interference in his personal life. If I want to remain a part of his life I ask no questions."

"Why is that? You're his mother. I thought that there was an unwritten law that no matter what age a woman's child is their mother reserves the right to question their actions and decisions," Ducette commented.

"That is not the case between Cody and me."

"Do you have other children, Mrs. Reynolds?"

"Yes, I do."

"Where are they?"

"Visiting with different friends. They each had sleepovers last night."

"So, why are you out here?"

"To visit with my son and my sister," Nina replied tightly.

"What time did Cody arrive at your home last night, Mrs. Reynolds?"

"About 10:00 p.m."

"What time did you leave?"

"About midnight."

"What were you doing from 10:00 p.m. until midnight?"

"Visiting with my husband, Detective Ducette," Nina replied, again with a tight smile.

Deciding it was best not to push her into confirming or denying what Cody had told them, Morgan interrupted Ducette.

"I think we have all we need right now, Mrs. Reynolds. Thank you for your cooperation and the delicious supper." Morgan stood and extended his hand for her to shake. She also rose.

"I wouldn't dream of not cooperating, officer. May I go to my son now?"

"If you like, although I agree with Detective Ducette, I really think he may not want any company right now. I may need you and your sister to come down to the station and sign a statement this week. Would that be a problem?"

"Absolutely not. I will do whatever is necessary."

As Morgan and Ducette were leaving Morgan heard a sound from the living room.

He stopped and turned to Leotie. "Do you live alone?" he asked.

"No. Tehya lives with me," Leotie replied.

"And she would be?"

"My friend's granddaughter."

"Is she here now?"

"Yes."

"Was she here last night?" Morgan asked.

"Yes."

"All night?"

"Why?"

"I'm simply trying to solidify Cody's whereabouts for last night and if she was here and either saw him last night or heard him that would help him," Morgan explained.

"Tehya! Come here," Leotie commanded.

A very tall, robust girl rounded the corner and stood in the living room doorway. She stood with her hands stuffed in her pockets and her eyes downcast.

"Did you either see or hear Cody at all last night?" Morgan asked.

"No," she replied as she continued to avoid his searching stare.

"Were you out last night?"

"Yes."

"Do you remember what time you arrived here?"

"No," she responded.

"Where were you last night, Tehya?"

"Around."

"Around here? On the reserve?"

"Just around. I went for a run and did some weight training."

"Are you training for a specific sport?"

"Wrestling."

"So, you didn't see or hear Cody's arrival on the reserve?"

"No."

"And you have no idea what time you returned back here to the house?"

"I already said no. I have homework. Are we done?" she questioned quietly but defiantly.

"Sure. Thanks," Morgan responded as they left the house and headed for town.

"Well, at least you found the kid an alibi."

"What're you trying to say?"

"Come on, Morgan, his only alibi is his mother. If I'm not totally convinced of his innocence why would a jury be?"

"Why aren't you convinced?"

"I think the burning question should be why you're so eager to believe him?"

"I know what I saw when we found him and I have interviewed for enough years to sense when someone is lying. Cody is not lying. I am convinced that we need to add to our list of suspects to try and find out who actually killed that girl."

"I agree that we need to keep digging for information but I think we've already found our man. Oh, and you know *that* girl is lying."

"Tehya? Yah, she is definitely holding something back. What about the latest scalped victim? Do you think Cody's responsible for her, too?"

"No."

"So, it's just a coincidence that both bodies ended up beside each other?"

"They weren't exactly beside each other and it could be a coincidence," Ducette defended his position.

"Cody said Megan was lying in the snow with her hands crossed over her chest and that she looked like she was sleeping. She was posed like *the scalper's* victims? Kent, that information has never been released. Only the scalper would know to lay her out like that," Morgan explained.

"Like Cody? Or maybe she was never even laid out like that at all. Maybe he saw the latest corpse and figured if he said that was how he had found Megan it would take the spotlight off of him. Okay . . . okay," he held his hands up as he realized that Morgan was about to interrupt. "Let's suppose that there was a third person on the riverbank before you guys arrived. Let's say Megan's murderer stumbled onto the latest victim when they were leaving and decided that placing Megan in the same way would lead us to believe that she was murdered by *the scalper*."

"Want to know what I think?" Morgan taunted Ducette.

"Shoot."

"I think Megan went to meet Cody and when she rounded that last corner she interrupted the scalper. I think he did kill her. It was out of necessity, and I'm going to prove it."

"You go ahead and dig for your proof and I'll dig for mine and then at the end of the day we'll see who wins."

"So far there are no winners, and even if we do find her killer, Megan, Cody, and their baby still lose."

Not another comment was made as the two made their way back to the station. Reports had to be written before either of them could head home for the evening. Morgan had envisioned other evening activities and knew Dabria had as well.

~ ~ ~

Dabria and Detective French had finished up not long after Morgan left to go to the reserve. This time she was glad she had her car. It was dark out now and having not lived here very long she was unsure which streets were best avoided. She poured herself a bowl of soup after soaking in the tub again for half an hour. At this rate her skin was going to be so dried out she was going to have to soak in a tub of moisturizer just to get it back to normal. She just couldn't get rid of the chill that seemed to have settled into her very bones. Soaking in a hot bath at least temporarily warmed her up. Lounging on the sofa, wrapped in a blanket, she promptly dozed off while reading a pocket book. At 11:30 p.m. Dabria's door buzzer jolted her awake.

"Hey, did I wake you?"

"I was just dozing on the couch. Come on up." She poured herself some water and opened the door and then leaned against the counter drinking it while she waited for him to come up.

Morgan walked in and immediately reached for Dabria. She had planned to be standoffish when he returned but the weariness on his face and slump of his shoulders tugged at her softer side. Shrugging off her protective armor she welcomed the embrace and allowed him to enfold her into his arms. They simply stood and held each other for a long time without speaking. Dabria was the first one to pull back.

"I'm sorry I snapped at you," she apologized as she brushed an unruly curl out of his eyes. "Have you eaten?"

"Cody's mom fed us a bowl of stew and bannock. But I could use a snack."

"I made soup."

"Soup would be good. It's not too late for you?"

"No. I'm a night owl. How are you? How's Cody?"

"I'm fine—just tired. Cody will survive, at least as long as it takes us to find Megan's killer."

"So you don't think Cody did it either."

"No and obviously neither do you."

"Do you want to talk about it or *can* you even talk about it?"

"I can tell you this much. We interviewed Cody, his mother, his aunt, and a young girl that is living with his aunt to try to corroborate his story and confirm some time-frames. That's all I can tell you at this point."

"Has he been charged?"

"Not yet."

"But you think he will be?"

"It's a definite possibility."

"Well, for tonight I won't ask you another thing about it. How's the soup?"

"It's excellent."

"Will you stay?"

"Do you want me to?"

"Yes."

"Then I will. Come and sit down and tell me what you have planned for this week. I don't want to think any more about today."

Dabria regaled him with the scheduled events of her week, from planned lunch dates to moving into her tiny cottage on the weekend.

"I'm assuming you're going to need some help."

"Actually, I hired movers. How about you just come for supper on Sunday night?"

"It's a date. I'm on afternoons all week and now with this I probably won't have a free moment to myself anyway. Come on, let's go to bed. I hope you don't expect a command performance tonight."

"How about we just hold each other and try to get some sleep. I know we're both tired and neither one of us has anything to prove tonight, do we?"

"I'd like that." Dabria had put away his dishes and he stood, took her by the hand, and led her to the bedroom. She headed for the bathroom and returned in a t-shirt and boxers. He peeled his clothes off and after having a quick shower he joined her in bed. He pulled her into his arms and gently kissed her on the forehead. Despite coming straight from the shower his distinctive scent enveloped her as she snuggled against him. It was comforting and after indulging in a big yawn Dabria promptly dozed off.

Dabria awoke with her nipples straining against her t-shirt as Morgan's hand unconsciously glided from her navel up to the swell of her breasts. She guided his hand to the crest and coaxed him into kneading it. As she arched into his hand her bottom ground into his crotch and a groan escaped his lips. Taking her free hand she grabbed a condom off the nightstand and using her teeth ripped the packaging open. Shifting, she sheathed Morgan and then returned to their original position. He was awake now and a full participant in the proceedings. Pulling her leg over top of his he slid into her from behind and they started their week with an unhurried early morning loving.

Chapter 16

By the time Dabria reached her office she had heard the radio station's take on the events that had occurred the day before. They reported the finding of two deceased females on the banks of the river and indicated that these may be the latest victims of a serial killer that had been stalking the women of the area. They released only the age of Megan and stated that at this point the identity of the second victim had not been confirmed. Dabria was one of those souls who had never taken something at face value and after her own personal dealings with the press she was again disturbed by the power of the media to lead the public in a certain direction. Knowing some of the key factors of this case she was disgusted by what she knew the general population of P.A. was going to be concluding once they discovered that Cody had been found with Megan. She was terrified for Cody.

She walked into the office and headed directly to reception to check Brad's whereabouts and to see if he was tied up. Sarah walked in right behind her. After confirming that he was in and had no early morning client she headed for the stairs.

"Kent told me you found the women," Sarah whispered as she followed her. "Are you okay?"

"I'll be fine. I can't image how Megan's family is making out, though."

"You know that the boyfriend may be charged."

"Yes, and I'm going to do everything in my power to make sure he's okay if he is."

"You think he's innocent."

"I know he is."

"They're saying that one person killed both of them."

"I think they're right. But it's not Cody. I'm heading up to talk to Brad now and fill him in on the weekend's events just in case he hasn't already heard."

"Sounds good I'll catch you later. I've got court in half an hour so I've gotta run," Sarah said as she headed for her own office.

Dabria climbed the third set of stairs and knocked on Brad's open door.

"Come in and close the door," he directed. "I understand you've had a very traumatic weekend. How's your head?"

"Some stitches, but I'll be fine."

"You found the women on the riverbank."

"Yes."

"Do you need to take some personal days?"

"No."

"Might I recommend that you check with *Lawyers Concern for Lawyers* sometime this week and see if they can set up an appointment for you? I don't think it would hurt for you to talk to a professional."

"Is that a *strong* recommendation?"

"Yes. The mental health of my staff is important to me."

"Although I've heard of them I've never had any dealings with them."

Brad handed Dabria a card he dug out of his desk drawer.

"This is the phone number to call. You're privacy will be guaranteed as they do not require your name and instead assign you a number. They set up an appointment for you anonymously. You call back in with your number and they give you the details of the appointment."

"Thank you, Brad. I'll call today."

"Is there anything else I can help you with?"

"Actually there is," Dabria responded. "There's a chance that the boyfriend of the teenage victim is going to be charged and we may be representing him. I know I can't represent him but I'd like to help with his defense."

"Dabria, don't you think you have enough on your plate? And besides I can guarantee that our criminal lawyers are extremely experienced. Don't you trust my staff to provide the best representation possible?" he asked with raised eyebrows.

"I would never question your team's ability," Dabria assured him. "However, I know Cody didn't harm his girlfriend because I personally saw his disbelief and his grief. I want to help because I'm terrified that that boy is going to pay the price for loving the wrong girl. Please let me help," she entreated.

"You think he's innocent?"

"Brad, Cody didn't kill either of those women," she vehemently assured him.

"I can't allow you to assist, Dabria, and you know that. But I do appreciate your analysis. Anything else?"

"No. Thank you," she said with a sigh. Dabria *had* known the answer before she asked but she wanted to make sure Brad knew there was no doubt that she believed in the boy's innocence.

"I'm preparing for a trial this afternoon. Was there anything else?"

"No, sir," she said as she stood up and made her way to the door.

"Promise me you'll make time for some personal counseling. If they recommend you take time off, I'll ensure that it happens," Brad promised. "And, take it easy today, okay." he suggested as she left his office.

Dabria made her way to her own office and closed the door. She wasn't in the mood for any questions from the other staff and she wanted to get that appointment made so that she could concentrate on her very full schedule. Dabria followed the procedures and was surprised when she called back half an hour later that she had an appointment for after lunch that same day. She flung herself into the tasks listed in her agenda. The morning flew by uninterrupted and just before noon Sarah popped her head in.

"You have to take a break and eat. In or out? Alone or with company? Your call."

"Let's order something in. I'm really busy this afternoon so I don't have time to go out. And I would love to have some company if we can talk about something besides yesterday."

"Done. Chinese?"

"Sounds great. Do you mind ordering?" At Sarah's nod Dabria rattled off her request. "I'll have ginger beef, fried rice, beef and broccoli, and chop-suey."

"I'll let you know when it gets here." Sarah disappeared back out into the hall and closed the door behind her.

Half an hour later Dabria's phone rang.

"Soups on! Come on over."

Dabria grabbed her keys and leaving her desk as it was, locked her door on the way out. Sarah had cleaned off her own desk and had their meals set out.

"So, how were your *interactions* with Detective Vaughn this weekend? He was very protective of you at the hospital, Friday night. And may I just go on record saying he is one fine example of the males of our species!" she exclaimed with a giggle.

"Yes, he is and he was very attentive *all* weekend long."

"*All* weekend long? Do tell!"

"A lady never kisses and tells but I will say he was the perfect nurse and weekend companion. So, did any of the girls spill the beans about the paint-ball game?"

"They all claim they didn't tell." Sarah reported as she recognized Dabria's "not so subtle" change of topic.

"Well, Morgan definitely suspects something. At this point he knows we cheated but I don't think he's taken the time to figure out how . . . . yet."

"I don't suppose we could have round number two this weekend?"

"No. I'm moving this weekend."

"Do you need help?"

"I hired movers but if you want to come out and keep me company that would be fine."

"Great, I'll bring munchies."

Dabria and Sarah finished lunch and Dabria headed off to meet with the psychologist. She arrived right on time and was promptly whisked into her office.

"Good afternoon, Ms. Abdulla-Smythe. My name is Dr. Julia Robinson. How can I help you this afternoon?"

"I'm a new lawyer in town and my boss recommended that I see a psychologist and chat about the events that occurred over the weekend."

"So, you don't really want to be here, do you?"

"I can think of better ways to spend my time. But, since I'm here can we get down to it?" asked Dabria bluntly.

"Of course. Please explain what happened this weekend."

Dabria gave a brief overview of what had transpired. When she was finished she folded her hands on her lap and looked directly into the doctor's eyes.

"That's all of it. And by the way my mother is a psychologist so I'm well aware that talking through trauma often helps. I have a friend that was with me through the weekend and if I feel the need to unburden myself further I can discuss things with him."

"Ms. Abdulla-Smythe, if your mother is a psychologist then you should realize that what we do does have value and we can help people if they allow us to. Instead of treating this as if it's a punishment from your boss, why don't you treat it as an opportunity? Haven't you ever had a time in your life when you needed an objective listener?"

"Sure, but not now. I have another appointment shortly so I'm afraid we'll have to end off here. Thank you, for your time. I'll make sure to tell Brad that this helped." Dabria rose and thrust out her hand in parting.

Dr. Robinson also rose but did not extend her hand.

"Is Brad your boss?" she asked quietly.

"Yes, Brad Howell, the Executive Director of Legal Aid. Why?"

"I apologize, Ms. Abdulla-Smythe. I should have asked you earlier where you worked."

"Why is that?"

"Brad is my husband and you may feel it is a conflict of interest for me to speak to you."

"Are you going to tell Brad what I told you?" Dabria asked bluntly.

"No," she sincerely responded.

"Then rest assured that there is no conflict especially since I won't be seeing you again."

"I hoped I could be of some assistance to you," Dr. Robinson gently expressed. "But, I don't believe that this session was very beneficial to you. I do, however, believe that it would be helpful for you to continue counseling with another psychologist." Dabria's flip manner didn't fool her for a second. This was a woman that was hurting. Her defensive attitude indicated that although the events of the weekend had been traumatizing she had obviously survived far worse trauma and had yet to deal with it.

~ ~ ~

If Dabria thought she was having a crappy day it was nothing in comparison to Morgan's. The "shit hit the fan" at the detachment when Morgan was called into his supervisor's office around noon.

"I see we had a lot going on this weekend. I read your reports and I have a few questions about some of the omissions," remarked the Staff Sergeant. "Sit down. This could take a while."

"Omissions?"

"Yah, and don't get smart with me. First of all your *girlfriend's* statement indicates that she heard the kid talking to *his* dead girlfriend but she is *unsure* of what he said. I have more than one officer that claims they heard him say straight out that he had killed the girl."

"I . . ."

"Don't bother interrupting me. I'm far from finished. You interrogated a suspect without a lawyer present and talked him into giving you a statement, a DNA sample, and fingerprints. Some lawyer is going to claim that while under duress, your suspect was coerced by the police into cooperating. You then released the kid without checking with me first and actually gave him a ride home. Next, you proceeded to question his mother, again without council present. Are you aware of whom this kid's mother is married to?" When Morgan was about to respond his supervisor put up his hand to silence him yet again. "Then the icing on the cake is that you sneak the kid into the morgue after dark to say goodbye to his dead girlfriend." He shook his head in exasperation. "You have been here less than three months and in that short time you have disregarded procedures on a regular basis. Despite the fact that some of your unorthodox methods have paid off in the past this is not Toronto and you are not the "King of the Drug Lords" here. Judge Reynolds called me first thing this morning and wants an explanation as to why he wasn't informed before you questioned his wife. Where do you want to begin?" The Staff Sergeant sat up straight in his chair, with his hands steepled, glaring at Morgan, and waiting for a response.

"I asked Cody to tell me what happened and when he questioned whether he needed a lawyer present I assured him he did not. He *didn't* kill either of those women and he didn't *admit* to doing it either. What he said was that he felt *responsible* for Megan's death. There's a huge difference."

"I have sworn statements, Morgan, that say he did admit to killing her."

"From fellow officers that are taking his comments out of context?"

"That may well be, but they still heard what they heard."

"There are omissions in my report because Cody asked me to keep some things that we talked about private, to protect his mother. I am well aware of whom his mother is married to and I have read the reports on Cody's past behavior. He volunteered the DNA and the fingerprints."

"Why would Cody need to protect his mother?"

"Is this off the record?"

"There's nobody here but the two of us. Spill it."

"Judge Reynolds has been abusing Cody and his mother for years."

"And you know that how?"

"Cody told me and I confirmed it by speaking to the school psychologist, the family doctor, and other family members last night and this morning. If I had allowed Mrs. Reynolds to contact her husband before speaking with us, he may have prevented her from telling the truth about her whereabouts on Saturday night and Sunday morning. The kid's only alibi is his mother. I couldn't risk that her husband's interference might change her story."

"Well, guess what? The story has changed already. Judge Reynolds claims you intimidated his wife into backing up her son, when in reality Mrs. Reynolds never left town until after midnight. And that was only after her son showed up on their doorstep, obviously distraught. Apparently, she then took *him* back out to the reserve to calm *him* down and then spent the rest of the night there. Did any one of these people you questioned actually witness this abuse or have proof? And by proof I mean pictures of bruises or x-rays of broken bones?"

"No."

"So, your *witnesses* are useless."

"They aren't useless to me. I just have to find some way to prove their claims, which is why I didn't include that in my report. The only reason I'm telling you this now is so that you understand why I've done the things I have and so that you allow me to further investigate Judge Reynolds."

"Checking out the Judge is on your own time and, for now, without the approval of this office. Understand."

"Absolutely."

"Fine. So, you believe the kid's story but at this point he has no alibi. The physical evidence as well as your witnessing him with Megan is going to prove that he was there. We have on record that the kid has a history of violent behavior. We have no other suspects. So far the only defense this kid has is that he had no motive. Am I missing anything?"

"Yes. Megan was pregnant," Morgan reported with a sigh.

"You've got to be kidding?" the Staff Sergeant shook his head in disbelief. "*Now* we have potential motive."

"Yes, and I'm sure the DNA will prove that the child was his."

"Okay. You give me your theory and tell me how you're going to prove it."

Morgan gave his captain the same story he had given Ducette the night before.

"So, you felt sorry for the kid and that's why you snuck him back into the morgue last night."

"Yes."

"At this point the only people that know are the Chief ME, the kid, you, and I. I'm hoping that all of us are smart enough to keep this under wraps. As for the rest, unless you can find me some other suspects within the next forty-eight hours we will probably be charging Mr. Saddleback. For now this kid has only got one thing, wait, possibly two things, going for him and that would be you and your *girlfriend*. Detective French doesn't believe for one minute that she didn't hear exactly what Cody said. And, neither do I. I don't want to see or hear about any more showboating. Got it? From now on you better be keeping me apprised of every new development within hours of that said development. Understood? Since Ducette and you started on this case the two of you will continue to work together with a team. I'm appointing you team leader." Shaking his finger at Morgan he dismissed him with a final command, "I expect a verbal progress report before midnight tonight."

"So," Ducette asked as Morgan returned to his desk. "How'd that go?"

"Better than I expected, actually. We have a team of four and forty-eight hours to find Megan's killer. So call Sarah and say goodbye, because for the next two days we are *on duty*."

Morgan called his team into a conference room and they set up a timeline of events, posted crime scene photos on a bulletin board, and drew up a list of potential suspects. Finally they made a list of duties, including interviews that needed to be conducted, information regarding the autopsy, etc. Once the list was complete and duties delegated they each headed out. Morgan's immediate focus was the Medical Examiner's Office. The chief ME had supervised Megan and the latest *scalper* victim's autopsies himself. Morgan met him in his office. After confirming with the Staff Sergeant that Morgan was indeed still the detective in charge of Megan's murder investigation and that he had the right to access of information regarding the scalped victims he answered Morgan's questions freely.

"I guess the obvious question is what did she die of?"

"A broken neck. He clearly came up behind her and snapped it instantly since there are no defensive markings at all. She never knew what hit her."

"You say *he* because?"

"It's doubtful that a woman has the kind of strength to execute a maneuver like that."

"Why do you think it was an attack from behind?"

"The way the bones broke indicated that he came up behind her and wrenched her head up and to the left. That also tells me he is taller than her and probably left handed. She wouldn't have made a sound nor even bled one drop of blood. He then placed her on her back in the same pose as the scalped victims with her hands resting on her chest."

"What leads you to that conclusion?"

"The postmortem lividity or livor mortis indicates where the blood pooled."

"Can you tell me time of death?"

"Not as precisely as you would like me to, I'm sure."

"Why not?"

"Because predicting time of death is far from an exact science. There are three sources of evidence that we use to estimate time of death. They are corporal evidence, environmental evidence, and anamnestic evidence. Basically, what this means is that we need to determine the answer to nine basic questions. Algor mortis or core body temperature is the first. Because she was laid out in the cold snow her body cooled off much quicker than if she had been inside where it was warm. According to the weather service Saturday night's temperature was around -20° Celsius. There was a slight breeze and some light snowfall. She had several layers of clothes on and she was pregnant. All of these factors affect the rate a body cools after death. Before we transported her we inserted a thermo couple into her liver and took a reading that way. When I saw the initial printout my immediate guess was that she had died within the last couple of hours despite the outside temperature. That was before I knew she was pregnant."

"The next question is rigor mortis. The cold slows the process of rigor. Simply put, under perfect circumstances if rigor seems to be progressing, death has occurred between two and nine hours previously, again depending on several factors."

"From what I saw she was in full rigor. She was stiff as a board. What's the time frame for full rigor mortis?"

"Again I stress, under perfect circumstances, it would indicate that death occurred more than nine hours previously. Unfortunately, you're wrong about her being in full rigor. After we brought her back here and warmed her up full rigor didn't actually set in until after your boy came to say good-bye last night. She appeared stiff earlier because the rigor was progressing and she was half frozen."

"Okay. So, what's the next thing you check?"

"Postmortem lividity, which I already explained. Postmortem decomposition is next. But again this is affected by the external temperature. Anything below 10°C and the rate of decomp decreases dramatically. The concentration of potassium in the vitreous humour of the eyes can also be telling. A white film seems to form over the eyes making them look cloudy. When the eyes are closed this takes between twelve and twenty-four hours."

"Next," Morgan prompted, swiftly becoming totally disheartened.

"Six and Seven would be Adipocere, which is the transformation of fatty tissue into a wax-like substance, and Mummification. Both of these are not factors for this case. That leaves us with Maceration and stomach contents."

"Which is?"

"The decomp of a fetus still enclosed in the amniotic sac."

"I have a DNA sample of the alleged father. Can you do a DNA test for me from the remains of the fetus?"

"Absolutely."

"How pregnant was she?"

"She was seven months."

"Seven months!! Christ! That means the baby was alive after Megan died."

"Yes."

"Boy or girl?"

"It was a girl."

"So in reality we aren't looking for only Megan's killer but also her daughter's. What information can you tell from her daughter's death?"

"Basically that she suffocated. She needed Megan's oxygenated blood to breath. When Megan's blood stopped pumping so did the oxygen source. I can't tell you exactly when she died either, simply for the same reason that I can't give you an exact time of death for Megan."

"Are you telling me that you have no idea when Megan died?"

"No. The last thing I checked was stomach contents and I discovered she had eaten an apple about two hours before she died. Do we know who the last person was that she talked to and what time that was?"

"Yes. It was her boyfriend at around 10:00 p.m. Apparently he left her a message at midnight and she returned his message with one of her own shortly after. I'll have to check the time stamps on their cell phones. Thankfully we found hers close to where her body was laying. I'll ask him if he heard her eating anything while they talked."

"See that helps. If you can confirm that she left a voice message at or after midnight that's a place for me to start. On the assumption that Megan was killed by the same person that killed the fourth scalped victim, she was laid out around the same time the other victim was. Although, Megan had been moved, by her boyfriend, the other victim had not and she was covered by a dusting of snow. According to the weather station it didn't start to snow until after midnight, and then only lasted for about an hour. That fact along with the other *guestimates* and what you have just told me roughly puts her time of death sometime between midnight and 2:00 a.m."

"Is there anything else I need to know?"

"She had sexual relations sometime in the last forty-eight hours as I found motile sperm in her vagina. Her only distinguishing mark was a tattoo on her lower back of a "phoenix." Beyond her neck there was no evidence of assault or trauma. She was in excellent health and physical condition."

"You didn't happen to find a ring in her personal effects?"

"No. Here's a list of what I did find though."

Morgan quickly skimmed the list.

"Could you go back and check her ring finger and see if she could have been wearing a ring that might have been pulled off?"

"Of course, but, if it was loose there would be little or no damage to her finger."

"I understand. Okay. What about the other victim?"

"Again, I have similar problems due to weather. However, I can tell you she died the same as the other scalped victims. She bled to death. Her killer cut the femoral vein in her thigh and simply let her bleed out. He washed her body with lavender soap and then dried her. Her degree of frozenness was more evident since she had obviously bled out at least a couple hours before he transported her. Plus, she had no clothes on for insulation and no heat source due to pregnancy."

"Did she have any defensive wounds?"

"No. But like the others, there were marks on her."

"Such as?"

"Identical incision in the femoral artery, vaginal bruising and bruises on the breasts like the last two victims, and this time very obvious IV punctures, with slight bruising from prolonged use."

"Did the others not have IV punctures?"

"Not as apparent."

"So these women are drugged and then raped."

"Yes."

"Do you know what drug he uses?"

"Succinylcholine"

"What?"

"Succinylcholine. Its trade names are Anectine or Scoline. It causes paralysis, but with no loss of sensation or consciousness. It is commonly used in combination with two other drugs for anesthetic. It is a white crystalline substance that is highly soluble in water."

"You don't think these women are conscious when they die, do you?" Morgan asked disgustedly.

"Unfortunately, I think it's a distinct possibility. The drug allows the killer to have a totally captive audience. He can talk to her and she hears. He can touch her and she feels. She can see him and smell him but her responses are only those that are autonomic like breathing. Meaning she can't make herself move or speak. There is evidence of sexual activity in the form of bruising on their breasts and inside their vaginas, as well as latex residue inside the vaginas of the last two women. The drug is difficult to administer and if not monitored and doled out correctly the results can be lethal. Sometimes it's used as the paralyzing agent for executions by lethal injection. I can tell from the toxicology reports from brain tissue extracted from these women that each new victim has a lower level of drugs in their systems. That may be why he has to keep finding new victims. The original woman died because he unwittingly overdosed her and her heart simply stopped beating. The next one became catatonic and he was forced to kill her. I believe they're useless to him if they aren't conscious of him."

"When does he scalp these women?"

"After he's ex-sanguinated them, or bled them dry."

"How do you know that?"

"There's soap residue on their bodies but not on their skulls."

"Do you think all four of these women were killed by the same man?"

"I do."

"Despite the fact that he didn't scalp Megan?"

"Operating on the premise that the killer cut a young lady in the bar on Friday night and witnessed the mess that made, I'm guessing he didn't want that kind of mess near the sterile, perfect death pose of his latest victim. Megan was different, anyways. She was young, innocent looking, and more importantly looked nothing like the rest of his victims. She was fair skinned and blond."

"Well, sir, you have been a fountain of information. Thanks for your time and insight."

"I'll let you know about the ring," the coroner promised as Morgan moved to the door. He headed back to the station to check on the cell phone situation.

Chapter 17

As Dabria's day drew to a close she was interrupted by a knock on her door. Brad stuck his head in and with raised brows questioned if he could come in.

"Come in, come in."

"So, how was your day?"

"It went fine and if you want an update on the psychologist, not only did I make the appointment but I already had the session."

"I know."

"Wow, word travels fast. I thought it was anonymous?" Dabria swiveled her head around scanning the ceiling, then peeked under her desk pretending to look for a surveillance camera, and finally picked up the receiver of her phone and gently banged it on her desk searching for bugs. Brad patiently waited for her to finish her theatrics. "Let me guess. Jaimie told you I was gone to an appointment?"

"Yes, and I have come to the conclusion that you are a *take the bull by the horns* kind of girl who doesn't tend to put things off if they can be dealt with immediately" he answered. "What are your thoughts on how things went?"

"Dr. Robertson was very professional. She allowed me to relate the events of the weekend without interruption and when I informed her that venting had been helpful she indicated that she was glad."

"And from your point of view that should be that?"

"Yes. My mother is a psychologist. So, I know how the whole thing works. I've been under analysis my whole life. However, Dr. Robertson did suggest that I continue counseling with someone else."

"Are you aware that Dr. Robertson is my wife?"

"I am now. However, since I won't be seeing her again it is really a mute point."

Brad had sunk into a chair upon arrival and now straightened up.

"If you decide to continue with someone else and need time off you know that is a non-issue, right?"

"Yes, thank you."

"Are you wrapping things up for the day?"

"Not yet. I have a few things I'd like to finish."

"Don't work too late. Tomorrow's another day. I'll see you in the morning."

"Good night."

Brad left her to reflect on their conversation.

Her reflections were cut short when seconds later her cell phone rang.

"Hey. It's me. Have you got time to grab a bite?" asked Morgan.

"I was planning on working late tonight and I'd really rather not interrupt the rhythm I've got going. If you want to pick up something and bring it here I'm game, if not I'll have to pass."

"I have some other interviews to conduct away from the station so I'll get something and stop in. Any requests?"

"I had Chinese for lunch so anything but that. Call me when you get here and I'll run downstairs and let you in. The doors are locked at 5:00 p.m."

"Great. See you in a bit."

As Dabria signed off another knock interrupted her and Craig stuck his head in.

"I see I'm interrupting," he commented without apology as he heard her sigh and witnessed the look of dismay that creased her brow. "Are you in for the long haul?"

"A few more hours at least. I didn't get much accomplished this weekend so I'm playing catch up."

"I heard there was some excitement after I left the bar on Friday night. Are you okay? I tried to call you Saturday after I found out, but you must have an unlisted number."

"I do. All of my friends and family have my numbers and I don't believe that the general public needs them. The girls in reception have both my home and my cell numbers if it's an emergency."

"Makes sense," Craig continued to lounge against the doorframe deliberately refusing to ask for the numbers, despite the fact that Dabria knew he'd take them down if she offered.

Rather than making this into something it didn't need to be, she wrote the numbers on a sticky note and without comment passed them over to him.

"Thank you," he responded knowing full well that she could just as easily have kept them to herself to further reinforce the shield she had surrounding herself. "Here's mine," he whipped a business card out of his pocket with his cell number written in pen on the back of it and passed it to her.

"You're welcome. And I'm fine. I have a few bruises and a few stitches, which itch like the devil, but otherwise all is well," she informed him as she accepted his outstretched card.

"I'm glad to hear that. So how's the rest of the week?"

"Really busy."

"Are you moving this weekend?"

"Yes."

"Do you need some help?"

"I actually have movers coming, but you can stop in for a visit if you like. Sarah already said she may stop by."

"I think I will then. I'll let you get back to it. Talk to you later. I'll leave your door open and lock up downstairs since you and I are the last ones here."

"Thanks. Detective Vaughn is on his way over. If you see him, please let him in. See you tomorrow," Dabria quipped. No sooner had Craig left then Dabria's cell phone rang again.

"I'm here."

"That was quick. What are we having, vending machine cuisine? Craig is on his way out. He can let you in and lock up behind you."

"Okay." Moments later Morgan appeared in her doorway empty handed.

"Morgan. I don't have time to go out," Dabria complained, exasperated.

"Settle down. I've ordered something and they'll call me when they arrive."

"Sorry. How was your day?"

"Let me sum it up this way. I've got forty-eight hours to find some other viable suspect or they're gonna charge Cody. And you?"

"I requested to help if Legal Aid represents him. The answer was a resounding NO. I also got to go see a shrink this afternoon." They both shared the events of their day and somewhere in between all that, their supper arrived. By 6:30 p.m. supper was done and it was time for both of them to get back to work. He gave her a long slow goodbye kiss.

"Call me on my cell when you leave tonight."

"You want me to check in with you?" she pulled back in his arms.

"Yes. I want to know you're safe." He looked down at her without letting her go.

Dabria pushed out of his arms.

"Morgan, while the sex is great it doesn't give you the right to control my movements."

"I wouldn't classify worrying about your safety as controlling, would you?" Dabria had moved back behind the desk, not so subtly, creating a barrier between them.

"Dabria, I'm not trying to scare you off, but I don't look at this weekend as just a booty call. That, however, is a totally separate issue from *this* issue, which is safety. I'm asking you to take a few seconds out of your life to assure me of your safety so that I can concentrate on finding this freak. Why is that threatening to you?"

"I don't know. I'm just not used to reporting in to anyone. I haven't had to answer for my actions for years."

"You're taking this all wrong. I want you safe. It's that simple. Will you call me—yes or no?"

"I'll call."

"Thank you. Promise me you'll stay alert when you're out and about. I have a feeling that if our killer finds out who you are, you're gonna become his number one target."

"Seriously?"

"Yes."

"Well, I promise not to take rides from any strange men or to change my profession any time soon."

"Not funny, Dabria. Serial killers are often people that blend right in. It's not like you're going to recognize him by what he wears, his profession, or where he might hang out. Although his targets so far have been street walkers that doesn't mean he isn't what society would classify as respectable and responsible. Just stay alert and let me know if you have any funny feelings like being followed or watched."

"I promise. Now that you've totally freaked me out I'd like to get back to work."

Morgan leaned across the desk and gave her a quick peck. "You can't hide behind that desk all night if you want to get some work done, because you have to lock me out."

Realizing she had forgotten that very important point she joined him by the door and they walked down together. After locking things up, Dabria returned to her office and put in another couple of hours.

The ringing of Dabria's cell phone startled her as she was absorbed in her work. With a pounding heart she checked the display and then answered.

"Dabria?"

"Hello Colin."

"Hey. So, are you all packed and ready to move in?" he asked.

"Pretty much, thanks."

"Is there anything we missed or anything I can help you with?"

"No, I'm good."

"I'm not disturbing you, am I?" he questioned as he noticed her responses were brief and she seemed distracted.

"Well, actually, Colin, I'm kind of in the middle of working on a case and really should get back to it."

"Oh, sorry, I didn't realize you were working."

"That's okay. Was there something specific you wanted?"

"I just thought I'd make sure things were going well and see if you needed help moving."

"Thanks, but I've hired movers."

"Good. Well, once you're moved in, maybe we can catch a cup of coffee sometime?"

"Colin, that sounds nice. I'm kind of overwhelmed right now with work but if I get a spare moment maybe we can."

"Great! Well, I'll let you go. I'll meet you at the cottage Saturday morning. See you then."

"Bye, Colin." That was unexpected. She had never really played the dating game and so having Morgan, Craig, Marshall, and Colin ask her out was flattering. It wasn't as if she hadn't been occasionally asked out by other men over the years but all of her childhood friends and her previous co-workers knew of her relationship with David. Maybe she should play the field a little, rather than focusing only on Morgan? All four men were very different and interesting in their own ways. Meeting Marshall for a coffee at this point probably wasn't the best idea though. And Craig *was* still a co-worker and Colin *was* still her real estate agent. So actually, Morgan was the only one that couldn't profit or benefit professionally from their association. For now maybe she should just concentrate on her new job, her new home, and enjoy great sex with one hot cop. Shaking her head she refocused on the file in front of her.

After another two hours she stretched, tidied her desk, and dialed Morgan while she locked up.

"I'm leaving now."

"Fine. Call me when you get home."

"Yes, sir. I've a couple of stops to make first."

Dabria picked up some milk and a couple of newspapers, one local and two provincial. She then swung past the post office to pick up her mail. After locking herself inside her apartment she called Morgan back.

"I'm home, safe and sound."

"Good, sweet dreams. I'll talk to you tomorrow."

"How's it going?"

"I'll let you know tomorrow."

Dabria signed off again and poured a bath. While she soaked she flipped through the papers looking for any articles relating to the events of the weekend. Unlike the previous three murders, this one made the front page of the city paper and was on the second page of the two provincial ones. Suddenly, since a *respectable* young woman had been murdered there was interest and outrage on the part of the reporters. All three papers promised further articles as the information was released by the police. How sad that Megan's death had to be the catalyst to make the public stand up and realize someone was murdering the young women of this area.

~ ~ ~

Morgan decided it was time to head home and get some zzzs. The other members of the team had left an hour earlier. He had stayed to make up a new list of unanswered questions for them to focus on in the morning. Although they had answers to some of their original questions those answers led to more questions. At this point without Cody's mom to back up his alibi things were not looking really good for the boy.

~ ~ ~

Despite following up every lead they had and interviewing everyone who could possibly shed some light on the case the conclusion was that at the end of the forty-eight hours the only person with possible motive who had proven access to the victim was Cody. If his mother had stuck to her original claims of being with him from 10:30 p.m. Saturday night until noon on Sunday he would have had an alibi. Because it was his mother, that alibi still would have been questioned, but at least it might have created enough doubt in the minds of Morgan's superiors to hold off on arresting and charging Cody. As it was, since his own mother wouldn't back him up, Morgan's law enforcement superiors were left with no choice but to conclude that he had in fact done the killing. The question of *the scalper* murders was still up in the air and not only French but the other officers on the case all agreed that they were looking for someone other than Cody. That was the added encouragement that Morgan needed to continue his investigation into Megan's murder. Not only did he believe that Megan's killer and *the scalper* were one and the same, but so did Detective French.

On Wednesday afternoon at 1:00 p.m., Cody Saddleback was formally arrested and charged with the first degree murder of Megan Thomas by Detectives Morgan Vaughn and Kent Ducette. After being properly read his Rights to Council, strip searched, and photographed he was allowed his one call. He made that call to Dabria.

Luckily, Dabria was in the office and available. She wasn't shocked by the call since Morgan had indicated to her the evening before, that things weren't going well.

"Good afternoon, this is Ms. Abdulla-Smythe. How may I help you?"

"Hey. This is Cody. Cody Saddleback. You found me by the river on Sunday."

"Hello, Cody. What can I do for you?"

"I don't know if you've heard but I've been charged with Megan's murder and I need a lawyer. Can you either represent me or suggest someone you think would be good for me?"

"Cody, I can't represent you but I will definitely find someone who can. I promise someone will be out to see you later this afternoon. Is there anyone you need me to contact, your mom or your aunties?"

"You could give my aunties a call and ask them to keep an eye on my place. Thanks."

Dabria immediately called Morgan. "What are the charges against Cody?"

"Did he call you?"

"Yes, and I need to know exactly what he's charged with before I go to Brad and inform him that Cody wants Legal Aid to represent him."

"He's charged with First Degree Murder and his bail hearing will be tomorrow morning."

"Where is he being held?"

"Here, for now. Dabria, I need to talk to him again about a girl named Tehya from his reserve. I think she knows something about that night and she's holding back."

"I'll see what I can do. Thanks. I'll call you later." Dabria then promptly called Brad and asked if he could spare a minute for a conference. He told her to come on up. She wasted no time heading to his office.

"Hi. I'll make this brief. Cody Saddleback just called from lock-up and requested that I represent him or recommend someone who could. He's been charged with First Degree Murder."

"I'll check into whose up for the next criminal case but I believe its Craig. You did tell him you can't represent him, right?"

"Yes, but I did say I would find someone who could and that they would go see him this afternoon."

"I'll take care of this Dabria. Trust me," he encouraged.

"I will, sir." Dabria made her way back to her office and continued to finish up the notes she'd been working on before Cody's call. Within the hour Brad had called her back up to his office. Craig was already sitting there.

"Okay. Here's the deal. Craig is going to be chief counsel. He will pick a team to work with him. I want to be given daily reports on the progress of this case since this is probably the highest profile case we have done in years and everything we do is going to be ruthlessly scrutinized by the public. We need to proceed with caution and stay strictly within the confines of the law. There is no room for emotional decisions. I know you believe he's innocent, Dabria, but without proof the only recourse we have is to make sure he is treated fairly and that his constitutional rights as a Canadian citizen aren't violated."

"Do you know if the police plan on continuing this investigation or if they are classifying this file as closed?" Craig interjected.

"I don't know what the official word is but I do know that Detective Vaughn will be continuing to investigate. As will I," she reaffirmed.

"You know you can't be part of the team, right Dabria?" Craig asked

"Yes. But that doesn't mean I can't continue to look for evidence on my own time. I would never do anything to risk Cody's defense."

"So if you find information that would help Cody you will inform me of it?"

"Of course, Craig. Also, Detective Vaughn mentioned to me today that he wanted to question Cody about a girl that lives on the reserve. She lives with Cody's Aunt and he thinks that she may be holding back something she knows about that night."

"I'll ask Cody about her. What's her name?"

"Teyha."

"Okay, Craig, go down to the station and talk to the boy. I'll stay here until you get back and you can give me a rundown of what he had to say," Brad directed.

Craig immediately headed to lock-up. Upon arrival he was directed to a private interview room and Cody was brought in minutes later shackled but dressed in his own clothes rather than in regulation prison garb.

"Hi, Cody, I'm Craig Martin. I work for Legal Aid. Before I get your story I need to confirm that you qualify to have me represent you. If you do I'll be the chief litigator and the head of your defense team. Can I get you something before I start?" Craig asked

"No, thanks. I'm good."

Craig had obtained a copy of Cody's signed statement from Detective Ducette upon entering the station and had breezed through it before Cody's arrival. After assuring that Cody did indeed qualify for Legal Aid he then had Cody retell the entire story and crosschecked that with his signed statement. The story matched almost perfectly—almost too perfectly.

"At this point my advice is to plead *not guilty* tomorrow morning at the bail hearing. Once I've had time to review the crown's case against you I'll determine if that plea needs to be changed."

"I don't understand why reviewing the evidence should have an effect on my plea. I didn't kill Megan. It's that simple."

"I'll see you in the morning, Cody." Craig totally ignored Cody's last comment and rose to leave.

"I said I didn't kill Megan. Do you believe me or not?" the volume of Cody's voice hadn't risen but he had stiffened up and glared defiantly at Craig.

"Unlike Ms. Abdulla-Smythe, I was not on the riverbank on Sunday. This is the first time I have laid eyes on you, or spoken to you and therefore I neither believe nor disbelieve your claim. My job is to give you the best representation that I am capable of. On that, I promise you I will deliver. At this point your innocence is irrelevant to me. There is a more important issue. What kind of a case has the police department built against you? Do you understand?"

"Completely." Cody now also stood.

"Did anyone explain to you what happens next and where you'll be kept?"

"Yes, Detective Vaughn did."

"Okay. Do you have any other questions then before I leave?"

"Yah, but at this point you don't have any more answers than I do. I'll see you tomorrow."

"Oh, one more thing, Cody. Do you know a girl named Tehya?"

"Sure. Why?"

"Detective Vaughn thinks she may have some information that could have an impact on your case. However, until the hearing is over tomorrow and I have some time to review your case I would prefer that you not speak with any of the detectives again," Craig warned as he saw Cody instantly stiffen up.

"Fine," Cody agreed.

Craig exited the police station and ran into Dabria.

"You aren't checking up on me, are you?" he asked.

"Of course not," she assured him. "I came to see Detective French. Apparently he had some more questions for me."

"Good. Because I would hate to think that you don't believe I can handle this case. I advised Cody not to speak with the police again until after I give him the go ahead to do so. So you can pass along to the detectives that no more questioning will occur without me present."

"I told you I would never jeopardize Cody's case. Why are you laying down the law on me?"

"You may be snowed by Vaughn but I don't trust that he's looking out for Cody's best interests. If *your* detective needs to question him again he can go through the proper channels on his side. Are you 100% sure that Morgan is convinced of Cody's innocence. Or is he using you to help build his own case? Also," he instantly quelled her urge to interrupt with a look of barely controlled hostility, "your sympathy isn't going to help Cody. He doesn't need *warm fuzzies* from you. He wants me to do my job, which is to convince a jury that he is *not* guilty. Since that isn't going to be an easy job to do, I need to stay focused on the end result rather than worrying about whether you and the police are privy to information you should not be."

Dabria stifled the gasp of alarm that automatically arose from the vehemence of his speech. This was a side of Craig that was unexpected but probably served him well when he was facing an opponent in court. If she could convince him of Cody's innocence his aggressive qualities could benefit Cody's cause. Stiffening her own spine and showing him she would not be cowed she replied.

"I am positive that Detective Vaughn and I both believe Cody is innocent. I agree with you that the primary goal is to get him acquitted. However, have *you* ever been charged with murder or even been suspected of committing a crime, and all at the ripe old age of eighteen?"

"No."

"Then try putting yourself in his shoes for a minute. How scary is his life right now? Add to that, the fact that your own mother just lied, which destroyed your alibi. Plus, let's not forget the woman you love *and* your child were murdered. Right now you can be the tough guy in front of him and I'll continue to search for the truth with or without your or the police's help," she promised him. "Don't be fooled into thinking that because I have expressed compassion for Cody and his situation that I can't be tough when I need to be. When someone I know is being unjustly accused I'm like a pit bull with a bone. I don't give up without a fight."

Chapter 18

After Detective French finished with Dabria she decided not to return to the office but instead to compile a list of questions that needed to be asked, and made notes on research that needed to be done. She knew that although Craig would request Cody be released, that request would be denied and bail would either be set extremely high or denied altogether. Now that the system had him they weren't going to give him up without a fight. The politics of the case decreed that someone pay for the death of that young girl. It didn't necessarily matter that they might have the wrong person. Since he wasn't being charged with the other murders, a new murder, unfortunately, would have no bearing on Cody's innocence or the opinions of the general public.

Cody's team arrived at the courthouse bright and early the next morning and supported him while the bail hearing took place. Not surprisingly, bail was denied, despite his plea and Cody was informed that he would remain in lock-up until his trial commenced. After being led from the courtroom in shackles, he was removed to an interview room to consult with his legal team. They spent the rest of the morning together while Craig collected a list of names and locations of all of Cody's friends, acquaintances—including Tehya—teachers, and employers, as well as his relatives.

They had him relate any incidents of skirmishes with not only people in authority but also his peers over the course of his life. Thankfully, he had pretty much stuck to the straight and narrow with that one exception of the incident where he was defending Megan's honor. Therefore, the only real area of concern, regarding his past behavior, was whether or not the prosecution would enlist the testimony of Cody's stepfather. He was definitely *a loose cannon*. Because of his alleged hatred of Cody and his proven control over Cody's mother, there was a good possibility that given the opportunity to disclaim Cody and have him removed from their life permanently, the good Judge Reynolds would jump at the chance. He was in the perfect position to add a few nails to Cody's coffin. He simply needed to indicate to the jury that Cody had been a difficult, defiant child whom often had to be sent back to the reserve because of his behavior.

~ ~ ~

Dabria's own amateur investigating turned up the fact that Judge Reynolds was Cody's stepfather and that there was no love lost between the two of them. She told Morgan that she would not be allowed to collaborate with Cody's defense team but assured him that she was more than willing to help him with his investigation. Morgan gently reminded her that although he would appreciate any help she gave him he would be unable to share everything he knew with her. Her hands were tied preventing her from hands on defending Cody and because Morgan couldn't allow her carte blanche with all the evidence in the case she almost felt like she was Cody's only true champion. That made her commitment to him even stronger since she knew with every part of her being that Cody was innocent. Strangely, she had a gut feeling that discrediting the judge was key to Cody's defense. She realized this was going to be a monumental task. However, Dabria's petite, pretty appearance belied her dogged determination when presented with a cause she was passionate about. If there were any skeletons in Judge Reynolds' closet, Dabria vowed to shake them out.

Dabria pitched her idea to both Craig and Morgan and they unnecessarily informed her that neither the police department's budget nor Legal Aid's budget included funds for hiring private detectives to investigate *prominent, well respected* judges—for no good reason. She promptly informed them that she would be footing the bill for the PI personally. Craig agreed to indulge her since he had been up against Judge Reynolds on several occasions and found him to be more arrogant than most, and as previously noted, quite eccentric. He wouldn't be heartbroken to have him taken down a peg or two. The fact that somehow Cody's mother's statement, regarding the events and timeline of Saturday night, had mysteriously changed after returning home to her husband, definitely entered into the equation. The question was how would Brad react to her investigations?

Surprisingly, Brad agreed to it. He indicated since it did not involve Legal Aid funds that he would allow the investigation providing that Craig sought out other forms of defense as well and that Dabria concentrated on Legal Aid cases during office hours. What he didn't tell them was that he had known Judge Reynolds before he ever became a judge and that the two of them had been in private practice together years ago. The partnership had dissolved due to his own questions regarding the legitimacy and suspect practices of the then "Counselor" Reynolds. If the PI was worth his salt it wouldn't take him long to discover that fact and once he presented this to Dabria and Craig, Brad decided he would volunteer his personal involvement and add a few tidbits to their investigation.

~ ~ ~

Downtown Morgan was busy working on other cases since his superiors informed him that as far as they were concerned they had their man and it was time to concentrate on solving other crimes. He did talk Ducette into going back out to the reserve to question Tehya to see what he could shake loose. Morgan was convinced there was something there that they were missing. Ducette's trip did produce one thing. She never said anything specific but Ducette was convinced by the time he left that she *was* definitely hiding something and strangely enough he noticed she was left handed. Thankfully, Cody requested a conference, in the presence of his lawyer, with Morgan and Ducette. He informed them that Tehya had transferred to his school that fall when she had moved in with his Auntie. They weren't friends exactly but he had tried to introduce her around at school and help her to settle in. She hung out with some of the same crowd as Cody, but since he had spent almost all of his time with Megan Cody didn't know that much about her. He said she was quiet and almost reticent. He assured them that Leotie would know more about her background as well as her personality. As far as Cody was concerned Tehya was a non-issue. Morgan secretly disagreed.

Ducette returned to the reserve to try to ferret out more information from Leotie. She was surprisingly accommodating. She informed Ducette that Tehya had come from a family that lived in a small remote northern community where, unfortunately, substance abuse was rampant. There had also been some evidence of physical abuse when she had first arrived. Leotie and Tehya's grandmother had grown up together. Her grandmother believed that Tehya's best chance at a normal life was if she was sent to live with Leotie. She had been working toward that end for many years. Once Tehya turned sixteen her mother had finally allowed her to go. She was a smart girl but behind in school so Leotie registered her in high school with Cody. She agreed with Cody that Teyha was reserved but pointed out that was hardly surprising considering how she had spent the first sixteen years of her life. Although her mother loved her she was neglectful and slovenly. Tehya was often secretive about her comings and goings but because she attended school faithfully and was doing well in it, as well as engaging in some extra-curricular school activities, Leotie didn't push her. She didn't bring friends over, but Leotie knew that she had some because she had witnessed her receiving and sending texts and occasionally chuckling out loud when reading them. Leotie confirmed that Tehya had no great love for Megan. She wasn't outright rude to Cody's fiancé but she certainly wasn't friendly either. When Cody was around Tehya was ever watchful and attentive. Despite Leotie's cooperation Ducette had a sense that she was holding something back. Unfortunately, Tehya appeared to be conveniently unavailable while Ducette was there. Leotie was unsure where she was. Ducette's suspicion that he was being watched was not unfounded. Hidden, haunted eyes gratefully followed his departure from the reserve, instinctively knowing this was only a temporary reprieve.

~ ~ ~

As Dabria prepared to leave for the day Craig sauntered into her office.

"I just thought I'd keep you in the loop since you're gonna find out soon enough anyway. I just got a call from one of the clerks at the justice department. Cody has been remanded to the Corrections Facility in Saskatoon. Apparently, P.A.'s Corrections is full and so he had to be moved. That's gonna be bloody inconvenient since I already have a full schedule and running back and forth to Saskatoon is gonna waste time I don't have."

"If space becomes available here can we request to have him transferred back?"

"Sure. But that could be weeks from now."

"Well, there's nothing we can do about it and frankly he might be safer there."

"Why?"

"Judge Reynolds could be acquainted with inmates here and if Cody is telling the truth about the abuse he's suffered for the last several years, then I don't think it's a stretch to be concerned. Cody just might become clumsy again and end up tripping and falling into doors etc."

"Okay, Dabria, I'm willing to agree that Judge Reynolds is weird and maybe even abusive but I know he's not a stupid man and he would never tip his hand by raising the possibility of having his name linked to an incident regarding Cody inside the jail."

"Really. I have a gut feeling that our good Judge is arrogant enough that he might use his influence to have that boy hurt. So far he has avoided any repercussions regarding his behavior."

"Alleged behavior."

"Yah, yah . . . . alleged behavior," Dabria dismissed. "Anyways, I believe that he's better off out of town."

"Maybe so. I know the Assistant Director of the facility. I'll give her a call and have her keep an eye on your boy. Will that make you rest easier?"

"Yes, thank you."

~ ~ ~

As Friday afternoon rolled around Detective Ducette received a call from Sarah requesting that he help her pry Morgan and Dabria away from work long enough to grab a drink and have supper with them. Since both had been putting in roughly fifteen hour days and moving day was tomorrow, Morgan agreed that he could do with the break and volunteered to be the one to convince Dabria. At 5:01 p.m. he had

Jaimie, the receptionist, call Dabria's office. She was not there but was in the building somewhere. Jaimie tracked her down in Craig's office. After getting the go ahead from Craig he waltzed into Craig's office to spirit Dabria away.

"Sorry, old boy, I don't know if you had plans for keeping Dabria's nose to the grindstone this evening, but I'm afraid I need to abscond with her. I promise to return her no later than Monday morning at 8:00 a.m."

"Funny, Morgan," Dabria brushed him off. "We have work to do."

"Actually, Dabria, I think I've got all I need from you for now" Craig sided with Morgan as he pushed himself away from his desk and stood up and stretched. "I'm sure you must have some packing you want to finish. I'll see you tomorrow."

"Alright, you win," Dabria packed up her paraphernalia and trouped off to her office with Morgan trailing behind. As soon as he entered her office she indicated he close the door with a nod of her head. The second the door was closed she quietly blasted him.

"Don't you ever barge in on me again when I'm working and demand that I quit what I'm doing and go play with you. I have never, nor will I ever, interrupt you while you're at work."

"Well, that's a shame."

"Don't be a smart ass."

"I'm not. That *is* a shame and if you continue to bury yourself in work for days on end I will continue to interrupt and continue to drag you away. I know that it's easy to get caught up in the urgency and importance of our work. But, I also know that if you step back and take a breather that when you go back you see things that you missed before. It's better for everyone if you take a break, especially Cody. He's in no immediate danger tonight and his trial doesn't start tomorrow." Morgan had followed her around the desk and trapped her in her chair. "Come on, let me kiss that scowl right off your face," he coaxed. Neither Dabria nor Morgan heard the light tap on the door the second before Craig strode in.

"Hey, sorry to interrupt, Dabria, but you left your coat in my office."

Morgan slowly straightened revealing Dabria's flushed face. Up to this point Craig had been hesitant to acknowledge that there might be more than a professional relationship between Morgan and Dabria.

Dabria's face left little doubt that she had just been very thoroughly kissed.

"Thanks. Just throw it on the chair," Dabria recovered her composure and stood, pushing Morgan ahead of her as she attempted to round the desk. Morgan dutifully allowed her to steer him right out of the door, forcing Craig to back out into the hall.

"I'll wait for you downstairs. Detective Ducette is expecting us in about ten minutes," Morgan cheekily informed her.

"You didn't tell me that," she accused.

"You didn't give me a chance," he responded as he turned and made his way to the stairs.

"Does this have something to do with Cody?" Craig inquired.

"No. I'm pretty sure this has nothing to do with Cody. I'll see you tomorrow." Dabria went back into her office to tidy up and retrieve her briefcase, purse, and coat. When she closed her office door and ventured into the hall she subconsciously registered that the hall was abandoned. Dabria assumed Craig had followed Morgan out. She was wrong. Dabria hastened outside and over to her car, where Morgan slouched.

As she loaded her car the hair prickled at the base of Dabria's neck and she had an uncanny feeling that someone was watching her. When Morgan returned to his own vehicle she quickly spun around and looked up just in time to catch a glimpse of a shadow as it retreated from a third floor window. With an unfounded shiver of dread, Dabria refocused her attention on stowing her gear and sliding into the Tiburon to follow Morgan. All of Morgan's warnings and a definite lack of sleep were making her paranoid. She noticed that Craig's car was still parked in the lot as she pulled out and so was Jaimie's. Jaimie had been less outspoken since the paint-ball expedition and had actually offered to help Dabria move. Dabria had declined the offer but invited Jaimie out for a visit. Jaimie had taken down the directions but made no commitment regarding whether she would go out or not. Was Craig the one that stepped back from the window or was it Jaimie and if so, why were either one of them watching her? Shaking off the disturbing thoughts that followed those questions, she concentrated on driving to the apartment. As she pulled into her parking space she noticed Ducette and Sarah parked across the street waiting for her, with Morgan parked behind them. Sarah and Morgan both exited and walked across the street towards her.

"This was my idea," Sarah confessed with arms outstretched to ward off any verbal blows that Dabria might be slinging. "I hope you're not mad. I figured you could do with a night away from work before the big move. Do you need any help packing up tonight?"

"No. I'm not mad. I didn't realize what time it was or how tired I actually am until I started driving here. I finished packing last night so why don't we just head out and get some supper and have a few drinks. Then I can make an early night of it. The movers are going to be here in about five minutes to start loading. I'll just run up and get my suitcases and get them pointed in the right direction and then I can meet you guys. Where do you want to go?"

"Let's hit that new pizza place. Are they just loading tonight or are they unloading, too?" Sarah asked.

"Just loading. I'm supposed to meet them and the real estate agent at the cabin tomorrow morning at 9:00 a.m."

"I'll come up and grab the suitcases for you," Morgan volunteered. "We'll see you in a bit. Can you order some appetizers when you guys get there, Sarah? I missed lunch today and I'm starved."

Dabria and Morgan went up to the apartment. While Dabria changed and added the finishing touches to her suitcases Morgan let the movers in and directed them to call her cell when they were close to being finished. As supper drew to a close Dabria's phone rang signaling the end to their evening out. They drove back to the apartment and gave the movers directions for the following morning. Dabria swept and washed floors while Morgan vacuumed and gave all the counter tops a final wipe down. They were finished by 10:00 p.m.

"Where are you sleeping tonight?" Morgan asked, not so casually.

"I thought I'd get a room."

"You mean like a hotel room?"

"Of course."

"Dabria, that's silly. Come on, let's go to my place. I can pour you a tub and massage all the stress right out of you."

"Morgan, I'm really not up for a *massage* tonight. I'd really like to just get some sleep."

Morgan tilted her chin up so she was forced to look into his eyes. "I know that and I wasn't suggesting a *massage*. I was suggesting a massage.

I promise to be good. Let's go before you pass out and end up sleeping on the floor."

They made it to Morgan's place and he kept his word. He drew a bath and then left her alone. After twenty minutes of soaking he went in to check on her and discovered her fast asleep. Gently, he woke her up, dried her off, and then carried her to his bed. After tucking Dabria in he returned to the kitchen. Too keyed up to sleep, he set up the coffee for the morning and then fired up his laptop. Around 2:00 a.m. Dabria woke up, disoriented, and after establishing where she was, discovered that she was still alone. She slipped out of bed and grabbing a shirt from Morgan's closet she padded quietly into the kitchen following the light emanating from the computer screen.

"What are you still doing up?" she whispered near his ear as she wrapped her arms around him from behind. "I thought you said that was enough work for the week."

"It is. I wasn't tired so I was checking my emails."

Dabria glanced at the clock. "For three hours."

"I had a lot of personal emails I haven't had time to check," he defended.

Morgan pushed his chair away from the desk and he attempted to rise. Dabria pushed him back into the chair and straddled him. The sides of the shirt she had flung on parted, revealing her nakedness beneath. As she leaned into him to tease his lips with her tongue, her nipples drilled pinpricks of sensation into his chest as her breasts flattened against him. While her lips focused their attention on his face her hands wandered up under his T-shirt and caressed the muscles of his back. The playfulness swiftly turned to feverish movements on both parts and with her legs wrapped around him he stood and while holding her with one arm swept the contents of the table out of the way with the other arm. He laid her back onto it and in record time had undone his fly and released his already throbbing cock. She handed him a condom that she plucked from his shirt pocket and tearing into the foil he sheathed himself and drove into her without breaking the seal of their lips. She stiffened into an arch with the sudden intrusion and he held back thrusting until she again relaxed. Watching his fully clothed body pump into her virtually naked one was certainly a turn on. With frenzied determination he continued to plunge into her until he felt her stiffen again and then he allowed himself to be pulled over the edge. Panting from the exertion he rested his torso on her and held her close as he tried to calm his pounding heart. Once things had settled down he straightened and, still connected, he shucked his jeans and boxers. Then drawing her into his arms he carried her into the bedroom and flopped backwards onto the bed.

Within moments he was gently snoring. Dabria slid off him despite his sleepy attempt to hold her. She went to the bathroom and returned with a warm facecloth to clean him up. He reached for her again and this time she allowed him to pull her back into his arms. Snuggling into his embrace she drifted off as well.

The shrill sound of the alarm blaring at 7:00 a.m. scared the living daylights out of her and as she bolted upright Morgan calmly reached over and shut it off. Wide awake now she gasped, "Is that how you wake up every morning?"

"Sure. I take it that was a little much for you?"

"Ya think?"

"Yah," Morgan attempted to pull her back onto him. She swatted his hands away and scooted off the bed.

"Playtime is going to have to wait. I want to be on the road by 8:00 a.m."

"Then we better get at it," Morgan jumped from the bed and chased her into the bathroom. "I was raised by two conservationists that drilled into me the importance of conserving fresh water, so sharing a shower is the only option in my house."

"Reallllly . . . ." Dabria drawled.

"Absolutely," Morgan confirmed, with a devilish grin, as he adjusted the jets and pulled her in beside him. The shower was like a mini car wash. It had jets of water spouting from above and from all sides. It also had a bench. After swiftly soaping each other up and washing each other's hair, Morgan adjusted the jets so that one side of the shower didn't spray. The obvious evidence of Morgan's arousal resigned Dabria to the fact that despite her claim that there was no time for "playtime" she was definitely going to have to make the time. Although her own arousal was far less evident and she pretended disapproval, she was hardly disappointed when Morgan picked her up, stood her on the bench, and then started kneading her buttocks and licking her belly button. Braced against the stream-less side of the shower with her legs parted Dabria coached his movements with her hands plastered to his head. With eyes tightly squeezed shut she registered the simultaneous sensations of the pounding warm water, the heaviness of the steam, which caused her breathing to be even more labored, his talented ministrations upon her most private parts, as well as the pleasure/pain caused by the sandpaper roughness of his large hands as they went from kneading to gently probing and stroking. As Dabria's legs began to quiver Morgan placed his hands on the outside of her hips and held her in place as he sucked her over the edge. With a gasp Dabria arched into him and then slowly slithered down the shower wall to rest upon the bench. The sight that greeted her as she slowly opened her eyes was Morgan resting on his haunches in front of her with the satisfied grin of a Cheshire cat on his face.

"Did you really think that some silly movers were going to get in between me and my playtime?"

Dabria smiled weakly and rose to switch places. She pushed him onto the bench.

"Wait here." She slipped out of the shower and returned a few seconds later with a towel and a foil packet. She placed the folded towel on the floor of the shower directly in front of Morgan and gracefully sunk onto her knees on top of it. She coaxed his legs apart and had him rest his back against the wall of the shower. The water continued to pound down on them as she skillfully administered her own brand of slow torture to Morgan. Unlike Dabria, Morgan's eyes remained open as he voraciously devoured the sight before him and mentally recorded every sound, movement, and sensation of the exquisite pleasure she brought him. As Morgan's balls tightened, his stomach muscles corded, and his restless hands stilled on Dabria's shoulders, she grabbed the foil packet, ripped into it and sheathed him without losing a stroke. Rising to her feet she climbed on top of him and promptly settled herself onto his engorged and straining penis. Although he tried to hold back to give her a well deserved ride, she had brought him too close to completion with her mouth and after only two bounces he grabbed her hips and ground her into him as he exploded inside of her. Now "playtime" was over.

Dabria did beat the movers out, but barely. Colin was actually waiting for her. She let him conduct the final tour before he handed over the keys and she allowed the movers to begin. He promised he'd be back later to see how she was making out. Morgan had stayed in town to pick up provisions for the company that would be descending, as well as the basics for the two of them to eat for the next couple of days. As the moving truck rolled out the furniture truck from the store in P.A. rolled in. By noon Dabria had all of her new furniture, except the custom made pieces, and all of her boxes of belongings from the apartment stacked in the appropriate rooms. For now the loft over the garage would be her main residence for everything but cooking. Except for appliances, cooking paraphernalia, and her wardrobe, the cabin itself remained mostly bare.

Morgan was surprised that the cabin was so small. Being several inches over six feet, the top of his head barely made it under the doorframes. As he strolled in, laden with bags of groceries, Dabria made room on the small kitchen counter. When Morgan made an attempt to unpack, Dabria grabbed his hand and pulled him from room to room and then led him outside. Chattering nonstop, which was extremely uncharacteristic for her, Dabria extolled all of the virtues of her new abode and the surrounding property. Morgan was enchanted by the tiny sprite that flitted back and forth, with flushed face and bubbling narrative. He had never seen her so animated. This was another example of Dabria's passionate nature on display. By the time they had finished the tour Sarah and Kent pulled up. While Morgan unloaded the groceries and made some sandwiches, Dabria enthusiastically started her tour all over again. As one tour finished another began since Craig had now appeared. Kent helped Morgan assemble the natural gas BBQ and patio heater they found in boxes on the deck, as well as set up the patio furniture that had also been placed there. Sarah went to work on making beverages for everyone and unpacking dishes and glass wear. Just as Dabria finished with Craig, Colin, the real estate agent, re-appeared.

"Afternoon, Dabria. How's the move going?"

"The moving is done but now the unpacking starts."

"Need help?"

"Nah. I'll pick away at it since I'm not really sure where I want everything to go."

"I forgot the extra keys this morning and here's a gift certificate to say thanks for the business."

"*Shay's*. Thanks, I know I'll make use of this." How cliché that Colin had picked the same place as Craig. She wondered if he hoped she'd invite him to share it with her. "Can I get you a drink, Colin? We're having kind of a little impromptu get together."

"Sure," he readily agreed.

As she headed for the kitchen Brad and his wife stopped in. She left the keys and gift on the counter and went to greet her new guests. Brad indicated they were out looking for property and just happened to recognize Craig and Dabria's cars so assumed this was Dabria's new pad. She ushered them in and introductions were made. Brad's wife, Alvina, did not draw attention to the fact that she and Dabria had met before. Next Barry, the lawyer from down the hall, and his wife Melinda and two kids appeared. She was nothing like Dabria had expected. Melinda was taller than Barry by several inches and while Barry was roly-poly Melinda was svelte. So far, the kids seemed to favor Melinda. Jaimie unexpectedly drove up and added to the social. Dabria led the last of her guests on a guided tour and then Morgan forced her to sit down and grab a bite before she fell down.

Sarah had arranged veggies and fruit on a platter and they all had munchies on Dabria's new patio. Up to this point the day had been unseasonably warm. Despite the snow, with the patio heater on and the sun blazing down the deck had been warm and inviting. The kids chased each other around the yard while the adults visited. Without warning a cold breeze from the lake picked up and brought an impromptu end to the socializing. Dabria's guests said their goodbyes and headed out. Dabria and Sarah returned to the kitchen and got busy unpacking. Morgan and Kent made their way to the loft. They built the second BBQ for the loft deck, hooked up the washer and dryer, set up beds, and then assembled bookcases, dressers, and nightstands. As the afternoon skipped into evening Sarah got out the fixings for supper and carried the supplies to the loft. They dined on burgers and beer and determined that since all the heavy lifting and building had been done it was time for Sarah and Kent to call it a day. Dabria washed and dried a new set of sheets while she and Morgan moved furniture into place and started to unpack the boxes in the loft. By midnight Morgan called an end to the work and Dabria returned to the cabin to lock things up and bring up the extra keys.

"Hey, did you see how many keys Colin left for me? I'm positive he left two extra sets. I can only find the original and one extra."

"No, I wasn't paying attention. But you can give him a call tomorrow and check. Come on, bedtime."

"Morgan, I'm way to wound up for sleep. If you're tired go ahead. There's a bottle of wine that has my name on it. I'm going to pour myself a glass and I think I'll go make a list of things to do tomorrow."

Morgan didn't argue. After last night's lack of sleep and the physical labor of today, he was done. "I'm gonna shower first. Have you found towels?"

"They're in the dryer with the bedding. I'll help you make the bed."

Dabria curled up in the corner of her comfy couch with a blanket and with most of the lights out and the windows cracked open she sat and sipped her wine listening to the sharp yips of coyotes and smelling the fresh scent of forest. Life had certainly taken a twist. A year ago she had been party to a sham engagement, had accepted only client's cases that could better her chances of becoming partner in a cutthroat law office, and was about to make choices that led towards a path of destruction and heartbreak. Today she owned a cottage on a lake in the woods, worked at a Legal Aid Office where a partnership would *never* be offered, was dedicated to proving a young man's innocence simply because it was the right thing to do, and last but certainly not least was involved in a racy little affair with a very sexy detective. Wow, life was great!

Chapter 19

Dabria and Morgan spent the next day unpacking and by mid-afternoon they were finished. Morgan suggested they go for a walk, get the lay of the land, and meet some of the neighbors. He figured it wouldn't hurt anything to let the locals know there was going to be a cop around. They wandered over to the resort and had a game of pool and shared some of their famous chicken wings. Morgan knew that introducing themselves to the proprietors guaranteed the permanent residents would soon know who had bought the old log place. Unfortunately, the owners had left their little operation for a wedding and so only a barmaid was in residence. Morgan was pretty sure word of his profession would get around anyway. So he made sure he introduced himself to the girl. They returned to the loft and spent a quiet evening with Dabria reviewing her list of things to do and Morgan volunteering to help her with some of the tasks she thought she'd have to hire out. Dabria refused to get a security system installed but did agree that a dog might be an option. Since they both had a big week ahead of them they turned in early.

The following week flew by. Dabria hadn't seen Morgan since Monday morning because of their ridiculously heavy workloads. Despite dogged determination on both Dabria and Morgan's parts, no new evidence came to light that would definitively help Cody's case. Although an interesting tidbit was delivered by the coroner. He called Morgan to confirm that upon closer examination of her ring finger there was a slight bruise as if a ring had been forced off but the real bright spot was the information the private investigator reported to Dabria

Thursday evening. He informed her about Brad's previous relationship with Judge Reynolds. He also apprised her of the fact that prior to his practicing in P.A. the good judge had gone to school in Victoria and had lived there with his first wife. She, coincidentally, was also of aboriginal descent. She had remarried and continued to reside there with her new family. A preliminary conversation indicated that all had not been good in the first marriage and that maybe there were a few skeletons hanging around. Dabria volunteered to jump on a plane and go interview her over the weekend. Since she had already put in over sixty hours this week, she felt no guilt in leaving early. Dabria informed Brad of her plans and he suggested she not go alone. Craig volunteered to go but asked that she hold off until next weekend since he was already booked for this one. However, he reluctantly agreed that if the first Mrs. Reynolds was available and willing to talk they needed to strike while the iron was hot. Using the particulars the detective had left them, Dabria called the former wife and set up a meeting for the following morning.

Dabria immediately called Morgan and asked if he could accompany her. He confirmed he was free for the weekend, could leave early today, and assured her he would handle the accommodations. She booked flights and a rental car for that afternoon. She and Craig went to Brad's office to confirm his connection to Judge Reynolds and to impart the other information the PI had uncovered.

"Yes. I was in a partnership with Richard and a couple of other lawyers for two years," Brad confirmed. "That was more than enough time for me to determine that not only was private practice not for me, but also that there were things about Richard that were strange. Plus, I just plain didn't trust him."

"What kinds of things?"

"He would not tolerate any questions about his personal life previous to his move to P.A. He only divulged the bare basics regarding his schooling. Although he seems personable enough he neither had, nor still doesn't seem to have, any close friends. To my knowledge no one has ever been invited to his home. Any entertaining he does is done in public."

"Okay. So, he's eccentric. That doesn't prove he's a liar or a bully, like the detectives are claiming," Craig pointed out.

"Detective Vaughn and Detective Ducette aren't just claiming that. They've given us copies of sworn statements indicating that they believed Mrs. Reynolds original recitation of events was the truth. That would indicate that he is a liar and a bully. However, you're right *I* have no proof of that. I do know that he has a wicked temper because I've heard it. Despite the fact that in public he appears calm and in control he is definitely a different man behind closed doors."

"Tell us more," Dabria enthusiastically prompted as she leaned forward and perched on the edge of her chair with her hands clasped in front of her.

"I had left the office early one evening and returned about an hour later after discovering I had left some paperwork behind. Richard thought he was alone since I had told him I was leaving and he had locked up behind me. Usually I would have called out letting him know I had returned, but the tone of his voice as I entered the outer office made me wonder if he was under attack in his own office. I quickly realized he was on the phone and that he was in the middle of an argument with someone named Waneta . . . ."

Dabria immediately interrupted him, "That's his first wife's name!"

"I know. He was yelling and swearing at her at the top of his lungs and ended up threatening her. Since I already had my doubts about him I continued to eavesdrop without a shred of remorse. The conclusion to the call was his slamming down of the phone and then picking it up and firing it across the room. At that point I let myself out of the office and pretended I was in fact just arriving. I called out to him as I walked in and while his door remained closed he acknowledged that I was there. Neither of us has ever spoken of the incident and I'm convinced that he isn't aware that I heard him. It was soon after that, that I informed the other lawyers of my decision to join Legal Aid. I hired my own investigator at that time to determine the identity of "Waneta" and confirm that he was no apparent threat to her. For the first few years I continued to get reports on her verifying that she was alive and well."

"So, what else can you tell us about her?"

"I agree with what your private investigator already told you plus I can add that she was training to be a social worker at the time of my last report."

"She is involved in the field of social work. When I called to set up a meeting with her I called her at work and the receptionist answered with "B.C. Social Services"."

"You have a meeting set up?"

"Yes. Detective Vaughn and I are flying out this afternoon for me to interview her tomorrow morning."

"Does she know you're bringing a cop with you?"

"No. When I talked to her I didn't know I was."

"I would find out what questions Detective Vaughn wants added to the ones you and Craig have agreed upon and then I would leave him back at the hotel. She may be more forthcoming with information if she feels she isn't under interrogation."

"I agree. Anything else we should know?"

"No, nothing that immediately comes to mind. See you Monday."

Dabria drew up a detailed list of questions and then she rushed home to pack and meet Morgan back in town. Once settled into their seats on the plane Dabria asked where they would be staying. He explained he had a reservation within walking distance of Waneta's home for Friday night and then a private home booked for Saturday. Since Salt Spring Island was only a ferry ride away from Vancouver Island Dabria correctly guessed that they would be staying with his mother the following night. After disembarking, picking up their rental, and checking into their hotel they decided to go for a stroll and not only find Waneta's house but also find a café for dinner. After dinner Dabria presented the list Craig and she had compiled and requested Morgan's input. Except for a couple of questions, they seemed to have covered pretty much everything Morgan wanted to know. He agreed with Brad and promised he would steer clear of the interview. They finished the evening off with a stroll around the harbor. The screeching sea gulls and the salty tang of the ocean breeze tugged at Morgan's heartstrings and made him long for the day when he would be able to return here permanently.

The next morning dawned bright and beautiful. After enjoying the panoramic ocean view from their balcony, while sipping on a creamy latte and munching on a fragrant, warm cranberry orange muffin, Dabria leisurely made her way to Waneta's home. Waneta answered the door herself and shooed a herd of rambunctious children and pets into the backyard. She swiftly closed the French doors shutting out the cacophony coming from the patio.

"Whew! Saturday mornings are a bit overwhelming even for me. I can't imagine what you must be thinking. Do you have kids? Dogs? Can I get you coffee or tea?"

"No. Neither. I'm thinking of getting a dog though. Tea would be great." The tantalizing aroma of fresh baking teased Dabria's senses.

"Get a puppy. They're great practice if you ever want kids. I have some blueberry scones I just pulled out of the oven. It's a new recipe I've been dying to try. Are you willing to be a test subject? They would go great with tea," she coaxed.

"I'd love one."

"Great. Now, before I answer any of your questions are you willing to answer some of mine?"

"Of course. Fire away," Dabria encouraged.

"Explain to me again exactly who you are and what your connection to Richard is."

Dabria gave her a rundown of what was going on and why she wanted some information on Richard.

"Basically, what I need is to confirm that Richard has a history of not only manipulating facts for his own purposes but also has displayed violent behavior. Although there are professionals willing to testify that they have been told of his inappropriate behavior and seen the psychological effects of his abuse they unfortunately have never witnessed it and so the only proof I do have is the claims of the accused. Can you help me?"

Before Waneta could respond the front door opened and in walked a forty something-ish, giant of a man. Waneta immediately rose and went to him. He grabbed her about the waist and pulled her into an intimate embrace. He gave her a fierce hug and then pressed a gentle kiss to her forehead. As he proceeded to travel down to her lips Waneta gently pushed at his chest and exclaimed, "Karl, we have a guest." Despite her admonishment he finished off his greeting with a lip smacking kiss. Dabria had directed her eyes to the antics of the brood in the backyard. Waneta strolled back into the kitchen with a dreamy expression and pushed Karl into a chair.

"Karl, this is the lawyer I told you about, Dabria Abdulla-Smythe. Dabria this is my husband, Karl. He just came off a twenty-four shift at the hall. He's the chief of our local fire department."

"Pleasure," Dabria sat up and shook his outstretched hand.

"I hope you don't mind if I make Karl some lunch while we talk. He's been up since 6:00 a.m. so he's usually starving by now."

"Of course not."

"So, where were we? Oh, I remember," she waved her arms to silence Dabria before she could re-ask her questions. "I can definitely help you out. Twenty years ago I was afraid of Richard. Not so, anymore. I married Richard right out of high school. He was older than me, very charming, and since my parents hated him I thought he was the greatest thing since sliced bread. He was going to university while I was playing the little wife. We had decided that I would support him while he continued to go to school and then once he graduated our roles would reverse. Everything was going great until I discovered I was pregnant. That put a real wrench in his plans since there were problems with the pregnancy from the start and the doctor suggested total bed rest after the first trimester. That was the end of me working. Richard would have had to either work and attend school or take a year off and work until after the baby was born. Since neither one of those options were particularly attractive to him he pushed me down the stairs instead," she related with detached calmness as she continued with Karl's lunch.

"What," Dabria choked on her tea and scone and with streaming eyes searched the faces of both Waneta and Karl for the evidence of mutual outrage. Karl's face had tightened but he spoke not a word as he continued to openly evaluate Dabria. Waneta placed a plate of sandwiches in front of him while she sank into a seat beside him. Her face conveyed nothing more than a sense of serenity. She picked up one of Karl's clenched fists and consolingly caressed it.

"And you claimed you fell," Dabria whispered.

Waneta shrugged and pierced her lips. "I lost the child and being estranged from my parents and too ashamed to admit to them that they had been right I remained with him until I was able to squirrel away enough to be able to leave him and disappear. I know you're appalled by this but you must remember this is twenty years ago and I'm a native woman. I had no contact with him again until after I met Karl. Karl showed me what love really is when he asked me to marry him despite knowing that I was already married and would never be able to bear children. I contacted Richard at that point and threatened him that if he didn't grant me an immediate divorce I would go to the police and file a report claiming spousal abuse. Despite the fact that it had been several years since the incident had occurred and my chances of proving anything were negligible my claims could have hampered his ultimate goal of becoming a judge. That was a risk he wasn't willing to take and so the divorce was granted."

"And Karl and you have married and now live happily ever after?"

"Almost."

"Almost?"

"I'm a social worker now, Dabria, and every day I see the struggles that young women still have with spousal abuse. In twenty years some things have changed but we've a long way to go yet. I decided several months ago that in order to continue to serve the needs of my clients to the best of my abilities, I need to confront my own demons. Although, Karl and I have made a family with several adopted children I can't forgive Richard for preventing me from having Karl's child. Richard needs to atone for that. Then I can move on."

"So what did you have in mind?"

"I want to testify that Richard was a liar and that he's been violent with me."

"What proof do you have?"

"After Karl and I were married he convinced me to go back and see the doctor that had treated me when I lost the baby. At the time the doctor told me privately that he knew I had been pushed down the stairs because he had seen the bruises on my back and had photographed them so that if I ever changed my mind and wanted to admit that I hadn't fallen, we had proof. He had kept the photos in the file and so he gave me a copy of both them and his report which stated he believed that I had been pushed. At the time I was unwilling to pursue the matter and simply brought my copy of the file home. After your call yesterday I checked to see if the doctor was still in practice and I've made an appointment to see him next week. Whether or not he'll testify in my favor isn't really important since my testimony alone should at least create doubt in the minds of the jurors as to his squeaky clean image, should it not?"

"May I ask why you didn't allow the doctor to act on your behalf all those years ago?"

"If you really are a family lawyer you already know the answer to that. He threatened to kill me and there was little doubt in my mind that since he had killed our child it wouldn't take much more for him to do the same to me."

"You know if I use you, you may be forced to actually see him?"

"I know. But, I'm not afraid of him anymore and besides I know Karl and our children will be at home waiting for me."

"I'll be with you, there!" Karl declared firmly, broaching no argument.

"*There* then," Waneta agreed.

"Let me know what the doctor has to say and I'll contact you as soon as I know if we can use your testimony. Thank you, for being so forthcoming. You were right about the scones. They are amazing. It was a pleasure to meet you Karl." Dabria again shook Karl's hand as she rose and let Waneta lead her to the door.

She met Morgan at the harbor and he insisted on taking her into the Empress Hotel for their famous tea and scones. Not wanting to disappoint him she related the events of her morning and excluded the part about the home baked blueberry scones she'd just finished, which just happened to be a lot better. After wandering back to the car they headed for the ferry and off to Salt Spring Island. Despite displaying outward calm Dabria was nervous. The only boyfriend she had ever had was David and she had grown up with his parents. Meeting Morgan's mother, whom he obviously respected and adored, was an honor that she knew shouldn't be taken lightly.

As they disembarked Dabria restlessly shifted in her seat. Morgan reached out a hand and trapped one of hers in his, forcing her to look over at him.

"Hey, she'll like you. Relax."

"I am."

"Right." He patted her hand and gave her a huge grin, knowing she was far from relaxed. They bumped down the road from Fulford to Ganges and hit the Saturday Market. Everything from blown glass to organic tomatoes enticed Dabria. After they sampled several vendors' wares Morgan bought goat cheese, pâté, baguettes, grapes, some organic veggies and fruit drinks. They settled on his newly purchased woven blanket for a picnic in Centennial Park. Music from the Market serenaded them as well as the squeals and giggles of children playing nearby.

"It's like paradise here," Dabria exclaimed as she tried to drink in all the sights, sounds, and smells surrounding her, while brushing the wayward strands of hair that were determined to swirl into her eyes.

"Umm," Morgan agreed sleepily, as he stretched out on the lawn.

"I don't know how you can stand to leave," she exclaimed as she popped a small blue/black grape into his mouth.

"I come back every opportunity I get. Once things settle down a bit maybe we can steal a few days and come back this fall," he suggested as he munched enthusiastically.

"I'd like that."

"Come. It's time to meet the clan." He jumped up and reached a hand out to pull her up.

"The clan? I thought we were meeting your mom."

"Yah. But you know my sister Amy lives here and since I don't come home very often mom called Shona and so her family also came over."

"Morgan!"

"Dabria, it'll be fine. I promise I won't leave you alone." After walking back through the market and picking up a few things, they returned to the car and bumped back down the road towards Fulford.

"We just came from this way."

"You're right. Although I grew up in the country near Fulford, I wanted you to see the market at Ganges, plus mom wanted me to pick up some things for her."

Morgan kept up a running commentary as they headed for his childhood home, hoping to distract Dabria. All too soon Morgan turned down a tree lined driveway where a painted sign indicated that they were getting close to *Natalie's Gallery*. As they rounded the last corner an ivy-covered stone arch framed Dabria's first glimpse of Morgan's birthplace. Morgan slowed down to allow Dabria time to get a good look at it. The drive split into a Y. A riot of spring flowers bordered a stone cottage and parking lot immediately to the left. To the right was a gate announcing *Private Drive*. That was the direction they headed. Morgan stopped in front of the gate, jumped out, and pushed it open. He jumped back in and drove through and then parked and closed the gate behind them. The lane continued to be tree lined and with Morgan's window open Dabria realized the sound of crashing waves was increasing. Suddenly the trees ended and nestled at the end of the lane a large two-story house came into view. Unlike the arch and the cottage, the house was not made of stone. It was a traditional cape-style house sided in weathered rough cedar planks. The color reminded Dabria of her own little log abode. Like the yard of the gallery this yard was also a riot of colors. Already parked in front of the house were a bright orange Smart Car and a large black SUV. As they pulled to a stop the front door opened and shrieking kids and barking dogs came bursting out. Dabria's eyes darted nervously between the bounding dogs that were on both sides of the car.

"Just give me a second to get the troops under control and then I'll introduce you." As he opened the door and slid out he was assaulted by the four. A bellow from the porch caused the two dogs to quiet down. Dabria followed the voice and was surprised to discover it was coming from the tallest of a trio of very tall women. As Dabria surveyed the women, without appearing to gawk, she opened her door and Morgan reached inside to draw her out.

"It's safe now," he whispered with a chuckle as he gave her hand a reassuring squeeze. He led Dabria to the porch, trailed by little boys and big dogs. Immediately upon making the introductions he was embraced by Amy and Shona and finally allowed to enfold his mother in a big bear hug. While the hugs continued Dabria became conscious of another body lounging in the doorway. He leisurely straightened and with an outstretched hand introduced himself as Shona's husband, Soren. Dabria's first impression was that Soren looked even more like an ancient Viking than Morgan or possibly the God of Thunder that he was actually named after.

Dabria felt like she had entered the land of the giants. She was shorter than most in the general population, if she was barefoot, but she normally wore four or five inch high heels making her almost average. Since she knew they would be hiking around today she had worn flats and so she wasn't much taller than the children. Soren offered to make everyone a cocktail before supper and the clan wandered back into the house and out onto the patio. Morgan directed Dabria to a loveseat close to the BBQ. He fired it up and checked the platter of raw meat that Amy brought out. The two boys promptly flanked Dabria on the lounger and stared at her inquisitively. Shona and Soren appeared from the kitchen bearing platters of appetizers and beverages. Shona scolded the boys for bothering Dabria. She immediately assured Shona that they were fine. Amy shoed her mother out of the kitchen and made her sit down and enjoy a cocktail while she and her siblings attended to supper. It wasn't long before the boys became bored with simply sitting and they soon jumped up and ran off to play with *Grannies' puppies* and dig for clams on the beach below the patio. If Dabria thought that Ganges was paradise then Natalie's backyard was surely heaven.

The family enjoyed a raucous meal with much laughter and loud storytelling. Although it had been months since the family had been together it was more than obvious that they were all extremely close. Late afternoon melted into evening and Morgan suggested a walk along the beach before dark. Naturally boys and dogs followed. Dabria commented on the distance of unpopulated beach they strolled along. Morgan informed her that his mother had owned several acres but she had the land surveyed and divided into four lots several years before. She had given each of her children one and then kept the homestead for herself.

"Are any of the other lots developed?" Dabria asked with interest.

"They each have a cabin on them. Mine is little more than a one room shack but Shona's is a fully modernized cottage and Amy is in the process of building hers. Come I'll show you." Morgan's was the farthest away and was indeed a shanty. It was spotless but contained only a bed, a table with two chairs, a fridge, and a two piece bathroom. The only appealing feature to Dabria was the overflowing bookcase on the wall outside of the bathroom. Dabria figured it was perfect for a hermit and she told him so. He teased her that this was where they would be spending the night. She giggled and assured him if he could rough it so could she. They walked back along the beach until she spotted a second trail that led up a switch-backed path to a deck above them. Two stories of glass and cedar beams greeted Dabria at the top. The cottage was gorgeous and the view was breathtaking. The boys had scrambled ahead and were eager to show off their bedrooms and the play gym they had in the yard. The foursome followed the graveled road to Amy's place. Amy's was a rounded, terra cotta, stucco bungalow that reminded Dabria of the smiling sea creatures Morgan had on his coffee tables in P.A. Designs had been molded into the curves of the house. They did a walk through and discovered that the only thing that seemed to be unfinished was the flooring. As they made their way back to Natalie's Dabria commented on the fact that the very different style of each of the houses showed off unique character traits of each of their personalities.

"Tell me what the houses say to you," he encouraged.

"Shona's house is open and airy and certainly sucks up every drop of sunshine that comes its way. She has the same sunny personality that seems to beg for company. Amy's house is earthy and more shaded indicating that she enjoys her solitude and has a deep appreciation for nature. Yours is a utilitarian refuge. It serves the purpose of keeping you dry, providing you with a place to lay your head, and hide from the world."

"And mother's?"

"Your mother's house is like a warm, welcoming haven. The colors inside are bright and cheerful, like she is."

"You like her."

"I do."

"She likes you, too."

"That's not possible. She hasn't heard me say more than a dozen words."

"She's very intuitive. And besides how can you determine that you like her but she can't have decided she likes you?"

"Because I liked her before I ever met her."

"Huh?"

"I studied those paintings you have of hers. Plus, you're a great ambassador for her. I looked around her home and listened to her children and grandchildren and that homey feeling I felt begins with her."

"Wow. You're very observant and apparently much deeper than me."

"Stop mocking me!" she punched him on the arm.

"I'm not. I'm serious. Come on, they should have had enough time to dissect you by now and I'm sure I saw the fixings for strawberry shortcake on the counter before we left."

Chapter 20

T he remainder of the evening proceeded pleasantly. After the boys were bathed and fed dessert they were put to sleep at Grannies' house and the adults played games. It was after midnight when Natalie stood up, stretched, and announced that she was heading off to bed.

"Morgan, make sure you show Dabria around upstairs. I've laid out towels for both of you in your room. First up makes the coffee. Soren volunteered to make breakfast so we'll see you all in the morning."

"Yah. I'm ready to turn in myself," Shona declared as she also stood to leave. Soren swiftly followed her out the door.

"Mark the date. I can guarantee we're gonna be seeing another bundle of joy in about nine months," Amy remarked dryly.

"Would that be so bad?" Morgan chastised.

"Absolutely not, since it takes the pressure off both of us to reproduce. I say GO SHONA!"

Morgan chuckled as he pulled Dabria up the stairs.

"I thought we were staying at the cabin?"

"I was just teasing. Besides I think mom wants us to sleep here. Is that okay?"

"*I* had planned to sleep here from the beginning."

Dabria was disconcerted to discover that Morgan's mom assumed they would be sleeping together in Morgan's room. She was hardly disappointed, but that would never have happened in Dabria's parent's home. Instead of wearing the sexy, lacy *next to nothings* she had packed for the weekend, Dabria had a bath and pulled on the same pair of boxers and oversize t-shirt she normally wore every night to bed. With Morgan's nephews across the hall, his bedroom positioned directly over his mother's, and the fact that his bedroom door didn't lock, cuddling was the only item scheduled for tonight's activities.

Dabria was extremely thankful the next morning that she had chosen appropriate sleepwear as she was abruptly woken up by a rambunctious Spiderman and Superman when they catapulted themselves onto Morgan's bed.

"Get up, Uncle Morgan. Get up!!!!!" they yelled as they bounced.

The smell of freshly brewed coffee assailed Dabria's nostrils as she disentangled herself from the *three* wrestling boys. She washed her face, brushed her teeth, and pulled on some sweats before heading downstairs to help with breakfast. Amy was already up making a fruit salad. There was no evidence of Soren or Shona.

"What can I help with?" Dabria volunteered.

"If you get out some bowls we can feed the rug-rats fruit and cereal and the adults can eat later."

After setting up the table for the boys outside, Dabria snagged a cup of coffee and settled into a comfy lounger on the patio. Amy joined her and they soaked in the beauty that surrounded them.

"Morgan told us you're a painter," Amy challenged.

"Mostly watercolors," Dabria responded casually. She had sensed last night that Amy was less than thrilled that Morgan had brought Dabria with him.

"Are you any good?" she asked rudely.

"I think so, but you know that all art is subjective. I saw the clay creatures you made for Morgan. I love the comic features of them and that bowl is absolutely inspired."

"I don't remember which one he has," she tested Dabria.

"It's a stunning combination of blues and greens with a splash of orange."

"Hmmmm. . . . Oh yes, I remember now," Amy feigned forgetfulness. Suddenly she sat up. "Look, I'm not going to beat around the bush anymore, since we could be interrupted at any second. Unless you plan on sticking around for several decades I suggest you find someone else to play with. Morgan has obviously fallen for you and when he sets his mind to something that's the course he follows come hell or high water.

He's ready to settle down and start a family. Are you?" Amy baldly blurted out.

"Amy!!" Thankfully before Dabria was forced to reply they were interrupted by Natalie. "Morgan's relationships are none of your business. He's a big boy and can take care of himself. Somehow, I think he should be the one expressing his undying devotion to Dabria, not you. I would love some of that heavenly smelling coffee. Can you get me a cup and a bowl of fruit, please? And apologize for your rudeness."

"I will not. We all want to know. You and Shona are just too polite to come right out and ask," Amy declared standing with her hands on her hips as she waited for an answer.

Dabria continued to sip at her coffee without comment. Disgusted, Amy snorted and marched back into the kitchen.

"Despite Amy's rudeness she is right when she claims we all want to know what your intensions are. I'm not going to put you on the spot like that but I do have something to say. Please don't hurt him," Natalie implored. "You're the first girl he's ever brought home and so we know he cares for you."

"I care for him, too," Dabria assured her. "I don't play games and would never deceive him into thinking I cared more for him than I actually do. He's a wonderful man and you should be very proud of him."

"Thank you, we are. Ahhhhhhh, here's my favorite boys, now."

~ ~ ~

Dabria and Morgan headed back home shortly after brunch. Conversation flowed naturally and Dabria wondered if in fact this might be that *someone* she could see herself with "several decades" from now. They headed for the cabin Sunday night and returned to the grind the next morning.

Morgan was greeted with the autopsy report on the latest *scalper* victim confirming what they already knew regarding her cause of death. Her identity was confirmed but again time of death couldn't be pinned down to an exact hour. Disturbingly, another prostitute had been reported missing over the weekend. Predictably her physical attributes matched those of all of the other victims. Detective French approached his superiors requesting that a warning be issued to the public stating that there was a predator in the area that was targeting young women with specific physical traits. They agreed. So while French and his team concentrated on *the scalper*, Craig concentrated on Cody's defense, and Dabria and Morgan spent all their free time trying to prove Cody's innocence. Dabria was able to verify the allegations of Judge Reynolds' first wife by interviewing Waneta's ER doctor over the phone. She then contacted Anthony (Tony) Tasos, the PI she had hired, to see if he had dug up anymore dirt. Apparently Richard Reynolds had appeared on the horizon about twenty years ago. Before that, there seemed to be no record of the man in Canada. The private investigator jumped at the opportunity to keep digging.

Within days Tony had new information for Dabria. He discovered that there were two boys that were born within days of each other about fifty years ago at an orphanage in Salem, Oregon, and had been left there. One of them was Richard Reynolds, the other was Benjamin Musgrave. They grew up together. Richard was awarded a scholarship to attend university when he turned eighteen. Although both boys were extremely intelligent and had both applied for scholarships Richard was the one that was actually awarded one. The priest believed that this was in part due to the fact that Ben was known to be a troublemaker with a violent temper while Richard was the direct opposite of that. They left the orphanage together on graduation night and were never seen or heard from again.

The priest who had been both boys' mentor had been murdered about a year later. The priest the PI interviewed was the only priest still at the parish that had known the boys. He indicated that the boys were similar enough in looks they could have passed for brothers. However, they had come from very different backgrounds. He couldn't divulge the actual identity of the boys' mothers due to privacy issues. Although Richard's mother had left her child with them he had never been adopted. Ben's mother had died giving birth. While at the orphanage Ben underwent several surgeries to correct a twisted foot and by the time he left his foot and leg appeared normal though he sported some impressive scars. Dabria faxed several pictures of Richard to the priest to confirm his identity. One had come from Waneta when he was her husband. It was a candid shot she had taken. She had indicated to Dabria that Richard seemed unusually shy around cameras and she assumed it was because of the scars on his right leg. There was no formal picture of him from graduation at the University and in fact, no pictures until he arrived in P.A. Although both boys had been given Social Security Numbers (SSNs) neither of the numbers had ever been used again in the U.S. after that June thirty years ago. There was no evidence of the existence of Ben after that summer. A Social Insurance Number (SIN) however, had been issued to Richard along with his citizenship in Canada two years later.

The priest's reaction to the pictures, along with both Waneta and Cody's descriptions of the scars on Richard's leg indicated that in fact Richard probably wasn't Richard at all. With every communiqué that Dabria received her confidence increased that not only could Judge Reynolds' integrity be questioned, but also his actually identity. Although both Craig and Brad had questioned the judge's practices neither one of them could have predicted that spending money on a good detective would yield the results it had. Brad assured Dabria the office would reimburse her for any of the PI's expenses that she had already incurred. He could see this already important case turning into a huge Coue for Legal Aid if they were able to reveal that a well respected judge had been living a lie for the past thirty years.

The next obvious course of action was to have the private investigator compile a list of male cold case murder victims in that area from the night that the boys had left the orphanage up to the time that the priest was discovered murdered. Two such cases were identified. One was of a local football player. The other one was a John Doe. The autopsy report was a gruesome description of the murder of a young victim whose identity was purposely meant to be forever concealed. The coroner reported cause of death as "unknown" since the body had been dismembered and so badly decomposed there was little left other than bones. The skeletal remains were missing both hands and feet and all the teeth had been smashed out leaving a gaping hole in front of the severed skull. The first question that came to Dabria's mind was where were the hands and feet? The report indicated the victim was a male of an age between late teen and early adult, as based on height and development of bones. Beyond that there was little else. The police report indicated that the body had been found in a shallow grave in the forest not far from the orphanage. One of the bones had been dug up by a farm dog and dragged back to his home. The farmer had intercepted it and enticed the dog into showing him where he had found it and then called the sheriff's department.

Dabria was drawn to this case like no other she had ever been involved in. The more they dug up the more obsessed she became in finding out the truth. She had known instinctively that Cody had been telling the truth about the judge's treatment of his mom. Her instinct had led her to discover things that no one in this town would ever have suspected. The obvious question at this point was—had the remains of John Doe been buried or cremated? Dabria was delighted to receive word that they had been buried and with special permission could be exhumed for DNA extraction. The next hurdle was to have the orphanage reveal the identity of Richard's mother and to find her and entice her into providing them with a sample of her DNA. Under normal circumstances cutting through all the red tape involved in a case that spanned several decades and involved two countries would have taken, at the least, several months and realistically years. Cody didn't have the luxury of waiting that long. Dabria needed some help. Putting her pride aside she contacted her father and asked him to request some favors from influential men in his circle of friends to expedite the process. Dabria wasn't disappointed. Within a week she had the permission they needed to exhume and extract a DNA sample. The next hurdle, which was a much bigger one, was to talk the priest into opening his files and revealing the name of Richard's mother. Dabria continued to work on the other cases that required her attention but every spare moment of personal time that she had was spent on Cody's case. With the approach of another weekend she made arrangements to travel to the orphanage and meet with the priest personally. Morgan again accompanied her.

Chapter 21

Dabria and Morgan travelled to Salem and despite the fact that she begged, pleaded, and tried to reason with the priest he refused to divulge the information they requested. Without the DNA results from the John Doe *and* a court order he calmly informed Dabria that he was bound by his vows to protect the mother's identity. Dabria had brought a recent picture that Tony had been able to snap of the good Judge Reynolds leaving the courthouse. Upon showing it to the priest he couldn't make a positive identification since it had been over thirty years and his eyesight just "wasn't what it used to be." He even confessed that he was unsure whether the pictures she had sent him before were of Ben or of Richard. He did acknowledge that he thought their case was convincing and agreed that the man claiming to be Richard may not be Richard. But, that was as far as he would go to help them at this point. Unfortunately, that was really no help at all. Disappointed but not totally disheartened Dabria and Morgan thanked the priest and returned to the parking lot.

"Hang on a sec," Dabria requested. "I should really hit the washroom before we leave." She hurried back into the manse hoping that the priest hadn't left. He had disappeared but a middle-aged woman was in the foyer polishing woodwork.

"Excuse me," Dabria interrupted her. "Have you a washroom I could use?"

"Of course, miss," the lady replied. "Follow me."

She led Dabria down the hall to a small private restroom. As she turned to leave Dabria had a sudden thought.

"Excuse me again. But I wonder if you might be able to help me with something?"

The woman stopped and went very still.

"If you don't mind me asking, how many years have you worked here?"

"Many," she replied without elaboration.

"Twenty? Thirty? More?"

"This is my thirtieth year," she confirmed.

"Did you ever come here as a girl?"

"Yes."

"Did you live here?"

"Yes. But it's not what you're thinkin'. I wasn't an orphan. My mother worked here and we lived in a little house behind the church."

Dabria swiftly grabbed the two boys' graduation pictures and the recent picture of Richard from her purse.

"Do you remember these boys?" she asked with anticipation.

"Yes," again she volunteered nothing.

"Please tell me about them," she implored as excitement built in the pit of her stomach.

With sad eyes the woman looked down at Dabria.

"I remember them well because we played together."

"What were their names?"

"Ben and Richard."

"Do you know much about their families?"

"No. They were orphans," she gave her reply in a puzzled manner.

"I know, but I thought there may have been some talk."

"I don't remember."

Dabria handed her the recent picture of Richard.

"Do you know who this is?"

She studied it for a while and then said, "It looks like a grown-up Richard."

"Really. Not a grown-up Ben?" Dabria prompted.

"No, Richard."

"How can you be sure?"

"Because I was in love with Ben and he would never have grown into a man that frightened me. *This* man does not look like he is a nice man."

"You're right. He's not," Dabria agreed with her. "My name is Dabria and I'm trying to save a young man from being wrongly convicted of a murder. Here is my card. If you remember any rumors you may have heard, please give me a call."

The woman did not offer her name but Dabria figured Tony would be able to find it out for her.

"Thank you, for the help," Dabria quietly called after her as the woman hurried away.

"Well, this wasn't a wasted trip after all," Dabria informed Morgan upon her return to the car. She filled him in while he drove to the airport. They returned home and set about procuring a court order to have the priest open the orphanage records while they waited for the DNA test results.

In the meantime, they concentrated on their other cases. At the end of the week Alvina called Dabria asking her if she would like to make another appointment. Dabria swiftly declined her offer but then paused for a moment after she hung up the phone. As the weeks had gone by, Morgan had crept into almost every aspect of her life. She couldn't honestly recall a day since her first encounter with him that she hadn't thought about him. They may go for days at a time without seeing each other but he made sure she thought of him every day. Morgan either called her, texted her, or sent her little treats. She was well aware that he was in full out pursuit and conquer mode. She was genuinely afraid that her little affair was actually turning into something a lot more permanent. She had loved before and been horribly betrayed. The memories of that betrayal were still fresh and despite her attempts to deal with the past several years of her life, the reality was that she hadn't dealt with anything. She had simply kept herself extremely busy and refused to allow the memories in. But when she slept, the nightmares could not be kept at bay and she often woke up sweating, shaking, and crying. Morgan thankfully had only been witness to these episodes twice and he attributed both to the attack on her in the bar. When he questioned her and tried to comfort her she remained evasive. Sooner or later she was going to cry out something that would make him realize she had some serious unresolved issues. Since Morgan was determined to make her fall for him maybe she should deal with some of them. Before she could change her mind she picked up the phone and called Alvina back.

With Alvina's recommendation she made an appointment with a colleague of hers. Tomorrow's appointment would be the beginning of what Dabria knew would be a heart wrenching journey that may very well destroy her. She only hoped that Morgan was up for the emotional rollercoaster ride ahead.

~ ~ ~

Dabria had hardly slept since just thinking about today's appointment had obviously brought all that turmoil to the forefront of her subconscious. She had gone from nightmare to nightmare all night long and finally gave up trying to sleep and dragged herself from bed at 5:00 a.m. She laid out several files from work and finished up notes on many of them before glancing at the clock and realizing it was time to get in the shower. As she soaped and sponged herself off a memory of Morgan doing the same thing sprang to mind. Knowing today was going to be an emotional challenge Dabria decided a little stress reliever was in order and she allowed her hands to follow the path Morgan's had taken. Bracing herself against the walls of the shower she caressed and stroked herself to fulfillment. Feeling revitalized and ready to take on her day Dabria dried off and walked to her closet to pick out today's battle gear. Despite the morning's dreary dawn and the trials that loomed over her, Dabria's disposition was surprising buoyant. Dressed in a fitted dark chocolate brown skirt and bolero jacket with a champagne silk camisole, she slipped on four inch suede pumps, grabbed her briefcase, and marched out to conquer her day.

"Wow!" Sarah exclaimed when she entered Dabria's office just before lunch. "Nice duds. Who's in for it? I didn't think you had court today."

"I don't but I do have an appointment this afternoon and when I feel good about how I look I feel more in control."

"What kind of appointment?" she asked as she sank into one of the client chairs.

Dabria debated the wisdom of answering honestly. Her hesitation caused Sarah to back off.

"Dabria, I'm sorry. It's none of my business. I didn't mean to pry," Sarah rushed to assure her. Although Dabria had shared some of her past with both Sarah and Kent, Sarah knew there was a lot that Dabria had held back. She attempted to rise. Dabria placed a hand on Sarah's arm and making the snap decision to trust and reinforce the friendship she was building with Sarah she answered.

"With a shrink and I'd appreciate it if you kept that on the QT. As in Kent doesn't need to know because he might feel the need to pass that on to one of his partners."

"Gotcha! I won't breathe a word. Does this have something to do with your attack?" she inquired as she resettled in her seat.

"No. I need to deal with some things from the past that don't seem to want to go away. I'm leaving at 3:00 p.m. and I won't be back for the day. If a certain cop is looking for me I hope to be home by 6:00 p.m. but I don't really want company."

"Why can't you just tell him that?"

"Because if he thinks there's something going on that he doesn't know about, it instantly becomes a challenge to find out and I'm not sure I'm going to have the fortitude to deal with him tonight."

"I'll make sure he gives you your space tonight. Kent already called suggesting an evening out with the two of you. That's why I came in here. I wanted to check out your schedule and see if we could decide on a place to eat. Consider me your champion. I will keep the boys busy and away from you."

"Thanks."

"Got time for lunch?"

"Sorry, with me leaving early I need to work through. I brought a sandwich. Why don't you and Kent come out for supper tomorrow night?"

"Sounds like a plan. I'll talk to you later. Good luck this afternoon." With a wave Sarah was gone.

When 3:00 p.m. arrived Dabria packed up and headed out to the lobby. As she was informing the girls she would be gone for the rest of the day Craig sauntered in.

"Any news," she inquired as she stalled to leave.

"No, nothing yet. I'm almost done for the day. Got time for a drink?"

"Sorry, I've got an appointment."

"Tomorrow?" he inquired hopefully as he opened the door for her. Since he had followed her outside and was out of earshot of the girls she decided this was as good a time as any to put an end to any further "dates."

"Craig, I'm kind of involved with someone. I'm sorry. Although I enjoy your company and would like to get to know you better I just can't play the field and date more than one guy at a time."

"I kind of figured. It's the cop, right?"

"Yah."

"Nuff said. I'll back off and keep it professional. Ya can't blame a guy for trying though. Have a good weekend." With a wave he retreated back into the office.

Dabria stowed her gear and headed off to the appointment. Upon reaching the clinic she was immediately ushered into the doctor's office giving her no time for last minute jitters or to effectively slip her defenses into place. A short round grandmotherly lady stood up from her desk and with outstretched hand introduced herself.

"Hello Dabria. I'm Dr. Rosemary Murphy. Would you be more comfortable sitting in the chair in front of me or moving over to the chairs by the coffee table?"

"Um," Dabria looked around the office and then stated, "I'd actually be more comfortable *behind* the desk."

Dr. Murphy chuckled. "I'm sure you would, dear. Dabria, this isn't an interrogation. I want to help you, not torture you."

"I know that. But I also know that it *is* going to be torture which is why I've tried to suppress it for so long."

"Come . . . . let's sit at the coffee table. What can I get you to drink?" Dr. Murphy headed to a small fridge that doubled as a coffee stand.

"A bottle of red wine would be great, but water will be fine." Dabria settled herself into one of the comfy occasional chairs.

Dr. Murray grabbed two water bottles and sat down.

"So, let me begin by telling you a bit about how I guide my sessions. And then I'll ask you some questions. Do you mind if I make some notes?"

"No."

"Okay then. The pace we set is mostly up to you. I'm guessing you have some unresolved issues that are affecting your ability to move forward. In order to do that we need to go back to the source of those issues, recall the situations, and then I need to give you the tools to deal with them. Agreed?"

"Yes."

"Okay. We're going to start with your background." Dr. Murray asked about her family, where she grew up, and what she had done since high school. Once that was out of the way she asked about her friendships. Dabria had kept her answers brief but honest. She attempted to gloss over her earlier relationships with David and Matthew. It was at this point that Dr. Murray stopped her.

"Dabria, why are you here?"

"I lost two of my best friends in the last year and I don't really know how to go on without them."

"Then from the beginning tell me how you really felt about David."

"I can't."

"Why not?"

"Because if I open the gate and let those feelings out I know I won't be able to stop the flood and I won't ever be the same again."

"You are absolutely right. You won't be the same. And isn't that the whole point? Is it better to go on as you have—keeping everything held tightly inside—or to move forward? Are you happy?"

"I want to be."

"Is there someone putting pressure on you to deal with your past?"

"Yes."

"Who?"

"Me," Dabria replied with a sigh. "I think I'm falling in love with someone who really doesn't know the true me."

"Dabria, what you are is an obviously intelligent, independent, strong, loving, and lovable young woman. That woman is not going to disappear and be replaced by something else. When we're finished you will only be stronger and more lovable. Believe that."

"I'm afraid, and that's not an easy thing for me to admit."

"I can see that. This is not going to be a walk in the park but I know you'll get through it. Trust me. I won't let you get lost or fail to reach your goal. Now let's try this again. Tell me about David. Tell me about your first memory of David."

Dabria sat and thought for a moment and then let her memories flow. She told Dr. Murphy not only about David but also about Mathew since for as far back as she could remember it had always been the three of them. When she stopped to take a breath and a sip of water she glanced at her watch and discovered to her chagrin that it was almost 6:00 p.m.

"Oh my God!" she jumped up. "Why didn't you stop me? It's so late. I'm so sorry."

"Dabria, it's fine. I think that's a great beginning. We'll stop here and we can continue next week. I can see you have some wonderful memories of the boys and someday soon when you think of them it will be those memories that stand out and not the things that came after. Go have a wonderful weekend with your friend and don't worry about next session. It will take care of itself. When do you want to meet?"

"The sooner, the better."

"I have some evening appointments. Is Tuesday evening alright?"

"That would be great!" Dabria agreed enthusiastically.

She fairly skipped out of the office. She had been so nervous that the relief she felt was almost overwhelming. She checked her phone and was thrilled to see a text from Morgan. He had talked to Sarah and despite his disappointment he was giving Dabria the night off. But he forewarned her to be prepared to see him on her doorstep first thing in the morning. She was in such a good mood that she decided to take the initiative and stalk him for a change. She texted Sarah to determine Morgan's whereabouts and then after picking up a bottle of wine headed over to his condo. She silently applauded her decision to wear kickass lingerie when she dressed this morning and was relieved to confirm that her antiperspirant had done its job today as well. Before she left her car she slipped her panties off and into her purse. Luckily a couple was heading out of the condo complex as Dabria headed in, so she didn't need to tip Morgan off to her arrival. When she stood outside his door she plucked the wine from its bag, fluffed her hair, added some lip gloss, and then with a "come hither" look in her eyes she pressed the doorbell.

Morgan was poring over the latest notes he had received from Detective French and making a new list of questions for their next meeting. He was relieved to hear the doorbell as he was starving and the pizza he had ordered was already fifteen minutes late. Without checking the peephole he yanked the door open as he reached for his wallet. He stopped dead when he realized that pizza delivery guys didn't usually wear sexy little brown pumps.

"So *Copper,* can you show a lady a good time?" Dabria purred as she sauntered past him licking her lips and dragging her finger across his chest.

"Uh . . . . you bet!" he slammed the door and followed her into the living room, just as the real delivery boy walked off the elevator. Before he caught up with her his doorbell rang again. Undecided as to whether to answer the door or take Dabria up on her invitation he briefly hesitated in the middle of the room and watched her as she shrugged out of her jacket and sank onto his couch.

"The doorbell is ringing," she prompted with a nod and a sardonic smile.

"Yah. I should probably get that," he shook himself out of his temporary daze.

"Uh huh. What I got, ain't goin' nowhere," she assured him as she draped herself over the couch.

He spun back towards the door, yanked it open, grabbed the pizza, and threw a fifty dollar bill at the kid.

"Keep the change," he muttered as he slammed the door again. He put the pizza on the counter, grabbed wineglasses, and a corkscrew and then headed back to the living room in record time. By now he had most of himself back under control. His penis somehow didn't care if he looked cool or not so it continued to strain against his fly.

"So, how was your day?" he asked tentatively.

"It's shaping up to be a great day. And you?" She passed him the wine.

"Yah. Great!"

"Since we're both starving why don't we tie into that pizza and then we can decide what to do about dessert."

"Ah . . . . sounds good!" Morgan headed back to the kitchen. Dabria had uncorked and poured the wine by the time he returned with plates, napkins, and the pizza. She asked him questions about his week while they ate. As he washed his last swallow of pizza down with a drink of wine, she leaned over, took his plate from him, and stacked it with hers. Then she leaned back over him and ran her nails up the fly of his crotch. His penis had never actually settled down since she had walked in, and so it was again straining to be released as she reached the waistband of his jeans. She unbuttoned his shirt and then skimmed her hands up his chest.

"God, you're beautiful!" she breathed. Before he could find his voice she placed a finger on his lips. "Shhhhhh . . . . let *me* play" she beseeched. Morgan didn't bother to attempt to answer he just opened his legs wider trying to release some of the pressure and let her play while he struggled not to make any noises at all. It was too much and as she unzipped him an involuntary groan slipped out. She grinned provocatively. *He* had unleashed her sensual side and so now *he* had to pay the price for that. He only hoped he survived with his manhood intact.

Mesmerized he followed the path of her lips and tongue as she made her way down his body. Afraid to touch her and thus distract her in any way, he spread his arms across the back of the couch and gripped the leather with ever increasing intensity. He was strung tighter than a bowstring and just before he came she stopped. She sat back on her haunches and pulled a condom from between her breasts. He almost embarrassed himself by coming right there and then. His knuckles dug into the couch and he could hear his breath sawing in and out. She pulled off his pants, sheathed him, and then hiked up her skirt revealing her gartered stockings as she slid her panty-less bottom on top of him. The instant she sank onto him he came with an explosion unlike any he had ever experienced before. As he grabbed her waist and ground her into himself he flung his head back and rasped out her name. She stayed still until his grip relaxed. He released his hold on her waist, smoothed his hands up and down her sides to ease the punishing grasp he had on her, and pulled her to lie against his chest. He buried his face into her neck as his hands caressed her back.

"Fuck, Dabria, you're gonna kill me," he hoarsely growled.

She chuckled and sat up.

"You just lay back and recover while I continue to amuse myself, okay?"

"Do with me as you wish."

"I plan to," she purred. While she continued to sit astride with him embedded up to his hilt she slowly removed her camisole. She slipped another condom out of her bra and placed it on the table in front of her. Next she undid her skirt and pulled it over her head. Lastly she undid her bra and slid it down her arms. She sat perched in only her stockings, garters, and sexy little kitten heels. She helped Morgan out of his shirt and then she slid off of him and removed the used condom. She patted him dry with his shirt and then grabbed the new condom and opened the packet. While he continued to watch fascinated, she perched one stiletto shod foot onto the arm of the sofa and dipped her fingers inside herself. With her other hand she caressed her own breast until the nipple beaded. When her fingers slipped out of her moist folds she rubbed them on the head of his penis and slid the condom over the top. His knuckles were white from clutching the cushions so tightly. He was ready and roaring to go again. He had never seen anything as erotic as she had just done and he knew that she *was* going to kill him before she was done. Not for one second had her eyes left his face. She straddled him again before that thought was finished and then continued to caress her breasts and pluck at her nipples. They were rock hard and the dark chocolate crests begged to be devoured. As she slowly began to ride him she stroked herself with one hand and continued to caress a breast with the other. Morgan couldn't stand it any longer and pulled her towards him so that he could suckle at her other breast. The second his lips touched her, a drawn out moan escaped and she let her head fall back. He shadowed the movement of her stroking and soon replaced her fingers with his. She gripped his shoulders with both of her now free hands, forced her head back up, and resumed her command of Morgan's total concentration. Her momentum escalated as he increased the pace of his stroking. He could feel her winding tighter and tighter and she began to gently pant.

"Yes . . . . yes . . . . yeeeees . . . ." Suddenly she stiffened, dug her perfectly manicured nails into his shoulders, and cried out. Her orgasm pulled him over the edge into his own and he again ground himself into her. This time she was as wrecked as he was and she slumped onto his chest without any coaxing. He held her tenderly and kissed her softly on the head.

"You know I've fallen in love with you, don't you?" he whispered. She instantly stiffened up. "Relax, I'm not asking anything of you. I'm simply letting you know how it is for me. Just let me love you." He carried her to his bedroom and lay her down on his bed. He slid out of her and went to the bathroom to wash up. When he returned she had snuck under his covers. He slipped in beside her and pulled her into his arms. She hadn't said a word since his declaration and continued to maintain her silence as she allowed him to wrap himself around her. He also remained silent and with a sigh, she acknowledged that he was keeping his word and that he wasn't going to force her to face her own feelings, at least not tonight. She snuggled in and was soon sound asleep. He knew it was going to take some time but he vowed he would mend her broken heart and someday soon she would accept that she was his.

Chapter 22

He tossed and turned caught in the grip of the increasingly frequent nightmare that plagued him. Like the old movies that were black and white and slightly out of focus, he saw himself running through a forest. The tree branches and leaves scratched at his face and arms as he plunged headlong into the woods. His breath sawed in and out as he ran, pushing at the branches, furtively checking over his shoulder. He had to get away—had to get away before they found him! Suddenly he tripped and sprawled face first onto the forest floor. He could smell rotting vegetation—rotting flesh! He lay draped over something that felt strangely like a body. A body he was familiar with. As a sickening sense of dread flowed over him he slowly propped himself up and stared at the thing he lay on. It was the thing he feared most! A headless body of a once living being with handless arms and footless legs splayed out before him. A friend . . . . his friend . . . . his *only* friend! A silent scream ripped his throat as he staggered to his feet and continued his flight. But with every footfall he knew he was not leaving the horror behind instead he was merely pursuing the first of the many unforgivable sins he had committed. As he came to the edge of the forest, despite trying to stop his progression, he was compelled to continue. Once he reached the shoreline of the lake it lapped at his high-tops while his eyes were drawn to the middle of it. Ripples appeared in the centre as something from below rose to escape its watery grave. He tried to back away but it was as if his feet were bolted to the ground. With horrified fascination he watched the bloated, fish nibbled, colorless remains of the once beautiful prostitute, with whom they had both lost their virginity to, ascend from the black depths of the lagoon. He knew it was her because the tattoo he had admired on countless occasions shone eerily in the moonlight and then suddenly began to ooze color into his monochromatic nightmare. Red . . . . dark red . . . . dark . . . red . . . gooey . . . . death!

Lurching upright he awakened with heart pounding and a throbbing ache in his leg. Breathing raggedly he dragged himself from bed and limped to the medicine cabinet for a pain pill. Damn leg must have spurred the nightmare, he silently cursed, as he headed back to the bedroom. Despite years of trying and multiple killings he could not control his dreams and make his original nightmare go away.

~ ~ ~

The next morning Dabria left with Morgan's promise to follow her out to her cottage after he cleared up a few details at the station. Before Dabria unlocked her door and walked into the cabin her instincts were screaming at her that something was not right. Her refuge had been compromised in some way. She backed away from the door and immediately began scanning the ground around the house. It hadn't snowed in a while so there were no discernable tracks in the driveway or footprints in the yard. She had only basic door locks but the door wasn't damaged in any way and the lock didn't appear jimmied. Shaking off her foreboding she unlocked the door and cautiously pushed it open. Instantly, she knew her first instinct had been correct. Someone had been in the house. The overwhelming stench of perfumes wafted over her. She immediately pulled the door closed, backed away, and quickly returned to her car to call Morgan.

"Hey. Can't stand to be away from me for even an hour?" he questioned with a chuckle. "What did you forget in town?"

"Morgan, this is gonna sound crazy but someone has been inside the cabin," she quietly stated.

Morgan was instantly on alert.

"Where are you now?"

"I'm back at the car."

"What did you see?"

"Nothing specific. I just had a feeling that someone had been here since I left yesterday and when I opened the door there was an overpowering smell of perfume."

"Go to the hotel and hang out there until I can get to the lake. I'm leaving right now."

"Okay. I think I will."

The fact that she didn't argue at all confirmed to Morgan that something was definitely not right and she was scared. The girl was no shrinking violet and knew to trust her instincts. Morgan's faith in his own instincts had kept him alive on more than one occasion. He swiftly left the station and sped out of town.

Dabria was sitting at the bar drinking a coffee and chatting with the bar owner and his wife when Morgan arrived. Mic and Ellen Pendleton had owned and operated the resort for several decades and knew everyone for miles around. Mic was the all purpose handyman, bouncer, bartender, and toy rental manager while Ellen was the chief cook, laundress, hotel and convenience store manager. They hired students in the summer to help them through the busy time but in the winter they mostly manned the business themselves. Taking his cue from Dabria's obviously relaxed manner Morgan casually pulled up a stool after he came in and sat down beside her. She introduced him as her friend and left out the cop part. She figured if he wanted them to know he'd tell them himself. She nonchalantly mentioned to him that their hosts had been very generously acquainting her with her neighbors. She learned that most of the neighbors on both sides of her were summer residents. The nearest year round neighbor was five lots down and elderly. At this point Morgan ordered a coffee and a sandwich and they asked him what he did for a living. They told him they had heard rumors a policeman might be moving into their community and assured him they would be thrilled if he did. He asked them if they had served any nonresidential customers in the last couple of days or noticed any unusual vehicles around. They immediately perked up sensing that he may be on a case or that at least they may learn some new gossip. He assured them he was only getting a feel for the area since Dabria lived out here alone and he didn't want to worry about her. They told him that the area was basically crime free and if they did see the occasional strange vehicle it was usually someone looking for property or coming to visit one of the known residents. They promised to call him if they saw anything unusual and said they would keep an eye out for Dabria and her place. Morgan tried to pay for his lunch and they waved his offer away claiming that all newcomers were given a complimentary lunch. He and Dabria thanked them and promised not to be strangers as they left.

They returned to Dabria's with Morgan leading the way. He waited by his Jeep until she joined him and then they walked to the front of the cabin together.

"I'm sure you think I'm being paranoid but I remember when I was waiting for you that I never did call Colin back about the number of keys he had left and I'm positive that there is a set missing."

"Okay. Who was here that day that might have taken them?"

"I believe that there are only two possibilities: either Jaimie or Craig."

"So, why would they do that?"

"Morgan, I honestly don't know. But this I do know, I can't get a read on Jaimie. She's extremely antagonistic towards me. Yet I have no memory of every doing anything that she should find personally offensive. Almost from my first day of work she has been blunt to the point of rudeness regarding my appearance and apparel choices."

"Is she like that with everyone or just you?"

"I don't know. I've never heard her commenting about anyone else. Plus, she only makes these observations regarding me when no one else is around."

"Okay. I'll see what I can dig up on her while you ask Sarah how she interacts with Jaimie. Anything else?"

"Yes. The night before I moved, you and I had been talking in the parking lot at the office. I could feel someone watching us. Right after you left I quickly turned around and looked up to the windows on the third floor. I caught a flash of movement and the curtain swung back into place proving that someone had been there. The only cars in the parking lot were Craig's and Jaimie's."

"So, besides the fact that Jaimie is a Fashion Nazi, there is no other evidence to support your assumption that she could be a thief. And then what is Craig's deal?"

"Craig and I went out on a *non-date* before you and I got together. He made it clear that he had every intention of pursuing some kind of relationship despite the fact that I informed him before we went out that I don't date lawyers."

"So why did you go out with him then?"

"Because I had just finished my first week of work and I wanted my new life to include some friends that I could socialize with. Is there a problem with that?" she challenged.

"Did you dress up? Did you put on perfume? Do you hair? Brush your teeth? Put on lipstick? Where did you go?" He countered with a barrage of questions of his own deliberately leaving hers unanswered.

"*Shay's*. You can't be serious?" the volume of her voice had begun to rise. "Because I take the time to personally groom myself before I go out in public I must be trying to make him want me. You're suggesting I'm a *cock-tease*?" she demanded as she stood ramrod stiff beside him clenching her fists and obviously fighting to control her temper.

"Dabria, I know how men think. I am one. If I asked a colleague out for supper to a fancy restaurant and she appeared in evening dress and smelling good I would take that as an encouraging sign that there may be some hope of eventually getting into her pants, despite the fact that she had claimed she never dated cops. Now if she showed up straight from work and we went out for a burger then that would be classified as a couple of co-workers grabbin' a bite and building a friendship."

Dabria was seething.

"You're a conceited, pompous ass!" she spat out.

"Probably, but that doesn't make me wrong. You were sending him mixed signals. I'm assuming you've told him that we are now *an item*?"

"*An item*? Actually, what I said was I only sleep with one guy at a time and for now, you were it!" she goaded.

"You would never have said anything that crass," he challenged.

"You'll never know," she sniffed.

"When did you tell him?" Dismissing what he considered a pointless exchange he continued with his questions.

"Yesterday," she gritted out. "Never mind. Just forget that I called you and get out of my way so that I can go into *my* house."

"I didn't say that I didn't believe you, Dabria. Did I? I trust your instincts as well as my own. I'm just trying to get some background so that we can attempt to figure out why one of them would want the keys to your house."

Dabria relaxed marginally but it was obvious she was still mad.

"Come on, let's go check this out."

The opened door revealed nothing obvious. They walked in and did a quick scan of the kitchen and living room. Nothing seemed to be out of place, but a nauseatingly intense smell continued to emanate from the bathroom. Dabria headed for the source of the stench. She glanced into her bedroom on the way but stopped dead in the doorway and gasped. Morgan instinctively pulled her out of the way and moved in front of her. Her closet doors and all of her dresser drawers were open and not all but most of her clothes had been taken out and left in a pile of tatters on the floor. Dabria tried to push him out of the way to assess the damage. He held her back.

"I'm calling this in. You can't go into that room until after I can get a crew out here to dust."

"It's got to be Jaimie. As if Craig would care enough about my wardrobe to come into my house and destroy it. But why? I don't understand."

Morgan moved down the hall before he called the station. The bathroom had also been purged of everything nice.

"Morgan?" Dabria questioned as she again tried to see past him. He stood aside. The medicine cabinet was open, as were all the drawers and cupboards. All of her perfumes had been dumped down the sink. Everything that either smelled nice or enhanced her appearance had been drained, smashed, or crushed and then thrown in the garbage. Dabria backed away sickened by the fact that someone had been inside her sanctuary and destroyed her beautiful things. She had never thought she was particularly vain but she had spent a fair amount of time accumulating her wardrobe and her cosmetics. The cosmetics were easily replaced. The clothing was a different thing as many items were from exclusive shops from all over the world. She and her parents had travelled extensively and she often shopped when she travelled. The more she thought about her destroyed beautiful garments the angrier she became. While Morgan talked on the phone she opened all the windows in the kitchen and living room to try to ease the stench.

"We need to check the loft as well," Morgan gently prompted.

"I know. I was waiting until you were finished on the phone." Her anger at Morgan had drained away and been replaced by sadness and fear.

Morgan grabbed her hand and together they went to the garage. It appeared untouched. Since her cabin furniture had arrived she had officially moved into the cabin rather than sleeping and working in the loft. Therefore, none of her personal things had been left in the loft. She hadn't had time to paint so none of her art supplies had even been unpacked. Her *intruder* may have been up here but there was really nothing personal to destroy. Morgan pulled her into his arms.

"You know I'm going to find out who did this?"

"I believe you. I just can't figure out what would prompt this kind of passionate display of hatred. I've only lived here for a couple of months."

"Dabria, you know there are lots of crazy people in this world. Let's go pack a bag so you can come back into town with me."

Dabria pulled out of his arms.

"I'm not going back into town to stay at your place. This is my home. I'm going to clean up the bedroom and bathroom after your guys leave and then I'm going to make the supper I had planned on making. I refuse to be afraid in my home. Monday morning I will have a security system installed with motion sensor lights and cameras and I will continue on with my life right here," she vehemently declared.

"Good. I expected nothing less. Let's go for a walk while we wait for my guys." Taking Dabria's hand again he led her out of the loft and down to the road. They walked and discussed the next steps that needed to be taken to prove Cody's innocence. After the forensic team was finished Dabria got busy cleaning the bathroom, removing her destroyed clothing, and making a list of the things that she needed to replace, as well as a list for her insurance agent. Since her losses far exceeded her insurance deductible it only made sense to put in a claim. As she sorted through the pile on the floor it became glaringly apparent that only those items that might be considered provocative had been destroyed—all of her lingerie, anything low-cut or fitted. What remained were her conservative court clothes, baggy t-shirts, and sweats—anything that didn't reveal her shape. Thankfully, her beautiful shuka was still intact. Assuming it was Jaimie, why had she fixated on Dabria? That was the burning question.

The rest of the day remained uneventful. Sarah and Kent came out for a BBQ and then they stayed for several rousing games of Kaiser—girls against the boys. Since neither team was willing to concede defeat the cards flew until early morning. Morgan stayed overnight and after a lazy morning loving they lounged in bed talking and playing. The phone rang and Morgan happened to be closest to it.

"Hello," his husky voice rumbled with laughter.

There was a distinct lack of response from the other end of the line.

"Hello," Morgan repeated more forcefully as his instincts went on the alert and he pushed himself into a sitting position.

"Uh . . . . Good morning. I'm looking for Dabria Abdulla-Smythe. Do I have the right number?" a very proper female voice inquired.

Morgan instantly relaxed while Dabria now stiffened up beside him as she heard and recognized the voice.

"Yes, you do. One moment please." He passed the phone to Dabria. "I believe it may be your mother."

Dabria promptly sat up herself and pulling the covers up to her armpits to cover her nudity, she accepted the receiver.

"Morning," she quipped brightly.

"You know she can't see you," Morgan teased in a whisper.

She batted his hands away as he tried to pull the covers back down.

"It's a little early for entertaining . . . . isn't it, dear?" her mother stiffly questioned.

"No, Mother, it isn't," Dabria firmly assured her. "How have you and Daddy been?"

"We're fine, Dabria, and speaking of that we determined it was time for a little break from our routine. Since we hadn't received any invitation from you, we elected to take it upon ourselves to visit your new home. Would that be a problem?"

"You know you're welcome any time and that you don't need an official invitation. Honestly, Mother, I have been trying to get comfortable with my new job and I only recently moved into my new house. I was planning to suggest a visit after the snow was gone so that you could see my beach and waterfront and maybe get in a round of golf."

"I suppose we could wait. We had hoped to leave the day before Good Friday and that way we could celebrate Easter with you. You do have a parish you attend, don't you, dear?"

"Ah, no. I thought I'd check out a few before settling on one. We could check out a couple when you're here and you could help me to decide. I'm in the middle of a big case right now, Mom, and I planned on working through Easter to get caught up. Would you mind holding off for another month or so?"

"I suppose that will have to work. Do make sure you fit in some time for us to get to know your new gentleman friend when we come to visit."

"I wouldn't have it any other way, Mother."

"Lovely. I'll keep in touch. Talk to you soon then."

"Love you, Mom. Say hi to Daddy." Dabria clicked off the phone, sighed, closed her eyes, and flopped back on the bed.

"Well, that was interesting," Morgan commented with a quirked eyebrow.

She popped back up, grabbed a pillow, and started pummeling him with it.

"Hey! Don't kill the messenger. I didn't know it was a problem if I answered the phone when your mother called. You *are* over thirty, you know?" he wrestled the pillow from her, forced her back onto the bed, and then promptly lay on top of her.

"Thanks. I wasn't aware. It's not a problem, exactly." Dabria sighed again and stopped struggling. Morgan immediately let her up, hoping she would tell him more about her family. She had said little over the course of the last several weeks. Morgan assumed it was due to the fact that David's and Matthew's lives had been so connected to her family that it was still difficult for her to deal with. Little did he know how right he was. If she kept herself immersed in her work and didn't think about her past at all she could keep out all of the pain.

"As you probably heard, my parents wanted to come for a visit. It's difficult to be around them. They were deeply affected by the deaths of David and Matthew. In some respects maybe more so than I was."

"How can that be?"

"Morgan, as you so kindly pointed out, I *am* over thirty. They not only hoped I'd be married by now but that I would have provided them with at least one grandchild. They adored David and are best friends with his parents. This whole thing has been devastating for them as well."

"I understand that but wouldn't they be happy to know that you are continuing on with your life and that you have a new relationship developing."

"I'm sure they would be if they knew anything about you and if they believed that I was actually moving on and not simply running away."

"So, Dabria, what is it? Are you moving on or running away?"

"A little of both. There are many things you don't know about my past, Morgan, and at this point I'm not ready to explain those things. Are you willing to give me some time?"

"Dabria, all I need to know is if you are interested in pursuing a relationship with me. If so then I'll absolutely give you some time. But if this is simply a diversion for you so that you don't have to deal with your past, then I'm not interested. I'm also over thirty, and as I may have indicated before, I want a partner. I want someone to share my life with and I want you to be that someone."

"I can't promise you anything. But I do want to explore what we have."

"Fair enough. So, who's making breakfast?" he asked as he pulled her up off the bed.

Chapter 23

"I understand there's a woman in town that seems to be sporting a very precise cut along her hairline. Some think that she's a link to the *scalper's* victims. How is that possible?"

"A copycat?"

"Hmmmmmm . . . . I don't believe so." A pregnant pause punctuated the statement. "What could you possibly have been thinking?" the voice quietly enunciated each word, clearly indicating the degree of anger. "Did you enjoy your time inside? I obviously misunderstood. I thought you couldn't wait to get out." Again there was a pause. "You can't practice your little hobby if they put you away again."

"Are you finished? I didn't have this particular hobby until you came along, remember?" he impudently challenged. "If I'm ever caught and convicted, guaranteed I'll make sure we're cellmates."

"Don't you *dare* threaten me," the voice hissed. "My little diversions supplement yours. Our relationship is symbiotic. Remember that."

"Look, I admit it was a lapse in judgment," he grudgingly acknowledged. "It was spontaneous. I walked around the corner of the bar and there she was, propped up against the wall and out cold. I've never cut one like that before and she was perfect. I needed to mark her. I had watched her all night long, dancin' and sluttin' around. She made it plain that no man would ever touch her, unless she wanted him to. No man except for *me*! She's always gonna wonder who I am! Who violated her? Shit, man, have you seen her? She's absolutely perfect. Trust me. You're gonna want her once you see her."

"I know exactly who she is and someday I will have her. But, ... that was still stupid. Marking her was a mistake! You jeopardize all we have when you take chances like that."

"Do the police have any leads regarding her little mishap?"

"Not to my knowledge. But I don't know everything they do. You need to hold off on getting another girl for awhile."

"Why?"

"I understand that killing the blond teenager was imperative to our remaining anonymous, but that has focused more attention on these trollops than I'm comfortable with."

"I didn't kill that girl. What are you talkin' about? I thought it was you."

"How could I have killed her? I wasn't even there. I never go to the drops."

"Since you check up on everything else I do, I just assumed you also check the drop sites."

"Well, you'd be wrong. I never see the girls after I leave the kennel. I have no need to."

"So it's okay for you to fuck 'em but you need to distance yourself from the killings. Why is that?" he quizzed. "Do you pretend to yourself that they aren't really dead? That your angels are just sleeping? Guess what? I . . . kill . . . them. I kill them when you're finished with them. I try to make it as painless as possible but I still . . . kill . . . them. They beg me, with their eyes, to let them go. They know me. They trusted me. Tears leak from their eyes until their hearts stop and then they just stare at me. I close those eyes and wash them and after I scalp them I wrap those girls in plastic and then I slide them into the dogsled. And then when I get to the drop I . . ."

"Enough! I am well aware of what you do to them and how you prepare them. Do you forget? I taught you. Now, let's get back to the point. If you didn't kill that teenager then who did? And what did they see? Did you see her truck or any other tracks around that night?"

"I don't use the road. The dogs and I travel better on the river. We're silent that way. That's why I drop them where I do."

"So, you saw nothing and you heard nothing? There's no way anyone could have seen you?"

"No!" he emphatically swore.

"Well, whether you want to accept it or not there was someone else out there that night and we need to find out who it was. Don't dismiss this threat so cavalierly. If only somehow we could hasten the conviction of Cody that would take the pressure off of that girl's real murderer. Hopefully then they'd keep quiet if they had seen something they shouldn't have."

"I'm pretty sure that even if her murderer did see something they're not about to go runnin' and tellin' anyone. Oh, and by the way, it's too late to decide we're finished for the season since I already have another one. This one has an interesting tattoo that may add to your viewing pleasure. She'll be ready tomorrow."

"Fine. I'll be out Thursday to play. But . . . . and I am absolutely serious, this one needs to be the last one this winter. We're running out of snow. Oh, and ditch the phone. I'll bring you a new one."

"Thursday it is."

Chapter 24

Since session one had gone so favorably and Dabria had been nightmare free all weekend, despite the break-in, she was actually looking forward to session two. She hadn't told Morgan anything about the therapy, mostly because she wasn't prepared to spill her guts yet. She trusted him more than any man she had trusted in a very long time. She could feel that he was honorable and fair and that she was safe with him, not only physically but emotionally. She suspected that once he claimed you as one of his own he would stand by you. Of course, that was providing you didn't do anything illegal or immoral. Unfortunately, that was the crux of the whole thing. Although it was comforting to know he would always have her back it was also scary as hell. What a standard to live up to. She was ashamed of many of the things she had done over the course of the last several years. And she was disgusted that she had been so easily played when she had known, deep down, that she was being used. For over a year she had allowed the charade to continue. And even now she still kept their secret. For what? The boys were dead! They couldn't feel pain anymore, only she could. Their secrets and the result of her one act of grossly misplaced loyalty could destroy *her* future. She needed to come to some kind of resolution and then she needed to tell Morgan. Their relationship could go no further until he knew the truth. She was so deep into her own musings that it took several attempts by the receptionist to catch Dabria's attention. Embarrassed, she jumped up and hustled into Dr. Murphy's office.

"Afternoon, Dabria. I take it you had a good weekend?"

"It was excellent. And yours?"

"Fine. Should we continue where we left off or do you want to go in a different direction?"

"Let's continue. I didn't have a single nightmare this weekend and I can't remember when I actually slept undisturbed three nights in a row."

"I'm happy to hear that. Carry on then."

Dabria continued with an accounting of their university days and revealed that it was at this point she and David had become lovers. She stated that despite the change in her relationship with David, the bond of the three musketeers seemed unchanged. If she hadn't been so naïve that fact in itself should have been a sign that something was not right. Human nature, being what it is, should have indicated that Matthew was jealous. He wasn't, and upon reflection, seemed almost smug around her. It was as if he knew something she did not. She was head over heels in love with her best friend and life couldn't have been better. It was simply an understood thing that once they had graduated and had their careers underway David and she would get engaged, be married, and live happily ever after. Matthew often went on double-dates with them. However, it seemed to be rarely the same girl twice. Dabria privately joked with him that he was her *favorite male slut*. David and she had separate apartments. Matthew and David shared a place. Therefore, when they wanted some privacy David simply stayed at her place. This arrangement continued even after the boys secured positions at the Conservation Station at Nordegg and she had landed a junior partnership in a law firm in Rocky Mountain House. Since accommodations were at a premium in Nordegg it only made sense for the boys to remain rooming together. Right?

She never suspected a thing until she caught them kissing each other goodbye one day when Matthew was dropping David off at her place. She had arrived home earlier than David had anticipated. Since her car was in the shop she had taken the afternoon off to make a special supper to celebrate the news of her unexpected pregnancy. When she went out on the balcony to water the plants she spotted them in the parking lot. She was devastated and had no idea how to react. Instead of immediately confronting David she made up the excuse of having an out of town appointment and sent him away. She then rented a vehicle for the weekend and left for Calgary.

"Were you planning on discussing the situation with someone there?" Dr. Murphy inquired.

"I honestly had no idea what I was going to do or who I was going to tell once I arrived. I only knew I had to get away from David and where else does one go but run to their family when they're hurting?"

"Indeed," Dr. Murphy concurred. "And so . . . . ," she prompted.

"And so, I was so bloody distracted I promptly ran off the road and into a very large tree about half an hour out of Calgary. The car was totaled and apparently it was a miracle that I survived."

"Dabria, was it deliberate?" Dr. Murphy asked gently.

"I wish I could assure both you and myself that it unequivocally was an accident, but unfortunately I can't do that. I honestly don't know, Dr. Murphy, that right at that moment I didn't wish I was dead. I do know, however, that after I regained consciousness in the hospital, about three days later, I was very glad things had turned out as they had. It was at that point after David had literally not left my bedside for three days that I knew at least some part of him actually did love me. I, of course, lost our child. The doctors informed David of that before I woke up. I was pretty banged up and it took several months for me to recuperate. Once I was released from the hospital I spent that time with my parents. I watched them and listened to them like I never had before. I had always known they were very close but until then hadn't actually realized how deeply they loved each other and how mutual their respect was."

"Therefore . . . ." Dr. Murphy again encouraged.

"Therefore, I believed that I should settle for nothing less than a relationship like that. I confronted David. He admitted that he was bisexual and that he and Matthew had been lovers for years. He begged me not to abandon him and swore he loved me. I believed him. And to a certain extent I still believe that he did love me. So, it was simply a matter of making a decision."

"Which was?"

"Could I live with his relationship with Matthew?"

"You decided you could."

"Initially, yes. Despite the fact that he had ripped my heart out that day, I still loved him. I had loved him for years. I didn't know how to *exist* without loving him. After I returned to work we became engaged. Despite David's attentiveness when we were together there was something not right. The final straw was when I started to suspect he was having an affair with his new partner. I saw him watching her at a social function and decided this sham of an engagement needed to end. We had a huge blow out and that was the last time I saw him alive," Dabria's voice caught as she stifled a sob. Her nails dug into the fine leather as her hands clenched the sides of her armchair. She fought for control by swallowing and closing her eyes. Dr. Murphy allowed her time to pull herself back together.

"Dabria, I'm so sorry," she stated with compassionate support.

"While the car accident hadn't killed me, the guilt from that argument almost did," she gave a harsh bark of bleak laughter. "I still can't seem to get past it. The things I said to him that night were ugly and malicious. I'm ashamed and appalled that I lost control like that."

"Do you believe that you were justified to be angry?"

"Absolutely. He played me for a fool for years."

"Are you sure?"

"No. But it felt like that."

"And now?"

"Now that I've had some time to reflect on it I don't know. David was always a restless spirit. He was always seeking the next thrill, the next challenge. And maybe that carried over into his sexuality as well. I mean, why wouldn't it?"

"Why indeed. Do you believe that you were kind and loving and faithful for all the years you were together?"

"Yes."

"Do you believe you were respectful and that you honored his right to privacy regarding his sexuality?"

"Of course."

"Are you still maintaining that confidence?"

"Yes. And that and the guilt are eating me alive."

"Who do you feel you need to tell? You've told me. Have you told your parents?"

"No. I didn't tell my parents. However, they do know because when Matthew was killed his parents, David's parents, and mine all went to help clean out the boys' house and found pictures of them together."

"And you have never had a discussion with them about this?"

"How could I? I would have to admit that I had known about their relationship before David and I were engaged. How does that make me look?"

"Do they know that the engagement had ended?"

"No. None of the parents do. David's and Matthew's parents begged me not to reveal the boys' relationship after their deaths and the R.C.M.P. assured us that it need never be exposed."

"So, I'm the first person you've told?"

"Yes, but I feel I need to explain all of this to Morgan before we continue on."

"Why are you holding back? Do you think he'll judge you and find you lacking?"

"Possibly. It certainly wouldn't instill in me a sense that that person was all together. It would probably make me question my choice in continuing a relationship with someone who was such a bad judge of character."

"Really?"

"Yes."

"Dabria, I think you're over-analyzing this and I also think you're doing Morgan a disservice. From the way you speak of him I don't get the indication he's that shallow. Give him a chance to show you his true worth. You know all men are not like David and Matthew."

"You're right."

"Is there anything else at this point that you want to share?"

"No."

"Okay. Then I think we should stop here. You need to decide when you're going to be comfortable with telling Morgan. Don't rush it. If you need time take some time."

"Thank you. When should I come back?"

"Give it at least a week. Then we'll talk some more." Once Dabria made her way out of the office Dr. Murphy added to her notes. Dabria was not revealing all that was going on. It was obvious to Dr. Murphy that Dabria felt guilty about more than the boys' secret. She obviously harbored a secret of her own. It was *that* secret Dr. Murphy was more concerned about. She feared that was the secret that could destroy Dabria.

~ ~ ~

Nina walked into Leotie's kitchen, arms overflowing with grocery bags. As she went to place them on the table Leotie grabbed a couple from her. Sunlight glinted off a ring adorning her finger. Nina stopped dead. She swiftly dumped the groceries and grabbed Leotie's hand.

"Where did you get that ring?" she croaked harshly.

"I found it," Leotie replied calmly as she pulled out of Nina's hand and twisted the ring carelessly.

"Where?" Nina again demanded.

"In the washing machine. What's the big deal?"

"Oh my God, Leotie," Nina sunk into a kitchen chair. "Do you know whose ring that is?"

"Yes. It's Megan's engagement ring," she again calmly stated.

"How would it end up in your washing machine? Why was Megan not wearing it the night she was killed?"

"How do you know she wasn't?"

"What are you saying?"

"You figure it out," Leotie said as she put food in the fridge.

"I don't want to. The implications are appalling," Nina shuddered.

"Where is your loyalty, Nina?" Leotie asked with disgust as she slammed a can onto the counter. "You've already thrown your oldest son, supposedly the child of your heart, to the wolves once to save your own skin. Who are you protecting now?"

"Cody won't be convicted. He never killed Megan," Nina bristled. "I had no choice, Leotie. Richard threatened to hurt his children . . . . *his own children*. You know how violent he can be," she defended her actions.

"There is always a choice," Leotie quietly reminded her.

"When did you find this?"

"The day after, the policemen were here to talk to you."

"What were you waiting for? Why didn't you say something? And why are you wearing it now?" Nina asked.

"I was waiting for Teyha to come forward."

"To say what," Nina exclaimed? "Hey Tante Leotie, I killed Cody's girlfriend last night and took her ring!"

"No, I was hoping she would say I followed Cody's girlfriend last night and I saw someone kill her . . . . then I took her ring."

"So which one is it?"

"I don't know, Nina. And besides there's a third possibility and that is she saw Cody kill Megan and is trying to protect him."

"Never! He would never have hurt her! You know how much he loved her."

"We will see."

"So, now what?"

"I've waited long enough for Teyha to say something. I'm going to phone that Detective Ducette. He can do what he likes with the information. Let's just hope it's her fear and not feelings of guilt that have kept her silent."

"Let's hope," Nina fervently agreed.

~ ~ ~

Hmm . . . . music. Hmm . . . . hmm . . . . hmmmmmm. Elevator music? Hey, I know. It's that Bach stuff. That's weird. I never listen to this shit. Wow, bright lights! I can't see a thing. Hey, where am I and why am I so cold? Yah, ... *why* am I so cold? Shit! I can't feel my hands . . . . or my feet. I can't move! I can't even turn my head!! Holy shit, am I dead? No. No! My heart is pounding. I can feel it. I can hear panting. I can *feel* myself panting. I must be alive. What's wrong with me? Wait. What's that . . . . a scraping sound? A door opening? Footsteps . . . . coming closer. I feel a draft. I *can* feel! I'm scared! This is NOT good!

God, my tailbone hurts! I must'a been laying here forever. And this ain't no feather bed. Something cold . . . . something hard. Oh my God, ... I'm naked!!! No wonder I'm so cold. *What* is that gross smell? Toilet cleaner! Why can't I move? Where the hell am I and how did I get here? Hey, a face. A FACE!!! I know you! Remember me? Help me! Help me!! I'll be good from now on. I promise! No more tricks. I swear! I'll do anything you want. Please. . . . You can't hear me, can you? I can't hear me!!!! Why can't I speak?

"Hey, beautiful, are you comfortable? Warm enough?"

No! I'm cold. Very cold! I can feel sweat running down my forehead into my hair. I'm sweating, but I'm freezing. Why are you strokin' my cheek? I can feel that, too. Stop. Please stop! Hey, stop!! You're creepin' me out. Why can't I move? I'm gonna die . . . . aren't I? I'm gonna die!! Shit, I think I just peed myself.

"Just relax. Don't cry," the voice gently coaxed as the hand brushes my tears away. "You're even prettier than I remembered. I'm so sorry. I know you trusted me." The hand moves from my cheek down my throat and across my breast. "I haven't taken very good care of you. Have I? I'm going to wash you and make you smell nice again. I remembered the lavender. Do you like lavender? I used to. My . . . . you *are* dirty! It's okay. You'll smell like your old self in no time. I'm being very gentle. Please stop crying. It won't help. I can't let you go but I promise I *will* set you free. I'm sorry. I won't ever hurt you . . . . I promise. I'm very good at some things. Very gentle. Don't be afraid. It will all be over soon."

Stop touching me! Stop touching me!! STOP . . . . TOUCHING . . . . ME!!!!! HELP ME! HELP ME!! HELP!!!

Chapter 25

After her session with Dr. Murphy Dabria determined it was time to take the bull by the horns and explain at least some of her sordid past to Morgan. She was definitely falling for him and before she allowed herself to care anymore she needed to give him the opportunity to run. She decided to pick up some Chinese food and surprise him at his place. As she was leaving the restaurant on Central Avenue she opened the door and walked onto the sidewalk and directly into the path of a man heading in. As she juggled the food he reached out a hand to steady her. A jolt zipped up her arm.

"Sorry," he mumbled as he brushed past her. A large man with a toque pulled down over dark hair was the only physical impression she had of him as she hurried to the car. However, a feeling that she had not only seen him before but had also been touched by him settled over her. As she secured supper into the back seat it suddenly came to her that she had danced with him that fateful night in the bar. He had been a lot more charming then. In fact, if she recalled correctly, he had definitely indicated interest that night. She dismissed the incident and returned to preparing her speech for Morgan.

~ ~ ~

"Are you free for the evening?" she inquired as she waited on the threshold of his doorway for an invite in.

"For you, ... always. Come," he drew her in as he relieved her of the tantalizing packages she carried. He set everything on the table and as he opened the boxes she washed her hands and brought out plates and cutlery. Before she could slide into a chair he swung around, grabbed her, and very thoroughly welcomed her with a lip smacking kiss.

"Hellooooo," she giggled nervously as he released her.

Although Dabria had provided tonight's sustenance it was obvious her mind was not on food. While Morgan wolfed his down she scooted hers around on her plate. Morgan made short work of his portions and then moved in for round two. Since his initial hunger had been abated he was able to slow down and while he casually chomped on dry ribs he prompted her to reveal why she had really stopped in.

"Okay. So, what's going on?"

"What?" she looked up distracted.

"You have something on your mind. What?"

"I, ahhh . . . . I guess maybe it's time that I explain some things about myself. You seem to think you know me and there are things from my past that you don't know and probably aren't gonna to like."

Morgan put down his rib, wiped his hands on a napkin, and looking directly at her calmly waited for her to continue. Dabria pushed her untouched plate away and clasping her hands began her tale. She basically repeated the story she had told Dr. Murphy. Morgan listened attentively without interruption. His expression revealed to her that he was surprised when she told him the details of her car accident and the loss of her child. Leaning forward he tried to compassionately grasp her hands. She pulled away from him so that she could concentrate on getting the rest of the story out. But, as her story continued Dabria had the uncanny feeling that the secrets she now revealed were not news to him. Before she finished she startled him by jumping up from the table and pointed a finger at him accusingly.

"You already know all this! You investigated me, didn't you?" she demanded as she planted both hands on the table and leaned towards him. "Why would you do that? Why would you go behind my back and dredge up stuff that was none of your business? If I wanted you or anyone else to know those things I would tell you. I didn't go digging into your past." Her knowledge of Morgan was based on only what he had told her and what she had observed herself. She felt betrayed.

"Hold it. I did a basic search the day I pulled you over, just like I do of everyone I have ever pulled over or arrested. After meeting you

I was intrigued and assuming I would never see you again, except of course for our court date, I decided to dig a little deeper," he attempted to defend himself.

"You had no right!" she exclaimed.

"Maybe not," he conceded. "But the reason I'm a good detective is because I follow my gut instincts and my gut said check this woman out. This is what I do, Dabria! This is who I am," he said as he stood and forcefully thumped himself on the chest attempting to drive his justification home.

"What else do you think you know?" she demanded.

Since this was obviously going to be the make or break point of their relationship Morgan decided to lay all the cards on the table.

"I know that you were investigated for being an accessory to attempted murder," he quietly stated, "and that you were never charged."

"Are you telling me that knowing what you do about my past you've been able to disregard that knowledge? Can you honestly say that the unanswered question of my innocence doesn't color every conversation we have? I don't believe I'm any more suspicious than you are of people and I know that not knowing the answer to that question must eat at you. It would eat at me! Well, despite what the reports may have told you I'm a woman who is very private and I don't trust easily. I've learned all this in the last year. I'm a different person than the one who lived in Rocky Mountain House. A year ago I would have naively excused your behavior. Today, I'm offended by your uninvited intrusion into my past. You, of all people, know there is more to a story than what appears on the surface. I can guarantee that not one of those reports told you I was devastated by the betrayal and death of David and overwhelmed by grief and guilt after Matthew's death. I am well aware that I was a prime suspect for the harassment and attempted murder of Annah Andersson. And, guess what Mr. Detective, you will never really know if I was involved or not since everyone else that was involved is dead! Believe me when I say that the only living person that knows the whole truth isn't about to share it with you or anyone else. Have a nice night, Detective. I have notes to finish for trial in the morning and I guarantee you, any personal interaction we had has come to an abrupt end." With that said she practically ran from his condo, slamming the door as she left. Scrubbing his hand down his face he made the decision to temporarily let her go and he sank back down into his chair. He'd been stunned and saddened by the information that she may have tried to kill herself and that her child had died. Before any kind of meaningful conversation could occur between them she would need to calm down. This was not the time to force his rationalizations on her or apologize for hurting her.

Dabria hustled out to her car and recklessly raced out of town. Tears poured down her cheeks and as her vision blurred she was forced to pull over onto an approach and give full reign to her depth of heartache. How could he? How could he? She refused to admit to herself that this latest debacle was a direct result of her poor judgment months ago. Wrapping her anger tightly around herself like a cloak she vowed to make Morgan pay for his duplicity.

Chapter 26

After yesterday's emotional fiasco Dabria determined she needed to spend more time on her working life and less time on her personal life. Work she understood and could control. Tuesday afternoon she received a call that blew that theory out of the water as well. Her caller gave her much to think about and his findings caused several new questions to crop up.

"Craig, I just received some information I need to share. Have you got a minute?"

"Sorry Bree, but I'm on my way to court. Can it wait until tomorrow?"

"Not really. Call me later," she stated. There was no way that Dabria was going to sit on this news until tomorrow. If only she could share it with Morgan. Despite the fact that the mature responsible course of action would be to leave her personal feelings out of it and maintain a professional demeanor so that she could use his expertise, she was not that big a person. Unfortunately, about eighteen hours wasn't nearly enough time to get over her anger and her hurt feelings. The next obvious choice was Brad.

"Brad, have you got a minute for me to give you an update and get some advice?"

"Sure, Dabria, come on up."

Dabria swiftly locked her office and bounded up the stairs. Before Brad had a chance to finish the note he was making on the file he was working on she was standing in his doorway gripping her notebook and pen.

"Come in. Come in. You look like you're about to explode. What's up?"

Dabria closed his door and swiftly plopped herself into a seat. Before she spoke she took a big breath and then let it out slowly. Brad gazed at her quizzically.

"Okay. My private detective has been earning his money recently. He called this afternoon and he has uncovered all kinds of new leads." Dabria stopped and flipped her notebook open.

"So, what's he got?" Brad leaned forward eagerly.

"First, Richard has dual citizenship for Canada and the U.S. so he can come and go as he pleases with no one asking questions. Coincidentally, or not, Benjamin Musgrave owns a residence in Willamette National Forest. For years someone has been occupying that cabin for a few days several times a year. Sometimes there is a woman with him, sometimes not. So question number one is—is it Ben—and if not, then who is it? The frequency of the visits has lessened over the last two years. Whoever goes to the cabin uses a rental vehicle and when the neighbors stop by there is never an answer at the door. No one around seems to have seen the guy's face clearly but the descriptions indicate that he has the same hair color and build as Ben or Richard. The cabin is fairly remote. You can't see it from any of the others around."

"Then who are these witnesses to his visits?"

"There are three other acreages on the same dead end road and so the neighbors have seen him driving to and from the property."

"Why has no one seen his face?"

"Because he wears large dark sunglasses and his vehicles always have tinted windows."

"Okay. For the sake of argument let's assume that Ben is in fact dead and that Richard is the one using the cabin. Now what?"

"First, we need to find out the identity of Richard's mother and force a DNA test to figure out if Richard is in fact Richard. Then if he is, we need to find out why he was using Ben's cabin and why he has stopped. We need to get a warrant to search the cabin and the surrounding area."

"Give me your hypothesis before we start throwing more money around and begging for favors across the border."

"I honestly don't know if we are dealing with Ben or Richard. What I do believe is that one killed the other and that the killer has also murdered women from that area. Over the past thirty years eleven young women have disappeared from the Canadian border down towards Salem. None of their bodies have ever been found. They all have the same physical characteristics as the women from P.A. I think the reason he isn't using the cabin anymore is because he is now butchering girls closer to home."

"Where is the PI getting his information?"

"From the Oregon State Police. When Tony showed pictures of the P.A. girls to Sheriff McLaren at the office in Salem he instantly perked up and started sharing what they had regarding cold cases of similar looking woman. There is a file on the eleven missing women."

"Okay, so back up. How does little orphan boy Ben end up with property in the woods but no one knows about it until now?"

"Apparently Ben's only living relative, who just happened to be an old hermit died not long after Ben and Richard disappeared. Ben may have known about the property and told his best friend Richard, or Richard did the same thing my PI did and that was to do a property search under Ben's name. The land was left to Ben according to his uncle's will. The taxes are paid out of a trust fund. There is no running water or electricity so therefore no other services to be billed."

"Back to an obvious question—why is either Ben or Richard murdering woman?"

"I don't know that yet?"

"What does your boyfriend think?"

"He's *not* my boyfriend and I have no idea!" she declared vehemently and then looked down at her notes.

"Dabria, we need police help on this. We *need* that DNA warrant and the warrant to open the orphanage records. If there is some issue between you and Detective Vaughn you need to remember you're a professional. You don't have the luxury of allowing personal feelings to get in the way of Cody's defense, which is ultimately why we're doing this, remember. If you still believe he's innocent then his case takes precedence over your sensitivities."

"Can I do some more digging on my own before I hand this over to the police?"

"I would prefer that you not. Investigating is not your job, it's theirs."

"Fine."

"Dabria, they have easier access to resources we aren't privy to. Be the bigger person here for the sake of the boy."

"I promise I will pass the information that we have so far onto the police."

"Thank you. Now is there anything else?"

"Yes. I'm meeting my PI in Salem this weekend to see what else we can shake out."

"Keep me updated."

"I will, sir, thanks for your input."

As Dabria left his office the wheels in her head were furiously turning, trying to come up with a solution to her cop problem. The one that first came to mind was to give the information to Ducette and let Morgan twist in the wind. Be the bigger person, huh! Brad was right. This was more important than her hurt feelings and she was not going to sacrifice that boy to spite Morgan. She marched back to her office, checked Craig's schedule, and promptly dialed Morgan's office number.

"Detective Vaughn," his clipped voice sent unwanted shivers of awareness down Dabria's spine and she inhaled sharply.

"Dabria?" Morgan questioned hopefully.

"Detective Vaughn, Tony has uncovered some information that may be helpful to your *scalper* case. Can we set up a meeting for tomorrow around 11:00 a.m.?"

"Sure or you could just tell me now," he recognized her chilly tone but continued to speak to her in a carefree, easy manner.

"I would prefer that Craig and Kent attend the meeting as well and Craig is unavailable until that time."

"I would think that the sooner the sharing of information occurred, the better for all parties. Wouldn't you agree? Therefore, I see no point in waiting until tomorrow."

"Unfortunately, you will *have* to wait until then," she quipped. "Where would you like to meet?"

"My office," the tone of his voice swiftly changed and made it immediately obvious that he brooked no argument. If she wanted to play it that way then he was more than happy to accommodate her. She may have the information that the case needed to proceed, but he had the muscle behind him that they both needed to get the warrants issued. Whether she liked it or not she needed him as much as he needed her. That is, as far as the case was concerned. Apparently, she was still mad at him and obviously nothing was going to be solved over the phone. Since she had ignored his calls and texts so far, he would need to make his move in person tomorrow after their meeting.

"Fine, we'll see you then.

"Dabria . . ."

"Good day, Detective Vaughn," she cut him off and hung up. Her heart was pounding and her palms were sweating so badly she could barely hang up the phone. She stood up, wiped her hands on her pants, and wandered over to open the window to take some nice deep fresh breaths. As she gazed into the backyard and single handedly massaged her tense neck muscles her thoughts wandered. She pushed all thoughts of Morgan out and concentrated on the details Tony had uncovered. She needed to make a list of questions before tomorrow's meeting as well as work on a couple of client files. Tonight was going to be a long night.

~ ~ ~

The meeting the next morning went off without a hitch. Dabria had briefed Craig and he informed Morgan and Ducette of the details. When Morgan asked Dabria a direct question she answered professionally but without elaboration. Morgan had decided he would honor her silent but obvious barriers until the meeting was finished. Craig indicated that they felt the next step was to procure the necessary warrants without Richard's knowledge. Therefore, they had to approach a judge who was known for his strong ethical morals who would keep their confidence. Although Dabria had been forthcoming with all the information that Tony had imparted she did not reveal what her weekend plans were. As they stood up to leave Morgan reached out his hand and touched her arm to detain her. With obvious disdain she looked down at his hand and then back up to his face. Flushing with anger, Morgan removed his hand and Dabria immediately stepped away from him.

"I would like to speak with you."

"Does it pertain to a case?" she questioned in a clipped voice.

"No. This is personal and needs to be taken somewhere more private. Remember where you are, Dabria," Morgan warned quietly.

"Oh, Detective Vaughn, I know exactly where I am," she assured him, equally quietly, but with flashing eyes. "This is your arena so I won't embarrass you in front of your co-workers but I don't wish to speak with you. So don't push me." With that softly but clearly stated she turned from him and walked away.

He allowed her to go despite the noticeable stares directed at him. He could feel the censure of his fellow officers for letting her leave with the last word. She was still obviously boiling mad and forcing the issue in front of others was not the way to settle the situation. He would let it go for today and start his attack of apologies and wooing tomorrow. Despite what she may believe their personal relationship was far from over.

~ ~ ~

Dabria was much more stubborn than he had originally assumed and not only was she able to remain unresponsive all week but then she disappeared early Friday for the entire weekend! Unbeknownst to Morgan, Dabria had flown to Salem to spend the weekend with Tony, *her* PI. Dabria knew Morgan would be livid when he found out but right now she couldn't have cared less. Tony met her at the airport and they had a late supper at her hotel while he explained what he had prepared for the next day.

They were up and on the road early. The plan was to head out to Ben's cabin. She wanted to get a feel for the place firsthand and hopefully meet some of his neighbors. The property was over an hour away from the outskirts of the city. Along the way they casually chatted about their careers—the commonality as well as differences. Dabria was also able to get Tony to elaborate on his background, which just confirmed for her that she had found the right man for the job.

The time slipped by and they quickly reached their destination. They veered off the main road and onto an overgrown side road. It meandered through forest and shortly opened up into a small clearing with a solitary building. The cabin was a clapboard structure with a sagging front porch. The shake shingles were covered in spongy damp looking moss and Virginia Creeper had twined itself around the supporting posts and trailed across the porch floor. It had been whitewashed at some point during the last half century but that appeared to be the only maintenance that had ever been done. There were shutters on the two visible windows and the only solid looking part of the whole structure was the padlocked front door. It appeared that no one had been in residence for some time judging by the vine's undisturbed trail. The second she stepped out of the car dread washed over her. Bad things had happened here. The sun shone brilliantly and it was a truly picturesque locale but it was not serene. A shiver rippled up Dabria's spine and goose bumps peppered her skin. Tony let her silently survey their surroundings. The scent of soggy rotting vegetation assaulted her nostrils, not unlike the smell of dead things. It had been raining for weeks and the lack of sunlight on the forest floor had prevented last fall's dead leaves from drying up and blowing away. The wind whispered gently through the aspen trees and ruffled their new leaves, scattering small shadows across the ground. The air was strangely absent of birdsong. When Tony finally spoke the sudden intrusion of sound made her jump.

"There's a trail behind the cabin that leads down to a creek," he pointed. "Sorry," he chuckled. "I didn't mean to startle you."

"It's soooo creepy. Can't you feel it?" she asked amazed at his composure.

"Of course, I can feel it. But I've been out here a couple of times now and at least this time I'm not alone—safety in numbers and all, ya know?" again he chuckled.

"Yah," she sarcastically agreed. She started snapping pictures of the scene from the road to the cabin and then walked up to the cabin and reluctantly turning her back on it quickly took pictures of the view from the porch. Tony walked around the building with her as she continued to click away. They headed down to the stream and she observed the overgrown state of the path. Tony informed her that the undergrowth had been totally undisturbed when he had walked in it the week before and that he had pics to prove it. The gentle sound of water tripping over rocks could be heard before they rounded the last curve. The brook was just as picturesque as the area surrounding the cabin and similarly it was unusually devoid of nature sounds. Dabria instinctively knew that over the years the woodland animals had been witness to horrific events. Again she snapped several pictures and then with one last survey of the vicinity she shook off a shudder and hastened back to the car.

Once they were back out on the main road she let out a long sigh as if she had been holding her breath for the last half hour.

"So, now what," Tony asked?

"It's not that I don't trust your interview skills but I wondered if we could possibly stop in and chat with the old guy that lives farther down the lane."

"The one that told me he found Ben's uncle?"

"Yes."

"Sure, maybe he'll have remembered something since I talked to him."

They pulled up to a tidy little bungalow that was exactly Dabria's idea of what a country cottage should be like. An elderly gentleman was sitting on the side of a raised garden box weeding. He continued to sit as they pulled up and then motioned them over rather than rising to greet them.

"I wondered how long it would take you to come back?" he directed his question to Tony. "And I see you've brought along a lovely companion," he turned his countenance upon Dabria.

"This is who is signing my paycheck this month, Gus. Meet Dabria Abdulla-Smythe, a lawyer from Canada. Dabria, may I introduce Gustav Gorbinski, a retired government translator."

"My, my . . . . that is quite some name," Gus commented with a quirked eyebrow.

"Please call me Bree," she quickly interjected.

"Bree it is, then. What questions do you have for me today?"

"Tony told me you were the person that found the body of the hermit that lived down the road."

"That's correct, old Hugh Musgrave."

"Did you ever have any interactions with him before he passed away?"

"Sure. I've had this place for years. Back then my family and I only used it as a retreat. Now I live here full time. Unfortunately, my wife passed away a few years ago. She saw him more often than I did and often spoke to him."

"Did anyone ever come and visit him?"

"Not that I ever saw, but my wife did tell me that he talked about having a nephew. It was his sister's child. He apparently took him one summer and was planning on raising him but social services came and checked him out and decided that the boy was better off at the orphanage. I know they wrote back and forth because we would pick up his mail in town and leave it at the cabin for him. My wife said he was expecting that once the boy was of age he would come back for a visit. That never happened and the kid didn't even show up for the funeral. According to the orphanage he took off the night after graduation and no one has seen him since."

"When did you find Hugh?"

"Beginning of July . . . . thirty years ago. In fact, it was the third of July. We had come out for the holiday and picked up his mail on the way. I left it on the porch under a rock like usual when his old dog came whining and nosing up to me. That wasn't typical. Whenever I had seen Hugh the dog was always right beside him. The dog licked my hand and then loped off. He stood at the edge of the path waiting for me to follow. When I didn't he came back to me, licked me again, and then went back to the path. I decided to follow the dog and I found Hugh. He was half in and half out of the creek, but very obviously dead."

"Did they do an autopsy?"

"Sure. They said he slipped and fell, knocked himself out, and then drowned."

"And that was the end of it?"

"Yes."

"How long was it before either you or your wife saw someone back at the cabin?" Dabria asked.

"Probably a of couple years later. And before you start asking me questions about that I'll simply tell you what I know. I never spoke to anyone over there. I only saw a man driving to and from there a few times over the years, maybe a half dozen, and twice he had a woman with him."

"Do you know if it was the same man?"

"I believe so. All I know for sure is that he had dark brown hair and that he wore sunglasses. He drove a rental every time I saw him."

"What about the woman?"

"Small dark girls."

"What do you mean dark girls? Not white? Dark like me?" she questioned in no way offended.

"Actually, yes," he said as he carefully scrutinized her. "You could have been one of them."

"So it wasn't the same woman both times?"

"No."

"Were you driving when you saw them?"

"No. I was hiking. I doubt he knew that I saw him."

"Did you see the women on their way to the cabin or on their way back?"

"Going to. One girl had the window open and she was laughing at something the man said."

"So, she didn't appear to be under any kind of duress?"

"Absolutely not. She was obviously enjoying herself."

"Can you think of anything else you might have seen?"

"I walked over there a couple of times and knocked on the door, but even though there was a car parked out front no one ever answered."

"Didn't you think that was a little strange?"

"Not really since Hugh never answered the door when I knocked either. I just figured the whole family must be a little eccentric."

"When was the last time you saw a vehicle or any activity over there?"

"About two years ago. It was right before Millie passed away. We were on our way to the hospital for one of her treatments and he met us as we headed to town. I never saw anyone around there again."

"Was he with anyone that time?"

"No, he was alone."

"Thank you, Gus, for your time."

"Any time. Would you like a cup of tea before you head back to town?"

"Uh . . . . yes, we would love one," Dabria accepted with a barely perceptible hesitation. They spent the next hour listening to Gus reminisce about his life with Millie. His devotion to his wife was as obvious as his loneliness. Dabria was glad she had decided they should stay. They headed back to the city and went their separate directions for the evening with plans of meeting up again the next morning before she flew out. Dabria called her other contact in Salem and left a message. She had hoped to catch the cleaning lady from the orphanage at home. Time would tell if she had the courage to call Dabria back.

The next morning Dabria suggested to Tony that they see if Gus would be willing to come into the city and check out the pictures of the missing women from the area. If they were really lucky one of them might match up with the two women he had seen. She would also like to see if he could identify either Richard's face with sunglasses or a computer generated picture of Ben's aged face with sunglasses. Gus was more than happy to agree since he assured them it was time to make a run to the city for supplies. They met him at the Salem Sheriff's Office and led him over to a desk covered with women's photographs. Straight away he picked out the photo of a young prostitute that had gone missing about three years ago.

"That's the girl that was laughing when they drove by. I remembered last night that she had a big colorful tattoo on her forearm. That's why I could hear her," Gus exclaimed excitedly.

"What? I don't understand what her tattoo has to do with being able to hear her," Tony asked puzzled.

"She had her window down and her arm lying along the window ledge of her door," Gus explained. Dabria jumped up and flagged down Sheriff McLaren.

"Is it possible to find out if this girl had a tattoo on her arm?" she asked as she pointed to Gus's pick.

"Maybe. I'll grab her file and see if there is any mention made of tattoos."

Tony and Dabria waited impatiently while Gus continued to peruse the other photos.

"Sorry kids, but that's the only one I know for sure," Gus stated with a regretful shrug.

The officer returned with the file and sitting opposite them with the folder open to only his view, asked Gus to describe the tattoo he had seen. Gus closed his eyes and concentrated.

"It fills up most of her forearm but ends before her elbow. It has many colors and lots of detail but I can't make out what it is. She's wearing a pink tube-top and her hair is long and dark brown and it swirls around her face as they drive by. She brushes the hair out of her eyes as she laughs."

"How fast were they driving?"

"Not very. It's a particularly rutted part of the road."

Sheriff McLaren passed a photo from the file to Tony, who looked at it, and then passed it to Dabria. She gasped and handed it to Gus.

"Is this the girl you saw that day?" The picture showed a dark haired laughing young woman in a pink tube-top with not only a tattooed right arm but a tattoo that curled round the left hand side of her neck and shoulder.

"That's her," Gus stated definitively. "That is absolutely the girl I saw."

Next the sheriff passed him computer generated pictures of Ben and Richard in sunglasses. Unfortunately, both men looked quite similar.

"I'm sorry but I can't say for sure. It could be either one of these men or neither of them," he stated apologetically.

"Gus, you have been exceptionally helpful. Your identification may be all we need to get a search warrant for Ben's property. And I'm hoping that by early next week we have the DNA warrant we need," Dabria's excitement was hard to contain. "Thank you, so much, gentleman for all of your assistance. I hate to run but I have a plane to catch. Tony, can you give me a lift to the airport?"

Chapter 27

"**M**organ Alert! Morgan Alert!" Sarah texted Dabria as she observed him waltz into the lobby. Thankfully Dabria's office door was closed. She swiftly slipped off her panties and stuffing them into a drawer, grabbed a condom. She walked over to her windows and stood looking out into the backyard. Dabria heard a tap-tap on the door just before it swung open.

"Can I come in?" Morgan asked calmly. A week had passed with her refusing his calls and declining his various, and he thought very generous, attempts at making amends. Plus on top of it all she had disappeared over the weekend. Enough was enough! It was time they dealt with things.

"Yes," Dabria did not move from the window. "Close the door and lock it," she quietly commanded. When she heard the snick of the old lock as it slid into place she turned around. Despite the fact that Dabria was still mad she couldn't help but appreciate the eye candy that stood before her and as she inhaled deeply she was assailed by his unique musky scent. He was plain and simply yummy.

"Dabria," Morgan began as it registered that she had just inhaled him and that her eyes had gone glassy with passion. "You have avoided me long enough, we need to talk," he stated as his traitorous penis twitched. "I've apologized every way I know how to and even a few ways that were suggested to me. Frankly, I'm at a loss. We have something between us and I know you can feel it, too. I didn't keep my silence to have something to hold over you. I did it because I needed to find out more about you, right from that first meeting. You captivate me.

After getting my initial report from Rocky I decided to stop digging and to let my own instincts take over to form my opinions of you. It was . . . . hey . . . . what are you doing?" Morgan asked taken aback, as he pleasantly determined what her intentions were. Dabria had closed the blinds and removed the condom from her pocket as she approached him. When he halfheartedly tried to push her away, she cupped his package and then trailed her fingers up his crotch. As things continued to swell to life she started unbuckling his belt.

"Dabria, stop!" he growled.

She persistently ignored his resistance and pushing him back against the door she forged ahead. After releasing his throbbing cock she slipped the condom on, checked the lock on the door, and then turning back around she bent over her desk with her posterior pointed at Morgan. She pulled up her skirt revealing her panty-less bottom.

"Jesus, Dabria, do you never wear panties?" he questioned with exasperation.

When she again didn't reply but instead simply looked back at him over her shoulder, with an obvious yearning in her eyes, he stopped fighting it and went over to her. Grabbing her hips and giving her no opportunity to change her mind he thrust into her. She was wet and ready to go. However, the sudden intrusion did cause her to gasp and grip her desk. He instantly stilled to let her adjust. Once her hands unclenched he continued to plunge and retract, gently and slowly at first. As her panting increased and his lust took over aggressively he brought both of them to completion. When Dabria stiffened and her uterus started to contract Morgan let the spasms pull him over the edge. With a cleansing sigh and basically no other recovery time Dabria wordlessly stood up and stepped back forcing Morgan to also step back. She then slipped off of him, tugged her skirt back into place, and walked around to the front of her desk.

"I have court in fifteen minutes. Please open the blinds before you leave," she instructed. With that said she grabbed her briefcase, returned to the door, unlocked it, and then glided out past him, closing it behind her. She figured she was being quite charitable by closing the door and giving him the privacy he needed to get himself put back together. Furiously, Morgan ripped the condom off, grabbed a Kleenex to dispose of it, and then stuffed himself back into his pants. Inwardly fuming he glared at the blinds and then stormed out of her office.

~ ~ ~

Dabria had headed directly to the women's washroom. When she emerged from her stall she wasn't surprised to find Sarah lounging against the counter of the sinks.

"So spill it. What was that all about?" Sarah probed. "Morgan just stomped past me, all but spitting nails," she reported. Taking one look at Dabria's face she relented. "Aw, Dabria, what happened? You look like you lost your best friend."

"I think I did," Dabria groaned with self-loathing. She slouched over the sink and hung her head. "Sarah, I was so angry with him. He had no right to investigate me," her voice raggedly wavered.

"No, he didn't," Sarah agreed. "But . . . ."

Dabria just stood at the mirror gripping the counter on the verge of tears, seemingly searching her own reflection for answers.

"I know he didn't keep it from me to be malicious."

"Okay. Then . . . . why the anger?"

"Because, Sarah, I've done things that I'm not proud of and I wanted to keep them to myself. Morgan has opened up a whole can of worms that I'm not sure I'm ready to share with anyone yet. I would have had to explain some things to him eventually but everyone has the right to some secrets. Don't they? Now, I have no idea exactly what the police force in Rocky revealed to him or what conclusions he's reached. Therefore, the only way we can move forward is for me to explain *everything* to him."

"Look, Dabria, your sessions with Dr. Murphy have been going great. Obviously you're making progress or you wouldn't be so tied up in knots over this. Are you in love with him?" she inquired gently.

"Yes, damn-it, Sarah, I am!"

"Okay, so do you think he's in love with you?"

"He said he was."

"Then you need to trust that regardless of what you tell him, he's still gonna be there tomorrow. And, you know what? If you share all of yourself with him that can only make you closer. Has he never done anything he's ashamed of? Come on Dabria, Morgan's human, too. Give him a chance."

"Gawd, Sarah, I was such a bitch to him today. I just lived up to everything that everyone in Rocky has always believed about me."

"There isn't a woman alive that can't make that admission. Every one of us can be a bitch occasionally. Come on. Do you have any appointments this afternoon or court?"

"No."

"Good. Go fix this. Get yourself together, apologize, and then have a heart to heart." Sarah moved towards the door. "He's not gonna dump you, girl. I can't imagine you revealing anything short of killing someone that would make him take a step back from you. I've gotta run. Call me later." The door silently swung closed behind her.

"Oh, Sarah, if you only knew," Dabria sighed. With quietly gasping sobs she pounded her palm on the countertop and raged at the universe for allowing her misplaced sense of loyalty and guilt over David to color her common sense and cause her to disregard her own morals. Although, she was angry with Morgan, this wasn't Morgan's fault. With no one to blame but herself she was overwhelmed with grief and self pity. This had been an opportunity at a new life, a new love. That new love was now in shambles and she was the only one to blame. She was also the only one who could salvage it. Straightening her skirt, repairing her make-up, and putting her shield of false confidence firmly back in place she marched back to her office.

~ ~ ~

When Morgan reached the parking lot he glanced to the right as he slid into the Jeep. Out of the corner of his eye he saw a flash of shiny black Tiburon. She hadn't left! She was still in the building. She had lied to him on top of everything else. Damn it! He sat seething in his car for several minutes. Only a fool would be livid that a gorgeous woman had just had her way with him in a very inappropriate place, in the middle of the day, surrounded by co-workers who could have interrupted them at any time. He was sure any other guy would consider it some kind of kinky fantasy come true. Obviously he was doomed. His *love* for her actually surpassed his *lust* for her! That was almost inconceivable since she was the sexist creature he had ever met. Once he had formulated a plan of attack he pulled out into traffic. Score one for Dabria, but Morgan vowed he would win this war!

~ ~ ~

The fact that the blinds remained closed when Dabria walked into her office only confirmed that Morgan was really mad. Putting her head down Dabria was determined to put in a couple hours of work before heading home to lick her wounds and come up with a strategy. After an hour of unsuccessfully trying to stay focused, she gave up. With a grunt of disgust she tidied up her desk and left.

How to fix this . . . . how to fix this . . . . her mind chanted? She decided a good start would be to feed him and then see how things progressed from there. She headed to the grocery store and picked up the fixin's for a good old fashioned roast beef and potato meal. Few men could resist pot roast and gravy. After she picked up a bottle of wine and some candles, she let herself into Morgan's place. Into the oven went the roast. Leaving her other purchases on the cupboard she decided to run home, change, and pack some clothes before the rest of the meal needed to be prepared. As she pulled out of one end of the parking lot Morgan was pulling into the other end. His cell phone had died so he needed to change batteries. He was surprised to see groceries on the cupboard when he walked in. Upon closer inspection he discovered the roast. Although all of this smacked of apology he wasn't about to let her off that easy. Grabbing the battery he continued to mutter obscenities under his breath as he headed back to the trenches.

Dabria changed into jeans and a sweat shirt. Her appearance was casual but she couldn't resist slipping into the naughtiest pair of underwear she could find. When she returned to Morgan's she prepared the rest of the meal, opened the wine to breathe, and checking the clock, lit the candles. Six o'clock came and went. Then seven . . . . and then eight. She drank the bottle of wine while she waited. At nine o'clock she packed up the now stone cold supper, put it in the fridge, and cleaned the kitchen. Just as she snuffed out the gutted candles Morgan walked in. He stood silently in the foyer staring at her. She stood just as silently by the table. The smoke from the now flameless candles curled upwards and dissipated while neither moved.

"I should have called," he growled as way of an apology. He toed off his shoes and hung up his keys.

"How did you know? I wanted to surprise you," she quietly stated.

"I stopped by after you were here the first time."

"Oh," she nodded.

"So, I'm surprised. Now what?" he refused to make this easy for her.

"Have you eaten?"

"No."

"Would you like a hot roast beef sandwich?"

"Sure. I need to shower first. It's been a long day."

"I'll leave it on the counter when I lock myself out," she sighed.

"No," he stated emphatically. "You'll stay until I'm done and then we'll talk."

She again nodded and then turned to the fridge.

Morgan hadn't meant to be so late. He had hoped to have this out with her about three hours ago and be on to the making up part by now. But, that was not how his profession worked. The second he had turned his cell phone back on it rang. Another victim had been found. This made victim six/seven. Unfortunately, the joint team was getting really good at processing the drop sites. They had finished it in record time. The general public might have assumed that the teams were getting blasé and that was why they had finished so soon tonight. The reality was that the team leaders knew their squad was getting not only tired but also disheartened. So, instead of working another night until after midnight French and Morgan sent the troops home and set up an 8:00 a.m. briefing instead.

While Morgan showered, he planned his speech. She had beaten him to the gun by showing up and feeding him. That didn't mean she wasn't still gonna get blasted. When he returned to the kitchen, shirtless and in a pair of sweats, he saw that his supper was on the table and the aroma was more than he could take. Choosing not to deny himself the opportunity to stave off his hunger, before having it out with her, he turned away from her. She stood in front of his living room window with her arms wrapped tightly around herself, gazing out into the inky blackness. The silence continued while he made short work of his meal. She didn't move. Morgan put his plate into the dishwasher and walked into the living room.

"Dabria, come and sit down," he quietly instructed. She turned back towards him and once she was seated he parked himself in the chair across from her. He admired her direct regard of him. She didn't hang her head or try to avert her eyes. She simply waited for his wrath.

"I will never again allow you to use me to simply scratch your itch or to use sex as a weapon against me. I don't play those games, Dabria, and I have never used any woman the way you used me today.

We either have an open honest relationship or we end this right now. I will not be lied to," he informed her emphatically. "I'm not in this for a quick fuck! I know you're mad at me and frankly I'd probably be pissed off, too. But, I'm not perfect. Up to now I haven't pushed you but tonight I'm going to. I'll come clean with you but you need to trust me. Now, you need to go first."

Morgan had noticed that Dabria was pale when he first came home but she seemed to be getting paler by the moment. Looking at him with a sick smile her eyes suddenly widened and she bolted for the bathroom. Sounds of retching soon emanated from the other end of the condo.

Morgan dragged a frustrated hand down his face. He had her so worked up she had made herself sick. This was not going at all as he had planned. Morgan paced until an even paler faced Dabria emerged.

"I'm sorry," she whispered. "I should never have treated you like a piece of meat this afternoon. I know I'm better than that."

"Yes, you are," Morgan agreed. "Come and sit down," he gestured with his hand. After she was settled he sat down beside her. "Are you okay?"

"I'm fine."

Morgan raised an eyebrow.

"Truly. I haven't eaten since lunch and I think the wine was a little much."

"Okay, how about *I* make you a sandwich while you talk?" Morgan suggested.

"I don't know if I can eat."

"I'm sure you'll feel better if you do. Come on," Morgan led her to the table.

"All right," Dabria agreed as they moved back into the kitchen. While Morgan sliced and diced, Dabria's story poured out.

She carried on where she had left off during her last attempt to explain herself. She admitted to accepting a relationship where she would be sharing David with Matthew for the rest of her life.

Morgan was shocked that this seemingly confidant, self-assured, intelligent woman actually had such low self-esteem that she would agree to that kind of arrangement.

"I had no idea," he gently encouraged her to continue as he joined her at the table.

"I told you that you didn't know me," she reminded him.

"I'm not judging you, Dabria. Please go on."

"Why do you never call me Bree?" she suddenly switched gears.

"Because, I've never been invited to call you Bree," he informed her. "I assumed it was one small way for you to remain aloof from me."

"Huh, maybe unconsciously, it was. Do you want to call me Bree?"

"Not anymore. I've come to realize that the people that truly love you, as in your parents and me, are the only ones that call you by your full name. And I Googled it and discovered it means "angel." And I like that you're *my* angel," he informed her with that heart stopping smile of his.

"I am hardly that, Morgan," she assured him. She continued by describing the arrival of David's new partner and her suspicions of an affair. She explained the details of his death, the subsequent funeral, and inquest. And then she paused.

"Do you want to stop for tonight?" Morgan inquired. By now it was past midnight.

"Do you need to be up early?"

"Yes, but that's irrelevant," he assured her.

"Morgan, I'm exhausted and you obviously had a long day."

"Okay, let's hit the sack. Do you have clothes here for tomorrow?"

"Yes. They're in the car. I didn't want to presume too much."

"Go grab them while I clean up," he gently propelled her towards the door.

~ ~ ~

"I love you, Dabria," Morgan reassured her after they had climbed into bed.

She turned in his arms and looking him in the eyes said, "I just hope you feel the same way after you hear the rest of the story." Before he could respond she placed a finger on his lips and whispered, "Please don't make a promise when you don't know yet if you can keep it."

Morgan kissed her gently and hugged her tightly. She slept soundly with Morgan wrapped protectively around her.

~ ~ ~

The next several days were extremely busy for both of them and they weren't able to get together again until Friday night. This time it was Ducette who called it quits for the day.

"Hey, man, enough already! It's 5:00 o'clock. Call your woman and get lost for the night."

"You're right. I'm outta here." Morgan dialed Dabria's number as he left the detachment. "You done?"

"No, but I'm packin' it in anyways."

"Good. I'll meet you at your place with supper fixin's in an hour."

"You're on." She clicked off, cleared her desk, and headed out. Spring was shaping up nicely. Almost all the snow had melted but the lake was still frozen over. The ice wasn't rotten yet or unsafe but it would only be a matter of time before it started breaking up. Dabria couldn't wait. Her beach at least was finally becoming visible, but she still had no idea what her shoreline or swimming area was like. She hurried home so that she could have a quick shower before Morgan arrived. Tonight would finally be the night of her reckoning. Since she didn't have a chance to show off her sexy new underwear the other night she put on the freshly laundered set in the hopes that tonight turned out favorably. Morgan roared in with grocery bags and a duffle.

"Staying awhile?" she casually inquired with a quirked eyebrow.

"Maybe permanently. We'll see, huh?" he challenged her.

"We'll see," she replied noncommittally.

After a barbequed supper and the clean up was done Dabria settled into the corner of the couch with a coffee. Morgan plopped down at the other end of the couch and pulling her feet towards him began to give her a foot massage. He didn't push her to continue her tale. Instead they talked about Cody's case and the developments since they had last talked. Dabria had a lot to tell. She admitted to going to Salem on her own and told him all she had learned. They had finally received some information that shed light on the identity of the John Doe. Ben's and Richard's mothers' names had finally been unsealed. Plus, Tony had come through yet again with a name and phone number for the cleaning woman she had met at the orphanage. Her name was Molly. Molly had talked to her mother after she left and when Dabria phoned her on Tuesday night Molly told her the stories her mother remembered.

Ben's mother had in fact died giving birth. She was a poor single mother with only an estranged uncle for family. When she realized she would not survive she made Molly's mother, who acted as midwife, promise to contact her uncle. If he was unwilling to take Ben, Molly agreed to keep the child at the orphanage. Unfortunately, Ben had been born with a twisted foot and neither his great uncle nor any prospective adoptees wanted him because of the many expensive foot surgeries he required. Therefore, Ben was kept at the orphanage and raised by the priests. Richard's mother was a Metis woman who was married to an influential foreign diplomat. She had an affair and had become pregnant. She knew her husband was sterile and would leave her if he discovered her betrayal. By the time she realized she was pregnant it had been too risky for her to have an abortion. Conveniently her husband decided to return to his homeland for a six month long sabbatical. She convinced him that she would be inconsolable if he plucked her from her home so he allowed her to stay and thankfully she gave birth while he was gone. Thus, he never knew she was ever pregnant. She abandoned the boy child at the orphanage and plied them with enough donations that they never allowed the child to be adopted out and they guarded her secret for her.

Unbeknownst to her, her name had been recorded in their birth book and since a court order had been issued for them to release that information the priest had no choice but to do just that. A DNA sample had been taken from the John Doe bones and compared to the court ordered DNA sample they had acquired from Richard's mother. They did not match. So, at least they knew that John Doe was not Richard. A DNA sample had also been obtained from Ben's uncle's exhumed ashes. Surprisingly it did match the John Doe. Therefore, Ben was their John Doe and apparently Richard was actually Richard. That, however, did not explain the scarring on Richard's leg. The next most pressing question however, was who killed Ben and why? If it was Richard, they had no motive at this point. They were obviously missing something. Morgan proposed that they look into the backgrounds of the girls that had disappeared around the same time as Ben's death. The boys had been almost inseparable all of their lives so the most logical explanation was that a girl had gotten in between them. Dabria wondered if another trip to visit Molly might be beneficial since maybe Molly was that girl. Regardless, she assured Morgan she'd get Tony on it immediately. She told him that Gus, the neighbor, had identified a missing prostitute from the Salem area and that he had seen her driving with someone that used Ben's uncle's cabin. The obvious conclusion was that it was Richard. But they still had to prove it. A search warrant had been issued for Ben's uncle's cabin and the investigator was dusting for fingerprints. If Morgan or Dabria could get a print from Richard they might be able to place him at the cabin. The investigation suddenly seemed to be rolling right along.

She had stalled long enough and so unprompted, Dabria continued where she had left off with her own tale. She explained that Annah, David's partner, had been harassed after his death and two serious attempts had been made on her life. Pulling her feet off of his lap Dabria got up and removed herself from his touch. She wandered over to the window and stared out at the silent darkness. Morgan knew that there was more to come and that he probably wanted to hear it even less than she wanted to tell it.

"I've never told anyone what I'm about to tell you and you need to understand that what I'm admitting to you is going to put you in a very awkward position because of your profession. Are you sure you want me to continue?"

Panic clawed at his gut. Suddenly he didn't want to know if she had been involved. Their lives would be changed forever if she admitted to doing anything criminal.

"Dabria, wait. I don't need to know," he blurted as he surged to his feet and advanced towards her.

"Morgan! Don't you dare cave on me now," she spat as she whirled around to confront him. "You're the one that forced me to deal with this issue. You're that one that gave me the ultimatum. Now *you* can't handle the truths I need to reveal? Well, to *hell* with you! You're gonna get the details whether you like it or not!"

"Stop it! I'm not caving on you. But you know if you admit to something criminal I have no choice but to turn that information over." He stopped short of actually reaching her.

"Do you? Do you really have no choice?" she demanded. "David is dead! Matthew is dead! David's mistress is dead!" her voice rose with every declaration. "And Annah and her little family are all alive and well. Charging me as accomplice would change *what* for any one of them? What would it fix?" she challenged.

With an indrawn breath and clenched fists Morgan carefully enunciated, "Were you an accomplice?"

Dabria turned away from him.

Morgan swiftly closed the remaining distance between them and yanked her around to face him. Grasping her forearms he shook her once.

"Answer me, damn it!" he demanded.

"Some might say so," she glared up at him.

"What the *hell* does that mean?"

As soon as she tugged to get out of his grasp he instantly released her and scrubbed a hand down his face. She rubbed her arms to take the sting out and he had the grace to look apologetic.

"I'm sorry. I didn't mean to hurt you," he regretfully expressed.

"I know," she casually dismissed his actions as she continued with her tale. "Matthew came to me and asked me to help him prove that David and Annah had been lovers. He convinced me that Annah had played an integral part in David's death and that she had tampered with her own rappelling ropes."

"Dabria, that's not logical and the inquest had already determined that she was not at fault. Besides what reason could she have had for killing her partner?"

"I don't know, maybe because the affair had gone south and she had set her cap for a bigger fish, namely Lachlan, her boss. David could be very tenacious when he wanted something and it was denied him. I justified that he hadn't wanted to end it and she needed him out of the picture."

"Did you actually believe that?" he questioned incredulously.

"Morgan, I don't know. But at the time I was devastated and looking for someone to blame. Our baby was dead, I had broken our sham of an engagement, and he told me himself that he thought he was in love with Annah. What was I supposed to believe? I needed some way to make the feelings of guilt go away. I knew she was involved with Lachlan and I wasn't convinced that she hadn't also been involved with David. I wanted her boss to know that she was a cheater and I wanted her to suffer for her actions. Just like I was suffering," she explained with a shrug. "Feelings are rarely logical, Morgan. They are often gut-wrenchingly illogical. I wanted her to hurt! Come on, you know the adage "There is no wrath like a woman scorned." Well, I was the *woman scorned* and someone needed to pay."

"What did you do?" he quietly asked again.

"Matthew told me he could get proof of Annah's involvement and he needed me to keep Lachlan occupied for about half an hour so that he could find this evidence in Annah's house. She would be picking up her kids after work and with all of them being away he would be free to do a quick search."

"Okay. So what happened then?"

"I made an appointment with Lachlan. I led him to believe that I may be filing a civil suit against Annah and the detachment. He agreed to the meeting. Just before I was ushered into his office he received a call from Annah informing him that someone had forced her off the road and into a frozen lake."

"That was the first attempt on her life. Wasn't it?"

"Yes, and it's a miracle she lived. I began to suspect then that Matthew was responsible for not only this failed attempt but possibly for David's death."

"So why didn't you tell anyone?"

"Who was I going to tell, Morgan?" she exclaimed frustrated. "I had no proof and besides then I would have had to explain the whole gay/straight triangle that had been going on. What if I was wrong? David was already dead. Should I destroy the illusion his parents held and possibly ruin Matthew's life as well?"

"Dabria, you know that cops can investigate matters and keep them confidential."

"Really! Well, I also know that people in the same profession share details of cases that they're supposed to keep privileged. Who told you about my suspected involvement and that the boys were gay? All of that information was supposed to remain under wraps for the sake of the boys' families. Apparently, it didn't."

"First of all your suspected involvement was not privileged information and *you* were the one who told me about the homosexual thing."

"Morgan, you can spin it however you like. The reality is it's defamation of character and if I find out who told you I can have them charged and force their resignation."

"Would you?"

"I said I could. I didn't say I would," she mumbled defensively.

"So, we're back to the big question. Knowing what you know now, do *you* believe that you were an accessory in the attempt on Annah's life?"

"Yes, I was," she calmly confirmed. "Now, what do you believe, Morgan?"

Several excruciatingly long seconds passed while Morgan stood simply staring at her. Dabria searched his face for some hint as to his conclusions. Finally Morgan responded.

"I think you've lived with your guilt long enough and the only way you're gonna be able to forgive yourself and move on is if you go talk to Annah and tell her what you just told me. It isn't up to me to absolve you or accuse you. It's up to her."

"Morgan, I don't know if I can do that. It's because of her that three people are dead."

"Come on," he said with obvious disgust lacing his voice. "You don't really believe that. Do you? It's not Annah's fault that David fell in love with her. If you're going to admit the truth, then bite the bullet and accept the whole truth. Stop your delusions and stop protecting those men," he paused and looked deeply into her eyes. "And Dabria, I do mean men. I think both of them acted like spoiled little boys who believe that they shouldn't be held accountable for their actions. But they weren't boys anymore. They were adult men who should have been making adult decisions." Morgan had taken off handling Dabria with kid gloves and had determined no purpose would be served in continuing to hold back his thoughts on the situation. Plain speaking was the order of the day. "David's irresponsibility was the catalyst for this entire fiasco. His infidelity hurt you, killed his child, and made Matthew crazy with jealousy. That in turn caused Matthew to be responsible for David's death, his other girlfriend's death, threatened the lives of Annah and her family, and ultimately devastated all three sets of parents. David and Matthew are responsible and only them. Both of them made choices. Now it's time for you to finish this and make your own choice." Morgan kept his distance while he waited for Dabria's reaction.

Dabria gasped. She was stunned by Morgan's brutal delivery of his conclusions. She groped her way back to the sofa and with slumping shoulders she plopped down into it. She braced her arms on her knees and covered her face with her hands. As she silently processed his speech she grudgingly acknowledged that his deductions were correct.

"Morgan, I'm so tired of all this. I just wish it would go away."

"It will, but only if you go make peace with Annah," he reiterated. "No one here knows you. You have a new life here and I think it's the beginning of a better life. Don't you?"

"Yes," she sighed. Sitting up she looked him straight in the eye. "Will you support me and come with me to explain to Annah?"

"Of course. My love for you isn't so fickle that I'll abandon you when the chips are down. When I love someone it's for life. Regardless of what you had told me today we would have found a way to work things out."

"So we're good?" she asked tentatively.

"Is there anything else you want to confess or does that about sum things up?"

"That's all of it," she promised him.

"Alright then, come here." He enfolded her in his embrace. "Yah, ... babe. We're good. I promise you whatever Annah's decision is we'll get through this together." He gently kissed her on the forehead and she clung to him as the turmoil slowly ebbed from her body into the stillness of the night.

~ ~ ~

Dabria contacted the Nordegg Conservation Office looking for Annah. She was frostily informed that *Annah* was off shift and that *Annah* would call her back at *Annah's* convenience. Obviously the receptionist knew exactly who Dabria was. Dabria was pretty confident that she was not well loved by anyone at that station. She knew the people of Nordegg had mistakenly characterized her shyness as someone who was a snooty little bitch. Then her display at David's funeral certainly would have fanned the flames of that fire. If Matthew hadn't held her back she would have leapt over David's coffin and scratched Annah's eyes out right in front of God and all of David's mourners. As it was, she was still able to make sure every person there knew her feelings regarding Annah's presence and that was only the beginning. Things had definitely gone downhill from there.

Surprisingly, Annah called later that afternoon. She agreed to a meeting with Dabria for Friday. Annah informed her that Lachlan would be present. Dabria informed Annah she would be bringing

Morgan with her. Dabria was both relieved and apprehensive about the scheduled appointment.

When she left the office Wednesday Jaimie was sitting at reception.

"I'm going out of town for a few days," Dabria said. "Can you let the other girls know?"

"I see you have new clothes," Jaimie accused without acknowledging Dabria's request.

"Do you like these better?" she asked with a quick pirouette.

"Not particularly."

"How do you know they're new?"

"Uh . . . . I mean different."

"Different from what?"

"Than before."

"Jaimie, I have a huge wardrobe. Just because you've never seen these before doesn't mean they're new."

"Yes, they are."

"How do you know that?"

"I just do!" she sputtered.

"Anyway," Dabria didn't pursue the matter since she was well aware of why Jaimie knew that the outfit was a very recent purchase. "I'll be gone until Sunday. I need someone to keep an eye on my house. Maybe check it out Friday night. I don't suppose you'd be willing to do that for me? I don't know a lot of people here yet and I'd pay you for your time."

"Absolutely not! I don't need your charity."

"I'm sorry, Jaimie. I didn't mean to offend you or presume too much but I thought you were my friend."

"Huh . . . . hardly," she scoffed. "So did you get lots of new clothes?" she returned to her obvious fixation.

"Some. Well, thanks anyway." When she left the building she couldn't help but smile. Morgan had done some digging since Sunday and discovered that David's mistress had a sister and coincidently her name was Jaimie. She just happened to live in Prince Albert. Jaimie had known who Dabria was since she had come to P.A. for her interview. Her venomous comments finally made sense. It became glaringly obvious that it was Jaimie who had taken Dabria's extra key and that she was the one who had destroyed her clothing and cosmetics. Apparently, she felt Dabria needed to be punished for her sister's death. A friend of Morgan's owned a security company and after the episode at the cabin he had a state of the art security system installed complete with high definition color cameras. The alarms were silent and when triggered, images were immediately projected to the alarm company. Dabria's cell was called first and then a call was made to the R.C.M.P. Dabria knew that Jaimie wouldn't be able to resist the opportunity to strike again. She had deliberately *not* changed the locks. This time she was gonna be ready for her.

Morgan and Dabria left early Thursday morning. She had decided to combine her appointment in Nordegg with a visit to her parents. If she was going to have a life with Morgan then he needed to know where she came from. They rolled into Calgary mid-afternoon. Dabria had grown up in a house that by most standards would be considered a mansion. It stood on a one acre lot and had been on the outskirts of the city at one time. That was no longer the case. This exclusive subdivision was now surrounded by many other subdivisions. The house was over a hundred years old and had been passed down from her mother's parents. It was made of sandstone and typical of the houses of the extremely wealthy at that time. Dabria's mother had taken great pains to maintain the integrity of it and yet to update it so that it was functional. The driveway was long and circular, reminiscent of a grand old manor house. Calgary was famous for its Chinook winds. Obviously one had blown in recently and the temperatures had remained above zero. Not a flake of snow remained. Spring often came earlier to this region and the gardens were just beginning to come into bloom. Flowers like crocuses, tulips, and daffodils colorfully dotted the many strategically planted perennial beds. The sounds of spring bird song filled the air and the smell of cool damp earth wafted through Dabria's open window. Morgan fully expected a butler to be waiting on the steps as he drove up and he was vaguely disappointed and then startled by the vision that confronted them as they rolled to a stop. The massive front doors were sedately opened by a statuesque, immaculately dressed, stunningly beautiful woman. He fleetingly wondered if Dabria had forgotten to tell him she was adopted since not only her skin color but also her stature was in direct contrast to that of her mother's. The only thing they seemed to share was their unusual eyes. Interestingly the color complimented both of them. Dabria's mother's auburn hair, light toffee eyes, and porcelain skin created a striking visage. She stood stiffly waiting for them to get out of the car and ascend the steps towards her.

"Hello, Mother," Dabria respectfully greeted her.

"Dabria," she gave Dabria a brief nod and a brisk hug. "You're father and I are delighted that you could find the time for a visit." It wasn't exactly a criticism but it wasn't a very warm welcome either. Morgan had pulled the suitcases out of the trunk and made his way to the house as well. Now he understood Dabria's remoteness towards her mother and her lack of encouragement regarding their requested visit earlier.

"Mother, I'd like you to meet Morgan Vaughn," Dabria introduced as they walked into the foyer. "He's a special friend of mine."

Morgan placed the suitcases on the floor and then extended his hand towards her. Instead of clasping her hand for what he knew would be a limp wristed shake he grasped it firmly and pulled her into his embrace for a proper hug. Caught off balance she was forced to grab onto Morgan to prevent herself from toppling over. Dabria grinned from ear to ear while her mother stiffened and squirmed. Once he released her she all but wiped his germs off of her as she needlessly tidied her flawless appearance.

"I've made up the *green room* for Morgan," she hastily informed them, obviously discombobulated by his affability. Quavering, she suggested they wash up and meet her and Dabria's father, whom she assured them, was expected home any time now, for a cocktail before dinner.

With that she promptly withdrew to a room across from the foyer. Dabria enlightened Morgan to the fact that her mother had retired to her private parlor. The strains of a classical ballad could be discerned emanating from within.

Dabria left her luggage in the foyer and directed Morgan to carry his suitcase to his room, which coincidently, or not, was on a different floor than her own. Once they reached the privacy of the *green room* he quietly closed the door and grabbing her to him thoroughly kissed her.

"What was that for?" she gasped.

"Encouragement for the evening ahead," he explained.

"For me or for you?" she giggled.

"Both. It appears it may be a long one."

"It won't be so bad. Wait until you meet Daddy," she assured him.

She gave him a tour of the rest of the house after they deposited her luggage in her own room. About the time she was finished she heard her father come in. Racing from the kitchen she flung herself into his arms. He pulled her in for a big bear hug and made her squeal.

"Angel, I'm so glad you've come for a visit!" he exclaimed. "Morgan, I assume?" he reached out both hands and clasped Morgan's in a firm welcome. "We are so pleased you've come to our home." Morgan now understood where Dabria's exotic looks and stature had come from. Her father was not a tall man and his skin was a dark chocolate brown. He could not be described as handsome but somehow his persona drew your attention towards him. He was obviously often quick to smile since deep creases bracketed his mouth. His eyes twinkled as he beamed at Morgan. Looking from father to daughter it was obvious that she was a delightful combination of both her parents.

"Does this mean you're keeping this one?" her father inquired as he turned back towards her.

"Daddy," Dabria admonished.

"I think she's still a little skittish, sir," Morgan stated "but, I have no intention of letting her get away."

"Good. It was time she was cherished by someone other than me," her father advised.

"She is," Morgan confirmed.

Caroline was perched at the entrance to the parlor and as Daniel reached her and affectionately kissed her she immediately relaxed and blushed. It was obvious she was still reserved, but no longer the China doll that Morgan had been introduced to.

The remainder of the evening continued smoothly. Dabria's father and Morgan got along famously. One would never call Caroline gregarious but she was the consummate hostess. While it was obvious that Daniel and Caroline were polar opposites it was equally obvious that Caroline was the yin to his yang. Daniel was not shy in his adoration of Caroline and despite her coolness those feelings were clearly reciprocated. Morgan could see the mutual love and respect they had for each other and he vowed that he would offer Dabria a lifetime of no less.

The urge to seek out Dabria after all the lights were out was stronger than his sense of propriety. Therefore, despite the knowledge that Dabria's mother would obviously not approve he stealthily crept up the stairs and into Dabria's room. An unfamiliar hum was the only sound to intrude upon the purr of pleasure softly drifting from the direction of Dabria's bed. Morgan stopped and listened trying to place the sound. Momentary disconcerted, he determined it was the sound of a battery operated appliance. She was using a vibrator! Quickly, he overcame his surprise, closed and locked her door, and started peeling off clothes in the moonlight that streamed through her open curtains. Even though she had obviously started without him he was not about to let his boldness go unrewarded. An *mmm* and a female sigh floated from Dabria. Spread before him like a tantalizing banquet lie a very naked, very sexy Dabria. Her hand caressed the distended nipple of her left breast while her right hand held a pulsing phallus that she was sliding in and out of herself. With her face in shadow Morgan couldn't tell if her moan was an expression of appreciation for his recently revealed manly form or from pleasuring herself. Either way, that sound and the fact that she was using a sex toy had ratcheted up his lust to a level never attained before. And that was saying something since he was almost always semi-erect when he was in Dabria's presence. She was the sexiest woman he had ever had the pleasure of bedding and it didn't hurt that he just happened to love her.

He slowly approached the bed and waited for her invitation. She knew it was only a matter of time before he snuck into her room and so she had amused herself while she waited. The forbidden encounter in her parent's house, in her childhood bed was no less alluring at thirty than it would have been if she was still an untried virgin at sixteen. She was so primed by the time he walked in and started stripping that she almost came just watching the play of moonlight flickering on his amazing physique as it shone past the leafless but budding tree branches that swayed in the breeze outside her windows.

While he positioned himself by her bed with all parts standing rigidly at attention, waiting for her direction, she bent her legs even more, slid the vibrator in and left it in place while she began to manually manipulate her clitoris. Having Morgan watch her masturbate was an unexpected but delicious turn on. With any other man she would have been self conscious rather than energized. Dabria's distinctive scent mingled with the appealing musk of impending completion. Without a word he knelt on the bed between her legs. He removed the vibrator and slid into her. Instead of simply discarding her toy he gently brushed her hand aside and held the vibrator to her already sensitized clit. Slowly—notch by notch—he turned up the speed. Although she tried to fight it to drag out her pleasure she was unable to hold off the inevitable. It only took moments to finish her off. She clutched the slippery butter soft bed sheets at her sides and bowing up, stiffened, and quietly groaning she came. He momentarily took the vibrator off of her. Before her contractions could completely subside he returned the still throbbing device to her and she peaked again. The whole time he had continued to slide in and out of her, absorbing her contractions and heightening his own pleasure.

Morgan could not only attain almost on-demand orgasms when his partner did, but he had also learned how to achieve multiple dry orgasms through concentration and extreme control. The benefit of this ability was that when he did allow himself to ejaculate the orgasm was more intense. He had never done this with anyone before, including Dabria during any of their previous lovemaking sessions.

Because of his love for her and his belief in her love for him he finally let down the last of his guard. Dabria knew that Morgan's refractory period was very short and that he would often initiate round two only minutes after finishing round one. She was intrigued by the fact that this time he had given her two orgasms without allowing himself one. However, she was so into her own pleasure that she was only vaguely aware of that fact and was totally unprepared for his continued onslaught. He had only just let her come down when he began driving her back up again. The sudden removal of the vibrator, tensing of his arms, and slight hesitation in his thrusting were the only indicators that he had allowed himself to reach orgasm. Then, taking a deep breath, he continued where he left off with her. Only this time the thrusting was more aggressive and he didn't resume the use of the vibrator. She was thankful for that, since with each orgasm her clitoris became more sensitive. It took only minutes to bring Morgan to orgasm again and yet again Dabria sensed it was not a full blown one. He stiffened, hesitated, and then slowly resumed pumping. It was like he was pleasuring himself while allowing her a slight reprieve. This session was like no other they had previously enjoyed.

And it was obvious that Morgan was far from finished. While still connected he leaned over her and began to suckle at her breasts. They were also highly responsive and so with little effort he was able to draw her up yet again. He had brought her to orgasm twice and allowed himself the same but neither had come together. He knew they were both hyper sensitized and so he decided to let go and ejaculate when he brought her to her third orgasm. He kissed her neck and nibbled her ears and sucked and licked down her body as low as he could go without disconnecting as he continued to slowly pump. This time he held off as long as possible by going as slowly and gently as his body would allow him to. When he could stand the strain no longer he returned the vibrator to her so that she could control her own clitoral manipulation and thrust into her like a jack hammer bringing both of them to a cataclysmic conclusion. Dabria actually cried out as she flung the vibrator to the floor and Morgan groaned out a guttural, primitive growl. He collapsed on her and then rolled and let her rest on top. They both lay spent in a tangle of legs and arms with their breathing sawing in and out. Dabria's clammy sheets were actually shredded by her nails from the clenching of her hands. She had never been so wrecked. Dabria's tears spilled onto his heaving chest and Morgan held her as she trembled.

"Did I hurt you? Was it too much?" he quietly sought approval as he soothingly caressed her sweat dampened back.

"No . . . . you could never be too much," she breathlessly vowed as she relaxed and peacefully slid into sleep. The vibrator had bounced and, thankfully, clicked itself off. Morgan's eyes were drawn to a puddle of moon light on Dabria's floor. Shit, it was a unicorn! A purple silicon unicorn! Who knew girls didn't just use plain old phallic symbols anymore. Apparently, vibrators had evolved. Shifting carefully Morgan chuckled and pulled the duvet over them to warm their moist, rapidly chilling bodies. He lie watching the shadows of the tree branches silently drift across the walls as he listened to the rhythmic breathing of Dabria and felt the steady beating of her heart close to his. Life couldn't get much better.

~ ~ ~

"Lovely spring morning," Dabria's father commented causing Morgan to flinch. Unexpectedly Morgan had bumped into Daniel as he backed shoeless and shirtless out of Dabria's room the following morning. He'd mistakenly thought 5:00 a.m. was early enough to creep back to his designated room.

"Uh . . . . yes, sir. That it is," he agreed with a resigned smirk pasted on his red face.

"Remember what I said, Morgan. Cherish her," Daniel cautioned as he continued on down the hall in his jogging gear. "Oh, and I wouldn't mind some grandbabies, too!" he commented as he stopped at the top of the stairs and looked back. "See you at breakfast," he cheerfully quipped.

"I'll do my best, sir," Morgan pledged.

After a leisurely brunch Dabria and Morgan headed to Nordegg. Annah was off and the kids were at school. The plan was to meet at Annah and Lachlan's house around 1:00 p.m. As she travelled the familiar path to Nordegg Dabria became more agitated. Strangely though, she seemed to settle slightly after they had passed the Conservation Station. She read the directions to Morgan that would lead them to Annah's. When they finally rounded the last corner and were greeted by the two-story log dwelling Dabria had worked herself into such a state that unbeknownst to Morgan she was close to throwing up. Annah may let the matter rest but Lachlan would probably be another story. From all of her dealings with him she believed he was fair-minded. But, if he felt that Annah was in any way threatened she knew he would be ruthless.

Before they could ring the bell Annah had opened the door and stood waiting for them to climb the stairs.

"Hello, Dabria," a very obviously pregnant Annah greeted them with a tentative smile. The smell of fresh baking and strong coffee wafted out in welcome.

"Annah, this is Morgan Vaughn. He's an R.C.M.P. detective from Prince Albert, but he isn't here in an official capacity," she hastened to add. "He's here as my friend." Having stated that fact she still wanted there to be no question in Annah or Lachlan's mind that she had someone in her corner.

"Pleased to meet you, Morgan, this is my husband, Lachlan. Please come in. Can I get you something to eat, to drink?"

"No, thanks, Annah. We won't be here that long. Can we just get this over with?"

"Of course, but, I'm unsure what it is we need to get over." Annah went and sat down with Lachlan standing behind her. He had not said one word since their arrival and was obviously sizing Morgan up. Morgan, on his side of the room, was doing the same thing. Dabria sat down across from Annah and Morgan sat on the arm of her oversized sofa chair. Dabria leaned forward and clasping her hands looked earnestly at Annah and explained, "I came to apologize and ask your forgiveness."

"Oh, I see," Annah shot Lachlan a look. He nodded and coming around the sofa sat down beside her and took her hand in his. "Please continue."

Dabria explained her involvement in the attempt on Annah's life and her reasons for that involvement. She stressed that she had been unaware of Matthew's intentions. She apologized for her behavior at David's funeral and for blaming Annah for David's death.

"Dabria, I've put myself in your position and I can empathize with you," she graciously assured her. "David was an excellent partner. I learned a great deal from him. He was a good Conservation Officer and he was a good friend to me," she charitably offered. "I miss him."

"I miss him, too," Dabria choked back a sob as Morgan squeezed her hand in support.

"Dabria, my life has turned out so amazing I wouldn't dream of carrying a grudge."

"Annah," Lachlan intervened, speaking for the first time. "I think Dabria wants your assurance that you won't pursue filing charges against her."

"Of course I won't. We've all suffered enough in the last year. Let's move on. I'm truly sorry for your loss, Dabria, and wish you and Morgan the kind of happiness that Lachlan and I share." Dabria stood up as Annah walked towards her. Annah hugged her and whispered, "Have a good life."

"You, too," Dabria hugged her back with tears in her eyes.

As Morgan followed Dabria to the door he shook Annah's hand and said, "You're an amazing woman. Thank you for your compassion and congratulations on the baby."

Lachlan turned to Dabria. "Thank you, for coming. That was very brave of you," he remarked gruffly.

"An amazing man found me and is helping me put myself back together. Better, I think, than I was before. He deserves most of the credit for my appearance today." Lachlan nodded at her as she stepped outside and walked towards the car.

"Don't let her con you. She would have made it here eventually. I just gave her a little nudge," Morgan clarified.

Annah grabbed his hand to stop him as he went to follow Dabria. "Love her Morgan. Having never met David you can't truly understand how brutally his betrayal hurt her. She needs someone to trust that truly loves and respects her," Annah quietly instructed.

"She has that someone," he assured her with a nod of his head.

Back to her parents they headed. They stopped in Rocky so she could show him her old law firm and her apartment. The radio was on and Dabria turned it up when she recognized Sidney York, one of her favorite Canadian singers serenading them with her song "Too Late." They returned to Calgary in time for a supper out at her favorite restaurant and then followed that up with an evening of dancing. She met several "friends" at one of her old haunts and introduced Morgan to them. The previous looks of pity were replaced with admiring glances from the females. Some asked where she was and how she was doing. She assured them she was doing fine and said only that she was working at a Legal Aid Office in Saskatchewan. No one pushed beyond that.

As they made their way back to the car to return to her childhood home her cell phone rang. It was the alarm company.

"Ms. Abdulla-Smythe?"

"Yes."

"There's been a break in and there's a man in your house."

"A man?" Dabria had expected it to be Jaimie. "Are you sure?"

"Yes. He picked the locks, went in and appears to be hiding in the dark."

"Don't alert the police yet. Just watch him," Dabria directed.

"No problem. We'll call back when there's a change."

Morgan had heard both sides of the conversation. "When they call back ask them if they can get a clear view of his face."

Dabria's phone rang again before Morgan finished.

"A woman just unlocked the door and walked in."

"Can you see their faces?"

"Yes. Oh my God! The man just attacked the woman!"

"Call it in!" Dabria yelled. "Call it in!" Dabria waited tensely on the line for the operator to come back.

It took almost five minutes. Finally they clicked back on.

"He knocked her unconscious, picked her up, and threw her over his shoulder. He left through the front door. He went down to the beach and then turned south. He's out of range now."

"Did you get still pictures of both of their faces and can you email them to me?"

"For sure," the alarm company guaranteed her.

"Send them on to the police department as well. Thanks for the update. Great work!"

They headed back to the house and as they pulled into the yard Dabria's phone alerted her that she had a message. They hurried to her room and plugged her phone into her laptop. The images displayed on her screen left them both speechless.

If Dabria hadn't been sitting beside him Morgan would have sworn that the woman in the picture was Dabria. It was her but it wasn't her. Upon closer inspection her real identity was revealed. It was Jaimie! Jaimie with makeup, different hair, and wearing one of Dabria's shirts. "What about the guy?" Dabria asked.

"He's familiar but I'm not sure why. Let me mull it over while you get some sleep."

"Are you kidding? I'm wired for sound now. Why would she be dressed like me? Why was that guy waiting for me? I don't get it. Obviously he thinks he's got me."

"I think he's our *scalper*, Dabria. And if not, at the very least, I think he's the guy that cut you in the bar."

"I'm the one he wasn't finished with," she heaved a sigh as she slumped onto her bed.

"I can sugar coat it if you like, but frankly, I do believe that."

"Okay, so now what?"

"We *hope* someone from the department recognizes him and knows where he hangs out. And we *pray* that they can find him in time."

"When you figured out who Jaimie was did you find out if she has parents or other siblings?"

"She has a mother. That's all."

"That poor woman!"

"Don't give up yet," he encouraged. "Come on, let's go to bed. We can't do anything by stewing about it. We have a long drive tomorrow."

They slid into bed and Morgan distracted her with childhood antidotes. Eventually she relaxed and drifted off to sleep. Morgan again lay holding her while she slept and he scoured his memory trying to come up with an identity for the kidnapper. Ultimately his lack of sleep from the previous night caught up with him and he also coasted into slumber.

Chapter 28

Morgan and Dabria were back in Prince Albert by suppertime. Since Morgan had slept little the night before and assumed he would be up very late Dabria drove most of the way home. She went to his condo and then he continued on to the station. The police had a solid lead. The kidnapper had been identified and every able-bodied policeman was searching for him and for Jaimie.

Assuming that Jaimie's kidnapper and the *Scalper* was the same person the police were disappointed that they hadn't figured him out sooner. He'd been investigated early on but dismissed as a suspect for various reasons. His business was in the perfect location to befriend the girls and then make the girls disappear. He owned a bookstore on Central Avenue. It was right in the middle of "the stroll." When some of the working girls were re-questioned they grudgingly admitted that he would let them come in and warm up when it was cold outside and that he often had given them something to eat and drink. Despite the fact that his store was closed at night he often worked late and although his front lights were out the girls knew his door would be open and that they were welcome inside. None of them had thought to implicate him. He was their friend. The girls felt safe around him. Even though he was offered sexual favors in return for his generosity he never took any of them up on their offers. In fact, none of the girls could ever remember him even touching them. They all assumed he was gay. He was a confidante, a safe place to come. They knew a good thing when they found it and weren't about to squeal on him.

The girls were wrong. He was very definitely heterosexual. What they didn't know was that he'd been castrated and had a penectomy performed on him when he was just seventeen. Apparently his first mistake was being white. His second mistake was to fall in love with a young native girl. His third and almost fatal mistake was to get caught by her papa having sex in the loft of the barn. Her papa figured appropriate justice was to knock the boy out and then nail his penis and scrotum to the floor with a spike. Then he left the boy there and disappeared with his daughter. The father had recently been informed of impending bankruptcy and then catching his only daughter *in flagrante delicto* it was enough to push him over the edge. At some point his conscience got the better of him and he eventually called the police and left an anonymous tip telling them where to find the boy. By the time help arrived at the barn the boy was half out of his mind trying to decide if he should cut off his equipment or slowly bleed to death. The damage was so extensive that the doctor's only recourse was to remove not only his testicles but also most of his penis.

Once he had recovered from the surgery his total focus was on revenge. He spent several weeks searching for his girlfriend and her father. Eventually, he found them in a run-down roadside hotel and despite his girlfriend's pleading, the boy killed her father. After the deed was done he simply walked outside, sat on the curb, and waited for the authorities to come get him. He knew he would never live a normal life and so what difference did it make if he went to jail. Although the judge and jury were all sympathetic the law is the law and he was convicted of first degree murder. Despite his repeated requests to remain incarcerated he had been released four years ago. Initially it hadn't turned out as he feared. He was able to access funds willed to him by his deceased parents which allowed him to set up a bookshop. Books had become his solace on the inside, and since he was virtually unemployable it was only natural that he became a bookseller. The police had ruled him out as a suspect since he had been a model prisoner, his crime was in no way related to the deaths of these women, and he didn't have the necessary equipment to rape them in the first place. However, things had gone horribly wrong when he had inadvertently breached his parole. Although, he knew he had been framed he had no recourse and when he was approached with the only solution that would keep him out of prison an unholy partnership was forged.

Terris Walker was a quiet, successful small business owner who sold used books and trained and raced dogsled teams. The general population had no idea that their friendly neighborhood bookseller was a convicted killer. They willingly supported him and cheered for his dog team during Winter Festival. So, the big question now was, where was Terris? He had closed up the store Saturday night and no one had seen him since. This was not unusual since he wasn't normally open Sundays. And since he seemed to have no friends other than his dogs there was no one but the girls to question regarding his whereabouts. When they checked with fellow mushers of the dog sledding club no one knew where he kept his dogs. A land title search indicated that he didn't own any land in the province of Saskatchewan, under his name or any known relative of his. Regrettably, that didn't mean he wasn't boarding his dogs on land owned by one of his former inmates from over the last twenty-five years.

The R.C.M.P. had searched in and around Dabria's cabin immediately after the call had come in from the alarm company. They had dusted for fingerprints and found none from Terris. However, they hadn't really expected any since the surveillance tapes had shown he was wearing gloves. They had removed two very distinct prints from the front doorknob and were hopeful that they would confirm Jaimie's identity. The prints did match the ones they took off the steering wheel of her car that was parked in the driveway. The police had followed one set of large footprints from the cabin down to the beach. They suddenly ended on the lake beside runner tracks and dog footprints. Sadly, those same runner tracks and prints were obscured by skidoo tracks not five hundred feet from where they started. He had deliberately guided the dogs to run on top of a well used skidoo trail. It was obvious that several sleds had driven over his tracks. So even with the use of tracker dogs they lost the trail and had no idea where Terris had taken his victim. They stopped at all cabins that had sleds parked outside to question the inhabitants as to whether anyone had seen a dogsled team. Frustratingly, no one had seen anything. And none of the cabins owners anywhere near Dabria's had heard anything either. Another dead end! The most exasperating part of the whole thing was that they didn't have conclusive irrefutable evidence that he actually was *the scalper*. He may very well have targeted Dabria for some other reason.

Although they continued to patrol past Dabria's place no one was assigned to stay there since it was decided that the manpower could be better used in trying to find Jaimie. There would be no reason for the kidnapper to return to Dabria's. Therefore, when the towing company called to say they couldn't find Jaimie's car to tow back to town the police were dismayed to conclude that someone else had taken the car. They immediately contacted all of the cab companies to determine if someone had rented a cab and been dropped off at Dabria's. They were surprised to be informed that a young *woman* had been driven out there and that she had taken keys from her pocket, unlocked the doors of the car, and driven away with it while the cabbie was turning around. When it was originally suspected that Jaimie had been kidnapped the R.C.M.P. had immediately put out a Saskatchewan Wide Alert. They now added her car with her license plate to that alert. An officer was sent to her apartment. Earlier in the day they had searched her place for clues. Pictures of her dead sister and newspaper articles mixed in with pictures of Dabria were found on her dresser. When they revisited the complex and questioned her neighbors one of them stated that someone had arrived about an hour earlier and then left again. But, those same neighbors couldn't confirm that it was Jaimie. When the police re-entered her place they found a blood smeared sweater that hadn't been there previously. Also, her closet doors were open with empty hangers left hanging. Had she returned and run or was someone trying to make it look like she had?

This was where Morgan re-entered the investigation. He reviewed all of the information they had up to this point and agreed with Detective French's determination that not much more could be done until morning. Unless an officer was lucky enough to find either Jaimie's car or Terris' truck they were better off starting fresh then. After debriefing, the assembled team was released to get some sleep. Morgan went to his condo and gave Dabria a brief summary. He tucked her into bed and then sat up making lists of questions for tomorrow and plotting out a plan of action which he added to his already bulging file.

~ ~ ~

"What the f*** were you thinking?" his steely control slipped. "I told you we were finished for now. No more girls until things settled down. You've got every cop on both police forces looking for you and that *stupid* girl you took. What did you do with her anyway?"

"Well, Richard," Terris deliberately addressed him by name. "I dumped her when her wig fell off and I realized she wasn't Dabria."

"What do you mean you dumped her?"

"Just that. I dumped her off the sled and left her."

"Dead or alive?"

"She was alive but unconscious when I rode away. She never knew who or what hit her when I knocked her out so I'm pretty sure she's gonna wonder how she ended up in the bush across the lake."

"Again I ask, what were you thinking?"

"I wanted Dabria," Terris stated simply with a shrug. "I figured if I was careful both of us would have a plaything for the summer. I've got the dosages figured out and I know how much nutrition they need to keep them not only alive but also healthy. I know how much physiotherapy I need to give their limbs to keep the muscles from atrophy. I've got it all figured out and she is gonna be my crowning achievement here. Then I'm movin' on, just like we planned."

"Moving on? Oh, Terris, I don't think you'll be moving on," Richard stated quietly and concisely. He removed a small handgun from the inside breast pocket of his suit and shot Terris squarely in the heart. The force of the gunshot at such close range propelled Terris through the open doorway of their little chamber of horrors and out into the hallway. As Richard bent over him to confirm that his aim had been true Terris clobbered him on the side of the head with a set of brash knuckles he had concealed in his fist. Richard slumped to the ground bleeding and unconscious. Terris pushed him away and staggered upright.

You don't survive years in a maximum security facility without learning how to defend and protect yourself. Bulletproof jackets could easily be procured if you had the right contacts. And Terris had the right contacts. He rubbed his chest when the bullet had hit. Damn, he was gonna have a good sized bruise to show for it. The problem with most people that came into contact with Terris was that they underestimated his intelligence. The judge had been no different. Terris had a brilliant if somewhat warped mind. It often was advantageous to him to downplay that intelligence. Terris knew that as soon as Richard found out about his latest little snafu that he would try to get rid of him. Conveniently, everything could be blamed on Terris if he disappeared. There would be no evidence to implicate Richard.

Now Terris' immediate problem was what to do with the good judge. Kill him and dispose of the body or let him live and then be forever looking over his shoulder waiting for the hammer to drop. There really was no choice. Richard had forced Terris' hand and sealed his own fate when he decided to end their partnership.

Terris knew it was only a matter of time before someone figured out where he kept his dogs and therefore discovered Richard's little playroom. Unfortunately, the back-up plan needed to be implemented earlier than scheduled. Terris had always known he was eventually going to have to dispose of the good judge. He hoisted Richard onto his shoulder and carried him back into the chamber. He injected him with his little sleeping concoction and then proceeded to strip him. Once Richard had been laid out on the table Terris strapped him down like he had the girls. After checking Richard's breathing and heart rate and confirming that the restraints were secure Terris left the chamber and returned outside to hide Richard's car, deal with the disposal of his truck, and to destroy the dogs. He parked the car in the old abandoned barn, covered it with a tarp, and rolled the barn door closed.

Terris cared for very little in this world but he did love his dogs. If there hadn't been the risk that the dogs would return and reveal his location Terris would simply have put them in Richard's car, driven them father out into the country, and then released them. Instead he hugged and kissed each dog for the last time, as he put them into their individual kennels of the custom made carrier in the box of his truck. The carrier was topped with his strapped down dogsled. He drove the truck to the riverbank where he knew there was an open stretch of water in the ice. He stopped at the very edge of the bank, put his truck in neutral, walked around to the back, and giving it a good push let gravity take over. The truck rolled down the hill and gaining momentum lumbered onto the ice. It broke through as it reached the edge of the open water. With the ice groaning and cracking the truck tipped over nose first and started to sink almost immediately. His well trained, usually virtually silent dogs began barking frantically as if they knew they only had a matter of moments left. Within less than a minute the entire truck had disappeared from site. The silence almost overwhelmed him as he stared down at the water's inky blackness until the ripples subsided. Shaking off his sadness and the sudden bone deep chill he felt, Terris walked away without a backward look.

It took him several hours to walk back to the abandoned farmhouse. He stuck to a route that kept him away from roads and other farms. By the time he returned the early signs of dawn were streaking the sky with pink and purple ribbons. He immediately returned to the chamber to see how his latest victim was fairing. Not surprisingly, Richard was awake and obviously the drug had worn off enough that he had some mobility back. There were rub marks where he had evidently been tugging at his restraints. He had, however, not regained the ability to speak coherently yet. He thrashed his head back and forth sending slobber flying as he grunted. Despite his obvious desperate situation his eyes still flashed condescension. So, Terris accommodatingly topped up his meds to stop his struggling and increase his awareness of his vulnerability. The look in Richard's eyes never changed. How amusing that he continued to believe he was superior to Terris considering the position he was in. Terris knew he could break Richard. It was simply a matter of time.

He returned to Richard's car and searched it from one end to the other to see if there was anything of value in it for him to use. Happily he discovered a police scanner and another gun. Until someone reported Richard missing his car was the perfect vehicle to get Terris back to town. He would then dump it and get a rental using the ID Richard had conveniently procured for him with his new identity. Supposedly the plan had been that when Richard decided things were too hot Terris would simply disappear. He had money stashed and the ID would allow him to vanish without implicating Richard in the process.

Terris' normal appearance was a full head of curly dirty blonde hair and a full beard. He promptly shaved his entire head. Sporting his new red headed wig and an oversized army coat he drove the car to town and cheekily parked it at the courthouse. Then he confidently walked down the hill, right past the police station to the nearest back alley with a dumpster visible and disposed of the wig, the coat, ski pants, and his big winter boots. He slipped on dress shoes he had hidden inside the coat. Despite his being downtown the chances of there being security cameras anywhere near him were slim to none. And that easily, his new persona was born. A man in a nondescript winter coat that covered a suit walked out of the alley and called a cab to pick him up in front of the mall. The cab dropped him off at the nearest car rental place and with his new credit card and driver's license in hand he rented himself an unremarkable cream colored Chrysler Sebring. He casually drove away and went and checked himself into a hotel. From previous surveillance he knew Dabria's schedule so it was simply a matter of implementing Plan B for her abduction. Plan A had obviously netted him the wrong girl. He was confident that Plan B would not fail.

Chapter 29

Morgan had a lot of unanswered questions. When you passed the most important questions of where were Terris and Jaimie, the next most obvious one was why? What was Terris' motivation for kidnapping, drugging, toying with the prostitutes, and then finally killing them? And who was his accomplice? Unless he was using a condom covered dildo, since there was evidence of latex inside the girl' vaginas, which simply made no sense, there was clearly another man involved. Was that man Judge Richard Reynolds? There was proof of penetration on all of the women. The penetrations had obviously been brutal, as there was considerable bruising and tearing in and around their vaginas. Morgan's conclusion to this was that physical pain was one objective of the torture and that psychological pain was another. *The scalper* or his accomplice wanted the women to know that they were being viciously raped and that they were powerless to stop the assault. Why was he punishing them? What did this excessive hatred stem from? The list of unanswered questions was getting longer, not shorter, as the investigation continued. Morgan finally gave up and snuck into bed with Dabria to try to catch a few hours of sleep.

When the alarm went off at 6:00 a.m. waking both of them up, Dabria rolled over and propped herself up on her elbows to bounce her own questions off of Morgan. Using each other as a sounding board they formulated a hypothesis. Terris was the kidnapper and the dumper. Richard was the rapist and the murderer. Each of the murdered women looked eerily similar to pictures they had obtained of Richard's mother. That could explain the deep seated hatred he appeared to have for them. Initial issues of abandonment had started his need to seek out specific woman to sleep with and rough up. Dabria suggested that the possible ridicule of his lack of sexual prowess by these women had fueled the rage and increased the level of violence. Unfortunately, these were mostly suppositions. What they did know was that Richard had been left at the orphanage by his mother and that he liked to smack woman around. Waneta had told Dabria that Richard seemed to have a hard time reaching orgasm unless he inflicted some sort of pain. Being a virgin herself, when she had taken up with him, she assumed that maybe this was part of the whole sex thing. Of course, she knew better now. Cody had also claimed that the sounds he heard coming from his mother's bedroom at night were not sounds of pleasure but rather stifled sounds of torment.

Since both had heavy schedules for the day the brainstorming session would have to be discontinued for now. When Dabria entered the kitchen she noticed Morgan's ever growing file sitting on the table. She picked it up to wipe the table down before she set it for breakfast. Juggling the haphazardly filled file and a wet dish cloth led to the shifting of some of its contents. Part of a picture of one of the dead girls slid out. It was a close-up of the girl's hand. Dabria set the dishcloth down so that she could stuff the picture back in. Dead bodies before breakfast tended to turn her off. As she pushed it back into the file she suddenly stopped. The girl's hand had French manicured nails and the thumb sported a decal Dabria had seen before—in fact quite recently. It matched the decal on *her* thumbnail. With an indrawn breath she called to Morgan.

"What's wrong?" he immediately came from the bathroom since the tone of her voice indicated distress.

"Which girl does this hand belong to?" she asked pointing to the folder.

"It should say on the back," he answered as he grabbed the picture from the file. "It's the Jane Doe—the first of the women that were found. Why?"

"I think my nail tech did her nails," Dabria held up her hand for Morgan to look at. "Maybe Brandy will know who this girl is," Dabria sank into a chair.

"Call her," Morgan directed as he released her hand and passed her his phone.

"I have her number in my contacts. Let me get my cell," Dabria rushed to the bedroom.

The phone rang several times and then went to voice mail. Dabria left a message for Brandy to contact her ASAP indicating it was a matter of some urgency that was more serious than the usual catastrophe of a broken nail.

After a hasty breakfast and quick kiss goodbye they both headed out to greet the day's challenges.

~ ~ ~

As Dabria hurried down the corridor to her office her cell phone buzzed.

"We are good to go, Dabria!" Tony updated as soon as she picked up. With barely contained enthusiasm he had called Dabria to inform her of their good fortune. He was hot on the tail of the detectives heading towards Ben's uncle's cabin armed with search warrants and a CSI team.

"I'm allowed to tag along providing I don't touch anything or get in their way."

"That is excellent news. As soon as you know anything let Morgan or I know. Thanks for the update. I'm heading into a meeting, so I gotta run."

"Talk to you soon!"

Dabria hadn't walked more than a few feet when her phone rang again.

"Hey, I just got a call from the Deputy Director of Security at the Saskatoon Correctional Centre and you were wrong," Craig said.

"How's that?"

"Apparently, Cody tripped and fell into a door in Saskatoon. So, it wasn't safer for him to be incarcerated out of town."

"No!"

"Yah, I happen to know Rachael, the Deputy Director. She and I went to University together and she assured me they'd be doing an investigation into the cause of the incident. These kinds of things are not something they take lightly."

"How badly is he hurt?"

"He'll been sporting a few scars but he'll survive."

"Did she give you any indication as to what she thinks happened?"
"They have it on tape and what they can see is that another inmate
approaches Cody and says something to him. Cody then jumps up
and throws the first punch. Within seconds he's surrounded by several
inmates who then start beating the crap out of him. Guards move in
and the whole incident is over in less than a couple of minutes. And,
Dabria, before you go jumping to any conclusions, there is no evidence
that Judge Reynolds had anything to do with this."

"I guess we'll have to have a chat with Cody and find out who this
inmate is to him and what he said. I'll reserve judgment until then."

~ ~ ~

The next several days were filled with court appearances, interviews,
and document preparation for Dabria. Morgan's days were occupied
with investigations, interviews, and mounds of report writing, until
Ducette called and informed him that they had been invited to a
private gathering. As Morgan ran out to the cruiser he noticed there
was already someone sitting in the front passenger seat.

"Morgan, I'd like to introduce Prosecutor Marsha Miller-Marsha,
Detective Morgan Vaughan."

"So, what's up?" Morgan asked.

"The Elders have requested a meeting with the three of us."

"The *Elders*?"

"Yah, the older, most respected members of Cody's band."

"Why?"

"I guess we're about to find out," he responded as they sped down
the gravel road towards the reservation. The consensus reached as they
drove was that this little get-together obviously involved either Cody
and/or Tehya and that Marsha had been invited to the party because
they were about to be propositioned to cut some kind of deal.

They parked in front of Leotie's house and before they could knock
on the door it was opened. Leotie appeared and beckoned them into
the kitchen. Seated at the table were several elderly native males and
a lawyer Ducette recognized. It was his cousin Joshua. Tehya slouched
with head down in the doorway of the living room.

"Please have a seat," Joshua invited as he introduced himself and
the men at the table. Ducette introduced his party since he was the

common factor of both groups and had been the one they had invited. The prosecutor accepted a chair and sat while both Ducette and Morgan remained standing. They waited expectantly for the lawyer to begin what was obviously going to be a negotiation.

"The Elders were wondering what kind of arrangement we might agree to regarding the exchange of information pertaining to a case that you might be interested in," the lawyer began as he sank back into his own chair and directed his question to Ducette.

Morgan had always suspected Teyha had been involved in Megan's death and now he instinctively knew that she had been. However, she obviously had also seen or heard something useful regarding the identity of *the scalper*, *the dumper*, or both. Now her *community* was hoping to cut a deal.

"Tehya, why don't you join the group at the table?" Morgan encouraged with an extended hand of invitation.

She grunted and turned away.

"Tehya," Leotie cautioned in a quiet but authoritative tone. "Come," she commanded.

Again Tehya grunted but she did turn around and shuffle over to the table. Morgan pulled a chair out for her and she plopped herself down into it. She kept her eyes downcast and her hands lay limply in her lap as if resigned to whatever fate was decided for her. Ducette had positioned himself against the wall beside the stove while Morgan, across from him, was now propped against the very doorjamb that Tehya had just vacated. It gave him the perfect vantage point to be able to observe the expressions of almost everyone around the table, with the exceptions of Joshua and Tehya.

"Tehya may have seen some events occur on the night that Megan Thomas was murdered."

"May have?"

"Yes, may have."

"And what do *you* want in exchange for that information?" Ducette prodded.

"Oh, Detective, it's not what *I* want. It's a matter of what the *community* will accept."

"I see. So what's the *community* seeking?"

"Because Miss Sakamoose is still a minor and the incident with Megan Thomas was an accident . . ."

"You mean her murder?" Ducette interrupted as he instantly straightened up.

"Her death," the lawyer refused to be drawn, "was accidental."

"Her neck was snapped and there was no evidence of defensive wounds or any other markings indicating that an altercation had occurred," Ducette revealed. "She was flat out murdered, Josh, and we both know that!"

"Detective Ducette," Marsha warned, "please let our esteemed counsel continue."

Ducette glowered at Marsha but maintained his silence.

"As I was saying," Joshua resumed, "we may have some information that could be beneficial to one of your other cases."

"Why don't you tell me what you have and what you want, and then I'll decide if we're interested?" Marsha suggested objectively.

"Miss Sakamoose might have witnessed the disposal of one of *the scalper* victim's bodies on the night that Megan Thomas died," the lawyer finally divulged. "Since she is a minor and Megan's death *was* an accident we are seeking community incarceration."

Morgan continued to appear nonchalant in his stance but mentally was at full attention. This girl's testimony could be crucial to convicting at least the accessory to the murders. They needed her testimony and they needed her cooperation to get the charges that were laid against Cody dropped.

"I can present a plea bargain to the judge that is assigned to this case," she assured the assembled group with unwavering regard. "Is Miss Sakamoose prepared to give us a statement?"

"Yes, she is. What do you propose?" Joshua pushed.

"If it is determined that Megan's death was in fact accidental and that the information Miss Sakamoose gives us pertaining to what she witnessed is accurate, then the Prosecutor's Office would be willing to recommend Community Incarceration for no less than 5 years. Is that agreeable to you?"

"Might I have a minute to discuss this with my client?"

"Exactly who is your client?" Ducette challenged.

"Why Miss Sakamoose, of course," Joshua replied with feigned innocence and a quizzical expression.

"Ah, we would be more than happy to honor your request," Marsha assured him as she rose and glared at Ducette and Morgan to follow.

In silence they headed to the car. Once the doors were closed Ducette all but exploded.

"That little bitch snuck up behind Megan and snapped her neck like a twig because she was jealous and Josh is using our ethnicity to try and get her off. A sentence like he is proposing will only add to the already strained relations between the white and aboriginal communities here. This is not going to help!"

"That's for the judge to decide, Ducette, not you," Marsha reminded him.

"I can't believe you haven't said a word," he turned on Morgan accusingly.

"I know how these things can go, man, and getting emotional in front of the suspect is not going to help our case. We need to keep our emotions in control and stay focused on the goal."

"What exactly is the goal? I seem to have forgotten," Ducette supplied sarcastically.

"The original goal for me was to find out who cut Dabria. That ballooned into finding *the scalper,* finding Megan's actual killer, and having the charges against Cody dropped. It now includes finding *the scalper's* accomplice, Jaimie's abductor, Ben's killer, the serial killer who has been praying on girls in the Salem area for the last several decades, and possibly Ben's uncle's killer as well. How is that for a goal?" Morgan asked.

"I would say overly optimistic," Marsha volunteered.

"Actually, I think it's obtainable. We now know who killed Megan and she is about to give us a positive ID on the accomplice. We simply have to prove that Richard is the serial killer and that should about wrap up all the cold cases of dead bodies that have been piling up around this case."

"I think they're calling us back in," Marsha pointed at the figure on the steps waving at them. They returned to the kitchen and resumed their previous positions.

"Miss Sakamoose has agreed to give her statement with the assurance that her plea bargain be recorded as accepted by her guardian, the Elders of her community, and you, Madam Prosecutor."

"Fine, Detective Vaughan will take her statement," Marsha directed.

Pen and pad were retrieved from Marsha's briefcase as well as a tape recorder. Tehya related the events of that evening almost emotionless. She claimed she had gone out for a walk and had happened upon

Megan talking on her cell phone. Megan was talking to Cody and telling him she would wait for him to come and get her. She said she loved him and knew his baby was as anxious as she was for them to be married and to become a real family. Tehya said she waited until Megan was off the phone and then she confronted her. She told Megan that she and Cody had been engaged since they were children and that Megan could take her bastard baby and find some white guy to pass it off on. She said Megan spit on her and then turned away. Teyha grabbed her hair from the back, Megan slipped, and Tehya fell on top of her, which supposedly is what snapped her neck. She flipped Megan over and realized that she was unconscious. Almost immediately after that she heard dogs, so she dragged Megan's body into the bush with her and hid. A dogsled team pulled up onto the shore and with the moonlight overhead she was able to see the face of the musher. She recognized him as the bookstore owner from the used bookstore in the city. She claimed she was about to request his assistance with Megan when he pulled a very dead naked body out of the sled and posed it on the bank not far from where she crouched. She waited until he and the dogs were long gone and had planned to drag Megan back to civilization with her. It was then that she realized that Megan was dead and so she decided to position her in the same way as the other dead girl only several yards away. Then she ran back home, hoping no one would ever find out that she was involved.

Tehya read over and then signed the statement that Morgan had handwritten and then silently got up and left the room. Tehya's lawyer and Marsha both signed that they had witnessed the recording of the document. It was placed in Marsha's briefcase and she assured the other party that she would be sending a copy to Joshua's office in the morning. Leotie saw them out and pressed a small packet into Ducette's hand when she stumbled and he reached out to steady her. He silently palmed the missive into his pocket and returned to his cruiser. Once they were back on the main road he dug through his pocket and handed the message to Marsha. It was a small tightly folded note with a diamond ring in it.

"Shit," Marsha exclaimed as she read the note. "Leotie claims this is Megan's ring and that she found it in the bottom of her washing machine. The only way it could have ended up in there is from the pocket of one of Tehya's pairs of jeans."

"Now where does that leave us with the statement? She obviously lied. That doesn't exactly make her a reliable witness does it?"

The three debated the credibility of Tehya's story and conceded that she had left some details out to make her actions appear less calculated and make Megan's death appear more accidental. Neither Ducette nor Morgan believed it was an accident. Morgan agreed with Ducette's earlier statement. She was jealous of Megan and being a wrestler she knew that grabbing Megan from behind and twisting her neck the way she had, would kill her. It was murder, plain and simple. In fact, since she admitted to knowing that Megan was pregnant it was a double murder. If she hadn't had something to bargain with she would never have come forward. Obviously Leotie had confronted her with the ring and forced her to confess. Tehya had counted on Leotie keeping the ring a secret. That was a foolish mistake. Cody was Leotie's blood, Tehya was not. Her loyalties obviously lay with Cody.

Chapter 30

D abria walked out of the courthouse and a very attractive, impeccably dressed, thirty-something-ish gentleman with a briefcase almost bowled her over.

"Wow, I'm so sorry," he apologized as he immediately set down his briefcase and then helped her gather the scattered contents of her purse. "I'm late for an appointment and was just not paying attention at all. Are you okay?"

"I'm fine," she assured him with an anemic smile. "These things happen."

"Hey, are you that new lawyer from Legal Aid?"

"Yes, and you are?" she asked without introducing herself further. She took a step back as he handed her refilled purse to her. There was something strangely familiar about him. He was undeniably attractive but an aura of menace seemed to radiate from him.

"TJ . . . . TJ Moffat. I'm with Moffat and Dunham out of Saskatoon," he introduced himself as he thrust his hand out towards her.

She reluctantly offered her own hand and it was swiftly enfolded in his firm cool grasp. His touch sent a tingle of recognition up her arm. As if experiencing the same sensation he quickly released his clasp and allowed her fingers to slide out of his hand. Dabria took another step back and deliberately searched his face.

"Have we met somewhere before?" she asked.

"I seriously doubt it. Trust me, you're not the kind of woman any guy would meet and then forget," he stated baldly.

She blushed and uncomfortably looked away, not from the compliment, but from the unnerving sensation of being drawn to him.

"Let me apologize again. I didn't mean to just blurt that out." He had however succeeded in distracting her enough that she was no longer trying to dissect him like some grade ten biology specimen. Obvious issues would arise if she recognized him.

Tenacity was one of her strong suits though and she continued her perusal of him.

"I really must run," he commented. "It was very nice meeting you. Maybe we'll get the opportunity to appear opposite each other some time. Bye for now."

She tipped her head in silent acknowledgement as he hurried off to his car. Dabria headed for her own vehicle as her mind feverously searched for a situation where she may have seen him before. After digging through the mess in her purse for her car keys she stowed her briefcase in the back then slid into the driver's seat. There seemed to be a strange but oddly pleasant scent in the car that she hadn't noticed previously. She determined that it was coming from her purse. She dumped the contents onto the seat beside her to see if something had spilled or broken when it had fallen on the pavement. Everything appeared fine but she was quickly developing a raging headache. She pawed more thoroughly through the disarray and discovered a broken perfume sample bottle that had leaked all over some tissues. Scooping up the whole sodden mess she deposited it in the parking lot garbage can near her car. When she returned to the car she took out more tissues and wiped off everything that appeared damp. Again she dumped the garbage in the can outside. She downed a couple of Advil with the dregs of the morning's coffee—which strangely enough tasted like her purse smelled—and pulled out of the parking lot to head home. Her cell phone rang and glancing at the display she determined it was Brandy. She immediately pulled over to the side of the road to answer.

"Hey, it's Brandy. I just got your message. We were out of town and I forgot my phone at home. What's up?"

Dabria asked Brandy how many girls used the decal that she and the Jane Doe shared without explaining why. Brandy said it was a funny thing since she hadn't used that decal for a couple years because she had actually forgotten she even had it. One of her clients had brought the decals to her and asked that she only apply them to her nails so that they remained exclusively hers. Brandy had put them in a drawer so that her other clients couldn't pick them and only brought them out when she did that girl's nails.

"So, why did this woman stop using them?"

"Oh, she didn't stop using them, she stopped coming in," Brandy explained.

"When?"

"Wow, I'm guessing about two maybe two and a half years ago."

"Why?"

"I don't know. She just stopped coming."

"Do you remember her name?"

"Sure, but I can't tell you cause that's confidential."

"Brandy, it's important. I think something has happened to her. Please help me."

"Something . . . . like we need to call the cops, something?"

"I promise whatever you tell me I will immediately pass on to Detective Vaughn, an R.CM.P. I know. Please Brandy."

"Her name is Luba."

"Luba?"

"Luba D. Her last name is some long Ukrainian thing. It started with a D."

"What does she look like? Do you know where she works or anything else about her?"

"She had short brown hair, brown eyes, petite, and curvy. She bragged that she didn't need to work. She had an inheritance and a new fancy "married" boyfriend. She said the whole town would be in a tailspin if they knew what was going on."

"Didn't you think it was strange when she stopped coming in?"

"Not really. The last time I saw her she was getting ready to go on a holiday and said that if things worked out well she may not be back. I'd tried calling her a couple times after she missed her next appointment but the last time I called the phone was disconnected."

"Thanks, Brandy. If you think of anything else let me know," Dabria requested. "By the way why, did you start using the decals again?"

"I was cleaning out the drawer and found them stuffed under a bunch of other papers. Crazy, heh?"

"Yah, crazy," Dabria signed off. Her head was pounding and she knew she needed to get home and go lie down. This was the worst migraine she had had in over six months. She called Morgan first and filled him in on what Brandy had revealed.

"We found Jaimie and her car," Morgan informed her. "They picked her up just outside of Calgary in a routine stop check. Apparently, she has *no* idea why she is being detained. I doubt she knows who kidnapped and then dumped her anyway. Also, Lena Reynolds reported Richard as a missing person a couple hours ago and his car has just been discovered parked at the court house."

Dabria asked if they could talk later since she was heading home and that she didn't feel well. She had just left the city limits when her vision started to falter. Immediately pulling over to the shoulder she grabbed her cell phone and speed dialed Morgan again. As soon as the line opened, without waiting for him to answer, she started to speak.

"Morgan, there is something seriously wrong with me. This isn't just a migraine. I . . . . am losing my vision . . . ."

"Dabria . . ."

"In car . . . . lake road . . . . help . . . . ," she weakly entreated and then went silent. The line was still open and Morgan heard rustling around the phone and then silence except for breathing.

"Dabria," Morgan yelled. "Dabria!"

He kept his cell phone glued to his ear while he radioed an emergency bulletin to dispatch. He requested that all units in and around Dabria's regular route to the lake search for her car as he raced to find her himself. The click of door locks opening and then the dinging of an open car door alerted him to the fact that someone had found her. Thankfully, before Morgan yelled into the phone, he heard a man's muffled voice.

"Aren't you lucky, Msssss. Abdulla-Smythe, that I just happened along?" the voice crooned acerbically as the sound of the car engine stopped. "In fact, I'm sure you'll soon be very grateful that I'm the one to rescue you. I'm very talented when it comes to satisfying a woman's every desire," the voice chortled wryly.

Miraculously, Dabria's phone had slipped from her fingers into the oversized pocket of her suit coat. Morgan could now hear the release of her seatbelt and rustling sounds like she was being picked up. He immediately depressed a button that allowed him to record every sound that was picked up by the phone. A car door was slammed shut. A grunt, ... more rustling and then another slammed door. The ding of a front driver's door . . . . the click of a seatbelt . . . . and then the start of a different vehicle engine. The rhythmic tic-tic of a signal light, the predictable racing of the engine's motor, and the subtle squeal of rubber on pavement indicated that Dabria's abductor had headed back onto the highway. Morgan mentally recorded what he heard as his own vehicle hurtled down the road, while his eyes desperately scanned the vehicles around him. He had put his cell phone on mute so he could listen but not be heard. Dispatch radioed within minutes to say that her car had been found but that it was vacant. The doors were locked, keys still in the ignition, and purse—with contents dumped onto the passenger seat. Morgan immediately pulled over and continued to listen intently while he urgently scribbled notes. Time of her call, ... time of abduction, ... minutes between abduction and location of her vehicle. There were officers that were only minutes away from Dabria and yet Morgan feared that she was just beyond their help. He knew after bundling her into the other vehicle the unsub (unknown subject) had pulled back onto the highway and then slowed down only a minute and a half after, signaled again, stopped, turned, signaled again, and then turned again and sped up. Somehow he needed to mobilize as many units as possible so that they could shut down all roads that could conceivably follow that timed pattern. As he talked to the dispatcher he discerned that Dabria's driver had again slowed down, signaled, and was turning. His signal stayed on as he continued to turn. Again he stopped. The consistent signal tic stopped and then resumed. There was a slightly different rhythm to the new tic-tic. He had switched the signals direction! Now he accelerated again. Morgan was convinced he had headed back to the city. Assuming that, he had either crossed the bridge, then headed East onto River Road or headed East before the bridge and was moving towards Candle Lake. Morgan strained his ears desperately listening for clues. The engine sped up and then slowed down, sped up and then slowed down. He had to be in the city! Signal on . . . . signal off. Stop. Go. Signal on. Stop. Go. Speed up. Maintain speed. Accelerate. Morgan started timing again. Fifteen agonizing minutes later, signal on. Gravel road! Timing again . . . . five minutes and stop.

"Final destination, Dabria, final destination," the voice announced with barely suppressed glee as the sound of the engine stopped.

Morgan continued to listen while he texted his observations to his superiors. Without knowing the type of vehicle the abductor was driving they would have to do a house by house search in the area that Morgan was guestimating she was being held and ask the residents if anyone had seen either Richard or Terris in the vicinity. The chances of finding her alive let alone unharmed were minimal at best. Morgan had never been so scared in his life, nor so driven to succeed. Unmarked cruisers were sent East through the city and also down the highway to Candle Lake. Using Morgan's sound/timing map they both drove as far as they could before encountering a discrepancy. The conclusion drawn was that she had been taken to an isolated location in the general area of La Colle Falls, which frankly only made sense. Now it was simply a matter of finding that specific location. Yah, simple!

~ ~ ~

Terris pulled into the farmyard and drove directly to the old barn. There was enough room left inside to park his latest vehicle acquisition. After rolling the central barn door closed he decided to temporarily leave Dabria in the backseat while he went to check on his partner in crime.

The second Dabria heard him walking away she quickly sat up to view her situation. Weak sunlight filtered through the grimy barn windows and dust motes and bits of hay swirled in the tiny shafts of light. She needed to get out of the car and hide immediately. With heart racing and shaking hands she tried the door handle. It wouldn't open. Shit! Her heart spiked as she panicked and yanked with futility at the door handle. Suddenly it occurred to her that she could simply unlock it manually and then climb out. Jerking the lock up she swiftly retried the door and a quiet sob escaped as the door popped open. Wasting no time she slid out of the car, quietly reclosed the door, and then determined her escape options. She searched for another exit and found two—the stairs to the loft and a backdoor to the barn. When she checked out the roof she concluded there was hay in the loft because she could see small bales piled up through the feeding chutes. She could go up into the loft and hide in the hay or try to make a break for it outside. Dabria hustled to the backdoor of the barn, opened it, and took a quick scan of the area. It was heavily wooded, but not knowing how long before her abductor came back or where she was, she concluded her safest option was to pick the loft. She left the backdoor open and ran up to the front of the barn and into the loft. The loft was full of bales! Quickly Dabria scrambled up the side of a stack. As she glanced to her right through a broken window she saw movement and horrified, realized that he was already making his way back to the barn. She immediately froze so as not to draw attention to herself and waited until he was out of sight. Then she instantly rolled behind the stack and pulled herself into a ball. She held her breath as the barn door opened.

"What the fuck?" an agitated Terris exclaimed.

~ ~ ~

Morgan was outwardly composed as the team assembled and waited for direction from their supervisor. But inside he was frantic. Every second of delay decreased Dabria's chances of a safe return. As soon as the chief arrived he issued directions to disperse the members to the various farms. Morgan bolted for his car with Ducette hard on his heels. They raced towards the first farm. As they pulled up into the yard a young boy and his dog stopped playing and ran back to the porch of the house. By the time they had stopped a woman had come to the door.

Morgan immediately flashed his badge.

"Good afternoon, Ma'am, my name is Detective Vaughn and this is my partner Detective Ducette."

"Afternoon," she responded warily. "Can I help you?"

"We were wondering if you could look at a couple of pictures. We are looking for these men and this woman," Morgan explained as he passed her the pictures.

She reached out and examined them.

"No, I'm sorry. None of them seem familiar," she said as she handed them back.

"Mom, can I see?" the boy asked before Morgan could ask her permission to show them to him.

"Uhh, I guess," she agreed hesitantly.

Morgan handed the pictures to the boy. There were two pictures of Richard—one in a suit and one in more casual attire. The boy flipped past them quickly. There was also one of Dabria. Again the boy flipped past it. But the two of Terris were different. One was of him in front of his store and the other one was of him with his sled dogs. The boy stopped at the picture with the dogs. He looked at it intently.

"Do you know this man?" Morgan asked expectantly.

"Maybe . . . . I don't know, but I do know the dogs. They live just down the road," he assured them with a smile.

"How do you know that?" his mother asked suspiciously, with her arms crossed.

"I uhhhhh, I'm not sure," he back-pedaled, suddenly uneasy.

"Ma'am, it is extremely important that we find this man as soon as possible. Please let your son tell us what he knows," Morgan entreated.

"Fine, go ahead Jacob."

"I was out walking Liberty and all of a sudden she took off like a shot. When I caught up with her she was standing at the end of a driveway and looking at this old barn. We snuck up to the barn and I looked in the windows. The barn was full of dogs. The dogs were looking at me and I was looking at them. Then Libby jumped up on the bale beside me. As soon as they saw her they all started barking, so I hightailed it outta there before I got caught."

"Do you know which farm he's talking about?" Morgan questioned his mother.

"I can show you," he volunteered eagerly.

"No, that's okay," Morgan assured him as he looked expectantly at the mother.

"Well, I'm guessing it's the old Danylovych farm. But it's been abandoned for years."

"What can you tell me about the farm and the family?"

"It belongs to a Ukrainian family. They were originally grain and beef farmers. The old man and his wife only had one daughter. She had a baby, dumped it with them, and took off. The baby was a girl. She was my age. The grandma died when she was just a little girl and so she was raised by her guido."

"Guido?" Morgan questioned.

"That's what she called her grandpa. He was a miserable, bitter old man and so as soon as she turned eighteen and finished school, she took off. He lived another couple of years and then passed away about ten years ago. I've seen her a couple of times over the years coming to or going from the farm so I'm guessing she inherited it."

"When's the last time you remember seeing her?"

"Gee, I dunno. Not for a few years. I'm guessing maybe two or so."

"Was she ever with anyone when you saw her?"

"Yah, actually the last time she was with a guy. She waved at me as they drove by."

"Please, look at these pictures again closely. Could she have been with either one of these men?"

"I'm sorry, I could tell you that the guy had dark hair and sunglasses but that's it. As soon as she started waving at me I concentrated on her and not him."

"But you recognized her?"

"Sure, we had been friends the whole time we grew up."

"Do you have any pictures of her?"

"Of course."

"Are they easy to find? I'd really like to see one."

"I have one on the mantle. It's our Grad picture. Come in," she invited as she opened the door and walked inside.

Morgan and Ducette eagerly followed leaving the boy and his dog on the porch. As soon as the door closed the boy quietly raced off like a shot. Something was going on at the farm and he figured if he got there first he could help the cops with their investigation.

"What was her first name?"

"Luba. It means love in Ukrainian."

The picture confirmed what Morgan had guessed. Her friend was the murdered Jane Doe—the girl with the fake nails in Morgan's file. They needed to get to that farm now! It was the obvious location of Dabria's abductor. As they turned to leave the house the mother realized that her son and his dog were gone.

"Where's Jacob?" she asked in a panicked voice.

"Damn it," Morgan cursed. They did not need a boy and his dog tangled up in this mess. Not only was it dangerous for them but they might innocently alert the kidnapper that someone else was coming to call.

"Does your son have a cell phone?" Morgan barked.

"Yes."

"What's his number?"

She rattled it off and stood there wringing her hands while Morgan dialed with Ducette's cell. His line was still open with Dabria's and except for the occasional rustling noise little else could be heard from her side. The phone rang and rang but Jacob did not pick up. When it went to voicemail Morgan disconnected and then texted instead.—Jacob. Stay away from that farm. Owner is a bad man and will hurt you and Liberty!

"If he comes back, keep him and the dog here," Morgan commanded.

"What's going on? Is he in danger?" she asked fearfully.

"Do you know what route he would take to get to the other farm?"

"Yes, there was an old path between our places. Follow me."

"Ducette, radio this in and request search warrants. I'll go in on foot." He rushed after the mother.

Jacob received the text and was unsure what to do. He wanted to help the police but if the guy might hurt Libby maybe he should hang back and wait a while until the policemen got there. Then he could just watch the action. As he was trying to make up his mind he heard running behind him. He grabbed Libby and pulled her into the bush beside him. He clamped his hand over her muzzle to keep her quiet and they hid. His mother was the first to rush past him. The cop was hot on her trail. Jacob immediately stepped back onto the trail so they wouldn't get too far ahead of him. Morgan instantly felt the boy behind him. He caught up with Jacob's mother and grabbed her arm to stop her. As she swung around to yank herself free, he motioned to her to be quiet. He pointed back down the trail. She instantly understood and hurrying back surprised Jacob as he attempted to follow them. Before he could utter one peep she aggressively made a slashing motion across her throat and then firmly pointed for him to go back to the house. Soundlessly, he dropped his head and then turned around and ran back with Liberty happily chasing behind. She gave Morgan a quick wave and then hurried after her son. Morgan two-way radioed Ducette to update him on the status of the boy and his mother and to inform him that he was going to continue in on foot. As he stealthily crept along the trail he silently prayed that they weren't too late!

~ ~ ~

Dabria hardly dared to breathe as she strained to hear below. Her heart was pounding so loudly that she had to sternly remind herself there was no possible way her abductor could hear it. She took deep even breaths trying to calm down enough so that she could come up with a plan that would keep her alive. She heard him swear and slam the car door. He obviously noticed the backdoor she had deliberately left open because she heard him making his way to the rear of the barn. Despite the fact that she had initially lost consciousness, not long after she had regained her ability to hear. She knew that they had returned to the city and then left again to travel into the countryside. She didn't know exactly where she was but she did know that she wasn't far from town. Unfortunately, her sense of direction was abysmal. As her panic decreased and her mind cleared she reviewed the events that had transpired since she left court. She concluded that the man who had knocked her purse on the ground was obviously the guy that had brought her here. Not only had he drugged her purse but he also must have drugged her leftover coffee. It had to be Terris. She recalled the pictures she had recently seen of him and compared them to the young man at the courthouse. She knew she had seen him before and suddenly it hit her. She had danced with him at the bar the night she had been attacked! She had also bumped into him outside the Chinese food restaurant. All three men were one and the same. The hair or lack of it was different. The eye color was different, glasses—no glasses, hat—no hat. But in the end it was Terris. So, he was her cutter. Was he simply copying Richard or did he scalp all of the women? There were still so many questions. She shifted and something hard dug into her hip. As she adjusted herself she realized it was her cell phone. She swiftly snatched it out of her pocket and before she registered that the line was open she tried to speed dial Morgan. As she fumbled with it she cut the connection Morgan had held open.

Panicked, he prayed that she redial and would be able to reconnect with him. His phone vibrated and he immediately opened the line.

"Morgan?" she quietly sobbed.

"Baby, are you hurt? What do you see? Did you see who took you?"

"I'm okay. I'm hiding in a barn and its Terris," she whispered.

"Stay there. We know what farm you're at and we're on our way. Keep your phone hidden and the line open. I'm going to go on mute but you can still talk to me. I love you, baby, stay strong."

The phone went silent but the light indicating the line was open remained on. Suddenly she realized Terris was back in the barn and was heading up the stairs. She slipped the phone into her pocket and listening keenly, she held her breath. She couldn't see him but she could hear him. He stood at the top of the stairs and then started to retreat.

As she silently sighed she looked above her and again noticed the dust motes from the hay dancing in the stream of sunlight that filtered in from one of the broken windows. Unexpectedly the urge to sneeze arose. The hay was no longer soft. It suddenly had the consistency of raw fiberglass scratching the back of her neck and her sweating hands. The sneeze overpowered her and despite holding it back a small kisnitch escaped. The creak of the stairs stopped. Instant silence descended over the loft. The creak of the loft stairs sounded again as he returned to the top level and then cautious footfalls sounded on the loosely scattered hay on the other side of the bales. She knew he was coming for her and she was trapped. Without making a sound and again holding her breath, she eased off her pump and clenching it in her fist she waited for her one opportunity to strike out. As his head popped over the top of the bale she swung up with all of her strength and clobbered him with the spike of her heel.

~ ~ ~

Morgan's heart almost stopped when a sudden high pitched shriek of rage came loud and clear through his cell phone.

"You bitch! You fucking bitch!" The ensuing tussle was punctuated by grunts and panting and concluded with a resounding slap.

"Stop it! Stop it! Gawd damn it! What a spitfire you are. You're gonna be a real treat for my little friend. Come along like a good girl now and I won't hurt you again. Recognize me yet?"

"Yes. You danced with me at the bar," Dabria responded. Morgan jolted with the delivery of that little piece of the puzzle.

"Very good. You found me attractive, didn't you? I could feel it," he taunted. "Two dances and then you turned away. Why? Too good for me, Little Angel?"

Dabria gasped.

"Ya, I know what your name means. I've researched you and stalked you for weeks. Richard figured you were his *perfect angel*—right down to the name. Boy was he wrong. In case you haven't guessed I'm the one that marked you," he chuckled. "Guess you're not perfect anymore."

There were sounds of movement again.

"Don't bother trying to run. Without your shoes you won't get very far. The grass is full of hazards and the ground here is uneven. Just head for the house and I'll reintroduce you to someone you may have appeared in front of before. Course he probably had clothes on the last time ya saw him and was lookin' all official," he chuckled. "Not so much anymore. I don't think anyone would find him very intimidating today." A door opened and closed.

"I've watched you fucking your boyfriend, ya know," he threw that out, trying to goad her into responding. Dabria remained silent.

Morgan continued to trot down the path listening, but slowed as he rounded a twist in the trail that appeared to open into a clearing. He could see the corner of a house at the end of the path. He dropped back closer to the ground so that if someone looked out of the windows they wouldn't catch a glimpse of him. The closer he got to the house the better the reception on the phone. He obviously had the right house. Morgan caught movement in the house and was able to watch Terris as he walked past the patio doors prodding Dabria to keep moving in front of him. Morgan's heart clenched at the sight of her. She truly did appear to be okay. Another door was opened.

"Down you go," Terris directed.

"I don't want to go into the basement," Dabria stopped at the top of the stairs, hoping that Morgan was catching everything they said.

"Well, that's a shame. Cause you're goin' down there anyway," Terris gave her a little nudge.

"I need to use the washroom," Dabria stalled.

"You can use the one downstairs. Keep going."

Unwillingly she started her descent. If Morgan and the troops didn't show up here soon there was a good chance she wasn't going to make it out of this basement. With each step her feelings of dread increased. At the bottom of the staircase she again stopped.

"Not into furniture much, are you?"

"It's not necessary. The playroom is through that door."

A lock rattled, the swish of a heavy door could be heard, and then Dabria's horrified gasp.

Morgan was afraid he wasn't going to be able to wait for backup. The second his intuition warned him that her life was in imminent danger he would be down those stairs in a flash.

"Dabria, welcome to your new home. Do you recognize the esteemed Judge Reynolds? I was right wasn't I? He doesn't look quite so daunting with all of his clothes off, does he? Good Gawd, Richard you're drooling. That's really kind of a turn off for most girls, ya know!" he chastised. "Okay Dabria, you can start taking your clothes off now."

"Why is Judge Reynolds naked and strapped onto that table?"

"So he can watch, of course. Come now I have waited long enough for this little drama to unfold."

"Why would I take my clothes off?"

"Because I asked you to and I want Richard to see *everything* he's never gonna have. He'll never be able to touch you, or taste you, or fuck you. But he'll get to watch *me* do all those things to you."

"And you think I'm actually going to *let* you do those things to me?" she asked incredulously.

"Ah, Angel, you don't have a choice. You either do it or I kill you in front of him instead."

"You're going to kill me anyway, so why would I comply with your wishes?"

"No, I'm not. When I'm finished with you I'm simply going to restrain you and leave the two of you down here."

"But Richard and I can ID you."

"Oh, by the time anyone finds you I'll be long gone and you'll both probably be dead."

"So, because I won't be surviving this event you might as well explain some things for me."

"Okay, since we have time I'll play a little game with you. For every piece of clothing you remove I'll let you ask a question. Sound like fun? Okay, you first."

Dabria removed one sock.

"Oh, come on now, at least both socks," he encouraged.

She removed the other sock and noticed that Richard was watching her every move. The metal table he lay on was a tilt table and he was inclined at the perfect angle to be able to watch everything that went on in the room. An involuntary shiver of revulsion tingled down her spine.

"I get the same feeling when I look at him," Terris acknowledged her reaction. "He's kind of gross, isn't he? No wonder he had to rape girls to get a piece of tail." Terris looked at her expectantly.

"I didn't ask a question" Dabria pointed out.

"Okay, that one's a freebee."

"I don't understand why the two of you are working together," Dabria commented.

"Oh, I would say we are definitely no longer working together. Wouldn't you?" he asked with a snort.

"Why *were* you working together?"

Terris shifted, crossed his arms, and waited. Dabria took off her blazer, folded it neatly, and with the pocket side up, set it on the floor beside the socks.

"He needed a fetching boy and so he made sure I was set up to break my parole and then approached me with a *deal of a lifetime*. Either accept his conditions or go back to jail. Since I won't ever go back to jail I had no other options. So, basically, I would catch the girls and he would fuck the girls."

"How?"

With a circular motion Terris indicated another piece of clothing was required.

Next she removed her blouse. A pale lavender satin demi-cup was revealed. A wet sounding moan emanated from Richard. Dabria refused to look at him and instead concentrated her attention on Terris.

"How?" she asked again.

"Well, the usual way, of course," Terris chuckled.

"I mean how did you catch the girls?"

"Another piece," Terris prompted.

"No, answer my question first," Dabria defied.

"Oh, all right, pretty much the same way I snagged you. The girls would come to the store. I would give them something to eat, something hot to drink, and then wait for them to keel over." Again the circular motion.

She slid out of her slacks revealing matching lavender tap pants. Again that awful wet sound oozed from the direction of the steel table. Involuntarily her glance darted to Richard. She was horrified to see that he was fully aroused. With a stifled gag she returned her gaze to Terris. He was almost bursting with anticipation. He couldn't have asked for a better reaction from her. She was absolutely revolted by Richard. That would feed Richard's rage and increase his impotent frustration. Terris stood up and approached Dabria.

"I think I'll help you with the remaining items that need to be removed," he volunteered.

"Question first," she held up her hand to halt his advance.

"Fine."

"So you catch the girls, he fucks the girls . . . ."

"Language, language, Angel. Come now, I know you don't normally talk like that. Don't lower yourself to their level," he admonished.

"So he rapes the girls. Who kills the girls and why?"

"Ah, ah, ah. That's two questions," he wagged a finger at her and shook his head.

She stood calmly waiting for his response.

"I killed them," he replied bluntly. "Now can I take your bra off?"

"I'd rather you didn't."

"Yes, well, I'd rather I did." He walked behind her and keeping his eyes riveted on Richard he reached his hands around her front and slowly, building the anticipation, undid the front clasp. Dabria could feel his hot breath sawing in and out on the back of her neck. Richard's hands clenched and unclenched as he wrenched at his restraints. When Terris pulled apart the sides of the bra Dabria's breasts popped out. Richard eyes seemed to glaze over as they greedily feasted on the bounty revealed. His penis twitched and again stifling a gag she turned her face away from Richard and focused on the wall beside her. Terris slid the straps down her arms and let the bra drop to the floor. Then he surprised her by returning to sit in the chair he had previously occupied without actually touching her at all.

Her gaze swiveled back towards him and she looked at him quizzically.

He did not respond to her unasked question. Instead he explained that he killed the girls for three reasons. The first was that Richard was bored with them and was interested in fresh entertainment. The second was because he believed his method of death was the lesser of two evils. Richard was into pain. Terris was not. He needed the girls to die virtually painlessly. The third hurt Dabria's heart. She recalled from the report that he had once been a victim. Although it hadn't been spelt out, there was a good chance that Terris had been raped by the other inmates almost immediately after his incarceration had begun. He had been a young man, he would have had a soft, almost pretty face, plus after his penectomy his lower anatomy would have resembled a woman's. "You can only be raped and degraded so many times before it does something to you inside and no matter how much you try, you just can't recover," he said softly as he looked directly into Dabria's eyes.

"So why do you scalp them?" she asked equally softly.

"I didn't to start off with. He did," he indicated Richard with a tilt of his head and scorn in his voice. "But now it's my job, too."

~ ~ ~

Morgan's two-way suddenly crackled.

"We're at the end of the drive, tell us what you know," Morgan's captain directed. Morgan quickly gave him a rundown of the clues Dabria had passed him regarding the house and what to expect when they entered it. As men swiftly moved into position Morgan prepared for advancement. He confirmed that the knife in his boot was accessible and he cocked his gun. He tightened his boots so that his entrance and walk through the house would be silent. Now came the hard part. He was about to sever all contact with Dabria. He needed to disconnect so that any sounds coming from the room below wouldn't give away his position to Terris. Almost instantaneously his palms began to sweat, his heart rate spiked, and his breathing became ragged. Focus! He needed to get himself back under control or someone was gonna get hurt. He needed to focus on the fact that he had faced situations like this before and as long as he let his training kick in and kept his emotions shut out his mission would be successful. Taking a deep cleansing breath he deliberately cut the connection and was immediately transformed into a warrior. But before he would take so much as one step his phone rang. Swearing softly he opened the line.

"Vaughn," he grunted in a hushed tone.

"Detective Vaughn, this is Tony Tasos. I tried to contact Dabria and I can't get through."

"She's a little busy right now, and so am I. Is it urgent?" he asked briskly in the same hushed tone.

"I figured you guys should know we dug up one body so far and then found what appeared to be several shriveled up pieces of leather in a drawer in the bedroom. Turns out they're human leather—as in scalps!"

"Thanks for the update, but I really gotta go. Is there anything else?"

"We're good for now. Talk to you soon. Bye!"

Morgan clicked off and then silently crept up the backstairs and gingerly opened the door.

~ ~ ~

"Terris, I'm missing something in the chain of events. Please fill me in so I understand."

Terris jolted at the sound of his name.

"How do you know my name?"

"I just remembered the other place I've seen you before. You own the bookstore and when I asked about you someone told me your name."

"Why were you interested in my name?"

"Because you were right about the night at the club, I did find you attractive and although I didn't recognize you as being the same man, I felt drawn to you."

"Don't lie to me," he flung out angrily. "I already told you I won't hurt you so you can stop sucking up!"

"I'm telling you the truth. You're an attractive man and if things were different who knows," Dabria stated sincerely. "As surprised as you are to hear me say it, I am equally as surprised to be able to acknowledge it." She looked at him truthfully with a slight shrug. "Tell me the rest, Terris," she gently encouraged.

With an unwavering look, his eyes locked on Dabria's and appearing to forget the presence of Richard he let the story tumble out.

Over the course of the last three years an unholy alliance had been forged between Richard and Terris. Richard was looking for an accomplice and searched the backgrounds of paroled convicts. Because Terris was a eunuch he was the perfect tool for Richard's purposes. He arranged for Terris' parole to be breached so that he would be able to "rescue" him when he made his courtroom appearance. Richard needed Terris' help to continue with his little hobby. Once he became confident of Terris' compliance his gigantic ego compelled him to brag about his exploits. Like Dabria had suspected, it had all started back at the orphanage and involved Ben. Richard had killed Ben because the two of them had shared a prostitute and she had died when Richard became too rough with her. They disposed of her body by stuffing her in a duffle bag, weighing her down with rocks, and flinging her into the lake near the orphanage. Despite Ben being the bad egg of the two, he was scared and didn't want to take the fall for her death. Somehow he knew that when push came to shove Richard would turn on him and implicate him if her body was ever found. Ben waited until Richard fell asleep and then attacked him with a knife. Richard had not been sleeping and although Richard was badly cut up he was able to disarm Ben and ended up killing him instead. That was why the scars on his legs were similar to Ben's. Terrified of getting caught he mutilated and burnt Ben's corpse so it couldn't be identified. He dumped the whole mess in a grave in the woods. Unfortunately, in the area he had buried the remains, the water table fluctuated a great deal and a dog found a bone only a couple of seasons later. Richard kept track of the news in Salem and knew when both the prostitute's and Ben's body had been found. However, despite the fact that the hooker was identified no suspects were ever charged and Ben's remains were labeled a John Doe. Richard believed that he had gotten away with not only one murder but two.

He continued to frequent prostitutes and abuse them but was careful enough not to get carried away and didn't kill again for many years. He hired a PI and discovered the identity of his mother. She turned out to be a Metis and was married to an influential foreign diplomat. She met with him only once and promised him she would destroy him if he ever contacted her again or tried to blackmail her into revealing their relationship. She smelled like lavender. His anger again led him to take his frustration out on a prostitute. Now he actively sought out hookers that reminded him of his mother—the mother who had thrown him away not only once but now twice. By this time he was getting better at cleaning up his messes and his obsession evolved. He researched drugs and for the right money was able to procure a drug that would paralyze his victims but allow them to still feel, hear, see, and taste.

Figuring out the precise dose to administer had been trial and error. A few died but more lived and since he picked them up in different locations and always untied his hookers and dropped them off alive after he abused them there was no trail of dead hookers for anyone to investigate. Once he had tested his drugs adequately he began to keep his hookers for longer periods of time and so motels were no longer viable. That was when he remembered Ben's uncle's cabin. The first order of business was to get rid of the old man. That had been child's play since all he had to do was smack the old geezer over the head and he toppled into the stream and drowned. Again he waited to see what the fallout was going to be. Luckily Ben had been named heir. Ben had disappeared but there was a fairly large estate attached to the property, so taxes continued to be paid and the land sat vacant. Richard now had the perfect hideaway and so he started taking his victims there.

This was all before he remarried. Then Cody's mom came along. He stopped with the hookers for a few years since he could do whatever he liked with her. He had almost total control over her as she refused to stand up for herself. By then he was a judge and she enjoyed the prestige of her position. He didn't need to drug her as she denied him nothing in their bedroom and she rarely made a sound while he did as he pleased. Then she got pregnant and he decided he wanted an heir. He started back up with the hookers again and restricted his activities to when he was out of town. Since this was no longer as convenient as it had been before, he realized he needed to find a place to keep his sex toys closer to home. He did his research and his first local pick-up foolishly took him to a piece of property in the country that she had inherited. Since the location was isolated and she had no living relatives to check on her he tied her up and kept her until he inadvertently overdosed her. This wasn't the first of his victims that was ex-sanguinated. For the last decade he had honed his skills in draining his prey of their blood, scalping them, and then posing them in graves on Ben's uncle's land. Since this was a new hunting ground and his activities had remained undetected for years he decided to leave his angels above ground where they would be found and appreciated. After verifying that the girl had remained a Jane Doe, no one else had claimed the land, and that the taxes continued to be paid out of her trust fund, he decided to set up his little love nest on her land. Since this whole little hobby of his had evolved, it had become too time consuming for him to maintain it and his current positions of judge, husband, and father. Now what he needed was someone to get him girls, prepare them for him, maintain them, and then dispose of them when he was finished. The perfect solution was Terris.

The house was still standing on the abandoned property and although animals had moved in it was an easy thing to clean up the basement and set up his playroom. His arrogance had increased with each victim and so now part of the game was to blatantly taunt the very system he was a part of. Instead of doing his own dirty work, now when he was bored with his latest "angel" he would have Terris kill them, shave them, and wash them in lavender soap. His mommy had smelled like lavender. Once they were prepared he would come back and scalp them—just like the Indians of years gone by who had scalped their white victims and taken their scalps as trophies. When he looked at them they no longer looked like his mom. Now they looked like angels, all white and innocent. He had freed them from their wicked ways. He had Terris leave his angels down by the river near the place he had left his first P.A. conquest. Terris explained that he had brought the corpses to the drop site by dogsled which was why the last three girls had been left in the winter.

Since Dabria filled the physical qualifications and her name meant Angel she was obviously a special chosen one. Terris knew that Richard was beyond enraged by the episode in the bar. The fact that Terris had marked her was inexcusable. Once she was safely restrained in *the playroom* Terris knew that Richard would want retribution. Terris had known the minute he saw Dabria that she was Richard's ultimate angel and since up to that point he had little control over who was picked and what he did with them, he felt the need to exert his own will. So, he did an "in your face" move that was meant to let Richard know that he didn't have exclusive command of the situation. Terris needed to leave his own mark on something and so by cutting Dabria he believed he had sent a very clear message to Richard. Richard had obviously misunderstood the message.

"So, what was the message?" Dabria asked.

"Simple. Until then he believed he had total control of the situation. I wanted to show him he did not," he looked directly at Richard now as he spoke. "Who's in control now, Richard?"

~ ~ ~

Morgan and several of his fellow officers had managed to access the farmhouse and as then moved into position he crouched outside the door of *the playroom* and listened intently to the tale that Terris told. A misplaced footfall caused one of the officer's boots to scrap the basement floor. All talking, from inside the room, immediately stopped.

"I think we have company, Dabria. Friends of yours, maybe?" Terris jumped to his feet and advanced towards her. She instinctively knew this was it and she tried to scoot out of his reach to stand behind Richard. Terris grabbed her around the waist and hauled her up against his body. She squeaked as the door to *the playroom* burst open revealing nothing more than dead air.

"What's in the coat, Dabria? A homing device?"

"No."

"Dabria," he cautioned.

"Terris, I'm not lying. The only thing in the pocket is my cell phone."

He bent down and grabbed the coat.

"Empty it," he commanded, "and put it back on. Could it be Officer Vaughn come to save the day? Please join our party," he taunted.

Morgan walked into the room with his gun drawn as Dabria slid into the coat. A quick survey revealed that she was unhurt and that Terris appeared unarmed but was obviously using her as a shield.

"Let her go, Terris," Morgan ordered.

"Not yet," Terris replied. "Although things did not go exactly according to plan A and B that doesn't mean that plan C can't be implemented." He slid his hand inside his jacket pocket and before he could slide it out again Morgan had raised his gun towards Terris' head.

"Get your hand out of your pocket and release her," he again demanded.

"No," he replied as he produced a small handgun. Instead of aiming it at either Morgan or Dabria his hand lay calmly at his side. He tightened his grip on Dabria and bent to whisper in her ear.

"You know I can't go back inside there. But I can make Richard suffer for the rest of his life. When I release you, fall to the floor and you'll be safe. Goodbye, Angel. Remember me," he kissed her gently on the cheek. Then Dabria's world went still and each moment seemed to be a freeze frame of images and distorted sound.

He released her, turning towards Richard, and shot him in the groin. Richard's body bucked, blood spurted, and a second shot rang out.

Richard roared an unnatural shriek and Terris' body crumpled onto Dabria.

The weight of his body seemed to jumpstart time back into its natural state and before Dabria could take a breath Morgan was flinging Terris' body off of her and pulling her into his arms. The room was suddenly full of officers and he rushed her outside of the room, up the stairs, and out into the yard. He held her away from himself and started to peel her out of the coat. She had blood and brain matter spattered on it and he needed to make sure that none of the blood was hers.

"Morgan, I'm okay," she tried to reassure him as he continued to pat her down and visually survey her. "Morgan, stop," she took his face between her hands and made him look directly at her.

Silently they stared at each other while Morgan's breath sawed in and out.

"Is it too late to say I love you?" she tremulously asked him with tears glistening in her eyes.

He let out a long relieved sigh and pulling her tightly against his chest wrapped his arms gently around her.

"No!" he assured her as he rained kisses over her face.

Epilogue

The last year had been a living hell in one form or another for Cody. All the charges against him had been dropped and he had been released from custody. But life as he knew it would never be the same. With all the bad did come a little good. Judge Reynolds was finally out of his life. He survived the shooting however, he was now officially a eunuch. He had been extradited back to the United States, charged, and convicted of the murder of eleven of the young women he disposed of at Ben's Uncles' cabin. Unfortunately, there wasn't enough evidence regarding the Canadian murders to charge him with those, yet. Tehya had admitted to causing the accident death of Megan and her unborn child and requested a Traditional Sentencing Circle. Her request had been denied. Jaimie had been charged with mischief and was sentenced to several hours of community service. She was released from her position at Legal Aid. Lena had sold everything Richard owned and relocated to parts unknown with her three other children. Dabria married Morgan after little persuasion and they were currently residing in her little log hide-a-way working on producing a grandbaby for the ever hopeful grandparents.

Cody walked from one room to the next confirming he had left nothing of value behind. He hoisted his duffle over his shoulder, stepped onto the deck, and locked the door for the last time. He purposely strode across the deck and then stopped at the top of the stairs surveying his surrounds also for the last time. The mere thought of living here without Megan turned his stomach. The sooner he left this place of great joy and even greater sorrow the sooner his life would move forward. The rumble of a cargo van bumping down the gravel road towards him pulled him from his musings. The van pulled up directly in front of the house and its trail of dust momentarily enveloped it. A delivery man jumped out and approached him with a package in hand.

"Looks like I just caught ya," he said with a grin. "Are you Cody Saddleback?"

Cody nodded silently.

"Ya need to sign for it. Right here," he passed him the package and an electronic scanning device.

"Who is this from?"

"Uh . . . . a Mr. Marshall Thomas," he informed him with the same friendly smile.

Cody signed the machine and passed it back.

"Have a great day," the driver said. He loped back to the van and then waved as he drove off.

Cody stared down at the package gripped in his hand. The duffle slid off his shoulder and dropped to the deck. He sunk down on the top step beside it and with shaking hands tore off the brown paper covering. A shoebox was revealed. Cody lifted the lid and inside laid a slightly bulging envelope and a journal that he instantly recognized. The envelope was addressed simply *Cody*. He turned it over, broke the seal on it, and watched Megan's ring roll out as he tapped the contents into his hand. As if mesmerized, he silently stared at the ring that lay glistening in the sunlight. Pain tore through him and he crushed the ring into the skin of his palm as he unconsciously made a fist. Lost in his pain he continued to grip the ring ever more forcefully until a drop of blood dripped onto his jeans forcing his attention back to the present. He loosened his clench, wiped his hand and the ring on his pants, and gently placed the ring back into the box. With gritted teeth he slid the letter from the envelope, unfolded it, and began to read.

Dear Cody,

When we cleaned Megan's room I found her journal. I started to read it and soon determined that you were the love of her life. She loved you, respected you, trusted you, and admired you. Watching you over the course of the past year proved to me that she was also yours. Your silent but constant vigilance at the trial confirmed for me how devoted you were and that your commitment to each other had not been given the proper respect by my family. I apologize for that. I've lost the opportunity to tell Megan how proud I was of her but I believe she knew how much I loved her. I wanted you to know that my girl chose well when she picked you to love and share her life with. Don't let this destroy your life. You have many years ahead of you and a whole world to discover. If I can help you in any way—financially, emotionally—please come to me. I've given you the journal because you deserve to know how deep her love for you was. The ring . . . . well maybe you can use it to start a new life. Thank you, for the joy you brought to Megan's life. Live a good life, Cody. Megan would want that.

Sincerely,
Marshall Thomas

Cody scrubbed his cheeks, wiping the tears away. He cleared his throat and refolded the letter. He put it and the ring back into the envelope and then placed it into the shoe box. He squared his shoulders, grabbed the duffle and the box, and purposely walked to the truck. Cody stowed his treasures behind the seat and without a backward glance drove away from the place that had once been his only consistent refuge but would from this day forward be no more than the place he was from.

Author's Note

For the purposes of this story, I've not strictly adhered to the rules of Canadian police and legal procedures. I created a fictitious Legal Aid Office, City Police Station, and R.C.M.P. Detachment. This book in no way reflects the actual police department of Prince Albert, the R.C.M.P. detachment of Prince Albert, or the Prince Albert Legal Aid office.

Sentencing Circles are a traditional consequence that can be requested by aboriginals after they have been convicted of a crime in Canadian court. For the purpose of my story I introduced the idea before the accused was actually charged.

Prince Albert is a real city in Canada. It is considered the "gateway" to Northern Saskatchewan which is comprised of hundreds of small lakes. The La Colle Falls Project was an actual development started in 1909 and was meant to provide the area with hydro electric power. Unfortunately, it was such a resounding financial failure that it was abandoned in 1914. The over $3 million debt nearly bankrupted the city. Decades later the city tax payers continued to pay. The unfinished cement remains are a desolate reminder of one man's unfulfilled dream. After hiking the area several summers ago it seemed to me to be the perfect dumping ground for the disturbed individuals of my little tale.